T0007463

Published by Semiotext(e)
PO BOX 629, South Pasadena, CA 91031
www.semiotexte.com

Special thanks to Mallory Curley, Robert Dewhurst, Raymond Foye, Nan Goldin, Chloé Griffin, Gracie Hadland, Max Mueller, Bradford Nordeen, and Janique Vigier.

Cover Art: Nan Goldin, Cookie at Sharon's birthday party with Lisette and Genaro, Provincetown, 1976. Courtesy the artist and Marian Goodman Gallery.

Design: Hedi El Kholti

ISBN: 978-1-63590-166-5
Distributed by The MIT Press, Cambridge, Mass., and London, England
Printed in the United States of America

10 9 8 7 6 5 4

Walking through Clear Water in a Pool Painted Black

Collected Stories

Cookie Mueller

Introduction by Olivia Laing

Edited by Hedi El Kholti, Chris Kraus, and Amy Scholder

semiotext(e)

Contents

Introduction by Olivia Laing

Cookie

In my favorite photograph of Cookie Mueller, by her friend Nan Goldin, she has one hand on her heart, one on a wall, and is laughing so hard she might fall over. Her wrists, fingers, ears are crammed with jewellery, her head's flung back and her enormous bleached lion's mane is damp with sweat. She looks a riot, like the most fun you could possibly have, the walking epitome of downtown style.

She was born in Maryland in 1949 and christened Dorothy. "Somehow," she explains in "My Bio—Notes on an American Childhood,'" "I got the name Cookie before I could walk," a nickname from her brother Michael, who died in a climbing accident when he was fourteen. As a teenager she dropped out of high school, hit the road, and did a hairy stint in the acid-fuelled Oz of San Francisco before crash-landing back in Baltimore, where at the age of twenty she met the wizard in the diminutive, moustached form of John Waters. Their first encounter, at the screening of his debut *Mondo Trash*, so enchanted him that she starred in his next five movies.

Actress and kohl-eyed muse in a monkey fur jacket, sure, but her strongest suit was as a writer. In 1976 she moved to New York, where alongside raising her son Max, dealing coke, and hosting parties, she wrote poetry, had a regular no holds barred advice column for *East Village Eye*, and did a stint as art critic for *Details*. In one column she jokingly predicted that in the future art history students would take modules on the painters of the East Village, as indeed they do; another reflects on the recent death of Basquiat, "one of the world's citizens who was translating the universe on a canvas." There's also a lot of gossip, grouching about gentrification and off the wall riffing, much of it enviably quotable.

She wrote her first book aged eleven, making a cover out of beer case cardboard and Saran Wrap and filing it on the shelves at her local library. This lost juvenilia (321 pages!) was followed by several collections of her writing, including the epistolary novella *Fan Mail, Frank Letters and Crank Calls* (1989) and the Waters-era memoir *Garden of Ashes* (1990).

The first I came across was *Walking through Clear Water In a Pool Painted Black*, published shortly after Cookie's death of AIDS-related pneumonia on 10 November 1989. I was given it a couple of years later, a precocious fifteenth birthday gift from an older cousin. Sarah had taken it upon herself to oversee my countercultural education, and Cookie was a must. The syllabus also included *Stripping* by Pagan Kennedy, *My Education: A Book of Dreams* by William Burroughs, and *Safe in Heaven Dead*, a Hanuman paperback by Jack Kerouac that fitted pleasingly in the pocket of my then-uniform, a man's suit jacket, on the back of which I'd scrawled in lipstick "Get Out of My Church."

All of those books left a mark, but Cookie Mueller was next level: a how-to manual for a life ricocheting joyously off the rails. It provided an introduction to the avant garde delights of John Waters and Fassbinder, but more importantly it was a primer for an outlaw way of life, in which every crisis or devastation was merely an opportunity to demonstrate unflappable worldliness and grace. Cookie careened through terrifying situations—abduction, rape, boat wrecks, car wrecks, house fires, a friend ODing—with languid ease, a good witch on bad drugs. Her style was neither macho nor touristy. She was merely reporting, hilariously, on the world as she saw it. As she said to an employer trying to inveigle her into an unwanted threesome: "Why does everybody think I'm so wild. I'm not wild. I happen to stumble onto wildness. It gets in my path."

This collection, first pieced together by Amy Scholder in 1997 as *Ask Dr Mueller* and now reissued in chronological order, represents the whole kit and caboodle of the Mueller oeuvre, complete with tales of piss queens and chicken-fucking, as well as advice on syphilis, loneliness, lactose intolerance and what to cut cocaine with (inositol). A monumental amount of drugs are consumed. In one single day, the young Cookie meets the Manson Family girls ("like ducks quacking over corn"), attends an LSD capping party, rides with the Grateful Dead to San Quentin prison for a concert, has a brief rest with some heroin, goes to a peyote ceremony, meets a Satanist who summons a footman of Beelzebub on top of Mount Tamalpais, escapes over a dissolving Golden Gate bridge, takes a bath, goes to a Jim Morrison concert, gets raped by a stranger, escapes again, and ends the night "talking about aesthetics, Eastern philosophy, Mu, Atlantis, and the coming of the apocalypse," this time on cocaine mixed with crystal meth. Other days were less eventful, but not by much.

Experience is a badge of pride. It matters to stay afloat, live on your nerves, keep smiling. The signature Cookie phrases are "too bad" and "oh well," the textual equivalent of a shrug. It's not that she thinks nothing matters or anything goes (rapists, she comments at one point, "ought to have red hot pokers rammed up their wee wees"); more that it's a point of dignity to poke fun at the terrors, to be able to metabolise whatever life throws at you, just as she casts aspersion on a boyfriend for sweating out his drugs.

I wonder at that tone now. Before rereading, I might have called it hardboiled or affectless, but that's not quite right. "There is a great art to handling losses with nonchalance," she observes. Some things, especially pain, don't need to be spelled out, but rather defanged, the raconteur's survival strategy, alchemised into material for a comic story, a transaction she once described as "sublime." What comes off these pages now is in no way anaesthetised or anhedonic, but rather a deep relish for adventure, a powerful, vibrating pleasure at the oddness of people, and the capacity of language to freeze even the most plainly terrifying or distressing material, to make it something that can be appreciated and shared, a communal pleasure rather than a private humiliation. It goes without saying that this is not the dominant style right now, which for this reader at least makes it all the more desirable.

It strikes me too that Cookie's world of happenstance and chance encounter has been obliterated by the internet, gone without trace. She never seems to pack a suitcase, let alone book a ticket or plan an itinerary. Her life is wide open, revelling in unscripted, unscreened contact and surprise. It's high risk, high reward. Getting a ride with a stranger might result in a gunpoint abduction, but her idiosyncratic approach to travel also generates new friendships, lovers, parties to attend, places to stay. I used to know a lot of people like that, in my own dropout days, but I can't think of anyone now who doesn't use Google as a prophylactic against the unexpected, a charm against getting lost that comes at a higher price than might have been predicted.

I'm not sure, but I feel like the internet's choirs of disapproval would have grossed her out too. "You're right about my mind being open," she writes in her advice column, "in fact it's so open that at times I hear the wind rippling through it." Never take yourself too seriously, another Cookie lesson.

By the late 1980s, she was HIV positive and addicted to heroin, as was her husband, the Italian artist Vittorio Scarpati. She wrote about AIDS frequently, dispensing not always accurate advice and dispelling stigma. I don't suppose she'd be surprised to know there still isn't a cure. Her writing took on a deepening tone of elegy, culminating in the beautiful, furious "Last Letter." Written in her final year, it eulogised the many friends already dead of AIDS, itemising what their loss meant for the culture at large. "Their war," she writes, "was against ignorance, the bankruptcy of beauty, and the truancy of culture. These were people who hated and scorned pettiness, intolerance, bigotry, mediocrity, ugliness, and spiritual myopia; the blindness that makes life hollow and insipid was unacceptable."

Well, I wish those people were still with us, but fortunately for us they've left a lot of themselves behind in forms more durable than bodies. Buy this book and give it to every young person you know. Tell them it's important to remember that we didn't always live as we do now, and that alternative modes remain a possibility. Cookie is a live corrective to conformity, conservatism, and cruelty. In a much reproduced statement, written at the end of her short life, she said: "you will never die. You will simply lose your body." As with much of her medical advice, I'm not sure how right she was, except in her own idiosyncratic, incandescent case. Turn the page, and there she is, grinning back at death.

Walking through Clear Water in a Pool Painted Black

"It is important that you recognize that there is no experience that comes into your life that is below your dignity."

— Dr. Peebles, a nineteenth century Scottish doctor

PART ONE

BALTIMORE, 1964–1969

Two People—Baltimore, 1964

I had two lovers and I wasn't ashamed. The first was Jack. He was seventeen and I was fifteen. The skin of his face was so taut over protruding bones that I feared for his head, the same sympathetic fear one has for the safety of an egg.

He wore his black hair all greased up with pieces spiraling down into his languid eyes. Jack owned only black clothes, and he wore his cigarettes in the rolled-up sleeves of his black T-shirts, showing off his solid pecs, which were big for a skinny person.

Once I visited him in the hospital; he had infectious hepatitis and sclerosis of the liver, resulting from his four-year bout with alcoholism.

He didn't look too good in there, all yellow in a murky blue private room.

His visitors had to wear hospital gowns and surgical gloves, also masks over their noses and mouths, which really frustrated him because everyone looked so morose, and sinister without smiles.

My nose and lips were the first nose and lips he had seen in two weeks … after his mother left I whipped off not only my mask and gown, but my pants, and hopped into the hospital bed with him. I wasn't afraid. I'd been as intimate as I could be right up until the time he got sick, but I kept my rubber gloves on anyway.

He was very sick, quite contagious, and looked ill, but sexy, like pictures of Proust on his deathbed. I was in love, and we were teenagers going steady.

He had been expelled from high school for bringing in real moonshine, corn liquor, from his uncle's still in West Virginia, and he'd gotten all his best friends drunk on the lunch break and tried to beat up on his American History teacher when the man had dumped out Jack's liquor.

Jack had a black Impala convertible with red rolled and pleated bucket seats, racing cams, dual exhausts, tire slicks, a roll bar, Laker pipes, big foam dice hanging from the rear-view mirror, and four on the floor, of course.

He drank sloe gin, or Laird's Apple Jack, or sometimes Thunderbird when he couldn't find anything else. He ate bennies (Benzedrine) like little candies. He called them crossroads because of the X on them.

This other lover of mine was Gloria. She sat three rows in front of me in algebra class. I watched her hairdos from the back. Every day they were different: beehives, barrel curls, air lifts, pixies, flips, French twists, bubbles, doublebubbles.

The things I liked best were the way her scalp shone through all the teasing as if her head was a mango and the spit curls pasted down beside her ears with clear fingernail polish. She also had bitten-to-the-quick fingernails. I even liked the warts and nicotine stains on her index and second fingers. On her, all this was heaven.

I began spending Saturday nights with Gloria when Jack had bloody cut eyes from fights. When he went in the hospital,

I stayed with her the whole weekend. I slept in her single bed at her parents' prefab house and first she used to feel me up. She kept telling me, "Just pretend I'm Jack. Just pretend I'm Jack."

In the beginning the cajoling was necessary, but in the weeks that followed I didn't have to pretend she was Jack anymore.

Jack and Gloria liked each other and no one ever suspected anything about Gloria and myself. For appearances, we were best girlfriends, both of us with our combustible hairdos, sprayed with lacquer and teased high as possible. We wore the tightest black skirts … so tight that they hobbled us … black stockings, white blouses with ruffles at the neck and cuffs, pointy bras underneath, and five-inch spike heels. With these shoes, and the hair, we were the tallest people in the school. Lesser women than we would have become acrophobic. We made people dizzy when they saw us.

We clicked down the high school hallways in our spikes, these shoes I had to keep in my school locker to change into when I got there in the mornings … my mother made me wear flats to school.

When Jack was in the hospital, we picked up guys together, smoked a lot of cigarettes, sniffed glue, and drank codeine terpin hydrate cough syrup for the buzz.

I stopped seeing Jack and took his initial ring off when he went to jail for a B and E (breaking and entering) charge. I stopped seeing Gloria when she got pregnant and decided to marry Ed, her longtime boyfriend, who she kept telling me she didn't love nearly as much as she loved me.

Years later, I found out that Jack, who was always pretty literate, was on methadrine writing a novel, never able to drink again because of his liver.

As for Gloria … that girl … born of a lightbulb it seemed, had died when she had gotten silicone injections for her little tits. It had spread all over her body, making tiny lumps arise on every inch of her skin, until finally it entered her pulmonary arteries and the aorta and she died of a silicone heart.

Alien—1965

I was always leaving. Every time I left I had a different hair color and I would be standing on the porch saying goodbye to the older couple in the living room. I didn't have anything in common with them except that we shared a few inherited chromosomes, the identical last name, and the same bathroom.

They would be protesting. Screaming. It became a tune, with the same refrain, and the same lyrics, "If you leave now, you'll have no future. If you leave now, you'll be a bum."

"I'll be back in the fall when school starts." Or "I'll be back after the weekend."

"If you leave now, don't dare come back. How are you going to live? You don't have any money. Why do you have to leave?"

"It's natural. It's a biological urge. Like little birds testing their wings. I can't help myself."

There were a bunch of people waiting for me, in the street in front of the house, honking the horn of a cream T-bird, or a black Impala convertible, or a pale blue Rambler.

"Bye, I'll see you soon."

"Do you want some money?"

"No. Thanks anyway. Bye."

We sped off. I told my friends in the car that I was an alien to my parents. It was better that I didn't hang around there too much. At this point it would always dawn on me that there was another problem. Not only was I alien to my parents, but I was an alien to my friends.

No Credit, Cash Only—Baltimore, 1967

When I was eighteen, I left my parents' nest for good and moved into a household of hippies and drug users. All of us were on our way to Haight-Ashbury; this was just a temporary home. There were five of us living there: Della, Don, Wendy, Nash, and me. Della was the only one who was working and bringing in money; she bitched about it every day. Finally Don, her boyfriend, got sick of her nagging and broke down and got a job, and then I did. I needed the money to get to San Francisco.

I started working in a men's clothing store in the center of Baltimore. The place catered to natty dressers. Baltimore city had an eighty-percent black population, and the clothes were designed with black men in mind. Their ads said they were "A quality designer's specialty shop for the fashion-conscious man about town." They said their clothes were "Handmade of fine imported fabrics." But I knew different. They were shoddy machine-sewn togs made of cheap homegrown textiles. They fell apart after three wearings. The ads also said "We have the latest chic European styles." And "We offer elegance for the individualist." But what they had on the racks, aside from an occasional conservative navy blue or gray pin-striped business suit, were lime green mohair Nehru suits, shiny two-tone sharkskin suits, loud sports jackets, and hot pink fake fur pimp hats.

The shop was tastefully decorated with plush wall-to-wall beige carpeting and mahogany woodwork. The clothes were really expensive, the most expensive in town, but it was all a sham. Maybe at one time it had been a haute couture shop, but in 1967 it was actually just a clip joint run by a crook full of snooty pretentious salespeople wearing too much cologne.

Somehow I talked my way into the assistant credit manager position. It was pretty good pay, but it was a nine-to-five office job on the fourth-floor credit department where chilly brain-dead adults pretended efficiency while they shuffled papers and yacked about last night's TV shows. I was always late and I didn't dress the part because I didn't own any office wear, but the worst part was what I had to do every day. It was my misfortune to be the one who had to make phone calls to people who were late with their layaway or credit payments. In other words, I had been hired to be the store heavy.

I was that dreaded voice coming through people's home phones demanding payment. It's the worst kind of phone call to get, and for a person like me, it was even worse to make. Every day, when the boss was around, I had to gear up to be nasty. I had to pretend to be concerned about the store and the money it made. I had to be mean and do ridiculous things like threaten lawsuits for a pair of slacks. I had to invade lives over the phone, disturb people while they were watching television or washing dishes or sleeping or having sex. It was horrible.

When the boss wasn't around, I never made any of those calls. When he returned and asked me if I called today's "delinquents,"

I would tell him I tried, but none of them had been home to answer the phone.

"I'm sure they're at work," I told him.

"Are you kiddin?" the fat oily boss said. "Them niggers don't have no jobs."

I didn't know what to say to that. What an asshole, a rude bigot stomping through life squashing everything to his level. He wore a ludicrous dark brown matted toupee and dirty gray pants he was too flabby for. The pants fit like a stuffed sausage casing with creases around the crotch area. One day he cuddled my butt in his hands as I was bending over the file drawers and since then, whenever he got close, my skin crawled.

I learned some interesting secrets, though, at this job. Aside from calling customers at home, I had to research new customers' credit history. When a customer downstairs in the store wanted to buy something with a credit card, the floor salesperson would ring me and I would call the Central Credit Bureau, give them the customer's name and credit card number, and they would look them up and tell me about the customer. They knew everything, all the details of that person's life. Apparently, they had credit detectives and FBI people who gathered information for them. It shocked me that they knew so much. For instance, if I called them about a George Johnson, first they would tell me that he was thirty-four years old, married for seven years to Alice Johnson, twenty-seven, had two kids, Andrew, six, Betty, four; he worked at Westinghouse Electric as a lightbulb inspector for twelve years, made $200 a week, was very late on a $30-a-month car payment, lived in a small mortgaged East Baltimore home that cost $200 a month, which he was having trouble paying for, because he also had a mistress named Louise Moore, twenty-three, and an illegitimate kid, Luther, two, whom he was supporting on the sly. He was a bad risk.

If a man was a gambler and played the horses, the Central Credit Bureau knew which racetrack he frequented. If a woman was a drinker, they knew which expensive liquor she liked.

Out of curiosity I decided to see what kind of dirt the Bureau would dish out about my father. Pretending he was a complete stranger, I called and listened to what the Bureau had to say about Mr. Mueller. My dad came up smelling like roses. He was the ideal credit customer: a notary, with no drinking or gambling problems, a model citizen. The only drawback, credit-wise, concerning the Muellers came as a shock to me—daughter Dorothy aka Cookie, eighteen, apparent hippie type, drug-oriented possible future money drain on family because of rebellious political attitude and neurotic behavior. Whoa! Who told them that? How dare they have this info about me! They knew everything and assumed more! I could hardly believe it. A whole new world opened up before my eyes. It was scary.

All this secret stuff didn't seem to interest anyone else in the office, and the people I talked to at the Central Credit Bureau sounded like all this was very humdrum and boring. As I saw it, this was a major invasion of privacy. It was scandalous, I was incensed, but all those credit workers didn't seem to notice or question any of it. They behaved like a numb herd of blockheads on Thorazine.

One day at the office, while I was stuffing some envelopes with bold-printed final notices and official-looking threats-of-collection-agency letters, the slimy boss came into my cubicle.

"I went over yar records laz night. Ya ain't doin such a hot job at collectin all these payments from these bums," he said, shaking his head. "You havta be meaner. Ya gotta shake 'em up. Lookit, lemme show ya how it's done," he picked up the phone. "Gimme a number. Anybody. I'll show ya how ya gotta talk to these people."

I handed him the first file from "delinquents." He looked at the number and started to dial. "I used ta be assitant credit manager years ago and how ya think I got where I am today? I collected the money for this here place here, damn fast, too. Whatsis person's name I'm callin? Leroy Washington. That's a nigger, for sure, with that name. Hello. This is Mr. Sanders from Nauvankauf's Men's Clothing Store. Is this Mr. Leroy Washington? Okay, Mr. Washington, I see here that yar very far behind in ya payments on that suit ya bought here … yes … well … but we been waitin a long time, Mr. Washington. You like da suit, right? And ya want ta keep da suit? So if ya want ta keep da suit, ya betta make this here payment right away … no not next week, Mr. Washington … tomorrow … otherwise, we just goointa repossess that suit. You know what repossess means, doancha? It means we come right to ya house and take the suit outta da closet and we take it back … yessindeedie … and ya gotta pay a rental for da time ya had it … and if ya speilt anything on it, or ifya busted any seams ya gotta pay for it, the whole thing … so ya got no choice here. Can we expect ya ta bring in yar payment tomorrow, then? Okay, well good, Mr. Washington, we'll see ya tomorrow."

Boss-man hung up the phone with a big smile on his mushy face. "Ya see, ya gotta yell at dem jungle bunnies like they was little kids. I scared the pants offim. He's bringing in cash tomorrow. Yool see. That's da way ya gotta handle 'em. Okay? Try that."

"Yeah, sure," I said. What an idiot he was.

"Try it. Call da next one. Do it, I'm goin ta lizzen on the extension," he said and handed me the receiver. I dialed a Mr. Thomas Andrews.

The phone rang and a man answered. "Mr. Andrews, this is Ms. Mueller from Nauvankauf's Men's Clothing Store," I said.

"Oh, yes … I know I'm late on that payment, but you see, my little daughter was in an automobile accident three weeks ago and she's in the hospital and you know the cost of hospital bills …"

"He's givin ya a story," the boss said with his hand over the receiver. "Tell im he's full of baloney!"

"Yes, but, Mr. Andrews, we've waited for five weeks for your final payment and we have been patient, but now we'll have to repossess the suit or turn over your records to a collection agency," I said, hating myself for every word. Suddenly, through the receiver, the beleaguered Mr. Andrews started to cry. He broke down and I knew he wasn't acting. I looked at ugly bossman Sanders helplessly.

He looked pissed off. "Just hang up the phone, I'll deal with this character," he said and then he really yelled at the guy, telling him that he was crying crocodile tears and what right did he have going around buying suits he couldn't afford. I couldn't listen, I left the office and punched out for lunch.

I hated that creep, Mr. Sanders, I hated the job, I hated the Central Credit Bureau with all their slimy secrets, I hated the whole thing. I was going to quit, but before I did, I had a plan. It occurred to me that there were no records of any customers' purchases and payments other than the records I had. It would be very easy to destroy all evidence of purchases and nonpayments. I could rip up bills and records right and left.

I went straight to my task after lunch. While Sanders was on his break, stuffing his face with carbohydrates, I called Mr. Andrews, the man who had cried.

"Mr. Andrews, this is Nauvankauf's Men's Clothing Store again. I have a surprise for you. This isn't a joke so listen closely. Forget about the rest of the payments on your suit. You're free and clear now. Don't worry about it, take care of your daughter's hospital bills. I'm destroying your records right now. Don't contact this store ever again and everything will be fine. Okay?"

"What? What's going on? Is this a joke?" Mr. Andrews was puzzled.

"No, it's no joke, Mr. Andrews, it's a gift, just wear the suit in good health."

"My God! This is wonderful! I can't believe it! What a surprise! Thank you … I can't believe it!" Mr. Andrews was happy.

"Good-bye, Mr. Andrews, have a nice life," I said, and hung up, feeling great, just like Robin Hood.

Next I called Mr. Washington, and told him that all the jive about repossessing was a pack of lies, and I was destroying his records so forget about making any more payments. The suit was a gift. Mr. Washington acted like he'd just won the lottery. He was really excited.

I called the most destitute people after that. Some of them didn't believe me at first, but I told them I was a gift-giver, and I asked them to please stop paying their bills.

"Don't call the store and ask any questions about this, and don't ask them where your bills are either," I told them. "Otherwise I'll be in deep trouble and so will you."

Some thought it was a big joke and they got a good laugh. It didn't matter if they didn't believe me, they would when the bills stopped coming. These people definitely wouldn't call wondering where their bills were, I was sure of that. One person, a Black Panther supporter, thought it was a political revolutionary action and he kept saying, "Yeah! Right on! All right! Power to the people!"

I was having a ball. I must have called eight or nine people before Sanders returned from lunch. I was very careful not to leave any evidence of the pieces of the ripped-up bills and records around. I put them all in my bag to take home and burn them. When five o'clock came, I couldn't wait to go back to work the next day, Friday. I decided it would be my last day.

At home, later that night, when Della, Bob, Wendy, and Nash were sitting around on the floor in candlelight, tripping on LSD and listening to Ravi Shankar on the sitar, I told them what I had done at work that day. Everyone except Della thought it was great.

"Far out!" they said. "Far fuckin out!"

"Wait a minute, wait a minute," Della said in horror.

"Did you stop to think about what you were doing? You were stealing! And if anyone finds out, the poor people who work at the store will have to pay for those clothes. And what if you're caught? Did you think about that?"

"First of all, the store can absorb the money for those suits, and secondly, there's no way anybody could find out. I destroyed all the records. Anyway, nobody remembers what was sold in there, they do so much business. And that store is a rip-off; you ought to see the cheesy way those clothes are made; those poor customers are believing all that hype and buying that crap!" I said. "I'm doing everybody a favor, the customers, and the credit clerks, too. It's less work for them."

The next day I felt like Santa Claus, or John Beresford Tipton on the old TV show *The Millionaire*. It was satisfying to hear all those worried people suddenly start laughing or crying for joy. Most of them told me that it was the first time anyone had ever given them anything.

I did one more thing before I left work for good that Friday. I called the Central Credit Bureau to find out about boss-man Sanders. There wasn't a lot of juicy stuff about him, but I got his address, 323 Oakland Avenue.

At five, I bolted out of there. I was so happy I never had to see that place again. I had a great weekend. On Monday I slept late, and called the office in the afternoon to tell Mr. Sanders that I had to quit because I had finally been called for a Baltimore county job that I'd been hoping for. This was an elaborate lie, a complete fabrication!

"It's a great job, Mr. Sanders," I said. "I'm going to be working with children. You see, the county bought this nice house on Oakland Avenue. It's going to function as a residence for these orphaned kids, and I'll be working there."

"Oh, Oakland Avenue? That's where I live! Ya know da address?" he asked.

"Yeah, I do," I said. "It's 321."

"Yeah!? Dats right next door ta me! An orphanage? I donno if I like diz ideer," his voice was sagging. "Hope dere good kids … ya know if dere good kids?"

"They're great kids," I said. "All under-privileged kids, all black." I heard him gasp. I think he almost dropped the phone. "Hey, see ya in the neighborhood! Bye for now!"

For once the tables turned on Sanders. He was getting the scary phone call instead of giving it.

That ought to shake him up for the day.

Haight-Ashbury—San Francisco, 1967

An earthquake rolled me off the mattress onto the floor. It woke me along with the rest of San Francisco. It was nothing too unusual considering the San Andreas fault; there were a lot of houses all over the city that were crooked from past tremors. This one was 5.6 on the Richter scale at 10 A.M., an uncivilized hour. It was too early to get up, but I decided I couldn't sleep any longer in the same bed with this person who I liked just fine yesterday when we liberated two T-bone steaks from the Safeway supermarket which we cooked and ate, much to the disgust of the vegetarians I lived with. After the steaks we drank a gallon of cheap Napa Sonoma red wine and took some LSD … Owsley Purple Barrels. But now he was sweating too much in bed, staining the one sheet I owned with all that wasted power from his pores. It meant he couldn't hold his liquor or his drugs, which irritated me so much I had to escape.

I went to the bathroom quietly so I wouldn't wake the eleven people I lived with. My roommates were spread out among five bedrooms. Five, if you consider the glassed-in porch off the kitchen that overlooked the dismal cement courtyard. We shared this courtyard with another building where Janis Joplin from Big

Brother and the Holding Company lived. On some mornings I could see her rattling her pots and pans in her kitchen. Sometimes we'd talk across the concrete abyss like housewives.

I put on my eye makeup. It was a throwback to the time when I plastered the makeup on thick and teased my hair. No one else wore eye makeup in the Haight … an occasional Day-Glo flower or a third eye on the forehead perhaps, but definitely no eye makeup. Then I went out on Haight Street looking for something new.

The first thing I saw was a school bus painted black with the words HOLYWOOD PRODUCTIONS (one L was missing in Hollywood) scrawled in gold by what must have been a retarded person. A tall hambone was sitting on the bus stairs. I asked him for a cigarette, just to strike up a conversation. I was curious.

"No cigarettes," he said, "but why don't you come in and smoke a joint with us?"

I followed him in and sat down among paisley throw pillows, bare mattresses, and hanging sand candles. The interior was painted sky blue with splashes of red. Five or six girls were lounging inside. They looked my age, but seemed younger. Maybe it was their dull eyes, maybe it was their girlie prattle, but they seemed like boring people, dressed like hippies. They were like ducks quacking over corn. I immediately felt superior. There was something missing here, faulty brain synapses, low wattage cerebral electrodes, maybe.

After we all smoked the joint and talked a little, one of the girls asked, "Would you like to join us? We're traveling up and down the coast in this bus." Everyone thought it was a good idea if I joined them. I thought it was rather sudden; I met them three minutes ago, but these people were weaned into peace and free love straight from their parents' Wonderbread and Cheese Doodles, so they were disgustingly enthusiastic.

I tried to picture myself traveling "up and down" the coast with them but my blood turned cold.

"I don't think so," said I. "I have a flat here with eleven other people so I'm sort of set up, you know? What's the situation on this bus? I mean, how many of you are there?"

"There's eight right now. Six girls and two guys. You should really wait for Charlie to come back from the store before you decide. He's really far-out and spiritual. He's in there buying oranges for us." She pointed to a fruit store.

I waited around for a little while, but then decided to leave, so I thanked them for the joint and left looking for a diversion from this bunch. It wasn't until years later while reading *The Family* that I remembered that bus. It was described in the book exactly as I remembered it. Those girls were Squeaky Fromme, Susan Atkins, Mary Brunner ... I just missed meeting Charlie Manson by five minutes.

Next on the street I noticed a gathering of women. I thought this was a little odd since this was long before the days when women felt it their duty to exclude men from their conversations. As I got closer, I realized the blond in the center of the group was extolling the virtues of Jimi Hendrix, after having fucked him the night before. I walked on by. It seemed silly. I'd fucked him the night before she had.

I moved on to Golden Gate Park. As usual, the sky over Hippie Hill was dark with Frisbees, kites, and seagulls. Hundreds of hippies' dogs were barking and walking on people lying on the grass. The air was thick with the smell of marijuana, patchouli oil, jasmine incense, and eucalyptus trees. Black guys were playing congas and flutes; white guys were playing harmonicas and guitars. It was as crowded as Coney Island on the Fourth of July. Hippie Hill was like this every day of the week.

I ran into some friends and sat around drinking wine. Noonish, I stopped back at 1826 Page Street, my home. An LSD capping party was in progress. It was the sort of party that only happened where an acid dealer lived.

The object of the party was to put LSD powder into gelatin capsules, but since the LSD assimilated through the skin, everyone got pretty high. The party went on in shifts. When someone got too high to continue, another person would take their place. So when Kirk, one of my roommates, dropped out, I took his place in front of a large mound of white powder. After filling about 300 capsules, I felt that familiar surge of LSD. Soon I didn't care about capping LSD anymore, and besides my fingers weren't doing my bidding. Someone took my place and I went back out on the street.

I walked down Page Street, which runs parallel to Haight. The sidewalk was now lined with hippies and dealers trying to sell anything you might want to get high.

I was high enough, and Haight Street was too crowded for me. So I went back to Page Street and walked to the Catholic church where I could be alone. It was empty except for an old lady in a pew who didn't notice me. It was near Easter, so the altar was dressed in purple and gold. It was peaceful.

Since I wasn't raised Catholic, the confessional booths had always fascinated me. I looked into them. There were booths on both sides of the priest's box, but the priest's box looked the best. It had a velvet armchair and gold and purple raiments hung over the backrest. The booth was bathed in blue light. On LSD it looked so comforting … a great spot to sit for awhile, so holy. I went in and closed the door. I was tripping my brains out so even if I had been a Catholic I wouldn't have thought this was a weird thing to do at the time.

A minute later the door opened. I thought at first it must be the priest, but no, it was some jerk. Maybe it was the janitor or someone like that, there to tell me to leave, but no, he fell to his knees in the cramped space. His glasses fogged up. He began sweating.

"Let me eat you," he whispered. "Please let me eat you."

Whoa, was this guy a pervert! This was disgusting. Who could think about sex on LSD in a confessional booth? I was feeling like a flaccid fungus, totally unsexy.

Where had this guy materialized from? He wasn't in the church when I came in.

I said something like, "No, my son, but you're forgiven. Go now in peace." I made the sign of the cross. But he didn't leave. He got physical, but I climbed over him and bolted out the door, past the pews and back into the eye-damaging sunlight of the street.

A flatbed truck came lumbering toward me, carrying amplifiers, guitars, drums, a group of hippies and THE GRATEFUL DEAD. They stopped, extended a hand and pulled me on board. We were on our way to San Quentin to give a free concert for the prisoners. Not much happened out there, but the music was good and the prisoners liked it.

By the time I reached home, everybody was snorting heroin to come down from the acid capping party. I helped myself to some and laid down for a bit.

A friend named Patrick, who I hadn't seen in a while, stopped by. He woke me and talked me into visiting his new guru, Anton LaVey, America's foremost demonologist and devil worshiper of the moment. It sounded interesting, so I went. First we stopped at Patrick's sister's house to borrow her car. She was having what appeared to be a sit-down dinner for a bunch of American Indians. What it turned out to be wasn't a dinner at all, but an authentic peyote ceremony. Her husband, a full-blooded Sioux, was munching on some peyote buttons. They all were. They offered us some; we ate them; they were nauseating. The Indians reminded us that we had to return the next day to drink each other's urine so we could get high all over again. It was part of the three-day ceremony.

"Oh, I'll be back," I lied. Are they joking? Drink the piss of those fat wrinkled Indians? Anyway what were they doing having a peyote ceremony sitting around on plastic chairs, in a prefab apartment, wearing polyester flowered shirts under fluorescent lights? Weren't they supposed to be out on the plains, under the stars wearing buffalo pelts? Their ancestors were probably rolling over in their sacred burial grounds.

When we got to LaVey's formidable Victorian house, which was painted black, all of it, down to the drainpipes and the ornate woodwork, Patrick asked me to sit in the living room and wait for him to return.

The living room looked like a film set for Poe's story *The Fall of the House of Usher*. LaVey entered wearing velvet robes. He seemed surprisingly cordial and human. He brought some sort of liquid for me to drink. Patrick returned carrying a bag. LaVey nodded to Patrick and left.

"We're going to have some fun now, Cookie," he said. "We're going to Mount Tamalpais to evoke one of Beelzebub's footmen. Whataya say?"

"Fine with me. Let's go." I was pretty sure LaVey was a fraud supported by naive fools like Patrick … although … at the same time I couldn't dismiss the creepy feeling I got inside the house.

As we crossed the Golden Gate Bridge, Patrick told me he had personally performed a black ceremony that resulted in the *San Francisco Chronicle* newspaper strike. I decided Patrick was nuts.

The summit of Mount Tamalpais was entirely too dark. There was hardly a moon that night and the trees, rocks, even my own feet beneath me were looking distorted. It seemed like spirits had invaded, making everything undulate and change shape. Maybe the knowledge this spot had been a sacred burial ground had to do with those sensations.

Patrick opened his bag and produced a bloodstone talisman, a jar of blood, a black-handled knife, a bag of herbs, the hooves of a goat, and a black book. He scratched a nine-foot circle and a pair of pentacles in the dirt. After seeing all this, I began suspecting Patrick might be dangerous. I knew enough from books about the black arts to realize when someone was taking themself too seriously.

When clouds began moving across the crescent moon it got so dark that the edge of the mountain disappeared and the earth beneath my feet was no longer visible. Patrick told me to stand in the middle of the circle. He said I would be okay since this was the protected spot. I thought, if this was the protected spot, why wasn't Patrick standing there with me? But I stepped inside the circle anyway and Patrick began reading from his black book. Just as I was beginning to relax, sure this was all ridiculous, I heard something in the distance running towards us. I heard footsteps and a screeching voice, half-human, half-animal. I was not imagining. Maybe it was a big wounded flightless bird? What else had only two feet in the animal kingdom? This thing certainly sounded like it was on two feet, not four.

I tried to categorize the sound … but fear overtook reason. I felt my body cold. My stomach sank. I felt like I must be going ashen. The little hairs on my body rose and waved like wheat in the wind. For the first time I knew the feeling of one's hair standing on end. I looked at Patrick, who was obviously not in command of the situation. He looked like someone being disemboweled. I guess he hadn't expected such dramatic results either.

If this was a test of courage, I lost. If this was a ritual for human sacrifice with me as the victim, I won, because I didn't wait around to find out. I couldn't stand it. No one with a shred of sanity would have been able to stand there.

So I ran, I left Patrick in the dust like the roadrunner in cartoons. I ran faster than I ever had in my life, probably crossed paths with the footman himself, jumped into the car, took the keys from under the floor mat and tore down the side of the mountain, tires squealing around the narrow precarious curves, gunning it full blast to the Golden Gate Bridge. When I finally saw the bridge lights (fear had altered my vision I think), the superstructure was melting and the houses on the other side were disintegrating. The road rose and fell like storm swells on the sea. I wanted to scream to the passersby but they looked shockingly inhuman. I kept feeling like there was someone or something in the backseat with me.

When I got home, I leapt out of the car and ran inside so scared that everyone was horrified (most of them were on THC and STP). They calmed down, and I calmed down. I took a hot bath and relaxed.

A little later we all decided to use Patrick's car and go out to Berkeley to see Jim Morrison play at some ballroom there. We wanted to distribute the Blue Cheer LSD that had gone through the laundry by accident. Susan had stashed it in the dirty laundry the day before. Mark hadn't known and washed the whole load (about $400 worth of the stuff) with the detergent Cheer. Now the whole batch of LSD was Blue Cheer and Cheer combined. We planned to give it away free, providing of course people didn't mind the accompanying side effects of the detergent.

Jim Morrison was good, as usual, and so was the LSD, despite the slight stomach cramps. We even handed a lump of the goo to him onstage and he happily ate it. After the concert, we left to smoke opium at home, leaving Kathy and Eve to go backstage to try and fuck Morrison. While smoking opium and listening to KMPX (the best radio station at the time), we heard an unfamiliar song. It was great, unlike anything else we'd ever heard. I offered, since we didn't have a phone, to go out into the three A.M. morning and call KMPX and get the title and the name of the musician.

While I was in the phone booth, after I talked to the KMPX DJ and found out it was a cut from a new album, *Doctor John the Night Tripper*, a black man with short hair walked up and stood next to the booth. I thought he was waiting to use the phone, but no, it was me he was waiting for.

"How do you like Stokely Carmichael?" he asked.

"He's okay. I don't really care one way or the other about him, to tell you the truth," I said, unsure of the relevance of the question.

"Would you like to meet him?"

"Not right now. It's a little late, don't you think? He's probably asleep," I answered.

But he drew a gun from inside an Iceberg Slim book. I looked around feebly for help. There was none.

"Come with me and we'll meet him," he said. He took me to his Lincoln and we got in.

We never met Stokely Carmichael.

Actually it would have been nicer to meet him because this turned out to be rape. It wasn't even done well and he was stupid besides, just like the young girls on the Manson bus. But he did give me a gift from his large glove compartment ... a musical jewelry box, the kind that has the ballerina in the pink tutu.

I ingeniously cajoled him to drive me back into my neighborhood by asking him to come home with me. I knew there'd be people walking around on the streets in the Haight, so I could just jump out of the car when he stopped at a red light or something. I told him I had wall-to-wall carpeting, air conditioning, a huge color TV set, and heroin waiting for him. When we got to the Haight, I saw a few hippies walking by, so I flung the door open, and clutching the music box, threw myself out of the moving car.

"That man just raped me," I screamed to them. They pounced on the car and pulled the guy out. There was a resident's hippie vigilante group forming in the Haight at the time, and these were some of them. They were taking the law into their own hands, to protect "their womenfolk" from things just like this. They didn't beat the guy up. Hippies didn't do that kind of thing. They gave him a big dose of LSD instead and took his gun away from him.

When I got home, a bit shaken once again, everyone was doing cocaine mixed with crystal methadrine. They got upset for a minute when I told them the rape story. Kirk asked me why I was always the one to have all the fun.

They offered me some cocaine and methadrine and we ushered in the dawn talking about aesthetics, Eastern philosophy, Mu, Atlantis, and the coming apocalypse. We recorded the conversation, not realizing we were all making the same points five or six times. It would sound foolishly cyclical the next day.

But it was already the next day … time for me to go back out on Haight Street and have some more fun.

Waiting for the New Age

One day in the park, a helicopter swooped in and dropped little pills of LSD on everybody. They said it was Owsley himself up there, but who knew for sure? We ate them. Didn't matter who sent them to us.

That day we were certain everything was finally going to happen like we'd been hoping.

The San Andreas fault and the old fault over there under New York City were going to act up, rumble, crack, and destroy California and the East Coast, Colorado would have beachfront property.

There'd only be a few places on the earth that wouldn't sink into the depths. Those would be the Power Places that existed on earth's meridians where life force energy accumulated. Places like where the Great Pyramid of Giza or Stonehenge stood, or the Nazca plains where UFOs have their airstrip, Machu Picchu, Mount Everest, Lake Titicaca, the Bermuda Triangle, Easter Island, and of course, Golden Gate Park in San Francisco.

Mostly everything would be destroyed, all the corporation buildings, banks, and industrial plants anyway, but communes, ashrams, retreats, and hippies' homes and gardens would stand. People who weren't wise or spiritual enough would fall into the cracks and go the way of the dinosaurs. It'd be the end for people of their kind.

Atlantis and Mu would of course rise again from the oceans and the new generation, the sons and daughters of the Light, the lost tribe, the descendants and reincarnates of Atlantis and Mu would inherit the earth, which of course would suddenly bounce back and abound with lush green, wonderful flora and fauna, and clean sparkling air and water.

We'd dance around in peace, love, sunshine, flowers. We'd swim with the dolphins and whales to share insights. Yes, we'd be the ones saved to start the new world. Things would be great. There'd be no wars, hatred, fear, or insensitivity … all living things would communicate telepathically, including our brothers and sisters, the plants.

There'd be plenty of other great stuff. Everybody would be able to see each other's auras as halo lights around their heads. White and blue auras would be the most spiritual colors. The healers would have green lights. Yellow lights for those in-between types. Some people would have red auras, which isn't so great but might be okay if they controlled their wild tempers.

Everything was all predestined and arranged and we knew these things without really having to discuss them.

We waited all day for the first rumble of the big quake, and the first crash of thunder, and force of wind that would beckon in the earth's rebirth. But it didn't happen that day. We didn't lose hope though. We waited until the next day and then the next three days. Then time stretched out and we waited through all the days in Haight-Ashbury.

Knowing that we were the blessed ones in states of grace, we lived clean lives in preparedness and took drugs to kill time. We got ready with our backpacks and energy granola.

We practiced astrology, yoga, levitation, transcendental meditation, astral travel, telekinesis, cabalism, prayer. We called on the spirits. We waited and waited, and hoped, but the world didn't fall apart. It was a big letdown.

Finally low-level energy swept through the Haight, destroying plans for the coming age. Some people gave up and became computer programmers or realtors.

But some people are still waiting, right there on Hippie Hill. Waiting and hoping. Still watching for the end.

"Look around," they say, "Mark our words. It won't be with a bang."

The Pig Farm—Baltimore & York, Pennsylvania, 1969

I was shopping for knockwurst, but it was the end of the day for the butchers at the A&P, and they were breaking down the meat section, so I settled for a package of frozen breakfast links. This was when I first saw Herb Eickerman watching me from the produce section, apathetically fingering the potatoes. He looked like a young blond Robert Mitchum, the hooded eyes, the unforgiving jaw, well worn Levis, muscles.

His expression changed the minute he saw me go for the frozen links. He approached me and put his hand on my package.

"Them sausages ain't no good," he said with a voice like Johnny Cash.

"Oh yeah?" I said, irritated. Who was this guy? "Are you an Oscar Meyer wiener salesman or something?"

"Those thangs are frozen even," he tried to pull the links from my hand, "I know pigs and these ain't from good pigs."

"One person's opinion," I said callously, thinking that this was a low display of meat sabotage. At this, the links slipped from his grip; his determination fizzled. I tossed my frozen links into my cart and wheeled away thinking about this man, this pork devotee. Maybe he was just one of those familiar cruisers, the grocery singles types, picking up girls in the meat section.

A moment later I ran into Bob, a friend known as the Psychedelic Pig because he was fat, he sold LSD, and had a huge collection of ceramic pigs: stuffed pigs, wooden pigs, pig clocks, pig lamps. His whole house was a porker menagerie.

He was there at the A&P with a cart full of Pepsi, club soda, beer, potato chips, dips, cakes, pies, doughnuts. It looked like he was having a party. He was, he told me.

"The main course is a roast suckling piglet," he laughed. "A friend of mine who owns a pig farm gave me the pig for the dinner. Isn't that perfect?"

"A pig farm?" I asked.

"He's around here somewhere helping me shop," he glanced around. "You're coming to my party, right? I thought you knew. It's my birthday."

When I got to the party, I found, as I had suspected, the blond Robert Mitchum was the pig farmer in question.

So … he actually did know something about pigs. This gave him credibility. He got more handsome at the party.

We talked. He was shy.

He told me that near York, Pennsylvania, he had a 9,000-acre farm … land that had been in his family for generations, when his great-great grandfather had left Austria with his famous opera star wife, a balding coloratura soprano who kept lots of wigs and pearls. This was Herb's great-great grandmother. He was very proud of his mother's side.

We left the party together to sit on the edge of the Baltimore Harbor, and watch the sun sink on the Domino Sugar refinery and the harbor's greasy water. With the sun bouncing red on the waves, it was difficult to see the true color of the brown water, difficult also to see the disgusting things unabashedly floating on the surface, things like rusty beer cans, plastic bags, used rubbers, occasional turds.

It was very romantic.

I went with Herb to his farm that night in his old muddy pickup truck. It took three hours to get there; he had to stop a few times to fix something under the hood; I guessed he was just showing off his mechanical acumen.

I was there for three days when Herb bought me a horse, a ten-year-old black gelding.

"I was buyin' some new pigs today at the market, and since they were sellin' horses too, I told 'em to go on an' throw inna nice horse for a little extra," he said.

"Go on down the barn and take a look at 'im. He's nice alright."

I decided to stay for awhile.

I took a trip back to Baltimore to pack some clothes and find a temporary home for my pet monkey. Then back at the farm, I rode the horse every day, while Herb rode his tractors, doing whatever it was that pig farmers do. I cooked a lot of pork; I sautéed vegetables but Herb didn't like them crisp; he liked them mushy, the way his mother made them.

We drank a lot of whiskey, and smoked a lot of grass at night, and he always sang and played the guitar before we went to sleep. He wrote new songs in his head every day. There wasn't any TV. His brothers and cousins were always around; they worked the farm too.

Sometimes friends of mine would drive up on the weekends from Baltimore. On these evenings with friends, while the biggest stars in the darkest skies spread out over us, Herb would take us for rides in the shovel tractor. In the dark we would all pile in the shovel and he would drive. He'd thunder across the land with us bouncing around and singing country hits.

I adopted one of the little piglets for a pet and brought him inside. He was so cute. Herb told me they were easily housebroken.

"Smart as whips," he said, and he was right. Pigs make good house pets. The pig would always scratch with his cloven hooves at the door whenever he wanted to go out or come back in.

The house was huge and cold, with no central heat. The main room was built a hundred and fifty years ago, and the rest of it was added on at the turn of this century. It hadn't been dusted or vacuumed in seventy years, so the dog and pig hair was so thick on the worn carpets that footsteps left impressions. All the furniture, the heavy drapes and the carpets that were probably vibrant seventy years ago were now the color of dried blood. Everything was monochromatic, the house and its interior, Herb's clothes, the dirt on the boots. Even the stove and refrigerator, which were probably white at one time, were so caked with grease and pork blood that they were dark brown too. Despite this, the place didn't look dirty, for some reason; it just looked earthy. I liked it. His parents didn't. They lived in a modern trailer home down the road.

I lived there for four months and liked being the farmer's girl. I rode my horse back and forth across the land every day, and got to know every acre … so when Herb was arrested for growing marijuana I couldn't believe it.

Where were those hidden acres? How had the police known about it?

I never did find out, but I saw pictures of the pot crop when I was taken in for questioning. In one color snapshot there was a fat cop standing beside a seven-foot-tall marijuana plant. He was posing like a proud fisherman with his giant dead fish strung up beside him.

The police tried to implicate me, but I was so obviously naive about the whole thing they let me go.

The worst part about it was Herb's father's reaction. He wouldn't bail him out.

On his own, Herb had no money ... didn't even have a bank.

I tried to get the money together myself but I didn't know anybody who had $25,000. At the time I didn't even know anybody who had $25 in one lump.

I stayed on at the farm without him for awhile, expecting that he'd be out any day, but the house became unbearable without him. I got very lonely. The pet pig got too big to keep indoors, so he ended as a regular pig. My horse disappeared, taken by the father or the brothers; I'll never know for sure.

I just sat on the red velvet sofa with the weak sunlight streaming through the muddy windows, my only companions the dust particles that floated around illuminated in the light. The trees became leafless; the ground turned hard with the first frost, so I went back to Baltimore and there found that even my monkey had died while I was gone.

I wrote Herb letters all the time but he never answered.

Finally I went to see him in prison.

He looked awful; his skin was sallow from being indoors; his blue eyes were empty; his hair was shaved.

I asked him why he hadn't answered any of my letters, and he said he couldn't read or write, and he was too embarrassed to ask any other prisoners to read him my letters because they were all busy reading constantly, and writing prison novels.

I had never known he was illiterate. I couldn't believe I hadn't known this.

So that's why all the books on the farm had been so dusty and upside-down on the shelves!

I read him my letters while I was there and I sent him a first grade English book. He had never gone to school, I found out, but that didn't make him stupid; he was one of the smartest people I've known.

What need did he have to go to school? His work was on the farm. What need did he have with the written word? He knew numbers; he was good at math; he could buy and sell pigs, and count them. He knew his relationship with the earth, and he knew all the carnal things, all the practical stuff.

He was born in that farmhouse on the same horsehair mattress that we slept on in the biggest bedroom. All his brothers had been born there, his father, his grandfather; in fact, his grandfather had died on it too.

"I'll probably die on this mattress," he once said when we were in bed together.

That day in prison he said something else. "I'm gonna die here in prison, Cookie. I feel my spirit ebbin' right outta me in this hell hole. It's a godforsaken place, this here prison."

"You'll get out soon, Herb. Hold on, honey. You just need to be out in the fields again."

"Ain't never gonna be the same. Ain't never gonna be the same."

It was painful to see him with all that steel and concrete around him, the proverbial wild thing in a cage.

Bored of singing and playing his guitar, sick of the street-wise cellmates with their talk of thievery and guns and bars, tired of doing endless push-ups, he taught himself to read in prison, and soon he was writing ten-page letters.

Grammar perfect, with spelling much better than mine, he finally found a way to write down the words to the songs he'd made up. He found out he'd been a poet all along, and found too, while consuming a book a day, that he was looking into a new world, and he responded to it like a man who'd been dying of thirst.

Eventually, after a year or two, I guess, I forgot what he looked like, the way he pitched hay, how he looked on a tractor, the way he sang. I stopped writing him letters and then he stopped writing me.

The next time I saw Herb was another year later at a Christmas party at my house. He'd just gotten out of prison, and he appeared all spiffy in his father's pre-World War II blue suit with a little squirming black-and-white piglet under his arm. He offered it to me as a token of his love and then he asked me to marry him, right there in the doorway.

"Oh Herb … I … this … I … I can't … I'm really … sorry … I'm with somebody else now. I tried to write and tell you this … but …"

"Who is this person you're living with?" He looked around, crushed.

I didn't recognize Herb at all. Who was this strange person on my doorstep? Everything had changed so much for me; things had been rushing in lightning speed. I'd totally forgotten about Herb. For him it was still two years ago, even though he was a different person, well read, well spoken, now on his way to becoming a very cultured person. Things had stood still for him.

I was the last woman he had seen. He probably jerked off thinking about me every night.

I felt guilty about that. I should have sent him some porno magazines, or found him a pen pal, or something.

"Who's this person? I'd like to congratulate him," he said. The pig began to squeal. "Can I put this baby down?"

I nodded. The piglet trotted under the kitchen table. I started crying.

"He's over there," I said and pointed to the rock and roll hedonist I'd been living with. He was one of those romantic slow poison types, very drunk at the moment, sitting on the sofa drinking gin from the bottle, talking to another drunk. He was very different than Herb.

Herb walked over to him. "Hi. I'm Herb Eickerman, maybe your wife told you about me."

"She's not my wife," my drunk said, "but yeah, she told me. You out of prison? Just in time for Christmas. Have a drink."

He handed Herb the bottle, but Herb didn't take it. "You want a glass or something?"

"Don't you know that heavy drinking is slow death?" Herb said to him.

"Yeah. But who's in a hurry?"

"I see darkness all around that man," Herb said.

I guessed that he was talking about auras.

I looked over at my rock and roller. He was sitting in dim candlelight, wearing all-black clothes, had dark-green eyes, black hair, and a three-day five o'clock shadow on his face.

No wonder he looked shady.

"Look, Cookie, I don't feel much like partying," Herb said. "Have a nice life, and you can keep the pig. Do what you want with him. Eat him, whatever."

"I'd never ..." I started to say I'd never eat him but he stopped me.

"I found Jesus while I was in jail. He's going to keep me company." And he walked out.

My boyfriend, that prince of darkness, came to the door to stand next to me.

"You wanted to be with him?" he asked, "I'll leave. Don't worry about me. I'll just jump off a bridge or something."

"No, you don't have to do that," I laughed. "Just get me a drink."

He handed me the bottle.

Years later when the rock and roller had long moved out, and the piglet pet got too big to be a pet, I heard that Herb had married a red-haired born-again Christian, and they were having little boy babies on the horsehair mattress.

Horsehair mattresses make a lot of noise, but they never lose their shape.

Breaking into Show Biz

Baltimore, 1969

I was living in a little cavelike hideaway on an alley called Lovegrove. The only door of this dugout lair opened directly on the alley, so that made it seem like secret chambers. It was odd. It had character.

This place must have had a seedy history, because it was alive with uneasy spirits. Maybe, in former days, it had been an all-night opium den, or the clandestine hutch for felons who have their pictures in the post office. It was definitely an undercover joint. Perhaps it was a speakeasy during prohibition, or a cubby-hole for occultists, even a bomb shelter. It just wasn't a normal living space, by any standards.

I still have nightmares about this place.

It had two rooms plus the kitchen and bathroom, which were always dark because the three meager windows that looked out on the alley never saw sunlight, just dense eternal twilight. I kept them draped with heavy velvet. Its low ceilings were covered with a jumble of exposed pipes.

Living there I felt like a mole.

The only way I could make the place livable was to layer it with dark fabrics and light it with tons of candles. All the heavy curtains and yard goods muffled city sounds. I could have been anywhere. The silence and the candlelight made reality impossible. It began to look cozy like a medieval padded cell for alchemist wizards.

I lived there with my pet monkey who liked cockroaches. He used to scan the fabric walls for them. When he saw one from all the way across the room with his primate super X-ray vision, he'd swing the distance on the ceiling pipes and deftly scoop up the bug with one hand, pop it in his mouth, and swing back to the curtain rod window perch where he lived. He was a good pet.

There were always a few people living there with me, they floated in and out, but a pretty lesbian named Babette, who never wore a shirt indoors, and a homeless philosopher hippie named Nash were permanent fixtures on the sofa. We lived primarily on LSD, poppy seed buns, and cheap champagne. Nash sold LSD from the place, so this paid the rent.

I was working on some novel, long since lost in the shuffle, and the word "future" wasn't part of my vocabulary. This was my status when I accidently broke into show biz.

At the time in Baltimore, there'd been word of a hometown filmmaker named John Waters who was showing his low-budget films in churches and bingo halls all over the city. One night, Babette, Nash and I went to one of his screenings of *Mondo Trasho* at a church bingo hall, right around the corner from Lovegrove Alley.

A door prize was offered and after the screening there was a random drawing of ticket stubs. I won.

The prize was twofold: dinner at a White Tower Hamburger joint and a screen test. Over dinner I discovered John Waters and he discovered me. We got along.

John was as thin as a string bean with shoulder-length brown hair and a pencil-thin mustache. He wore thrift-store shirts, drank Coca-Cola, and smoked Kool Midgets nonstop. He made me laugh.

He seemed driven, so driven in fact, that when he told me that he was premature and only weighed a pound at birth, I envisioned him as an infant, compact like a pound cake, lying in a clear plastic preemie life support box, while nurse's aides were off loafing, already rococo and bursting his bunting wrapper with his dreams and plans of film scenarios. I'm sure he was entertaining the other babies, making them laugh about the inept hospital staff, their moms and dads, and the oddness of being born. He's one of those kinds of people that you imagine was already an adult while still a baby. The same, just smaller.

When later I did the screen test and met the bunch of actors who were his constant companions, Divine, Mink Stole, David Lockhary, Bonnie Pierce, Pat Moran, Susan Lowe, Marina Melin, I felt like I was meeting my new family. I got a part in his next film, *Multiple Maniacs*. We were starting to shoot in a couple of weeks.

I'd found a new niche, a foray as an underground film actress. So there I was, way way underground, figuratively and literally, underground in the Lovegrove inner sanctum studying the underground script by candlelight.

Being underground times two felt right.

I came above ground when the alley home flooded during a four-day rainstorm and Babette and Nash left for a Russian River, California, commune. I moved to an attic apartment with lots of sunlight.

John Waters and the Blessed Profession—1969

John Waters was a rare bird in Baltimore in 1969. He still is. He was born rococo, with perceptions that surely confused his parents.

"I weighed one pound when I was born. I was premature," he said to me one day.

By the time he was ten years old, he'd been bitten by the show biz bug. He wrote plays and became a puppeteer. He told me that none of the neighborhood kids understood his kind of puppet theater, though. I guess it was way over their heads. I can only imagine what those puppets said on stage. The neighborhood kids' heads must have been spinning.

Most of his films had religious undertones, a few saints or angels performing miracles in laundromats or beauty parlors, so he thought church halls were appropriate places. I'd heard a lot about his films, he was the only maverick filmmaker in Baltimore, probably the only filmmaker in the whole city. He knew every aspect of filmmaking. He was the writer, producer, director, cameraman, soundman, lighting expert, editor, even the distributor. I liked him immediately. He always seemed very restless but not nervous, always self-assured but not ego-maniacal. His perceptions could make you laugh even when you were miserable.

When I met him, he'd already made four or five films shot with his own camera, budgeted at under two hundred dollars. These cagey, fast-paced, celluloid stories, scored with wild music and wilder action, were masterpieces. They were unclassifiable. They weren't exactly art; no one knew what to call them. Baltimore audiences were confused by his imagination.

He had a bunch of friends who always worked with him. The anomalous nobility, the only underground superstars Baltimore could call its own. They were a close-knit, clannish group, but I was ushered in, and they became like family, finally a family I understood.

The first time I worked in film was in his *Multiple Maniacs*, a film about maniacs, obviously, and a giant lobster-turned-rapist. I played Divine's wild hippie daughter. I danced around topless in shorts in the film and explained to my mom, Divine, how great it was to get tear-gassed in antiwar rallies.

I was terrible in this film, I couldn't remember lines for some reason, and after a million takes John got impatient. The more impatient he got, the less I could remember. John is the kind of director who shows you physically how to do a scene: he turns off the camera, hops onto the set, and demonstrates the scene for the actor. He would have been a great actor in his own films; he should have played all the parts himself, but someone had to run the camera.

In John's films you had to exude energy, and you had to shout. One reason for this was the low-budget sound equipment. If you didn't shout, no one was going to hear you. The other reason was purely a matter of style.

I began to observe the techniques of his veterans, Divine in particular. I watched Divine closely and tried to be calm but energetic, like him. I didn't quite get it, but Divine always put me at ease, he was a born star, a serious actor. In his Capri pants and Spring-o-lators, smelling from cosmetics like my aunt Pearl, he was very gentle in scenes with me. He knew I was nervous; it was my first film. He was just like a fairy godmother.

Everybody wanted to act in John's films, all the Maryland Art Institute students, all the druggies, even the redneck honkies, and John put them to work. But sometimes not as actors, so they objected. Everybody wanted to be in front of the camera, not behind it. My lesbian friend Babette hounded him so badly for a part that he finally put her in a crowd scene. Nash, my other roomie, proud of the blue aura exuding from his hairline, thought for sure John would notice it and give him a starring role as a messiah or someone like that. But John didn't see Nash's aura. I didn't see Nash's aura either. Only Nash saw it, in the mirror. When John didn't cast him, Nash packed up and left for Hollywood, where agents might see his aura, he thought. He wanted to be a star. Everyone wanted to be a star. Everyone, all over the world, wants to be in movies. It's modern human nature, a new biological urge, a twentieth-century physiogenesis. People feel compelled to be on the screen.

John was allowing a lot of people to fulfill these urges. He always had new featured people, new discoveries in each film. People who acted in his films got underground fame in Baltimore. Yes, he was the casting agent too, aside from everything else, but he never used a casting couch, even though he probably could have. After all, he was Baltimore's film tycoon. He just wasn't the sleazy type.

In those days he didn't get a lot of newspaper press, but it didn't matter. John Waters and his bunch got sort-of-famous in

Baltimore anyway. I guess I became sort-of-famous too, after *Multiple Maniacs*, but sort-of-famous people never know they're famous until someone asks them for an autograph, and no one ever asked me for one in Baltimore back then.

The ambitious low-budget film world was really exciting, we were all just over twenty-one, we were on the screen, we were close friends working together, and Baltimore was becoming our oyster. World fame looked like it was just around the corner. We were up-and-coming celebrities, our ships were coming in, our stars of fortune were rising, we were blessed people in the most blessed profession, the best business in the world. The entertainment business.

Route 95 South—Baltimore to Orlando

I don't remember why I went to Orlando with Lee. I guess I went because I needed some sun and there was a great place to stay. According to Lee, his brother's place was a mansion with a pool and gardens full of gladiolus and hibiscus flowers, grapefruit and orange trees.

"And, we'll have fun. He has lots of cocaine," Lee said.

It was dark when we left for the trip. We walked in the bitter cold across a glass-strewn parking lot; the pieces of broken bottles glittering in the orange crime prevention lights made it look like a huge field of fool's gold. The cyclone fence we scaled had garbage and a lone ripped brassiere plastered to it in the stiff wind.

Approaching the highway, I realized that none of the cars would ever be able to see us in the dark with our black clothes on. I was right, we were there for about an hour with no luck at getting a ride.

Lee, who didn't possess the appropriate negativism wouldn't give up and go home. He just kept putting that Johnny Walker Red to his lips while chanting Hare Krishnas.

"I chant to get rides," he said. "It works."

"Doesn't seem to be helping much tonight," I said.

"Wait. Be patient," he coaxed.

Another hour went by and we hadn't gotten a ride. I decided finally that he should hide behind the cement arch of the overpass and I would stand alone and hitchhike for awhile. It was the standard trick.

Sure enough a car stopped. I opened the door of the blue Ford and was a little disappointed to see that this person wouldn't do at all. He wore one of those psychosexual-disorder smiles. I closed the door.

Lee, as mad as I'd ever seen him, couldn't believe I turned the guy down.

"'I'd protect you," he said with his hands on his hips.

"You'd fall asleep."

"No. I would have sat in the middle," he said.

"He would have raped you too. I'm a good judge of deviates. He was one all right," and that was that.

Before Lee got back to his hiding place, a Mercedes stopped and I opened the door. The driver looked okay. He was skinny with highly lacquered blond hair, a full mouth of good teeth, very clean manicured bejeweled hands. Here was a male version of a nouveau-riche hillbilly Farrah Fawcett, way before her time. Jascha Heifetz was blaring on the tape cassette.

Lee and I got in. He said his name was Cleo. He was going to Arlington, Virginia, right outside of Washington, DC.

"I'm on a lot of amphetamines," he said. I fell asleep.

When I woke up the car was parked in front of a large brick colonial house tastefully covered in English ivy. I was alone. I wondered what was going on.

Cleo and Lee soon appeared from the back of the house with a stereo, a color TV, silverware and a metal box.

"What's going on?" I asked as they loaded up the car.

"I just had to stop here and pick up a couple of things," Cleo said and smiled.

We left his house but fifteen minutes later we were parked in front of another large Tudor style house. Cleo was picking up a few things there too.

By the time we got to the fourth house the back seat was piled with ultra-modern state of the art appliances: Mister Coffees, La Machines, high performance vacuum cleaners, Kenmore toaster ovens. They also hadn't forgotten various valuable objets d'art, a few loose bottles of Korbel Brut … you name it. I figured out that I was an accomplice to Breaking and Entering and Grand Larceny so I thought it would be best to get out at the next Howard Johnson.

I found my bag under all the stuff and noticed a little gold statue of Pan lying on the floor with a Maxfield Parrish print and a crystal jar of jelly beans. I liked that statue. Maybe I should ask Cleo for it. Oh, but why? He stole it anyway, so I put it in my bag without Cleo noticing. He had his back to me, driving.

"Take it," he said.

"I'm sorry. It was like impulse shopping. I can't believe you saw me do that." I handed it back to him.

"You can't hoodwink a hoodwinker," he said and winked at me in the rearview mirror. "It's yours. Take it."

I decided I wouldn't get out after all so we drove all the way with him until his turn off in Arlington.

He left us on the highway, after giving Lee a gas chain saw and his calling card. It had only his name and his phone number in lavender baroque script.

We got a ride by hanging out at a Howard Johnson and intimidating an old lady in pink foam curlers at the wheel of a gray Dodge. She was nervous; she didn't really want to pick us up at all.

"Oh, I understand totally," I said, "you don't really know us or anything."

She was leery of the chainsaw, she kept asking why we were carrying it. (Years later when I saw the film *The Texas Chainsaw Massacre*, I thought about this lady.)

When she dropped us off later Lee gave her the chainsaw as a gift and she was really happy. She'd always wanted one, she said.

The next ride was with a person in an Impala. Lee fell asleep in the back seat. This guy had something wrong with his neck. Big growths or something. He started talking about how he was turned away from the army induction center because of the varicosity in his scrotum and did I want to feel it? "Why don't you pull right over here on the shoulder?" I knew he would think I was going to take him up on the scrotum thing.

When the car came to a stop I jumped out and yelled at Lee, "Time to go, Lee. This guy is 4F."

By this time we were in West Virginia and we got a ride with some mountain hippie types joy-riding with marijuana, seconals and beer. We got stopped by the cops and had to help swallow the grass and the seconals so they wouldn't get arrested. It was the least we could do in exchange for the ride.

By the time the seconals hit we were in another car speeding as the sky changed into pale blue. The Cuban guy driving the car told me there was a Spanish word for this time of the day.

"*Madrugada*," he said. "There's no equivalent in English."

I asked him if it included in its meaning the horrible way one feels after being awake all night. My bones felt hollow.

Before the sun had come all the way up, and the headlights were still on, we ran over a rabbit. Right before we hit him the rabbit froze; I guess he was paralyzed by the lights. I looked right into his eyes and saw his final instant of panic. I felt sick. We didn't say anything to each other, but the driver just pulled over and let us out. I guess he was superstitious.

We were both so tired now that we decided to rest in the woods for awhile but we crossed a little shallow swamp to get there and came out with leeches all over our ankles. The only way to get them off if you don't happen to be carrying kerosene was to piss on them. It wasn't easy; we must have stood there for forty five minutes thinking of running water.

Back out on the highway, we got a ride with a couple going as far as Sarasota. That was great.

When we got to the bottom of Georgia, Lee smoked a joint he'd gotten from the mountain hippies. Then he started throwing the *I Ching* coins. I ignored him. After that, while the woman in the front seat was trying to sleep, Lee started playing his harmonica. Music was not his forte but he thought it was, so when the couple asked him four times to stop playing, he argued the point until the couple dumped us out at three in the morning on a section of the highway that ran directly through the Okefenokee Swamp.

There was no moon. The sky was like black cotton batting that enveloped us in a way that felt like walking through clear water in a pool painted black. Very clear and cloudless was the night sky, so it was thick with stars. We even saw clusters of the dust from exploded supernovas deep in space, thousands of light years away.

All around was a nocturnal cacophony; alligators roared, lemurs, birds, and weird insects were yelling at each other. We kept walking and walking, blindly in the dark, along the deserted road that we couldn't see underfoot. There were no points of horizon, no beginning, no end to the highway; if the stars hadn't been there we would have no constellations to lead us; we would have fallen off into the swamp's mouth that gaped at us on each side. In all this blackness, it occurred to me that vicious reptiles and angry mammals might be rearing up for attack; hybrid swamp snakerats could start licking at our heels at any minute.

Way back in the swamp were dim lights, probably the bunson burners of alligator wrestlers.

Lee played the harmonica until I grabbed it from him and tossed it into the darkness at the side of the road. It made a little splash as it hit the swamp water and all the animal sounds stopped for a moment.

We kept walking for hours until finally a Black man in a dark pickup truck stopped for us. We could hardly see him.

He told us he was going to Orlando. Perfect! He was cracking something in his hand and eating it, and offered us some of whatever it was from a paper bag that was audible but not visible. I reached in. Oval things. Nuts!

"Pecans!" I said. I was hungry.

"I'ze haulin' a load obbem," he said, "Y'all take da hol bag."

"Thanks." Then we were all cracking and eating, rumbling along in the slow pickup. When the sun rose, there was silver and gold and every shade of tree laden with dew, all over the place. Willow, cypress, oak, and cottonwood trees were dripping with Spanish moss; the land was lush, fluffy. The air was sweet and warm. A flock of noisy Scarlet Tanagers and Cardinals lit up a cherry tree. The cicadas started droning. A pink Cadillac convertible with a pink woman driving whizzed by in the opposite direction. There were never any other cars.

The man, who in daylight seemed like a cute smiling pocket gopher, pulled off the road and stopped next to a little orange shack with fatback cooking smoke coming from a gray pipe in the roof. There was a cardboard sign with the scrawled words "Brekfas 25 cent" taped with band-aids to the screen door.

"Les hav us som grits an aggs. And waatillya taaz dis beer coffee beer. Hmm hmm, ez good beer." He hopped out of the pickup.

"I'm buyin'," I said as the screen door slammed behind us. The place was humming with black farmers in scrubbed overalls, little girls the color of buckwheat honey with hundreds of plastic barrettes in their hair, and their mothers in thin cotton dresses and flip flops. I don't think I've ever had a better breakfast in my life.

When we got to Orlando, the man let us off not far from Lee's brother's house. It was regular suburbia. What a letdown. Lee's brother's house was not a mansion. It was more like a dilapidated pre-fab fake rancher. The place was overrun with weeds and the pool hadn't been cleaned in a long time; it was frothing green and slimy, with a thick surface layer of insect corpses riding on the little waves.

There wasn't much inside the house either except a TV set, a lava lamp and a few pieces of furniture covered with plastic. In the kitchen there were huge palmetto bugs and lizards scattering over the crusty dishes in the sink. The oranges and grapefruits were rotting on the ground, the flowers were all dried up and brown, and he hadn't seen any cocaine in a year.

The next day I took the golden Pan statue to an antique dealer and he gave me enough money to buy an airplane ticket back to Baltimore.

Next to me on the plane was a stranger who was putting out lines of cocaine on the little tray tables on the seat backs.

"Do this as we lift off. It's a rush," he said as he handed me a rolled up fifty dollar bill to snort with.

I thought about Lee and his brother doing nothing by the light of the lava lamp … well, maybe they were chanting and throwing *I Ching* coins on the stained wall to wall carpeting.

Far below was Highway 95 looking like an aluminium arrow with sparkling specks—cars. The distance Lee and I covered in three slow days would now take three quick hours. I turned to the generous person next to me and suddenly he didn't seem like a stranger after all.

Abduction & Rape—Highway 31, Elkton, Maryland, 1969

"They were just three sluts looking for sex on the highway," the two abductors and rapists said later when asked to describe us.

This wasn't the way we saw it.

A lot of other people didn't see it this way either, but these were women. Most men who know the facts say we were asking for it.

Obviously you can't trust every man's opinion when it comes to topics like rape. A lot of honest men admit that they fantasize about it and that's healthy, but the ones that do it to strangers, unasked, ought to have hot pokers rammed up their wee-wees.

The worst part is there's no flattery involved in rape; I mean, it doesn't much matter what the females look like; it doesn't even seem to matter either if they have four legs instead of two. Dairy farmers have raped their cows even.

"It's great to fuck a cow," they say, "you can fit everything in … the balls … everything."

So I guess it just depends on your genital plumbing as to how you see the following story.

True, we were hitchhiking. True, we were in horny redneck territory, but we hadn't given it a thought.

It was a sunny day in early June, and Mink, Susan, and I were on our way to Cape Cod from Baltimore to visit John Waters, who had just finished directing us in his film *Multiple Maniacs*.

When we told him we were going to thumb it, he said incredulously, "You three?? You're crazy! Don't do it."

"He's just overly paranoid," I told Susan and Mink. "Hitchhiking's a breeze."

It made sense anyway because we only had about fifty dollars between us and above all we needed a beach.

Mink the redhead was dressed casually as always in a black leather jacket with chains, black fingernail polish, and tight black Levis. Susan, the brunette, was dressed as was her normal wont, in a daytime low-cut evening gown, and I, the blond, was dressed conservatively in a see-through micro-mini dress and black velvet jacket.

This was not unusual for us, in fact benign, but in Baltimore at this time, the height of fashion was something like lime-green vinyl pantsuits, or other petroleum-based togs in chartreuse plaid or paisley that melted when the temperature was above 98.6. These clothes became one with Naugahyde car seats on a hot day. So people stared at us. They laughed right in our faces when they saw us.

"I hate to tell ya this," somebody would always take us aside, "but this ain't Hallor-ween."

To this day I can't figure out why we looked so odd to them. What did they see when they looked at their own outfits in their full-length mirrors?

In Susan's thrift-store Victorian mirror that was about as useful as looking into a huge silver-wrapped stick of Wrigley's, we put on our Maybelline black eyeliner lines and mascara, and were looking much better than any of the other displaced hilly-billy beau monde on South Broadway that day.

"FINE MAKEUP, SENSIBLY PRICED" the Maybelline ad on TV said. I thought to myself how true it was. Couldn't beat it for a long trip; waterproof, smudge proof, it sure held up.

For the twelve-hour trip, we didn't forget our two quarts of Jack Daniels and a handful of Dexadrine Spansules (they were new on the pharmaceutical market) and twenty Black Beauties. Aside from these necessities we had a couple of duffel bags of Salvation Army and St. Vincent de Paul formals and uniwear. We were all set.

On the street, we had no problem getting a ride due north.

The trouble started after about an hour into the journey.

We had been traveling in an old green Plymouth with a salesman and his Gideon Bible. He had run off the road into an embankment. Trying to follow our conversation, he'd gotten too drunk on the Jack Daniels, so we left him after he passed out behind the wheel.

"I don't think he was ready for us," Susan said, as we tumbled out of his car laughing.

"Let's make sure the next ride is going to Delaware or Connecticut," Mink suggested, "or at least a little farther north."

We had no idea that we were standing smack in the middle of a famous love zone, Elkton, Maryland, the quickie honeymoon and divorce capital of the eastern seaboard.

Men whose eye pupils were dilated with goatish desire stopped before we could even free our thumbs. We decided to be selective. Apparently we weren't selective enough.

After a long dull lull in traffic, we hopped right into the back of a burgundy Mach 4 Mustang with two sickos, gigantic honkies, hopped-up and horny on a local joy ride. They told us they were going to New York City, the Big Apple, they said.

It is a fact that retarded people do not know they are retarded; they just know that some people do not talk about stuff that interests them.

The conversation we were having in the back was beyond their ken; after a quart of liquor and five Black Beauties apiece, we were a bit hard to follow, even for people who read all the classics.

I suppose they got jealous. They decided to get our attention by going around in circles, north, then south, then north again, passing the same toll booth four times.

Mink, the most astute of us, realized that her instinctive internal migratory compass was awry.

"We're trying to go north," she reminded them.

They just laughed.

"We see that you're playing some kind of circling game with your car." She was trying to make herself heard over the din of some backwoods hard rock bubblegum music that was blaring on the radio.

"Yeah, guys, I saw this same cheesy truck stop whiz by twice already," Susan pointed to a roadside diner that was whizzing by for the fourth time.

"I think they're just trying to get our attention," I said, taking the psychological angle.

"No," said Mink, "these guys are assholes. They're wasting our road time."

She should not have said that, but Mink has never been afraid of telling people about their personality flaws.

"Assholes, huh?" the driver scoffed, and he veered the car right off the highway and into a field of baby green beans and then got back on the blacktop and headed north again. The tires squealed the way they hardly ever do in real life, only in squalid car chase movies.

"Round dees parts we don't call nobody assholes," he said. "That's kinda impolite. We call 'em heiny holes." And they laughed and laughed.

"Well at least we're going north again," I said and in the very moment I said it I realized that it was a ridiculous thing to say.

There comes a time when even the most optimistic people, like myself, realize that life among certain humans cannot be easy, that sometimes it is unmanageable and low-down, that all people are quixotic, and haunted, and burdened, and there's just no way to lift their load for them. With this in mind I wanted to say something to Mink and Susan about not antagonizing these sad slobs, but right then the driver turned to me.

"You ain't going north, honey, you ain't going nowhere but where we're taking you."

These were those certain humans.

"Let's ditch these creeps," Susan said.

"We're getting out at the next truck stop," said Mink and she gathered her duffel bag like a career woman in a taxi with her attaché case.

"Shut the fuck up," the driver said as a Monarch butterfly was creamed on his windshield. The wings mushed into his wipers as the blades squeaked over the splattered glass.

"Fucking butterfly guts," he said.

"We have knives," the guy riding shotgun said and he grinned at us with teeth that had brown moss growing near the gums.

"Big fuckin' deal," said Susan, "so do I," and she whipped out a buck knife that was the size of my miniskirt.

The driver casually leaned over and produced a shotgun and Susan threw the knife out the window.

Suddenly the effects of the Jack Daniels were wearing thin and the black reality of a speed crash was barreling in.

Mink began scribbling a note on a Tampax paper, "HELP!!! WE ARE BEING ABDUCTED BY ASSHOLES!!! CALL THE POLICE IMMEDIATELY!!!"

It was a note for the woman at the toll booth.

When we stopped there Mink started screaming and threw it at the woman. The note fluttered back into the car as we sped away.

"Have you ever fucked calves' liver?" Mossy Teeth said.

"How the hell ya supposed to fuck calves' liver?" the driver asked.

"Well, ya buy some fresh liver and ya put it in a jar and ya fuck it. It's better than a pussy."

Now that's disgusting, I thought, almost as disgusting as the popular practice in seventeenth-century France when men took live ducks and placed the heads of the ducks in a bureau drawer, put their dicks in the ducks and then slammed the drawer shut at the moment of their (not the duck's) orgasm. Men will fuck anything.

I suppose they also cooked the duck and ate it too.

They pulled into this long driveway. The dust was rising and matting the mucous membranes of our noses. Everybody sneezed.

I began to realize that for them we were party girls, that this wasn't something unusual, that girls around these parts were game for a good time, a gang-bang, and that threats of murder might just be considered all part of the fun.

We bounced full speed down this backroad for quite a while, passing vast stretches of young corn plants rustling and reflecting the sun on their new green leaves. I remember getting sliced by young corn plant leaves once, the same kind of painful wounds as paper cuts.

Mink and Susan and I couldn't even look at each other; our eyes hurt.

A white clapboard house came up near diseased elm trees in the distance. Some chickens ran away from the fenders. A rusted-out pickup truck was growing weeds and a blue Chevy was sitting on four cinder blocks right next to a display of greasy old auto parts and an old gray dog that was trying to bark. We pulled up right to the house and from the front door, screen door slamming, came a big acne-scarred man in his BVD underwear and a plaid flannel shirt with a sawed-off shotgun.

"I told you once before, Merle, get off my property," the man hollered, "I'll blow your fuckin' heads right off your shoulders."

"My cousin's a little crazy," the driver said to us and he laughed.

"You wouldn't do no such thing," he bellowed to his cousin with the yellowish drawers on.

"Oh yes I would," the cousin said and aimed his gun at the windshield.

"You think he'd shoot us, El?" the driver asked his buddy.

"Sheet," the other one said, "he'd shoot his granny."

The screen door slammed again and then next to the cousin was a woman with dirty blond hair and dirty bare feet. She was wearing blue jean cutoffs and a T-shirt that said MARLBORO COUNTRY on it. She looked forty-five but she was probably twenty.

A toddler of about two came to the door, pushed it, and fell out into the dirt. The baby started crying but nobody in the yard noticed. The baby got to his feet and stopped crying when he picked up a piece of car tire and put it in his mouth. He was teething, I guessed.

The woman grabbed the shotgun muzzle. "Put that fucking gun down, Henry," she said.

"Leave goa dis gun, woman," Henry said and shook her off, aimed again. She jumped for it again, and in this moment the three of us, Mink, Susan, and I started diving out of the car windows. Mink and Susan got out but Mossy Teeth, El, grabbed my thigh and held me fast. Merle spun the car around and we took off, making corn dirt dust in all the faces of everyone who was standing there in front of the house.

Susan and Mink tried to run after the car, yelling to me to jump. I couldn't now. It was too late. We were burning rubber up the gravel path while Merle and El were pulling me back into the car. They got me in the front seat with them. I was straddling the bucket seats.

I wondered what was going to happen to Mink and Susan, but I bet they wondered more what was going to happen to me.

What happened was this: I began to feel the mood change. As they were talking to each other I noticed that they sounded scared; El even wanted to get out and go home.

After a lot of fighting, Merle finally did let El go. He let him out at a backwoods package store.

Now Merle and his little brain began to wonder what to do with me. His buddy was gone. Who would fuel the fire?

I assumed that he would rape me. He wouldn't let me get away without that at least. Of course I didn't want to get raped so I began to think of a plan.

I have always been an astute observer of sexy women and unsexy women, and in all my years I've never seen a crazy woman get chased by a man. Look at bag ladies on the street. They rarely get raped, I surmised. And look at burnt-out LSD girls. No men bothered with them much. So I decided that I would simply act crazy. I would turn the tables. I would scare him.

I started making the sounds of tape-recorded words running backwards at high speed. This shocked him a bit, but he kept driving farther into the woods, as the sun was setting and the trees were closing in.

"What the fuck are you supposed to be doing?" he asked me nervously. "You a maniac or something?"

"I just escaped from a mental hospital," I told him and continued with the backward-tape sounds, now sounding like alien UFO chatter.

I think he was believing me, anyway he pulled off into the bushes and unzipped his pants and pulled out his pitifully limp wiener. He tried to get it hard.

For a second I saw him debating about whether or not he should force me to give him a blow job.

"Ya devil woman, ya'd bite my dick off wouldn't ya?"

He tried to force his semi-hard pee-wee rod into me as he ripped my tights at the crotch. I just continued with the sounds of the backward tape as he fumbled with his loafing meat.

This infuriated him. "I'm going to ask Jesus to help me on this one. Come on, sweet Jesus, help me get a hard-on. Come on."

He was very serious.

This struck me as deeply hilarious. Praying to the Lord for a hard-on was asking for the ultimate Bible text rewrite.

Not waiting to see whose side the Lord was on, I pushed his wiener quickly aside and threw open the door and dove out into the darkness. I ran faster than I'd ever run and I wasn't a bad runner.

As my eyes grew accustomed to the half-moon light, I saw that I was running into very deep woods. Aggressive brambles grabbed at my thighs, poison ivy licked at my ankles, and yearling trees slapped me in the face.

After a long time I decided to stop running, so I got under a bush next to a pile of rocks. I felt a bunch of furry things scuttle away. Rats, or possums or raccoons, I guessed.

I laid there for awhile trying to see things in the darkness. And then I heard his voice.

He was far in the distance yelling, "Girl! Girl! Where the hell are ya?"

Did he think I was really going to answer?

As he got a little closer I saw that he had a flashlight and I got scared again. If his light found me there would be no hope. My white skin was very bright in the bluish flood of the half moon.

I had a black velvet jacket on with a black lining, so I ripped out the lining in two pieces and wrapped one around my head and the other on my almost bare legs. Those brambles had shredded my stockings.

No light would bounce off me now.

I was awake for a long time and then I just fell asleep, sure that he had given up the search.

At sunrise, or thereabout, I woke up. I didn't even have a hangover.

I felt very proud that I had melted so well into the underbrush, just like Bambi.

Without too much trouble I found this little dirt road and I started walking to the right.

"All roads lead to Rome," I told myself.

I guess I was walking for almost an hour when I heard a vehicle rumbling up behind me. For a second I thought maybe I better dive back into the woods, maybe it was Merle again but I turned and saw it was a little country school bus, a sixteen-seater, a miniature version of the long yellow city buses. I stood in the middle of the road and waved it to a stop.

A woman was driving the bus and there was a load full of kids. I stood in the front of the bus and whispered my predicament; I didn't want to alarm the kids. She drove me to a ranger station and the ranger's wife gave me a cup of Lipton's.

I told my story and they were really peaceful sympathetic people. The ranger called the police station and I found out that Mink and Susan were there.

The ranger's wife liked me, I could tell, and they both drove me to the police station.

When they let me off the wife kissed me and said, "I hope everything goes well for ya, honey. That's a nasty thing ta happen. Watch yasself round these parts, there's some hanky-panky round every corner hereabouts. I know. My husband deals with it everday."

They drove off. I liked her.

Inside the police station the police weren't so nice, but they were patient with my story. They knew the guy. It was a small town.

"He was just released from Jessup's Cut," they said. "He's a bad ass for sure, always in trouble."

"His daddy's a religious man, though, had one hell of a religious upbringin'," one of them said.

Don't I know it, I thought. He believed the Lord would raise the dead even.

It was good to be reunited with Mink and Susan. They told me that they were beside themselves with worry until about ten o'clock. That was about the time I was finally relaxing in the bush, I told them.

The police brought Merle in for questioning. They wanted to hold a kangaroo court right there in the next building. The law is quick in Elkton, Maryland.

In the courtroom I didn't press charges. That would mean lawyers and coming back there and a whole long drawn-out scene. I would lose anyway. I just wanted to leave that town as quickly as possible; anyway Merle was going back to jail for a false insurance claim, or something like that.

The cops then drove us to the bus station and told us that they better not ever see us on a highway again.

While we were waiting for the bus we decided to go to Washington, DC, to the airport where we could maybe hitchhike a ride on a plane.

"Let's go in style," I said. "No more cheap highways."

At the airport bar we met a marine biologist who was working in Woods Hole, Massachusetts.

"I'm flying back to work. I'm working with endangered bass," he said. "But my buddy's flying right into the P-town airport. He'll take you there. No problem. He should be landing here in about twenty minutes."

In midair we told them the story. We laughed a lot.

His friend flew us right into Provincetown.

"Wow, what luck!" Susan said.

I didn't think it was luck. Innocent people are sometimes rewarded.

Anyway, after everything we'd been through, we deserved it.

PART TWO

PROVINCETOWN, 1969–1976

Female Trouble

There are some hairdos that make women look like they've just had a facelift. Very tight ponytails can do this, and tight pigtails too. But white women past twelve years of age look dumb in pigtails. I did.

The last time I wore them, I didn't have a choice.

"Your hair was all matted up and snapping off, you were thrashing around so much," the hairdo nurse said.

"I had a pretty high fever?" I asked her.

"Yeah, you were delirious, but you were funny," she laughed.

I'd just woken up in a hospital bed, I didn't know where, but it didn't matter, I felt great, clean, and very neat. My hair was parted down the middle with two tight braids ending in white surgical rubber bands.

John Waters and Mink Stole laughed at me when they saw me with this hairdo in the hospital bed.

"So it didn't turn out to be appendicitis, so what is it? What's wrong with you?" John asked and got comfortable on the foot of the bed.

"Female trouble," I said. It was a catch-all phrase and he found this term very funny ... so funny, in fact, it became the title for his next movie.

"What kind of female trouble?" Mink asked, woman to woman.

"Infected Fallopian tubes ... PID, you know, nothing too serious," I said. I didn't want to be in the hospital. I was missing the best part of the summer on Cape Cod, but I'd collapsed three days before in a cold sweat before the noon lunch whistle at the Provincetown Fish Factory where I had a job packing rock lobster tails and freshly caught mackerel. I didn't hate the job, I didn't even hate the smell of fish, or my black rubber apron, gloves, and swashbuckling boots that were caked with fish scales. I liked working with the tough townies, the "Portagees," the men and women who were descended from the Portuguese whaling people that settled on the Cape in the early 1800s. I liked their lingo. I got all the town gossip, the inside dirt the tourists never heard.

I guess this illness was going to end my fish career. From what the doctors told me, I was going to be in the hospital for at least two weeks.

"How did you let it go so long? Weren't you in pain?" Mink asked.

"Yeah, but I thought it was period cramps or something," I said. Actually I'd been in lots of pain and I was worried but I'd been raised to ignore pain like a strong pioneer woman with the good genes of the North Carolina Sawyers. If my mother's Sawyer theory for illness didn't work, then my German father's Mueller theory did ... a couple of tankards of husky beer always brought the cure.

"We were really worried when we saw you being taken away in an ambulance from Doctor Herbert's," John said, "Do you remember that?"

"I was kinda out of it," I said, "What'd I look like?"

"Your makeup was fine," Mink assured me.

"Ah … good ole Dr. Herbert," I smiled. He was Province-town's miracle worker, a rosy-cheeked jolly octogenarian M.D. who didn't believe in pain either. He went down into the annals of medical history as the only doctor who performed an appendectomy on himself. With mirrors. I must have been pretty bad off for him to send me away in an ambulance.

"Good thing the fish factory people brought you to him instead of Dr. Silva," Mink said. There were only two doctors in Provincetown at the time. Doctor Silva was the town's joke doctor. In his waiting room he had framed pictures of Robert Young as Marcus Welby, M.D., and Raymond Jaffe as Doctor Zorba. Vince Edwards as Doctor Casey, with his surgeon's Nehru collar agape wasn't there, and neither was Richard Chamberlain as Dr. Kildare.

"So when are you getting out?" John asked.

"Dunno," I said.

Eighteen days, and many injections of antibiotics later, my doctor came in to sign me out.

"You're fine now," he said, "The infection is gone, but I've got some bad news."

"Yeah?" I asked. It couldn't be so bad. I was going home.

"It looks like you'll be incapable of conceiving children," he said and after I didn't respond he said, "Of course I'm not really sure."

He left and while I was discarding my butt-revealing hospital gown and getting into my black Levi's and high-heeled mules, two other staff gynecologists came in and told me the same news. They looked really sad.

"Hey. It's okay, who wants kids anyway? We're already too many on the earth," I said. But when I envisioned my future, there was a child of my own in it. I guess I'd have to adopt.

Two years later I was back in the same hospital, but this time I was in the maternity ward.

Divine

There is a little hill right outside Provincetown where everything opens up big and wide, the sky, the bay, the sea, and the dunes. From this point you can see the end of the world, or at least the end of America, the very last tip of the Cape jutting into the Atlantic. It's called the Witch's Knoll because supposedly it's where the old broom riders met to toil and trouble over their bubbling brew on full moon coven nights. It's the windiest part of the Cape and the wildest.

From this vantage point on clear winter days, you can see whales blowing their spouts and flicking their tails among huge icebergs from Arctic flows.

The Cape highway runs right over this knoll.

The day Divine and I were traveling along this very spot the wind was kicking and howling, shaking and whipping the VW bus with a lot of force. There was some ice and snow on the road and we didn't have snow tires, but we were singing "Got no diamonds. Got no pearls. Still I think I'm a lucky girl ..." from *Annie Get Your Gun*, and the day so clear and fresh that we didn't care about slipping and fishtailing. We were zooming toward a thrift-store shopping spree down-Cape.

A mean hand of the wind caught us while we were on the second verse. "Got no checkbooks. Got no bank ..." and the bus just spun all the way around twice and then it just fell over onto the tall dune grass and almost into the wild cranberry bog. It just tipped over like an empty cardboard box.

A funny thing happens in all car accidents. Time changes. Everything goes into exaggerated slow motion. It's so bizarre.

Once I was in a really bad car accident with my parents when I was fourteen and while the car was spinning slow and mom and dad were flying out the doors in quarter time, I was marveling at the eerie time phenomenon. It was only when the car came to a full stop that time sped up again and got normal. The same thing happened this day except neither of us got hurt.

When the VW bus came to a halt on its side and time got regular again, Divine and I found ourselves in the back of the bus. I was on top of Divine. The windows were flush to the ground, and we were dazed, but nothing was broken. The engine was still whirring away.

"You alright, Cookie?" he asked me.

"Yeah. You?"

"Yeah. But that was weird. Like slow motion," he said and crawled into the front and pushed open the passenger door that was now the top of the bus. "Door works." He laughed.

"The windows didn't even break," I said looking around and crawling out after him.

We walked around the bus and stared at its belly. It looked fine. Nothing was falling off.

It wasn't even scratched.

"We gotta call a tow truck or something." I said but a phone was miles away and there weren't any cars coming along.

Divine didn't say a word. He just picked up the bus, the whole thing and stood it up, back on its tires. Just like Superman-woman.

I think I was just standing there with my mouth open.

"God, you're really strong," I said, "I can't believe you just lifted this thing. I'm flabbergasted. You oughtta go into wrestling or weightlifting or something." I couldn't get over it.

"Must have been adrenalin strength," he said and he got back in the driver's seat. "Well, get in," he said. "We going shopping or what?"

From that day on I always felt really safe when I was with Divine. He wasn't afraid of anything.

Provincetown—1970

It was December and all the money-spenders, the tourists, were gone. They had disappeared at the end of the summer; the town was quiet. With the tranquility came belt-tightening. Most of the year-round residents of Provincetown went on unemployment in the winter; there was no work without tourists.

I lived that winter in one of those clapboard salt-box houses, the kind that people who read *House and Garden* call a Cape Codder. I wasn't aware that devotees of early Americana would sell their souls for a home like this. To me a Cape Codder was a vodka and cranberry juice.

Between that house and the miniature Cape Codder guest house in the back, five of us lived: Divine, Chan, Marnie, George, and me. The place had been great in the summer, but that particular week in December, when it was below zero outside, the wind ripped through the minimal insulation, the toilets were frozen, and we could see our breath in vapor. That lovely little house was incredibly expensive to heat; every bit of money went for oil bills; we may as well have burned cash in the fireplace for warmth.

The kitchen was the only warm room because we kept the gas stove going night and day. Like the rest of the town, we were getting food stamps so at least we had food. We would crowd together in the kitchen with Divine's dishes of steaming pasta; it was the only time we ever took our coats off, or talked with each other without our teeth chattering.

One day when Divine was really sick of being cold, he left the house in a blizzard with the TV under his arm and traded it for a tank of oil. He's always resourceful in a pinch.

We took daily trips to the town dump in the station wagon in search of good stuff we could sell at our Saturday yard sales: clothes, shoes, furniture, appliances. We always found something. I remember Divine standing in his full-length mink coat on top of mountains of garbage, his head crowned with circling, screeching seagulls.

Marnie always found the best stuff, she had that knack, but she stopped going to the dump with us when she started showing signs of losing her mind: secret messages on the radio directed to her, acute insomnia, preoccupations with strangers who didn't exist. We'd known of eighteen other nervous breakdowns she'd had before this, so we thought she'd get better sooner or later.

Urging her to go see a doctor didn't work until one day, returning from an early-morning solo dump trip, I found everybody sitting around the kitchen wearing the living-room drapes, watching feebly while Marnie cut up her own clothes with a pair of scissors. All night she'd been cutting up everyone else's clothes into little scraps. I was the only one who wasn't wearing a curtain toga.

Dressed in curtains and blankets, we took her to the Tauton Mental Hospital in Rhode Island, and she was admitted and dressed in a clean white hospital gown and ushered into warmth and medication. Seeing this, we were all pretty jealous.

A few weeks later, I accidently got a job working two days a week as a housekeeper. The house was spacious and warm with all kinds of stuff to make work easier: a stereo, washer, dryer, and color TV. The only real problem was Wendy, the woman who lived there with her husband, Chris.

She was there most of the time, so I couldn't totally relax when I cleaned. She stayed in bed though, all day, lying in her flab with crumbled candy bar wrappers and empty peach brandy bottles clustered around her form like decorations.

I didn't blame her for lying in bed. She couldn't walk. She was crippled from an accident in Mexico when her husband Chris haphazardly ran over her legs with the Volkswagen camper.

I felt sorry for her. Had it been me I would have divorced and sued this Chris person. He kept insisting that the reason she couldn't walk was a psychological disturbance. He sounded like that misogynist idiot Sigmund Freud.

I cleaned around her.

One day I found some wild photos of Wendy and Chris. I think one of them left them out especially for me. There was a picture of Wendy spread-eagled, inserting huge bowling pins into her vagina. There was a picture of Chris trying to stick silver balls up his ass. There were pictures of the two of them and some other girl. She was tied up and they were all over her. I wonder who took that picture?

Because of these snapshots, I was prepared for anything, and sure enough, the day after, while I was relining the stove with tin foil, Wendy called me up to her bedroom. She motioned for me to sit on the edge of the bed.

"Cookie," she said, "you might as well know that Chris and I aren't getting along very well."

"Oh?" I said, trying to sound interested and involved.

"I think it's my legs. They're not really pretty anymore … well, I know it's deeper than that. Anyway, I want you to help us put our marriage back together again. You'd do that, wouldn't you?"

"Well, sure, whatever I can do to help," I said, and thought *oh no*.

"Well, I'd like you to come over here tonight, around two in the morning, and get in bed with Chris. I'll be sitting in that chair over there, and I'll just watch. We'll play it by ear, okay?" She readjusted in the bed, propping herself up with more pillows.

"I don't know, Wendy …" I said. Wild horses couldn't drag me into hopping into bed with that husband of hers.

"Please, it would really help out," she said.

"I'll think it over for a couple of days, okay?"

I went back downstairs and stood there for a couple of minutes. Was she joking? I hated threesomes. Somebody was always getting left out. I didn't want to fuck her husband, I didn't want to fuck her. I didn't want to be an upstairs maid! Next thing, they'd have me wearing a little fluffy black-and-white mini-skirt maid uniform with no underwear. I went back upstairs.

"Look, I don't think that's my cup of tea," I said.

"I thought you were wild," she said.

Why does everybody think I'm so wild? I'm not wild. I happen to stumble onto wildness. It gets in my path.

"You're supposed to be so wild," she almost screamed.

"Well, I'm all finished for today," I changed the subject. "I relined the stove with tin foil, and I even swept under the refrigerator and I …"

She sighed, "Oh, go away."

I did. I went home and I didn't go back to Chris and Wendy's.

Too bad. I needed that money for Christmas. I wanted to buy everybody in the house something special. Oh well.

At home, as Christmas was drawing near, poverty made everyone joyless. Everyone except Divine seemed depressed. He was planning a huge Christmas party, a buffet feast for forty.

He bought crown roasts of lamb, vegetables, and dessert supplies with our combined monthly supply of food stamps. With what money we had we bought liquor and a tank of oil to heat the house for the party. But we didn't have enough money to buy a tree, and we wanted a big fat one. We didn't have any money for tree lights or decorations, either.

"There's tons of pines on the dunes, we'll just go out and chop one down," Chan said, and we all piled in the car, riding around in the vast miles of dune forests looking for a good tree. We trudged around for hours in the dark searching for a tree that was pretty. All we saw were dwarfed, wind-deformed scrub pines, the kind that grow near the ocean, low and almost flush to the sand they grow in.

"None of these are going to be any good," Divine said. "We need a big full Douglas fir or blue spruce, something really special."

"We can't afford one of those," Chan said. "Here, look at this one over here." He walked to a little scraggly tree and put his hand on its thin trunk. It was sad looking. "This one's okay."

"Yeah. Let's just get that one. I'm cold," George said. He was shivering.

"We could make one of these trees look really minimal, Japanese, you know, Bonsai-style." I was trying to be optimistic.

No one said anything. We all pivoted around, taking in a complete 360-degree view of the horizon of twisted pines. I was thinking how great a big blue spruce would look in our living room. Then I got an idea.

"Hey, I know where there's a perfect blue spruce!"

"Where?" they asked.

"Well …"

"Oh, no. I know what you're thinking. No. No. That's not a good idea," George said.

"I'm not going to be part of that either," Chan said. Everyone knew the blue spruce I was talking about. A couple of doors down from us, on a front lawn, there were these full blue spruce trees, four or five of them.

"I could dig it up, the roots and all, then I could put it back after Christmas. Why not?" I said. "We'll just borrow a tree."

We got in the station wagon and Divine and I dropped off George and Chan. I got a shovel. We went to the blue spruce house. I picked out a good one and started to dig it up, very quietly in the dark. It took forever, the roots were impossible. Finally I gave up trying to be nice with the tree and sawed it down. They'll never miss it, I thought.

We brought it home and decorated it with Marnie's pearl collection and my earring collection. Divine made huge red roses out of the red satin bedspread. Later George got some little white lights. I don't know where he came up with those.

It was the best-looking Christmas tree anybody had ever seen.

Christmas day was great. All the things we'd collected for each other from the dump were wrapped up and under the tree, the food was incredible. All the guests had a ball. People who'd been eating toast for three months, starving since Labor Day, were really happy. Everybody was there. Even Marnie got out of the hospital for the party.

A couple days later when Divine got some money together, he bought a little blue spruce from a nursery and late at night we put it in the ground in that neighbor's yard. It looked just fine. It almost made up for the one we removed.

To this day, I don't think those neighbors ever knew the difference.

Sailing

Roy was a nice Jewish boy from Long Island, an asthmatic manic depressive who was really fun when he wasn't suffering. He came to visit me in Provincetown and enthusiastically told me he had just invested in a sailboat. He was going to the Caribbean, leaving from New York the day after tomorrow. He was really excited.

"You're really lucky, Roy," I said. "I wish I was going."

"HEY! Maybe you can! You want to? Why not? Yeah. You know how to sail, right?"

"A little," I said.

"We need a cook. You want to go?"

I didn't even think about it. "Sure, yeah. I've never been to the Caribbean. Why not?"

"I don't know how to sail at all," he laughed, "but I guess this is the best way to learn. Right?"

He had bought the boat with two other guys, "veteran sailors," he assured me. It all sounded okay to me; as long as the other two knew more than I did about sailing everything ought to be fine. I packed some cruise wear and went with Roy the next day to Long Island where the boat was docked.

It was a forty-two-foot sloop, made in the thirties, all teak-wood, well cared for and seaworthy; resting in the water near Roy's house, it looked graceful and sophisticated with the waves licking its smart hull.

The other two proud boatowners were Tom, the red-haired alcoholic navigator, and Jerry (I'll call him Jerry, because he looked and acted exactly like Jerry Lewis with a hangover at the end of a flop *March of Dimes Telethon*.) His real name I have mercifully forgotten.

The sun was sinking on Long Island Sound when we shoved off, but it wasn't red; in fact, you couldn't even see it for all the ash-colored clouds moving in. That wasn't a good sign, but we left anyway.

By the time we passed between the shores of Queens and the Bronx it started to rain and the water was slapping up, spitting and splashing us in the faces in the dark. As we started rolling into the bottleneck of the Narrows, Jerry was having a hard time maneuvering around the big freighters. I couldn't figure out why the sails were still up, why we weren't using the engine. Considering all the rain and all the ships we were almost hitting, it just didn't make sense.

Roy got an asthma attack from fear, on top of being seasick. He should have gone up on deck for air but he couldn't bring himself to do that, so he was throwing up all over the cabin. He obviously wasn't cut out for sea travel; I think it was the first time he'd ever been on a boat. He kept saying he wanted terra firma.

While I was busy cleaning up after him, paper towels in hand, I happened to look up to the deck, starboard side, and saw a ship so close that I was able to look right into one of its porthole windows and read 60 Watt on a bare lightbulb that was hanging in there. The ship looked like a floating World Trade Center.

In my peripheral vision I noticed two other monster ships barreling portside, blowing their horns. Jerry did some amazing acrobatics at the wheel and we missed all three ships. It was just luck.

I was really angry and getting scared, so I climbed up on the deck and started inching my way out to the jib sail.

"What the hell are you doing?" Jerry screamed at me.

"I'm taking down the jib sail and you're going to take down the main sail and turn on the motor. We're going to die out here if you don't," I screamed at him with a mouthful of seawater. Swells were hitting me from all sides.

"The motor doesn't work," he screamed back and a wave smacked him in the kidneys.

I was mortified. I didn't know what to say to this, so I went back to the galley. Did he think we were going to go all the way to Jamaica without a motor? That was insane.

In times of crisis, on TV, someone always resorts to making coffee. Maybe coffee was the right thing at this moment. I tried to light the stove, but I wasn't too familiar with propane; I guess I opened the lever too far, so when we hit a dip in the wave, the propane leaked from the stove's face and it ignited the whole stove. The flames started licking the teak cabinets and I looked around for the fire extinguisher but I couldn't find it. I'd seen it somewhere … where?!? Never mind, there wasn't time to look. With all the adrenaline strength I could muster I picked up the flaming two-hundred-pound stove and tossed it up to the deck. Tom and Jerry jumped back, but then they picked it up and threw it overboard. They must have burned their hands.

No one said a word.

Around midnight he put in at Sandy Hook, New Jersey, and Jerry started screaming about the stove, how he'd paid so much money for it, how HE wasn't going to buy a new one; I had to buy a new one.

"It was all your fault!! Why the hell didn't you use the fire extinguisher?"

"I couldn't find the fire extinguisher!" I screamed back at him.

"Look. It's right here. Right here." He looked around and couldn't find it either. "Well, it was here." He found it laying on his bed in his cabin room.

"Good place for it," I said.

"Who put this in here?!?" he demanded. Nobody answered.

Through all this, Tom the navigator was drinking rum, not saying a word, just fixing the engine, covered in black grease. Roy was packing his bag. He still looked green.

"I'm getting off here. I don't think I'm cut out to be a sailor. I'll meet you in Jamaica. Call me when you get there, I'll fly down." He hopped on the dock. "Have a great time." He paused a moment, wondering why he felt unsteady, "God, I'm swaying. I must be really sick. I feel unsteady." He sat down on one of the pilings. "I'm going to see a doctor."

"Don't worry about that, Roy. What you're feeling now, every old salt feels when he jumps on land. Those are your sea legs," I told him and laughed. Roy did not think it was one bit funny. He was the classic hypochondriac.

"That wobbly feeling goes away in a little while," Tom said.

Roy took out his hankie and blew his nose, then he got up and wobbled away fast, down the dock and onto the shore, leaving me with these two strangers. I never ever saw Roy again. I wonder what happened to him.

We started out the next day at dawn. The engine was all fixed, but I found that the sloop couldn't take most of the inland waterways; its main mast was fifty feet tall so most of the bridges were too low for us to fit under. Not only this, the boat drew six feet (its underside ran six feet deep) and most of the waterways weren't deep enough. The inland waterways were for small craft, cabin cruisers and sailboats with more sensible proportions, so we had to travel along the coast in the open ocean and it was hurricane season. The three of us weren't so enthusiastic about the open ocean anymore; we wanted the easier route, the calm man-made canals of the inland waterways.

Every day the sky was mottled with black clouds, the sea was high, it looked fat and angry. People who've never traveled on the ocean have no idea how scary it is to be on a little boat out there with no land in sight, waves towering over you while you go into the valley of a swell with nothing to see except water ... water and sky, no other boats anywhere, no semblance of any kind of firm reality at all. The main thing one shouldn't do is imagine things. One shouldn't think about the boat tipping over; just falling over and rolling under. Things like that happen all of a sudden. A gigantic three-story-high wave could wallop the boat broadside. Splash! Whoops! You're gone! No hint of a boat in about three minutes! If you don't get sucked under with it, then where are you?

I decided not to think about this aspect of ocean travel, so I opened my book, *Interviews with Film Directors*, and started reading aloud, trying to concentrate on how Alfred Hitchcock wanted to print the film *Vertigo* on latex instead of celluloid so he could stretch it and make audiences dizzy. I wanted to ask Jerry to head the boat toward earth but I didn't dare. He would have just gone further out to sea. He was still angry with me.

By dusk Jerry was heading toward shore and thank God, there was Atlantic City on the right. Far, far in the distance the

Ferris wheel was the size of a dime, but I swear the smell of hot-dogs was reaching me when the wind blew in our direction. It was like the smell of the earth.

That night we put in around Atlantic City and Jerry yelled at me all night about the stove. Two days later after one night at Cape May, New Jersey, the sky broke, the sight of the sun made everything seem less scary in the open ocean; it was the first really bright day we had. We made it to the waters of Maryland.

In familiar waters, with the sun out, and Tom singing, and even Jerry in a good mood, I decided that I'd do some fishing.

That was a ridiculous idea.

Moving along at that speed, the baited hook was just trailing along the surface of the water way behind the boat. Fish couldn't even get a nibble.

A seagull started following us. After a while he swooped down into the water, and when he flew back up into the sky, there was something obviously wrong with him. I noticed then he had my hook in his mouth, I had a bird like a kite on a string. This was horrible. He was screaming like a human being.

I didn't know what to do. I couldn't leave the hook in his mouth, I had to get him out, so I started to reel him in.

"Cut him loose," Tom suggested.

"Oh, I can't do that, he'll die."

"Let's get into that inlet there and get the hook out!" I pleaded with Jerry.

He was already heading there. Maybe Jerry was alright after all. Did he like birds? People who like birds can't be all bad.

In the Chincoteague Inlet I reeled in the bird. He was all mus-cle, flapping and screeching; it wasn't easy. It was like fighting with a five-hundred-pound tuna. My arms were aching. Tom and Jerry wanted to help but I had to do this myself; I had to. When I finally got him aboard I put him under my arm. He bit and scratched me until my hands and arms were bleeding, but from his mouth where the hook was, he was bleeding worse. I was crying; the bird was whining, and it took forever, but I finally got the hook out and let him go. He flew away wailing and bleeding. I wondered if he'd die. He certainly wouldn't be able to eat for a while.

This was too much, not a good sign. It all seemed too much like the Ancient Mariner with the albatross. I wanted to end the journey, pack my bags and leave. After everything else that had happened on this trip, I took this for an omen, a harbinger of further problems. Besides, it had taken five days to get from New York to Ocean City, Maryland. Definitely it was an outmoded way to travel. Too much for a modern girl.

"I have to say goodbye here, fellas," I said and I don't think they were too sorry to see me go. "Let me know where you are in the Caribbean and I'll try to send you some money for that stove."

"Never mind, Jerry can well afford to buy another stove. He's just too cheap." Tom spit out these words, like he'd been dying to say them for days. Jerry glared at him and said something like fuck you or up yours … something lame. They were still fighting as I walked the length of the pier and turned toward the town. The next person to jump ship would be Tom, I guessed. Then what would Jerry do?

I had gotten off the boat only forty miles from where my sister lived. That was handy. I called and told her I was on my way; then I hopped on a bus and was there in an hour.

"What took you so long?" she asked.

Long? That wasn't long. If I'd been sailing here, it would have taken two days.

The Birth of Max Mueller—September 25, 1971

The night Max was born mongrels roamed in packs. The moon
had turned to blood and the hungry hounds were howling for it
in wild lunar lust.

I was in pain in the maternity ward of the Hyannis Hospital,
but this wasn't plain pain, no; this was the kind of pain that for
reasons of sanity, the mind doesn't allow a woman to remember.
It was relentless, unbearable, hideous, appalling, horrifying. I was
undergoing internal gut-ripping tubal-wringing, organ-stretching,
muscle-pummeling, bone-cracking. I was the grand martyr.
Prometheus knew no pain like this. Lamaze had lied.

I couldn't believe that women went through this to have children. After this why would anyone want to have another one?

In my hallucinations caused by pain delirium, I watched
dozens of night birds throw themselves, screaming, against the
glass of the windows … or was it just hail?

Every sound was magnified. Everything roared.

The fluorescent light was buzzing like a chainsaw, the clock
ticking on the wall was Chinese water torture, the cries from other
women in the next rooms were as earsplitting as the wrong songs
of distressed humpback whales. The white tiles on the floor were

so clean they were whistling. Even the usually silent plants on the windowsill, benevolently doing their miraculous carbon monoxide to oxygen exchange, were wheezing with asthmatic photosynthesis.

From my antiseptic bed with the stiff flash-pasteurized sheets in a severely blank hospital room I could see, though the window, the black sky and the Libra constellation of stars rising in fast motion. Other galactic nebulae and meteor dust were swirling backwards, the red moon was closing in, but maybe it was really a UFO with atomic power pack problems, reverse electromagnetic damage.

Was this happening?

I abandoned all hope. I was sinking into the bed; I was drowning; I was falling. I was being sawed in half like the woman in the box with the magician.

So … this was childbirth? Nobody told me about this part. This wasn't fair. Men didn't have to do this, but they couldn't ever deal with this anyway. Men can't stand pain without snapping into idiocy or vegetable-dom.

"What the hell is the deal here?" I yelled at the nurse who walked in eating a ham and swiss on rye and reading *House and Garden*. Mayonnaise was on her weak chin.

"Just calm down, my dear. It'll all be over before you know it. It's not so bad."

"Have you ever done this?" I asked. I needed real sympathy.

"Well, no … but I've seen it thousands of times." The mayonnaise on her chin must have been imitation mayonnaise, because it wasn't melting into her pores. It was just sitting there, getting on my nerves.

"If you've never done this you don't know anything about it. Why don't they hire some nurses around here who can be sympathetic? Some nurses who've had children?" I hissed.

"Why don't you try your Lamaze breathing again?"

I was incredulous. I just gaped at her.

"THE LAMAZE METHOD! Are you kidding?!? Don't you think I've already tried that?" At this point the Lamaze Method was about as useful as sandals in a blizzard.

She just looked me over with eyes very dead. Shark attack victims have described shark's eyes that looked like this.

I wanted to escape. I decided to get to the window and jump out to die to end the pain, but the nurse wouldn't let me.

"Lie down," she said, "just lie down."

"This isn't a natural position for childbirth … lying down … I want to squat. Why can't I squat?"

"We can't let you squat."

"This is really stupid. All I want to do is squat. Women in Africa dig a hole in the ground and squat over it when they're giving birth. The baby comes right out."

"Look, do you want pain medication?" she asked like a heroin dealer, smiling. I remembered that line about the first one being free, which isn't true in real life.

"No. I'm a martyr," I screamed, "can't you see that?" I was not a martyr; I was delirious. I had quit drugs and alcohol for the whole nine months of pregnancy; I hadn't even taken an aspirin; why take something on the last day?

I tried to sit up, roll over, squat, stand in bed, turn, thrash, but she kept holding me down.

"We're going to have to restrain you if you keep trying to move around," she said.

"I can't believe this. What is this place? Dachau?" I screamed. I should have stayed home and had the baby. Friends of mine who had their babies at home were up and active until they felt the baby coming out. Then they just squatted in an easy chair and dropped the baby.

I was so angry I wanted to cry. I held the bridge of my nose the way Marlo Thomas did on the *That Girl* show when she was trying not to cry.

"I'm really thirsty. I haven't had any liquid for twenty-four hours," I said. "Can you get me some water?"

"We can't let you have water. Just in case we have to anesthetize you, we don't want anything in your stomach."

I knew all that. They didn't want me to get sick on the anesthesia, and throw up, and have the vomit caught in my esophagus. If only they knew; it took a lot more than a little anesthesia to make me puke.

"Jesus, I have to pee," I said. I did have to pee and while I was in the bathroom I could drink some water from the faucet.

She wouldn't even let me go to the bathroom.

"I have to pee, " I screamed. "That's all. Just pee!"

"We can't let you get up," she said. "I'll get you a bed-pan. Wait."

While she was out I got up, went to the bathroom and took a piss. I also put my parched lips on the faucet and sucked water, like a person who had been lost in the desert.

The nurse came back. She caught me while I was shuffling back from the bathroom. She was irate.

"I can't believe you got up when I told you NOT TO! Get back in bed and lay down!" She tossed the bedpan aside and handed me a weird oblong yellow thing on a lollipop stick. "This is the only thing you can have before an operation. It'll take your thirst away. Suck on it."

I did.

On this whole planet, there are not too many things eatable or suckable that I cannot easily recognize or give nomenclature to. This yellow thing was one of those things. It was a preoperative horror on a stick, but it was sweet, sort of, so I used it, and it did put some moisture on the tongue. I had been in labor for almost twenty-four hours and I was dry. Anything remotely wet was fine.

When the next contraction came, and the pain was even worse than before, I decided I was dying. Women die in childbirth all the time. I had to think of something else. I forced myself to relax.

Okay. If this was the way it was going to be, then it better be worth it. This kid had better be as formidable as the pain. This kid had better come out of the womb speaking quantum physics, or be telekinetic, or have white hair and purple eyes, or be able to levitate, or have a blue aura, or be the new messiah, or be clutching gold in his little fists, or at least speak like the dolphins speak.

A couple of hours later, he just came out. The head and the shoulders were a push, but the rest of the body just slipped out. It felt like a fish sliding out, like a bloated mackerel.

My baby was a boy and he looked like all the rest of the babies I had seen the day before in the nursery, red and shriveled and screaming. The umbilical cord looked exactly like a gray coiled telephone wire.

The doctor looked him over: "It's a boy. OH! ... but what's this?"

Naturally I panicked. "WHAT'S WRONG WITH HIM!?!"

"Oh ... ahh ... ahh, it's nothing. I'm sorry ... I thought ..." The doctor was laughing then. "It's just a birthmark, a black birthmark where he'll never see it in his life ... under his scrotum."

There was nothing else weird about him except for his hair. He had the longest, blackest, thickest hair anyone had ever seen at that hospital. And he had a cowlick, ridiculously sticking straight up from nine months of amniotic hair setting. The nurses' aides all went wild about his head of hair. They gave him an Elvis Presley pompadour for his hospital photos. That was something worthwhile.

When the dad saw his son for the first time, he looked pleased, but he told me he was terrified.

I held my kid in my arms when they brought him to me to breastfeed. He was like a little monkey, wiry and solid … no fat at all, with strong legs like a mature frog.

I drifted to sleep with him beside me.

"Goodnight, Max," I said to him, "I'm going to sleep now."

I had a dream that Max spoke to me. "It's a good idea to get lots of sleep now, while you have a chance," he suggested in baritone, "because for many years to come, you're going to need it."

I woke in horror. "I'd better get a Doctor Spock book," I told myself, then I fell asleep again. It was to be the last time I slept soundly for sixteen years.

"What's the worst thing that can happen to me when I eat the dogshit?" Divine asked us, while we were sitting around the set waiting for John Waters, who was doing some exterior shots. Van Smith, the makeup man, was painting Divine's face. David Lockhary was arranging his blue hair and drinking coffee; Mink was putting her contact lenses in; Bonnie was reading the *Baltimore Sun*; I was trying to remember my lines.

There was no question that Divine would eat the dogshit. He was a professional. It was in his script, so he was going to do it.

"We'll find out what'll happen," I said.

It was a secret. Only a few people involved with *Pink Flamingos* knew about the shit-eating-grin scene at the end of the film. John wanted to keep it quiet. Maybe he was afraid some other filmmaker might beat him to it, steal the shit-pioneer award. Anyway too much word of mouth, now, would deplete the surprise for the filmgoer later.

"We'll talk to a doctor," Van said, pausing mid-stroke with the liquid eyeliner brush.

"I'll do it if it doesn't kill me," Divine said and laughed.

"Pretend it's chocolate," Bonnie suggested.

In the world there are many brave people: those who climb Mt. Everest, those who work in Kentucky coal mines, those who go into space as astronauts, those who dive for pearls. Few are as brave as actors who work with John Waters.

We didn't think he was asking too much. We didn't think he was crazy, just obsessed.

"Call a doctor right now," Mink said.

"Call a hospital. Call Johns Hopkins!" I said, and handed him the phone.

"Why belabor the situation? Why worry? Get it over with," said David.

"Dial the phone," said Mink.

"Call pediatrics. Tell them your son just ate dogshit. See what they say," Van suggested.

Divine started dialing the hospital and reached a doctor.

"My son just accidentally ate some dog feces," Divine said. "What's going to happen to him?"

"What's he saying?" Bonnie asked.

"Shh ..." he said to Bonnie. "And then what?" Divine asked in the phone. "Hmmmhu, hmmmhu, okay, then. Thank you." He hung up.

"So?" asked David.

"He didn't sound too alarmed," Divine said. "I guess it's just a routine question for a doctor. He said all I have to be careful about is the white worm."

"What's that supposed to mean?" Mink asked.

"Tapeworms," Divine said, "that doesn't sound too dangerous."

"You don't have to swallow it anyway," Van said.

"He said to check out the dog. Take it to a vet," Divine said.

"John is doing that," I said.

"What kind of dog is it?" Mink asked.

"A miniature poodle," said Divine.

It was suggested to John to do the take in two shots, first the dog does his duty, then cut. Replace the real shit with fake shit. Divine eats it. Cut. But John knew, we all knew, that audiences wouldn't fall for that.

"No. NO. Everybody would know we replaced the real shit for fake. Divine's gotta scoop it right up still warm off the street," John had said a few days ago.

This was show biz. Divine didn't balk and he wasn't the only one. Mink Stole was going to do a big scene that called for her red hair to catch on fire. The dialogue would be: "Liar, liar, your hair's on fire." She didn't seem afraid at all.

"I'll do it. There'll be fire extinguishers there."

"You could use a wig," I said.

"Somebody already suggested that to John. No. Audiences want the truth," Mink said.

The day John was about to shoot the hair-on-fire scene, he changed his mind; he decided it would be too dangerous after all. They tested a piece of Mink's hair and it just smoked and sizzled and smelled awful. There'd be no dramatic effect; it wouldn't have burst into flames. John was a little disappointed but he'd think of something else. Mostly when John came up with these kinds of ideas for his actors, he was testing us or half joking; the actors were the ones who took him seriously, we were the hams. Actors know scenes like these make stars.

"Aren't you supposed to do some scene where you get fucked by a chicken?" Divine asked me.

"Fucked by a real chicken?" Mink asked me.

"How?" asked Bonnie.

"In the script it says Crackers cuts off the head of a chicken and he fucks me with the stump," I said.

"Oh that sounds easy," Divine said.

"Yeah, that's easy compared with what you have to do," I said to Divine.

"Chickens scratch pretty bad," David said. "Even without their heads."

"Bird wounds can be dangerous," Van said.

I thought about Hitchcock's *The Birds*, but those were seagulls and I knew just how powerful seagulls could be. Compared to them, chickens were jellyfish.

"I'm not worried about some little scratches," I said.

"But I don't think I can watch while the head's being cut off."

"Oh come on. Chickens don't know they're dying. They're not smart enough," David said.

There were a couple other scenes in the film we talked about.

"The whole trailer has to burn to the ground. That could get out of hand, couldn't it?" I asked.

"John's going to have a fire truck there," Van said.

"Doesn't Linda Olgeirson have to be artificially inseminated on camera? Down in the pit?" Mink asked.

"She'll have a stand-in," Bonnie said.

"It's a close-up beaver shot. Nobody will know it's not her. She doesn't want to expose her pussy for the audience. I wouldn't do that either," I said.

"No, I wouldn't either," said Mink.

We would all eat shit, catch on fire, fuck chickens, but we wouldn't do close-up crotch shots. There has to be a line drawn somewhere.

"I have to show my dick," David said.

"But you're going to have a turkey neck tied on it," Mink said. "That doesn't count."

"Elizabeth is going to expose her tits and her dick, David. So what are you complaining about?" Divine said, and we all agreed.

Making this film, we went to bed every night really excited for the next day's shoot. Perhaps there are other actors who can tell you that making films is really boring. This film wasn't. On big-budget sets, actors go into their private trailers, waiting for their camera time. Not on this set. We were all in the same room between takes, busy changing costumes, remembering lines, bitching about bit actors stealing scenes, layering makeup, getting ready to emote. There were no private trailers around.

Making low-budget films is work, but it's fun, it's more fun than working in big-budget films. If you're an actor, there is nothing more rewarding, despite the meager pay. On small films you get to know the whole cast and crew in a day, and all of these people are much more inventive because of the limited budget; they create effects that wouldn't have been born if there was more money. Necessity is the mother of invention; this is true. John is a master at this, his imagination runneth over.

Before we started shooting *Pink Flamingos*, I was living in Provincetown with two-month-old Max and Tom O'Connor, Max's stepfather of the moment. Max and I were staying with my mother in the Baltimore suburbs for the duration of the filming, but it wasn't turning out well living there with Mom and Dad.

My mother knew there was filming going on, but I didn't tell her Max was one of the stars, cast as the newborn infant bought by a lesbian couple, and I certainly didn't tell her I was going to have to fuck a chicken.

"Let me read the script," she'd say all the time.

"Ah … well … I don't have the script here. I left it on the set."

"Then tell me about the movie. About your part," she'd say.

"Not much to tell. It's the story of two rival families. I play the intermediary, the spy," I said.

"What's the rivalry? Are they criminal families?" she asked.

"Not really, but sort of," I said. How in the world could I describe that film to my mother?

A few days later, when John came to pick up me and Max for the day's shoot, my mother stopped me from leaving.

"Where do you think you're going?" she demanded.

"I'm going to the set," I said.

"OH NO YOU'RE NOT, " she screamed, "I FOUND THAT SCRIPT AND I READ IT AND YOU'RE NOT GOING ANYWHERE NEAR THAT SET!"

I sat down in the Victorian chair for a second. "Mom, it's not like you think. This movie's going to be funny. It's not porno. It's a whole other kind of film … it's art … it's …" I was at a loss for the right word, the label that would legitimize the film for her. How could she ever understand?

"ART?!?!?! ART!?!?! THIS ISN'T ART!!" she sputtered, and threw the script at me.

"Mom, hold on. Sit down," I said, but there was no calming her. She has quite a temper, that woman.

"AND YOU'RE GOING TO EXPOSE YOUR POOR DEAR LITTLE BABY TO ALL THIS NONSENSE?!?!? THIS GARBAGE?!??! THIS IS THE SCRIBBLING OF THE DEVIL HIMSELF … THIS SCRIPT, THIS ART SCRIPT! HA! HA! ART!!!" She was really wild now.

All I could do was start packing. Fast.

I threw Max's clothes in his little bag, grabbed his Pampers box, stuffed my clothes into my suitcase, and put Max in my arms.

"WHERE DO YOU THINK YOU'RE GOING?!?!? PUT THAT CHILD DOWN!"

Outside, in the driveway, John innocently started beeping his car horn. I cringed.

"IS THAT MANIAC OUT THERE?!? I'M GOING TO GIVE HIM A PIECE OF MY MIND," she yelled and flew out the front door, me following. I hopped in the car with Max and my bags before she reached it.

"Make tracks, John," I said to him. "My mother's on the warpath."

He sped down the driveway. My mother was standing on the front lawn flailing her arms around.

"YOU'RE BEELZEBUB," she screamed at John as we tore down the street.

"Did she read the script or something?" John asked. He was upset.

"She sure did," I said, looking back at her. She was still on the front lawn screaming.

"I guess she didn't exactly love it," he said and laughed.

"Not exactly."

"You shouldn't go back there. You can stay with me," John said.

"Yeah. I can't go back there. Did you hear her? She called you Beelzebub."

"Who's Beelzebub anyway?" John asked.

"One of the devil's footmen," I said.

"Was she serious?"

"She was brought up in the Deep South as a Southern Baptist. That was high drama. She's an actress," I told him.

"Maybe I ought to give her a part in the film," he laughed.

"I feel kinda bad just packing up and leaving so fast. You sure it's okay that I stay with you for a while? I know you're under a lot of pressure with the film right now but Max doesn't cry much. I can put him in a dresser drawer. Dr. Spock says to put your infant in a drawer when you're traveling."

John started laughing, "You're joking."

"You're not supposed to close the drawer or anything," I said.

He just kept laughing.

We went to the farm from there and got ready to shoot the chicken scene in the chicken coop. It went well, but we had to reshoot four times, the chickens weren't too compliant. Danny (Crackers) had to kill eight or nine of them; I didn't watch him slice off the heads.

Just as David had said, even without heads they were a lively nasty bunch of fowl, flopping and kicking with all their might. I got completely scratched up by their sharp claws. I was getting hurt for real. I'd underestimated these chickens, even while I was feeling sorry for them.

In the next scene Max was great as Little Noodles. He upstaged even the bulldykes.

Later on, after we finished for the day, with the sun sinking beyond the horizon of winter's leafless trees, we roasted all those chickens, had a big feast for the whole cast and crew. Those chickens I'd felt so sorry for earlier sure were delicious.

British Columbia—1972

I accidentally burned a friend's house to the ground once. The friend didn't approve. True, it wasn't entirely my fault; I was a guest along with three other guests.

The friend was away for the burning that evening, Friday the thirteenth, November 1972.

I had just left Baltimore after filming *Pink Flamingos* with John Waters and needed a vacation somewhere other than where I was living, Provincetown, Massachusetts.

I went to visit my friends, Tony and Laura, in British Columbia, right on the edge of the Canadian Rockies, minutes from the Kootenay River, outside a little town called Nelson.

They were married and it was their first home. They lived there with a girl named Vickie who was part owner. There were three bedrooms upstairs, with quite a view from the guest bedroom, where Max, Howard, Don, Loo, and I slept in two beds.

It was land with no boundaries, no discernible perimeters anyway, and there was a barn where the boarded horses were supposed to be kept, except they were too wild to feel comfortable in a barn. There, too, was a half-finished log cabin, and a two-story tree house with blue glass windows Vickie was building all by herself.

There were lots of animals, a mean male goat tied to a plum tree, three mild-mannered milk goats, four horses, three cats, two dogs, an intelligent pig, and very dumb chickens.

I've known a few chickens in my time and they're all really stupid, even though they lay perfectly good eggs.

The first couple of weeks I stayed there, my only interest was riding the horses, except they were practically uncatchable; they romped in their acreage of fenced woody hillsides, hiding behind trees, galloping away whenever they saw somebody coming with a bridle and a pail of oats.

The only horse I could ever nab regularly was the big brown gelding, Mory. He was fairly docile once bridled, but had been hit by a Mack truck years before, so he was spooked. When anyone was on his back, he always hallucinated obstacles in his path, so he would leap suddenly to one side or the other with no warning, throwing the unwary equestrian's fanny into the dirt. Since there weren't any saddles it was always a test.

I once caught the smart young mare, who was fast and hard to handle. She was an incredible ride; I had a great time until she threw me and came back to trot on my stomach. I never thought I could lose interest in horses so fast.

The night the house burned down, Tony and Laura were across the river at an all-night party. Vickie had gone to Vancouver for the weekend on an antique buying spree. The house was full of the stuff. The guests, Don, Loo, Howard and myself were busy that evening with Don's cocaine and old photographs. Max was crying upstairs; he didn't want to go to sleep at all. Finally I brought him down with us. I was really angry at him.

When we ran out of cocaine and photographs, Don went out to his little Volkswagen to get more.

He wasn't gone for more than five seconds.

"THE ROOF ..." he screamed. He was all choked up, his mouth was moving but he wasn't making any sounds. We thought maybe he was ODing on cocaine or something. "FIRE ... ROOF ... THE HOUSE ... IT'S ON FIRE!!! "

"What?" we all asked.

True, we had been getting warmer all along; we'd been shedding layers for a half an hour; we had all commented on it, but we thought it was the coke or the whiskey.

"THE TOP OF THE HOUSE IS ON FIRE!"

We threw back our chairs and ran out to see most of the roof blazing. Max had been upstairs only an hour before.

"CALL THE FIRE DEPARTMENT!!!" I screamed. I picked up the receiver but it was dead. The phone lines on the roof must have burned already.

"DON'T THEY HAVE A FIRE EXTINGUISHER SOMEWHERE?" Loo shouted.

"DON'T KNOW!" Howard screamed.

"I SAW ONE IN THE BARN!" I yelled. The barn was so far away.

"SOMEBODY RUN AND GET IT!!" we all shouted and Loo made tracks.

"I THINK IT'S TOO LATE FOR A FIRE EXTINGUISHER!" Don sweated.

"LET'S GO UPSTAIRS AND THROW BLANKETS ON IT!" Howard took the stairs five at a time.

Behind him, Don and I couldn't go further than the top of the stairs. Instantly our eyeball retinas were singed, our eyelashes gone with the heat. By now all the rooms were roaring red and gold; it wasn't just flames; it was a massive inferno. There wasn't any need to say anything; we just tumbled down the stairs.

"LET'S SAVE WHAT WE CAN DOWNSTAIRS!" Howard looked around frantically.

I picked up Max and a bunch of coats that were hanging on the door. I ran out and untied the goat from the plum tree and tied Max to it. I ran back inside. Don and Howard were breaking windows and throwing valuables out. I picked up a huge antique gold-framed mirror, but I dropped it on the way and even the frame fell away, but I took one piece out anyway, then I ran back in. Everything was whizzing out the windows, chairs, books, pots, pans, vases, lamps, the stereo.

Howard and I hysterically grabbed a huge plastic container with a lid on it. We carried it out carefully, whatever it was; we would risk our lives saving it. Later we found out it was the garbage.

"GET THE COATS!" Don yelled.

"GET THE CATS!" Howard had breakables piled in his arms.

"CATS ARE OUT!" I remembered seeing all three of them huddled near the woodpile outside.

Loo came running in wincing from the sudden blast of heat on her face, "I COULDN'T FIND THE FIRE EXTINGUISHER, BUT I RAN TO THE LASSERS' AND CALLED THE FIRE DEPARTMENT!" The Lassers were the people who owned the farm way down the road.

"AND?" we asked.

"THEY SAID THEY'D COME BUT THERE WASN'T MUCH THEY COULD DO!"

"WHAT'S THAT SUPPOSED TO MEAN?"

"DON'T KNOW!" she said.

Don was gathering sleeping bags and silverware while Loo picked up some blankets and rugs and crystal stemware. Howard and I carried out the Victorian blue velvet couch, the hanging

Tiffany lamp, a mahogany rocker, radio, clock, some food from the refrigerator, and three bottles of Canadian Five Star Rye whiskey.

After these trips we came back in and looked around like maniacs. We looked at the walls. All the paintings were hanging there waiting. We went into instant art panic. It was getting dangerously late to be in the house, the roof was about to fall.

"THIS ARTIST IS MORE FAMOUS!" Howard yanked a painting off the wall.

"BUT THIS ONE'S WORTH MORE!" I grabbed another. We hadn't much time.

"NO TAKE THIS ONE! IT'S OLDER!" Howard pulled one down.

"BUT LOOK AT THESE BRUSHSTROKES."

"NO! THIS ONE."

"GIMME THEM ALL. I'LL CARRY THEM ALL!" I realized it was completely ridiculous to be standing there fighting over art while the house was beginning to crumble in flames. I stacked as many as I could under my arm. Howard scooped up some more paintings and piled them on his back with the wires around his neck.

We decided it was to be the last trip back inside.

I went over to the plum tree where Max was roped. He was thirteen months old at the time, a toddler who wobbled away every chance he could. Toddlers know no danger; the minute you put one of them down they run off, right into anything, traffic, a deep pool, a canyon. If I hadn't tied him he would have toddled as fast as he could into the flames.

Right then he was as happy as a clam, pulling the ears of one of the cats and smiling at the bright orange fire.

I untied him and held him on my hip and we all looked at the house totally engulfed by flames. As I looked through the living room window, I saw Max's boots hanging on a nail on the mantelpiece. I'd put them there to dry before we'd had dinner; because he ran into the river earlier that day. My boots were there too. They got soaked when I ran after him. I looked at Max's feet. He was totally barefoot; so was I but I just hadn't noticed during the panic. It wouldn't do at all to be barefoot in November in the Canadian Rockies.

"Hold Max a minute," I said calmly to Loo and I attempted to walk back in through what was left of the front door.

"Where you going?" Howard grabbed me.

"I have to get Max's shoes."

"You can't go back in there." He looked at me like I was crazy.

"I have to. Max is barefoot." I released Howard's grip and started again, but Howard pushed me aside. He went back in himself, literally risking his life.

"HOWARD! NO! IT'S NOT YOUR RESPONSIBILITY!" I screamed at him, but he was already in there. We held our breath.

Howard did not lose his life. Instead, he lost his eyelashes, eyebrows, and a lot of his hair. He got Max's boots and mine too.

Then we just stood there watching it burn.

The fire department came eventually, but there wasn't anything they could do; there weren't any fire hydrants within twelve miles.

"Don't you people carry water on the fire engines?" Loo asked. They sort of laughed at this, but were actually very sympathetic.

They cut some wires and soon left.

We spread some blankets on the ground, opened a bottle of whiskey, and sat watching the upstairs start to crumble into the downstairs. What the hell were we going to say when Tony, Laura, and Vickie came home? The five of us had lost all our clothes and money, but they had lost everything, including their home.

I looked in the window again and saw a metal lamp melting. It was an inferno inside with solid white hot flames and fleeting sparks of green. The rest was Halloween orange.

We killed two bottles of whiskey, but it didn't make a dent. By the time the morning birds were singing, there was nothing left except a glowing stone chimney, that skinny two-story monolith, standing over a smoking mound of red-hot rubble.

Dawn is fine when you've slept well with a clear conscience, but a dawn like this was a hard thing to face, especially when you're freezing with nowhere to go.

We decided that we'd pile into Dan's Volkswagen bug with all the blankets and the sleeping bags, but that didn't work too well. Even with Max comfortably sleeping in the little space behind the backseat, there wasn't enough room to stretch out. That's all we wanted to do. Our bodies were aching.

Loo and I gave up trying to sleep and we left the guys, who had snoozed off. It's a fact that guilt rarely affects a man's sleep.

We decided that we ought to milk the goats, so we went to the barn. In there it was gray and cool and still, with the first glints of the sun shooting stripes of light through the chinks of vertical wood. The cobwebs in the corners swayed a little in a slow breeze and pieces of hay from the loft floated down once in a while. Everything looked soft, as if there were no sharp edges. Mourning doves in the rafters murmured and rustled their wings, and the goats were casually chewing hay like it was any normal day. Despite this, I saw there was something accusatory in their eyes. Goats have the strangest eyes in the world; the pupils are slits in bright light; in semi-darkness the pupils are diamond-shaped, not unlike snake eyes.

We gave them some oats and sat down, back to back, on the little stool next to them. It is not an easy trick to milk an animal; it had taken me days to learn it from Laura.

After we got a squirting rhythm going, Loo asked the question we'd all been thinking about.

"How do you suppose the fire started?"

"Lord, I don't know," I shook my head slowly. "An act of God?"

"I think we stoked the wood stove too high. The flues were wide open. I remember Tony telling us not to open the flues all the way."

"Yeah? … OH NO!! … Yeah! He did say that, didn't he?" My heart sank. It was our fault. He had told us quickly before he left that with the flues wide open sometimes chunks of burning wood fly up the chimney, because that stove was really too big for that size chimney. It created updrafts or something. Because of this, chunks of burning wood could fall on the roof.

"But who opened the flues all the way?"

"Nobody's going to admit to that," Loo said, "and there's no point accusing anybody now."

She was right, of course.

After we milked the goats, we dropped into the hay and fell asleep from sheer exhaustion.

I guess it was around noon when I heard Tony and Laura's pickup come rumbling down the gravel drive. Loo and I hopped up from the hay and stopped the truck before it could go any farther. From the distance of the barn to the house, one could only see the top of the chimney over the edge of huge Douglas firs.

The truck radio was blaring some country hit, but they turned it off when they took a look at our faces. They knew there was something wrong.

How in the world does one tell a friend that their house burned to the ground?

Loo started. "The house ... it caught on fire ... and ..."

Tony and Laura just stared at both of us.

"It burned to the ground," I said, and looked down at my sooty cowboy boots.

"No it didn't," laughed Laura. Loo and I looked at each other. Hey, maybe it didn't, I thought. Maybe it was just a dream. Maybe over the hill the house was standing like it always had. I looked at the chimney top. Maybe the whole house was under it, with Don cooking soup at the stove and Howard sitting in the living room reading. Maybe it hadn't burned down, just like Laura said.

Loo and I got in the truck and we slowly drove up the drive. The whole scene opened up after the trees and it looked so bad. Laura began to cry, and Tony just stopped driving and turned off the motor.

Two hours later, Vickie came home and she was hysterical when she saw it. By then Tony was walking around in the rubble with the bottoms of his boots smoking, looking for stuff from upstairs.

We slept in the barn that night. Tony put up a huge tent and piled hay bundles around it for insulation from the cold. We cooked our dinner outside over a fire. Fortunately we had saved all those sleeping bags, so it was really cozy, all of us in a row sleeping in the tent. We even laughed a lot that night.

The next day we started work on the log cabin. I had the job of chinking the logs with a combination of horseshit and mud. With all of us working furiously we could have the place built in a matter of days.

Word got out in the town that our house had burnt down; and later that very day, families came from all over with food, and warm clothes, and more tools. They just picked up hammers and chainsaws, and then there were twenty people working. We finished that house in three days.

Then we started in on the tree house. That was a bigger task, but after another two weeks or so, both the houses were really in order, and that's when I decided to move on. I hated to leave, but I had the feeling that Tony and Laura and Vickie wanted to get on with their lives without a bunch of guests. Don and Loo had already gone two days before, and Howard was only going to stay another day or two, and then return to Provincetown. I didn't want to go back to Provincetown immediately, but I didn't have any money, and there really wasn't anybody to ask for some to borrow.

Howard was the only one, really. He'd saved his bag from the fire. It had been downstairs. He loaned me fifty dollars and that seemed like plenty. Don had given me some cocaine to sell when I got where I was going. Laura had offered me some from her bank account but I just couldn't take it.

The night before I left, Tony went into the mountains and shot a bear, and we invited everybody from the town who'd helped us for a grand outdoor bear feast.

Before we skinned him, we gave him his last rites. He was so big and handsome with gigantic brown eyes. We all started crying before our guests came.

I left the next day with Max on my back. Somebody from town was going to Eureka, California, a two-day drive, so I drove with him that far, and hitchhiked the rest of the way to San Francisco to visit Divine.

But that's a whole other story.

Tattooed Friends

Susan unscrewed a bottle of rotgut port, the kind laced with formaldehyde, and sat down at the kitchen table where black mollies swam in a blown glass oval and a potted hibiscus was folding up its red blossoms for the night. Mardi Gras beads at the window moved and clicked in the first timid breeze of the twilight. It was as if the rising moon had exhaled a cool sigh.

The sun sank on the wood plank terrace right out the window, where Susan had left her unfinished canvas and open tubes of paint.

"Oughtta cap up those tubes, Sue," I said.

"They'll be okay," she said. "It's not gonna rain tonight."

"I'll do it," I went out the window and put the caps I could find on the tubes. The sky was getting dark royal blue and there was the moon like a white banana. Next to it was Venus, the first star to appear at twilight and the last one to fade at dawn, as large as a glowing ping-pong ball.

"This would make a good tattoo," I called to Susan and she looked up from the table at the configuration of Venus and the crescent moon. We'd been talking about tattoos earlier, in the heat of the day.

"Too Turkish," she said.

"Yeah, you're right. It looks just like their flag." I went back into the window.

"Why don't we give ourselves some tattoos? Right now." She was all excited, "I have all the stuff to do it."

"I guess it's time to have a tattoo," I nodded. It was inevitable. I was following in my grandfather's footsteps. He was a sailor and a tugboat captain, with lots of girls and anchors on his arms. My mother hated them, the same way she would hate mine.

"What though?" I asked Sue. While I pondered, I started drawing little experimental designs on pieces of paper. "It has to be something I won't get tired of since I'm going to have it for the rest of my life."

"How about this?" she pointed to the spot right below her left elbow on the topside where she'd just penned her Capricorn astrological sign on her skin.

"Good idea," I said.

"Why don't you put your Pisces sign in the same place?" she suggested.

"Great!" I said. "Let's do it."

This was perfect. We wouldn't get tired of these little tattoos. She would always be a Capricorn, I'd always be a Pisces. That wouldn't ever change. It wouldn't be like tattooing the name of your current boyfriend.

I drew a quarter-inch Pisces symbol in the same place on my own arm where Susan had drawn hers. It looked good.

Susan brought in some sewing needles, white cotton thread, a candle, and India ink. We wrapped the sewing needles with the thread, sterilized them in the candle flame, dipped them into the

India ink and started punching our flesh with the needle points, following the outline of the penned-in symbols on the skin.

"I knew this one guy who tattooed himself in jail with the point of a guitar string," she said, "I guess they didn't have any sewing needles."

"Why is it only people in jail do tattoos?" I wondered.

"I guess they're bored," she said.

"Or maybe they just don't have any paper to draw on," I said.

These were our first tattoos. We needed tattoos. We didn't know why. It was something bigger than both of us. Maybe we'd both been North African Berber women in past lives.

After this first tattoo, I was hooked. Through the years, I couldn't stop tattooing myself. I thought of it as body decoration. I never wanted to be too nude, even without clothes. Now, I'd always be a little dressed.

Six tattoos and four years after the first one, I used to go to this nude beach called Ballston Beach in North Truro, Massachusetts, on Cape Cod. This nude beach scene was a one-summer phenomenon. It was a mini Isle of Levant, quite a show, before the tourists came to gawk and the police started jailing people for indecent exposure.

On beach blankets bare butts were broiling in the sun like luscious ham hocks. Pubic hair unfurled in the breeze. Nude people played volleyball with their dingdongs dangling and boobs bouncing in tune with the game scores.

Everyone was naked as jaybirds and my tattoos were turning heads. Nudies were wearing hats, and some of them sneakers, but no one was wearing a tattoo, except for this old nude Wellfleet oyster fisherman, who was always doing pencil sketches of the girls frolicking in the surf.

This was before it became sort of fashionable for women to have tattoos. The untattooed masses saw my Pisces sign on my arm, the moon on my shoulder, the falcon on my wrist, the dots on my fingers, and an eternity symbol, a lizard eating its tail, on my leg. Strangers started approaching me.

"I love your tattoos," they'd start. "What's this one on your thigh? What do the ones on your hands mean? Are these occult symbols? Did it hurt? Who did them?" When I told them I did them myself, they all wanted me to tattoo them. I started bringing the India ink and needles to the beach with me. Every day under the sun, I tattooed people who were committed to a life of wearing insignia.

"This isn't a decision to be taken lightly," I told them, "You're gonna have this for the rest of your life, so you better think about it."

To the people that asked me, "So what do you think I should have?" I told them to go home and think about it for a week. To the people that came around and said, "Right here I want a pyramid and an eyeball," and they had already penned it on the skin spot, I got out the sanitary needles and was ready to punch it in.

Everybody wanted tattoos that summer. I worked on shoulders, ankles, backs, breasts. Thighs, asses, and foreheads. I tried to talk people out of having tattoos of Mickey Mouse or Huey, Dewey, and Louie ducks, or their girlfriends' names. People on LSD or mushrooms wanted stars or third eyes in the middle of their foreheads, but I told them to come back when they felt a little more grounded, less far-out.

"You might regret it someday," I'd say. "Suppose you wanted to become a film actor someday. How many movie roles do you think people with face tattoos might get? Put the third eye on your ass instead."

A lot of people got tattoos that summer. Some got hooked.

That following winter, in Provincetown, tattoo fever overtook the town. Everyone was tattooing themselves. The Provincetown art supply store ran out of India ink. There was a run on sewing needles at the five and dime, needle prices went sky high.

All over town, around the candlelit tables, over bottles of ink and painkilling 151-proof rum, sewing needles were stabbing designs on skin. The liquor store ran out of 151 rum, but we didn't stop, we moved on to tequila.

Cape Cod winters can be brutal and boring or lonely, but not this one. We got to know each other. Tattooing stirred conversation.

It was better than hanging in a bar, more sociable than Canasta, more exciting than Monopoly, as challenging as Scrabble, and cheaper than gambling at poker.

In the old traditional New England way, it was an arty masochist's version of a sewing bee.

Jamaica—1975

A bunch of Jamaican airport loafers jumped on us when we got off the plane in Kingston. They were all dressed in worn, sun-bleached, abbreviated clothes and held in their hands all kinds of things they were trying to sell: scarves, carved wooden animals, marijuana, fruit, edible green weeds.

"These people must be really poor if they're hitting on us," Shaggy said.

To Jamaicans, we looked rich. To Americans, we looked like what we were—welfare recipients.

"Goin ta Montego Bay? Or Negril?" the very thin man in green cutoffs asked us. "I an I tik ya dere cheap almoss nutin. All de touriz tey go dere."

"No, we're going to Cedar Valley," I said and he looked surprised and sort of backed away like we'd told him we were contagious. We were going to Cedar Valley to visit Vickie from British Columbia. She had gotten a job as a contract school-teacher with the Jamaican government.

"Cedar Valley? Why ta tere? Ja knoo Cedar Valley?"

"Nootin in Cedar Valley," said a man who was squashed in a seam-busting blue jumpsuit. He fell in step with us like the other one.

"We have a friend there," Shaggy said.

"Ya mus rentta car ta get tere," he said.

"Nooo, maahn," the green cutoff man said to the jumpsuit man, "I an I drive dem tere. Cheap!"

"We don't have the money for that," I told him.

"An, aow ya spect ta arreev dere? Kenna goo ba feet! Dats laang wee! See oova tere?" Yankee Fan pointed to a ridge of mountains that were teal blue and way off in the distance. "Cedar Valley ez oova tere, upon ta Blue Mountains."

"I an I tik ya fa da rentta car. Ya foolow I," Jump Suit said.

What was this "I and I" stuff? I wondered. Do Jamaicans think of themselves as two people, like schizophrenics? Whatever it was, with these two it was trouble squared.

"I know there's a bus that goes there," I said, scanning the horizon that was shimmering in the heat. "Either one of you know where to catch the bus?"

"Derz noo bus ta Cedar Valley," green shorts said and laughed.

I took in a 360-degree view. We were in an almost empty airport parking lot; there weren't many cars and there weren't many people except anxious tourists with flocks of ragged salesmen clustered around them. There were a few taxis doing good business so I walked over to one of the drivers, who was wiping his forehead with a rag. "Where can I catch a bus to Cedar Valley?" I asked him. He looked surprised, like the other two guys had when I mentioned the place. He told me I had to catch a bus to town to catch the bus to Cedar Valley. He made it sound really complicated.

"Ya, ta Honey Bee bus gooz ta Cedar Valley, but ya don waanta tik tat bus … noo, tat bus a frightful ride, laang ride, veery laang. Noo tourist ever ride ta Honey Bee. Betta ya rentta car. Why ya goo ta Cedar Valley? Nootin dere."

A couple hours later, we found the Cedar Valley bus. It was blue and green with yellow-and-black bumblebees painted on the side. Honey Bee was written front and back in red script.

It was a hot bus, seething with people. Toasting on the tin top were men and boys in rags with live chicks stuffed in crates, peeping and squawking, and boxes of mangoes covered with blisters of fruit sweat. Only the mangoes were quiet.

Inside were skinny old men, too feeble for the roof, women with baskets of food, fanning themselves with big green heart-shaped leaves wedged next to the glassless windows. In the aisle and roped to the last seats, two nervous goats were bleating, coughing, and stamping their cloven hooves. The goats smelled, like all goats do. Their smell was pungent, but not something familiar like the smell of old Limburger cheese or dirty socks and jockstraps in basketball locker rooms. They reeked of something gamier, like a she-wolf's perfume. Eau d' Call of the Wild.

It was thick and steamy inside; everyone looked on the verge of being poached.

We found two seats; Max sat on my lap.

"Look tat face, look tat cunnin face," a woman behind us said and pinched Max's cheeks.

"Rasta boy?" another asked.

Max was three. His skin color was café au lait; he'd been in the sun. He had long hair, almost to his waist, that was matted and sun-streaked gold. I had given up trying to brush or cut his hair, he screamed too much.

I watched the scenery but everyone else was watching us. I guess we were the only white people these people had ever seen close up; besides, we probably didn't look much like the other white tourists they'd seen from bus windows. Shaggy was dressed in something that made her look like a cross between a blond Japanese Sumo wrestler and a gypsy fortune teller. I was wearing my everyday drag: black drapes, Tibetan monk bones, monkey paws. Max was in his little black Levi's with sticks hanging on his belt loops. The sticks were his pretend rifles. I never believed I should buy him toy guns, so he devised his own. Little boys like guns, there's nothing any ex-hippie parent can do. Kids aren't reproductions. Friends of mine who raised their kids as macrobiotics were disappointed when their kids turned out to worship at the shrine of McDonald's Golden Arches.

After Kingston, a town of mostly corrugated tin shacks, the bus headed for the Blue Mountains. The woman in front of us told us that Cedar Valley was the last stop, and that it was in the St. Thomas Parish, high up. She had laughed when we told her we were going there.

"What do you suppose is so hilarious about Cedar Valley?" I asked Shaggy.

The bus driver was flooring it toward the ridge. Once we started gaining altitude, the mountain road became a series of hairpin curves, but he didn't slow down. He was whipping around those loops that dangled high above dense tropical green so lush that forest floors far below were indiscernible.

The farther we climbed into the mountains, the more disoriented I felt. Quasi-civilization had slipped away an hour ago. Even shantytowns were getting sparser. This was jungle land, territory I had no frame of reference for. At every shack and goat path, half hidden in green, the bus would stop and drop off passengers laden with their fruit and livestock. As the altitude grew, the bus got more empty. Soon there were no shantytowns or shacks at all and even the roadside folks, women in flowered dresses balancing big bundles on their heads, kids leading goats, and barefoot old men with walking sticks, began to ebb away to nothing.

The last person I saw, aside from the bus driver and the skinny kid who worked collecting fares, was a little old woman with a basket of peaches who'd been sitting across from us. When she got off, it was just Shaggy, Max, and me rumbling up the hills, while the day got older and everything around us got weirder.

We traveled for hours, expecting to see some kind of town looming up over a hill, but it never arose. As the sky grew darker and duskier, with the tropical time-warp jungle roaring all around, I began wondering what we had gotten ourselves into.

When the bus stopped and the driver got up and stretched, the skinny kid came up to us and told us that we were in Cedar Valley. We looked out the windows.

To the right was jungle, to the left was a cement bungalow with a tiny car sitting in front of it; next to that was a little tin and wood store with colored lights on a string, and beside that were some other lean-tos made out of tin cans.

"This is Cedar Valley?" I asked. How could this be a town?

"Ja, Cedar Valley," the kid said. "Where ya gooo nooow?" he looked deeply into our six eyes. Here was a child that worried like an adult.

"Ah, well …" Shaggy said to him. Then she and Max looked at me, "Hey, this was your bright idea to come here. Are we in the right place?"

"I hope so," I said looking around. "But how do we find her? She doesn't have a phone. I wonder if she ever got my letter."

"Whoo ja liikin foor?" the kid asked, but then he suddenly brightened, as if a lightbulb went off in his head and dissolved the furrows in his brow. "I bit I neoo, ya, ya, I neooo. Ja liikin fa Meez Vickie?"

"Yeah! You know where she lives?" I jumped up.

"Everbooty neoo Meez Vickie heer reound," he smiled. "Sheez schooltetcher heer. All St. Thomas Parish tey goo ta school ta leoorn weeth her. I shoolda kneoown ja lik fa Meez Vickie. Cooem fallaw me. I tiek ja reet dere, weer sheez libban," he said. He was really excited, "Ez noot fa ahwaay."

We grabbed our bags and followed him down the bus stairs. It was almost dark.

Cedar Valley wasn't what I thought it was going to be. When I had heard that Vickie had gotten a British Columbian three-year contractual job in Jamaica as a schoolteacher, I thought she was going to be set up in a swanky sun-drenched beach villa, palm trees swaying, ocean surf licking the marble columns of her terrace, restaurants, bars, discos, moments away. I could not have envisioned her as the jungle missionary schoolteacher type.

When we got to her house, a one-floor cement box with glassless squares for windows and a doorless rectangle as an entrance, the bus kid led us right in. Vickie was shocked to see us.

She looked better than she'd looked in British Columbia: her olive complexion didn't look sallow, she was gold from the sun. The woolen things she'd worn in the northern cold had covered muscles I didn't know she had. In the green cotton bag dress she wore she reminded me of one of the rubber trees outside her door.

"You took the bus?" she laughed. "That was brave, it really was. I mean, I take the bus all the time now, but the first time …

Hey, thanks Jan, for bringing them here," she said to the bus kid. "Sit down!" She hauled some cinder blocks to the Formica table and gave us some plastic cups of rum from a jar.

In this poured cement kitchen, she was surrounded by three little barefoot kids and two skinny ladies. One of the women was very pregnant, and she was cutting up some green leaves and some kind of root vegetable. A pot of rice was cooking on the electric hot plate.

"I'll put on some more rice for you," Vickie said, and then introduced us to everyone. "You're staying, right? I'll lay some mats out for you. You must be really tired. Did you just get to the island? Today?"

"Yeah, we came straight off the plane to here," I said. "I really didn't expect …"

"I guess it's kind of a culture shock," she said looking around. "You know, this is the St. Thomas Parish, the poorest parish in this country. Isn't that right, Tuanna?" she said and turned to the pregnant woman.

"Ja kin see tat agaaiin!" Tuanna said and laughed.

"I'm the only person with electricity in the whole town, aside from that little store in the center, the one with the colored Christmas lights," Vickie said.

"Ooonly oone weeth reeunning waata, too," Tuanna said.

"Meez Vickie feed ta whole tooewn when we're hoongey," the other woman said. "Eez a goooed friend! Geenarooz friend!"

"I like to have people over for dinner because they do the cooking. I hate to cook." The ladies laughed.

"Shee doon keoow heow ta boil waata," Tuanna said and when she laughed her loaded belly went up and down.

"Hey! Look at Max, he's big. Wonder if he remembers the house bonfire episode in British Columbia!"

"I'm glad you can laugh about that," I said. "Are you sure it's okay if we stay here for a couple days?"

"Of course, don't be silly. Don't worry about this house ever burning. It's all cement!" Vickie let out a howl and doubled over laughing.

"Day after tomorrow, we'll head for Negril or somewhere," Shaggy said.

"Well, Negril is alright, but it depends on what you want. If you stay until the weekend, I'll take you down to Port Antonio and set you up in a little place a friend of mine owns. How about that? Port Antonio's nice."

"That'd be great," I said.

"Tomorrow I'll show you the school where I teach. I think you'll find that interesting."

Later on, after everyone was asleep, I listened to the rumble in the jungle. It was bedlam out there. Caterwauling insects and mooing birds were booming the night anthem. A honking cantata started from somewhere high up on the peak where the moon sat and then a chorus started moving down the hill like an army. I had never heard anything like this and I imagined a battalion of creatures who were a hybrid of locusts and hairless rats on the warpath, yodeling and plundering, coming to overtake the house and clean our bones while we slept. Who knew what spirits stalked the night in this thicket?

Lying there in the blackness with the cool blue moonlight on the windowsill, I looked out and saw huge green leaves and clusters of things that looked like human heads nodding in the breeze. I turned my head toward the other window, but sitting on the sheet, on my leg, were two tiny fluorescent green eyes, the same size as the O's in the word spooky.

It crossed my mind that I had come to Jamaica for the ultimate rendezvous with the spirit world. What was this little green-eyed thing on my leg? I lay there and soon the green eyes disappeared. I fell asleep.

When I woke up the sun was pouring over everything. The cluster of human heads outside was a bunch of big pink blossoms on a bush, and the thing with the green eyes was a Jamaican lightning bug that was now sitting on little Jesus' wooden hair as He hung on His crucifix on the wall.

A goat stuck his head through the window and brayed just as Vickie came into the room.

"Did you hear those tree frogs last night coming down the mountainside en masse?" she asked me. "They do that every full moon. Lovelorn frogs looking for mates. When I first heard them I was tripping on mushrooms and I was so scared. Did you sleep well?" She took a cup and squatted next to me with an egg in her hand. "Once I was staying in Red Ground in Negril near the beach. It was the middle of the night and I heard clomping coming up from the beach. It sounded like an army. Then all these little kids with torches and sacks were trying to catch these clompers, which turned out to be huge land crabs, and the kids were catching them to cook them. These animals were like three-feet-tall hard-shelled spiders. There's some strange animals in this country," she said.

Vickie drank the raw egg and ate a piece of breadfruit. Then she left for work. We followed her through the jungle to her school. It was a small corrugated tin building with no more space than a hopscotch square. Kids were coming from every direction, barefoot with pet goats and chickens following them.

"Think Max would like to sit in on this class?" she asked.

Max was already sitting on a log scribbling on some paper. "We'll see ya later at home," she said. "Leave him. He looks content."

Shaggy and I wandered around in the mountains that week.

On the weekend Vickie took us to Port Antonio and set us up with some Rasta guys who owned a small reggae nightclub and a little beach bungalow that we rented for a week. It was perfect.

I said good-bye to Vickie.

"Thanks, Vickie, you've been great. I'll write to you when I get back to the States."

"Okay, do that," she said. "I'd like to know what's happening in civilization. Right now I like it here. I like this country and I really like working with kids. Both are green. The land and the kids. There's no limits, no limits."

I haven't seen her since.

Someone told me she had moved to Brazil, working with some anthropologist fighting with cattlemen over the preservation of the rain forests.

Maybe I'll run into her again in some jungle. She'll be cooking up monkeys and three-toed sloths, kneeling at the turnspit with a poker. The local kids will be crouched in their loincloths around her, looking wide-eyed. The jungle schoolmarm.

For Vickie no green is too dense.

The Stone Age—Sicily, 1976

There are plenty of sex perverts in Sicily; all of them are men. The whole island, as I see it, is a man's primordial porno playground. The place pulsates with the vibes of undulating male loins.

Of course it's all very hush-hush ... all very covert and Catholic. I don't think Sicilian wives are very much aware of this, but who really knows the truth except the priests in the confessional booths?

Wherever we went, we were plagued with randy dandies and horny honchos. Guys were always walking along beside us whispering in dialect about their balls and other organs. Along paths in mountains, where we thought we might find respite from all these biological urges, we would see lust areas in the underbrush where sex parties took place at night. We'd always catch a few guys jerking off in the magenta crush of bougainvillea blossoms.

They followed us everywhere; the fact that we were both blonds had something to do with it. The fact that we were lesbians on a honeymoon didn't make much difference to them. Four year old Max was with us too, and that didn't deter them either. Maybe they thought he was a very short pubescent girl. Everyone is short in Sicily anyway.

"I'm tired of walking everywhere in this country," Shaggy said.

"I want to go back to the beach," Max whined.

"I just thought you two might want to walk in the mountains for a change," I said. We were walking up a quiet road into the hills. A boy, barely nine years old, pulled up to us on his Piaggio. His motor was hot. He smiled and said something to us.

"Another pervert," Shaggy said. She knew a little bit of the Sicilian dialect from her mother.

"Whadhesay?" Max asked.

"He was telling us about his personal history," I told Max. "Just ignore him."

We decided to rent a car to get around. After being haunted by guys on Vespas and wild groups of cruisers in Fiats everyday, we thought it would be a better idea. We went to a fly-by-night rental place where there were rows of navy blue Fiats waiting in the sun. To rent us the car the man didn't want money or a credit card; we didn't own one anyway and he didn't know what a credit card was.

"One of you will have to leave a passport," he said in his English. Since Shaggy and I had both given our passports to the pension people, Max's passport was the only one we could give him. That was fine with him. "Mario, the man who runs this place, isn't here now, but he'll take care of the money when you bring the car back. Okay?" he said. That sounded fine.

I jumped into the driver's seat and we barreled off. I loved the car. It was the size of an ordinary kitchen table. It handled like a small bathtub with wheels. Now the horny grape growers and olive farmers wouldn't bug us. We would leave them in the dust. We were mobile.

We still ran into problems when we stopped at intersections. There'd always be a man on a corner who would notice us quickly and he would immediately expose himself by dropping his scrubbed drawers around his ankles. In Sicily, all the men's underpants are very clean. Their wives or mothers don't have much else to do during the day except wash clothes.

"I'm beginning to think there's sexual repression in Sicily," I said as I turned the corner away from the butt-naked man.

"They seem healthy to me," Shaggy said, looking back at him while he was pulling up his pants.

"Maybe it's us," I said. "Maybe our clothes are too tight or something."

"I think it's because we're Americans and we're blond," Shaggy said.

"Maybe it's your eye makeup," Max said from the back seat. He was pretty astute for a four year old.

We were staying in a pension in a little town called Rocalamare. It consisted of that pension, an empty beach, a restaurant, a cigarette store, a grocery store, and a variety store. The population was about eighty children, forty-five men and three fat women. We spent most of our days on the sun-baked beach next to the placid water of the Ionian Sea, burning the retinas of our eyeballs reading books to fill the vacant hours.

Rocalamare was very close to Taormina, where we had wanted to stay because of the annual Taormina Film Festival. We had plans to meet with some German independent filmmakers there but because of the festival there weren't any vacancies in any of the pensions we could find in Taormina.

The first night of the festival, we drove into Taormina. The festival films were all shown in an ancient Greek amphitheater which sat on the edge of a mountain overlooking the sea and the active volcano Mount Etna. We found our German director friends there.

"Ve von't haf time fa dinna," Werner said as he ran along with his Japanese wrist watch. "But I haf dis bottle orf red vine. Ve'll haf dis, no? Ve'll vatch the films, den maybe ve eat somesing afta, no?"

None of the films made any sense to us. We'd forgotten that they were all in Italian. Even the German and American films were dubbed in Italian. I hated dubbed films, even when they're dubbed in my own language; it just ruins everything.

By the time the films were over, all the restaurants everywhere were closed and the opening night festival party was a flop, so Shaggy and I returned to the Rocalamare pension, drunk and hungry.

I'd left Max there with a ten year old daughter of the pension owner and there he was sitting in the big family kitchen under a faulty florescent light at a high marble table with skinny white cats scattered around eating cold pasta on newspapers. Max was drawing on butcher paper with waxy crayons.

The ten year old babysitter looked like she was about forty years old. It occurred to me maybe she wasn't a child at all, just a short adult. She had been waiting on tables in the family restaurant for five years, all the kids waited on tables in Sicily. Waitress jobs make girls look old before their time.

"I don't like it here," Max said the next day, sitting on the bed crying.

"I don't either," said Shaggy. We started to pack. I didn't really like it either.

We paid our bill and said goodbye to the family, then we packed up the Fiat and left to return the car to the rental place. On the way, we came to some railroad tracks where the red lights were flashing and the bells were bonging. A train was coming. I stopped the car and waited for it to pass.

I had stopped the car in the wrong place. The red striped two ton metal pole that lowers automatically to warn cars on road crossings was slowly smashing the roof of our Fiat. We were wedged under it.

I felt like a complete asshole while the people in other cars laughed at us. I tried to back up, but we were pinned. As the pole squeeched metal on metal, I looked at Max in the back seat to see if he was okay. He was laughing. Shaggy was laughing. The roof was smashing in.

"Get out of the the car," I screamed. "We're going to get crushed." They weren't taking this very seriously, but they jumped out. The car was shaking and its steel body was whining under the weight. Then the pole stopped descending. We waited. After the train passed, the pole lifted and the little blue Fiat bounced up into position on its rubber tires. The roof was all smashed in, sway-backed, like a birthday cake someone had fallen into.

"We're going to jail now," I said. "We don't have the money to pay for these damages."

"Get back in the car," Shaggy said. "We'll take our chances at the rental joint."

"Don't mention the roof until they do," I told both of them.

"Maybe we could just leave the car there with some money and keys in an envelope," Shaggy said.

"Let's just leave it by the side of the road," Max said.

"You're forgetting about your passport," I told him.

We drove the car back to the rental lot. I turned off the ignition and sat there for a few minutes. I knew we would all go to jail or something and this was our last day of freedom.

I walked into the office and met Mario, who was sitting behind the desk. I handed him the keys.

"Okay, let's take a look to see how many kilometers are on the car," he said and slid off his seat. He stood no taller than my waist! I couldn't believe it! Mario was a midget! This was divine providence! He looked the car over, checked the kilometers, kicked the tires … but he couldn't see the top of the car. He was too short.

He gave us back Max's passport and we paid the small sum for the rental and left.

There's an old superstition in Sicily about seeing a midget. It brings luck.

PART THREE

NEW YORK, 1978–1984

Go-Going—New York & New Jersey, 1978-79

In the beginning I just couldn't bring myself to do floor work. Bumping and grinding while lying on the floor looked completely ludicrous to me.

I would have made more tips if I had; the girls who did floor work always had stacks of one-dollar bills in their G-strings. They wore the money like a tiny green fringe tutu flapping around their hips.

Those girls brought their own personal floor mats on stage with them for their half-hour sets. They'd just unroll their fake fur bathroom rugs on the stage floor and lie down and start undulating.

It seemed so inane … convulsing there on a dirty Dynel shag pad on a "stage," which was usually nothing but a flimsy fly-by-night platform the size of a dinner table, while stone-faced male loners sat in a circle around it, clutching their overpriced drinks, watching intently this twitching female flesh parcel.

No, that wasn't for me. I just danced. On two feet.

I had decided to topless go-go dance when I first moved to New York from Provincetown. It wasn't something I especially wanted on my résumé but I had been casting around, looking for work … something to pay the bills while I was making a start at designing clothes, searching film parts, and writing. I was down to thirty-seven dollars. That kind of money doesn't go far in New York, especially when you have a kid.

I'd tried waitressing when I was sixteen and found out fast it wasn't my calling in life. I always screwed up. People were always bitching about the missing side orders. I spilled everything, had a lot of walk-outs. It's a horrible job, demanding, demeaning. I started hating people. I wound up throwing food.

I'd worked in offices when I was eighteen, and that always turned into a fiasco; anyway the pay was so low and it took all day, five days a week. I needed some kind of job that didn't have such long hours and paid really well.

A go-go friend suggested dancing. She gave me her agent's name. I got the job.

The agent was straight out of a cheesy '50s gangster B-movie, second generation Italian, the good-looking-twenty-years-ago type, flare-collared polyester Nik-Nik shirt, pasta belly, lots of big rings on the pinkies.

He sat in a greasy office filled with cigar smoke, pictures of broads on the walls, the telephone ringing.

Every Monday the place was packed with girls getting the next week's bookings and picking up their checks. He called everybody sweetheart or honey. He was close: all the girls had phony names like Jujubee, ChiChi, CoCo, Sugarplum, Dumpling, BonBon, Sweetie Pie.

Most topless bars in the city had eight-hour work shifts, noon to eight or eight to four A.M. The bars in New Jersey had five-hour shifts.

I liked working in Jersey more, where topless was against the law; the dancers had to wear a little something on top. That eliminated my stretch marks and sag problem that came with the pregnancy and breast-feeding package. It was less sleazy in Jersey; the bars were local hangouts for regulars; the customers didn't feel like they were getting ripped off because drinks were cheap. Dancers made more money in Jersey anyway, and there, no one would ever recognize me from John Waters movies, not that they did in Manhattan go-go bars, but I always had this horror. People in Jersey didn't go to those kind of movies.

Actually it wasn't a horrible job, when I thought about it. I was just there exercising and getting paid for it. I was never in better shape: tight buns, strong legs, flat stomach. Working in Jersey, I began to wonder why every woman didn't want to go-go.

But then, every time I worked in a bar in Manhattan, I discovered why all over again.

Manhattan go-go bars are really sleazy. The owners sometimes want you to go in the back rooms to do hand jobs on the creeps. They made customers buy outrageously priced little bottles of champagne; some managers demanded that you "flash" … show your puss, when they knew you could get busted for that.

Of course, right over on the next block a guy could walk into a strip joint and get a bird's-eye view deep into the internal structure of a vagina for a dollar; in fact, he could stick his nose right in if he wanted, but in topless places, because they served liquor, nothing like this was supposed to go on.

I was working the day shift at the Pretty Purple Pussy Cat, doing my half-an-hour-on, half-an-hour-off. I was working the same half-hour as Taffy, on stages facing each other. The other two girls, Marshmallow and Lollipop, went on after us. With those names, the place could have been a candy store.

Taffy was wallowing on her bathroom rug, with all the customers at her stage, ogling. She had piles of bills tucked in everywhere, mostly ones, but when somebody wanted her to flash, she'd do it for a five.

I was on the other stage, knocking myself out doing flips, splits, high kicks, triple spot turns, with nobody watching me, thinking that somebody with respect for a real dancer would soon toss me some fifty-dollar bills. Nobody did.

I watched Taffy. She was lying there pumping her hips and looking right into the eyes of the men. She was turning them on, obviously.

I was exhausted. I'd been up since seven thirty getting Max to school; then I had this early interview at Macy's to show some buyer a couple of silk blouses I'd designed. After that, I'd gone for a cold reading for some low-budget independent cable TV movie.

All I wanted to do was lie down.

When the half hour was over, I put my little mini-dress over the pink sequined G-string and got off the stage. In Manhattan the dancers are required to hustle drinks from the customers … or at least try. Nobody was buying drinks for me, but Taffy called me over to sit next to her and a customer.

"Buy her a drink," Taffy told the guy and he ordered me a vodka soda.

Taffy pulled her chair next to mine.

"Sweetheart, I've been watching you bust your ass over there and you ought to give it a rest, girl. You ain't making no tips. Look here," she looked down at her G-string, "I got a mess of money here," she flipped through the bills hanging on her hips, "and I got more in my pockets here." She put her hands in her mini-dress pockets and pulled out handfuls of ones and fives, even a lot of tens and twenties. "And I didn't make this working too hard."

"For some reason," I told her, "I just can't bring myself to lie down up there. It looks so stupid … I mean, you don't look stupid, the idea is so stupid."

"I know just what you mean," she said. "I used to feel the same way when I started working these bars, but you get over it."

She lit a cigarette and put her Revlon Cherries in the Snow lips to my ear.

"Look," she whispered, "these guys just want to look at something they can fantasize about. They like to feel horny, it makes them happy."

"I think I'd feel like an asshole," I said.

"Oh shit, forget it. You want to make money or not? Just try it next set. Lie there and look right into their eyes. Remember to do that part, otherwise it doesn't work. You have to make it personal."

The next set I took my scarf on stage with me and I laid it on the floor. Nobody would want to lie on the slimy platform without something under them.

Feeling dumb, I got on the scarf and put my head back and looked at the ceiling while I did some sort of cold Jane Fonda–type floor workouts. There was a customer sitting there in front of me but he didn't look very interested.

"That ain't it," Taffy yelled to me from across the room. She pointed at her eyes.

So I made myself look into this guy's eyes. It worked immediately. He started peeling off the ones and handing them to me. This made me start putting some sex into the workout. I undulated all over the place, just like an eel in heat.

Other customers started moving over to my stage looking for something hot, I guess. They loved it hot.

By the end of the set I had twenty or thirty dollars and it was so easy on the heel bunions and the toe corns, so relaxing for the calf muscles. Wow! What a job!

"I should'nta told you nothin'," Taffy said, "you took all my paying customers."

So I had graduated. Every working day I'd dance the first half of the set and when I got tired I'd just lie down and stare into eyes and pump the hips, do leg lifts, things like that.

I worked this job for a year or so, two or three days a week, saved some money. I worked in Jersey mostly, taking the Path train to Newark, and then taking a cab. There weren't too many problems except for having too much to drink during the day. It would be an ideal job for an alcoholic, I often thought.

One day I was working in a Manhattan bar where sometimes the owner would try to act like a pimp. I hated working there, but it was the only place the agent had left on a Wednesday, since I forgot to see him on Monday, booking day.

I was doing floor work in front of a customer and he was handing me dollars. He asked me to sit and drink with him when I came off the stage. So I did.

He was a young guy from Brooklyn, a blond meathead who wasn't unlike all the other meatheads who hung around go-go bars everyday. He was buying vodkas, and he was getting drunk and I was getting drunk. He was telling me his life, his astrological sign, the standard rap.

"Ya read about dem tree peoples killed in Brooklyn yesterday?" he asked. "Was inna *Post* and da *News*. Sawr it onna tube too, late night news."

"Yeah, I saw it. Terrible," I said. I had seen it. Pretty grisly, it was too. Torsos in green garbage bags, with treasure-hunt notes leading to the heads, which were in black garbage bags.

"I did dat," he smiled. "I killed dem. Cut 'em up. Waddn't too easy eitha."

I turned and looked at him very closely. He was proudly smiling but he looked really serious, although he didn't look like a killer, except maybe for his eyes … but then I don't know if I'd ever looked in the eyes of a killer before.

"You didn't do that," I laughed.

"Oh yeah, I did. It kinda bodda me a lill, but dey was ass-holes. Ya don know. When dey died der was no human lives lost. Dey was animals. Deserved it. Fugging animals." He looked into his sixth vodka and drained it.

When he started to cry, I half believed his story.

What could I say? Could I say something like: "Oh, don't feel so bad. Tomorrow's another day. Forget all about these heads and bodies. You're just depressed." That wasn't really appropriate under the circumstances.

"Ya know, I have dis gun, heer, in ma coat," he looked around to see if anybody was watching, then withdrew it quickly and showed it to me.

I was beginning to believe him.

"I have dis index finga too from onna dem animal." He pulled out a plastic Ziploc bag with a human finger in it. The blood was caked around the stump. He put it away fast.

I think I just sat there staring at his pocket for a while.

"Well …" I just didn't know what to say. What could I say? What would be the right thing to say when something like this happens?

Maybe I could say, "Oh. Isn't that interesting looking!"

I thought that maybe I should say something to the bouncer though, but this guy would figure it out if I told him I was going to the bathroom and instead started whispering to the tough guy in the corner. He might go on some wild shooting spree. No, I couldn't say anything. I just drank the rest of my vodka and tried not to stare at him aghast.

The other dancer, Pepper, got off the stage and it was my turn.

"I need to talk ta ya sommoor," he said. "Comon back afta. I'll be real pissed if ya don't."

I certainly didn't want to piss him off.

"Don't worry, I'll be right here in front of you and I'll sit with you again after my set," I said and he smiled.

If I hadn't been slightly drunk I think I might not have been able to dance, maybe not even able to undulate on the floor. Considering the circumstances, I was very nonchalant, but I decided not to do any floor work in front of him now. I didn't want to get this guy aroused or anything. I just stepped around on the stage while he smiled at me.

Pepper started to sit down with him to ask him for the drink.

"Gedda fug outta heer," he pushed her away. Then he felt bad. "Hey look, girlie, I'm sorry, ba I'm savin' my dough fa dis chick heer," he pointed to me. "I like er."

Great. Just great, I thought.

While I was dancing and trying to smile at him, thinking about garbage bags and heads, a bunch of men came in the bar talking to each other.

One of the guys stopped to look at me and he handed me a fifty-dollar bill.

"Come have a drink with me after your set," he said and winked. Then he walked to the end of the bar and sat down with his buddies. They were all talking to the owner and looking at the girls, nodding and laughing.

The gesture wasn't unusual, but the fifty was.

I loved the fifty but the killer didn't.

"Ya ain't gonna sit wit im. Are ya?"

"No. Never."

"Yall havta give im bak dat fifty," he looked over at the guys.

"Yeah," I said, "I was going to do that anyway."

Then the bar owner, one of those Grade-D bad eggs, walked over to me and whispered in my ear, "This group of guys back there are friends of mine. They want to party with you, Venus, and Fever. In the back room. Go there after the set. They got lots of money. We can both make a little."

He walked off before I could tell him I wasn't interested. First of all I didn't go to back rooms and then of course there was this angry young man sitting here ...

He was getting angrier by the minute. He'd heard what the owner asked me to do so he kept looking at the guy who gave me the fifty. He clenched his fists, ground his teeth, bit his lip. His face was getting all red. There was going to be trouble.

What could I do? Getting shot or beheaded wasn't the way I had planned to go out. I didn't have many options: (1) I could sit the rest of the evening with the killer, but at closing time he'd probably follow me home. (2) I could maybe call the police, but the killer might see me at the phone, get paranoid, and shoot me. (3) I could go to the bathroom and climb out the window, if only the bathroom had a window. (4) I could quit the job and walk out while the killer was in the bathroom, but he looked like he had a good bladder.

"Hey, ya name again?" the Brooklyn Butcher yelled up at me over the music. I told him.

"Dat ain't ya reel name," he sneered. "Tell me ya reel name."

"That is my real name."

"It ain't," he barked.

"Okay," I said, "you're right. My real name is Charlene Moore." Any name would do. The kid swallowed his next vodka and started on another one, then another. His eyes were very green and the whites were very red after those twelve vodkas.

"I'm gonna tell dat fugging asshole bak dere dat ya sittin wit me afta ya dance." He got up and stumbled to the back of the room. I froze.

When he got there he started poking his finger at this fifty-dollar guy. The guy stood there taking all this abuse and then he just hit the kid killer in the face, really hard. The kid butcher fell on the floor, and his gun fell out of his pocket and slid across the carpet, and disappeared under a huge stationary space heater radiator thing.

He saw it when it slid, and they saw it, and everybody pounced on the space heater and started wailing in pain because the heater was so hot.

Then the kid just scrambled for the door and left the bar, fast.

The bouncer and the owner let him run. They all started bending around the heater, but they couldn't find the gun because, first of all, the bar was so dark, and the heater was so wide and hot.

Finally somebody got a broom and pushed it out.

I got off the stage and walked up to them while they were all huddled around the gun. I told them all about the kid, the whole story. Nobody believed me.

The owner took the gun and disappeared into his office; the rest of the guys just started drinking again; the girls started dancing again, so I went back to the stage.

All the party boys forgot about their party even before I finished my set. They left, all fired up, talking about how "they were going to find that little motherfucker."

I made a phone call to the police. I described the kid, told them everything he told me about himself. They weren't too interested until I told them about the finger. I didn't mention the bar or the gun, I just said I met this kid in some restaurant. I told them my name was Charlene Moore. They thanked me and hung up.

That was the last day I worked as a go-go dancer; I never wanted to see any of those sleazy joints again. I didn't want to writhe on another floor in my life. I didn't want to be forced to talk to any more creepy dummies in dark smelly dives; I was perfectly capable of finding creepy dummies on my own time. I didn't want to be in the same room with murderers or birdbrains or desperate people anymore.

After all, I'd made my first fifty-dollar bill that day. Not a bad way to finish up.

When I got home I hung up my pink sequined G-string, and there it hangs to this day, gathering dust. It still sparkles just a little when the sun hits it.

Careening Around in Career Vehicles

As a small-time operator in the fashion business, people were telling me I was doing alright. I had a label, I had a couple of people sewing my designs, I had orders to fill. The way I saw it, though, things weren't going so well. I was in deep debt, and up to my belly button in stumbling blocks.

There were a lot of sleazy dealers in the rag trade and I was sinking into the mire with them. I had even stooped as low as to bribe a large fabric mill executive into slipping me some bolts of solid color rayon challis that wasn't on the market yet. It was the hot new fabric for next year's spring season, and this fabric company had the inside scoop.

The night I quit the fashion business I had met with this man in the cover of darkness at his huge office building on 7th Avenue. I handed him cash, and he gave me the stuff. I brought the heavy bolts home in a Checker cab, and was proud that after weeks of trying to find this fabric, I had finally scored. At home I laid out the bolts of fabric on the kitchen floor and I sat down beside them and just looked at them. I was happy. The future looked bright.

While I was just sitting there on the floor, gazing at this fabric, the coveted tokens of my future success, things began to crumble.

Literally. The kitchen ceiling above my head started to make a lot of noise. A large part of the plaster overhead started to come down, then half the ceiling gave way. Brown water and 100 years of dirt and plaster fell all over the rayon challis. It was totally ruined. If I hadn't scrambled under the kitchen table when I did, I would have been brained with chunks of heavy plaster. I probably would have died. At the time I wished I had.

I found out later that the new sub-letter in the apartment above me had flushed his toilet and suddenly the plumbing went haywire. His bathtub had started filling with brown water from the drain and the toilet started overflowing and he couldn't stop it. My ceiling had just given way.

This was the proverbial last straw, the climatic end to a bumpy career. I cried under the table, but the sense of relief was something I hadn't expected. In truth I hated the fashion business, I hated the hours, I hated filling orders, I didn't like the way the buyers talked or walked and I couldn't stand the contrived way the fashion business people wore their clothes, or their accessories. They were all dressed up for automatic pilot. No, the fashion business wasn't for me.

That very night I dumped the ruined fabric on the street, threw away my labels, disbanded my sewers, and ripped up my orders.

The next day I decided to get back into a career I almost forgot I still had. Show biz.

In an H.M. Koutoukas play, I got the part of a Doberman dog and it didn't matter that I had to go through the whole play on my hands and knees. It was New York City show biz. That was all that mattered.

The next play I did was a John Vaccaro hit.

The seriousness of Off-Off Broadway was apparent the first day of rehearsal when Vaccarro said, "There's no excuse for missing a rehearsal. The only excuse is death ... AND NOT IN THE FAMILY!!" In other words if you died you couldn't make it, if you were alive you had to be there.

After that I made the rounds with head shot photographs and resumes. I took singing lessons, acting lessons, went to casting calls and did cold readings.

I got a job entertaining at a barmitzva, sort of a go-go dancing stand up comedy routine I invented. I was the only gentile there. It didn't go over very well.

I wore a paper bag over my head in another play, I was attacked by a slimy monster in the film *Smithereens*, I wielded a chainsaw in a beauty salon in another film, I played a dominatrix in a rubber torture dress for a cheap made-for-tv-movie scheduled for channel nine at four in the morning on a Monday. I did voice overs for tin can company industrial films, I danced with live goats for a SoHo art piece, I played a whore in an Amos Poe film, a slut in an Eric Mitchell film, Sharon Tate in a Gary Indiana play, I did extra work in big budget films, got hit by cars, water, guns, fists, whips in all kinds of low budget bombs. I answered all casting calls.

One day I answered an open call for a film that looked like it was right up my alley. It was written up in the actor's newspaper, *Backstage*, and said something like this: "U.S.A Film Productions is casting an independent quasi-docu-drama film. Seeking circus-type people: bikers, hillbillies, acrobats, animal workers, singers, dancers, comediennes, show people. Non SAG. Men and women from ages 21 to 75, all races. Low budget but average pay."

That sounded pretty good, but rather general. There would be tons of actors vying for parts at the casting call. The average pay part was weird. What did average mean? I'd find out.

I went to the call and there were hardly any other actors there. I thought that odd, considering that eighty percent of all the actors in Manhattan were out of work. The casting agent turned out to be the director too, and he looked slimy.

A couple of other things made me leery of the production: I got the part too easily, there was no real script, he asked me to bring along any male actor friend—preferably my boyfriend—to do my scene with, and he was shooting my scene the day after tomorrow. The average pay turned out to be two hundred dollars for a day's work, so I took the part, whatever it was. I didn't really know what kind of part I had. I kept asking, but he told me it would be so obvious it didn't need much explanation.

That night I called an actor friend of mine named Louie. He agreed to do it, no questions asked.

Two days later we met at the same place where I'd gone for the casting call. It was nine in the morning and the director was there with some camera equipment and about eight other meat-head crew members. Some men and women who were supposedly actors were there too. We were going on location, out to Long Island to Riverhead Prison in a van. None of the other actors knew what their parts were either.

When we got out to Riverhead prison, Louie and all the male actors had to get into prison uniforms. The director told them they were playing prisoners who were all being let out on a weekend pass, conjugal visits, to see their wives. I was playing one of the four wives there to meet their prisoner husbands. Wardrobe had me dressed in a skimpy, sleazy mini-dress. When we saw our husbands coming we were supposed to jump into their arms and kiss them exuberantly. Then we were all supposed to climb into the van and we would be smooching and hugging while the van took us somewhere else with one of the actors as a prison warden driving.

We were driven into an old age trailer park and let out there in a main building that was the community center for the geriatric bunch that lived in the trailers. All the old people were gathered there watching tv, playing cards, eating, talking, and sitting around in wheelchairs entertaining each other. There was food set up for the cast and crew. Louie and I waited around for our scene.

Finally, I got some sketchy information about the film from one of the crew members. She told me that this segment of the film dealt with a new experimental prison policy called conjugal visiting. It was to be filmed realistically, as any docu-drama film would. That was all she told me. I began to suspect the worst.

When Louie and I were called for our scene we were taken to one of the trailers. It had the tackiest interior I'd ever seen, like a parody of tastelessness, except it wasn't a parody, it was for real. The cameras were all set up in the bedroom. Two black actors, the fake prisoner and his fake wife were sitting on the bed looking confused. The director was handing them some mixed drinks. "Here," he said, "Loosen up with these. We'll get back to your scene after we shoot the scene here with Louie and Cookie. They look like a couple of professionals," he turned to us, "I'll get you two some drinks also. You like Vodka tonic?" He left to get the drinks from the kitchen. I looked at the black couple. They looked at me and shook their heads.

Everything was coming in clear now. I should have known before. This was a porno film!

I looked at Louie.

"Let's get the hell out of here," Louie said.

"Fast as we can," I said.

We left out the back door, without saying a word to anyone.

By this time, it was dark out and we started wandering around among the trailers trying to find the community center. We got lost.

"I think it was this way," I told Louie, but it was a maze of trailers. Every turn took us deeper into mobile home hell. We tried every direction, but we couldn't find our way back to the community center.

"Let's ask somebody where it is," Louie said, but there wasn't anyone walking around to ask.

"Let's ask at one of the trailers," I said and I walked over the lawn and looked into the window of a beige one. There was an old couple sitting on the sofa watching tv and eating with trays in front of them. We knocked at the door. They looked up, then the old man got up slowly, walked over, and looked out through the glass of the front door. His mouth fell open when he saw us and he started screaming, "No! No! Go away!"

I couldn't figure it out. Why was he so paranoid?

"Betty, there's an escaped prisoner and desperate looking honky-tonk woman at our door," he screamed at his wife. She jumped up and spilled her tray of food on the floor. She picked up the phone and started touch toning, "I'll call the police," she screamed.

At first I wondered who they were talking about. I'd forgotten Louie had that prison outfit on. Across his breast pocket it said in large black print : RIVERHEAD STATE PRISON. Did I really look like a desperate honky-tonker? Louie and I laughed.

"No. No, don't be afraid," we yelled through the glass, "We just want to know where the community center is."

They didn't answer. Betty just kept screaming into the phone.

We decided to try another trailer, but this time I'd do the asking without Louie. At this other trailer I got the directions to the community center from a nice old man.

We returned to the community center where all the old people were playing Bingo. Louie put on his own shirt.

I went over to the crew member who I'd talked to before, "Why didn't you tell me this was a porno film?" I asked her.

"A porno film? I didn't know it was a porno film," she said but she was obviously lying, "Did you do your scene? How'd it go?"

"We didn't do it. We don't do porno," I huffed.

"We want to go back to the city," Louie said, "How are you going to get us back there?"

"You're not going to do your scene? You don't want your money?" she asked.

"We're not doing porno and you can keep the money. We just want to get back to the city," I said and sat down in a vacant wheelchair.

"Well, okay," she said, "One of the crew is leaving right after he finishes this game of Bingo. He'll take you back." She pointed to one of the crew members who I'd seen reading the light meter earlier. He was obviously enjoying himself playing Bingo with the old people.

We waited a little while, but the game was interminable. The numbers caller didn't have his bifocals on.

"They're playing for a microwave oven," an old man who was hovering around told me, "You two actors with this movie, hun? What kinda movie is it anyway? We're all curious."

"It's a docu-drama about prisoners," I said and let it go at that.

"You all finished with your scenes?" he asked.

"Yeah," I answered, "We're all though."

"Then why don't you two join in on the Bingo game? You know how to play Bingo don't ya? You're kinda getting in on the tale end, but you could still win that micro-wave while you're waiting," he said.

Louie and I got some Bingo cards and chips, and sat down at the long tables with the old people.

"I 22," the Bingo caller said.

"I got I 22," Louie said.

"G 7 ... O 9 ... N 15 ... Nobody's got Bingo yet?"

Sam's Party—Lower East Side, NYC, 1979

It was his party and he'd die if he wanted to.

Sam was that kind of guy. He never let anyone down, especially himself.

This particular party was for his birthday, at the apartment he shared with his lovers, Alice and Tom. All his loyal friends were there, the famous, the infamous, the washouts, the successful rogues, and the types who only have fame after they die. They were the representatives of the New York alternative subculture, the people who went to sleep at dawn. And never held a nine-to-five job because they were too odd-looking, or sassy, or overqualified.

Because Sam had an MFA degree, he never had any money, but he always gave great parties ... never pretentious ones, always wild ones. He wasn't short-handed with the food or liquor.

It wasn't even midnight but the party was already jammed and jumping. Alice hadn't even gotten around to lighting the candles on her attempted Cordon Bleu birthday cake when I noticed Sam thanking a rock star for a very small birthday present, one of the many very small presents he'd received all night, yet another glassine bag of heroin, his drug of choice. He'd been using it off and on for the past five years.

He immediately went to the bathroom with Tom and locked the door.

At first no one missed the host. The party was too good. The stereo was blasting rare old hits and obscure unreleased new stuff, people were dancing, laughing, drinking. The layered smoke in the rooms was a gray veil. The place was wall-to-wall celebrities and future stars, who all knew each other and were still speaking.

I was dancing on the sofa when Mary approached me looking a little worried.

"Where's Sam?" she asked. "Have you seen him? I want to light the cake."

"I think I saw him going out for more beer," I lied because Alice didn't like Sam using heroin, especially if she didn't get some of it.

Alice went to the door. Shoeless in her fishnet stockings, she walked out into the misty November night where the party was spilling over into the street.

"Sam?" she screamed lamely into the abyss of the Lower East Side tunnel of tenements. "Sam!?"

"Didn't see him out here, Alice," the people sitting in Sam's blue Pontiac convertible said. There were people on the stairs and on the ledge too, but they hadn't seen him for a while either. Meanwhile I knew Sam was very busy in the john and by this time there was a line at the locked door. Everyone was getting impatient with their bladders full.

It wasn't three minutes later when Tom slipped out of the bathroom, closing the door behind him and holding the door-knob, making sure no one got in. He looked nervous.

"Hey, Tom, you finished in there or what?" a drag queen film star asked him. She was the first in line.

"Go out on the street and piss," he said just as nicely as he could, and the drag queen thought this was not a bad idea, so she headed for the street. So did a couple of others in line.

While Tom was standing there holding the doorknob, I noticed he looked ashen and awful, like the blood had just drained from his head. Frantically scanning the room, he saw me looking at him and called me over.

"What's wrong, Tom? What's going on?" I asked him after I fought my way through the crowd. Tom's hands, and even his hairdo were trembling. He was sweating all over his party silks.

"Come in here." He wedged the door open so we could squeeze in over protests from the line.

"Hey, come on ... man. I was here first, Cookie ..."

"Lettus jes take a quick pee."

Inside the bathroom, Sam was lying on the floor in a fetal position. His skin was the color of a faded pair of blue jeans. A syringe and a bunch of crumbled empty glassine bags were on the floor next to him.

"Obviously he's ODing!! Do you know what to do?" Tom was beside himself. He guessed I might know because for years I'd been writing a sort of "health in the face of drug use" column for a downtown newspaper.

"Yeah, don't worry, Tom. There's time before somebody dies shooting too much heroin, it never happens in a flash despite what you've heard. DON'T PANIC! Just go to the kitchen and get some salt ... and some ice cubes," I said. "And hurry."

While he was gone, I filled the bathtub with the coldest water possible and tried to lift Sam into it, clothes and all, but he was dead weight, he may as well have been a Buick. I had to wait for Tom but he was probably having a hard time making his way through the mob of plastered party people. When he finally returned, Alice was with him. She started to wail, and tried to kiss Sam awake, which never works.

"Let's get him into the tub," I said, so we lifted him in.

"This water's freezing," Alice cried.

"It's supposed to be," I told Alice.

"I DON'T HAVE TO PEE, I HAVE TO SHIT," someone outside the bathroom door said, banging on the door.

"Do we have any time?" Tom asked.

"He's going to die … on his birthday … he's going to die!" Alice was weeping over the tub, her tears falling on Sam's blue face.

"He won't die," I said.

"WE KNOW YOU'RE DOING DRUGS IN THERE! WE DON'T WANT ANY, JUST LET US PISS!" The banging at the door kept up.

"Any ice cubes?" I asked Tom.

"None. I was fighting over the last ones in somebody's vodka." Tom was sweating again.

"DAMMIT, GUYS … WHAT THE HELL YA DOIN' IN THERE? COUNTING TOILET PAPER SHEETS?" Somebody was really mad.

"What's the ice cubes for?" Alice looked at me with her black eyes, the same kind of orbs on orphans in Keane paintings.

"The cold gets the heart moving. But never mind, we don't need them really, just hand me the salt and the syringe."

With Sam's teaspoon in my hand, I tried to calmly pour a little salt into it. I couldn't really remember exactly how much to use, but there was little time to belabor the question, so I just used an arbitrary amount and put in some tap water; swished it around, and drew this saline solution into the syringe, forgetting about the cotton.

"That works?" Alice demanded.

"That's an antidote?" Tom asked.

"WHAT KIND OF PARTY IS THIS WITH NO BATHROOM FACILI-TIES!?!" The line was getting riotous.

"You're taking too long, Cookie ..." Tom was wiping the sweat on his forehead with a big beach towel that had a print of a Coca-Cola can on it with the words IT'S THE REAL THING.

"He's going to die," Alice was sobbing.

"I told you he's not going to die, Alice!" I said but I was terrified.

"He'll be brain-dead!" Alice screamed and threw herself against the toilet.

"He won't be brain-dead either," I said, but I wasn't really sure about this part.

I guess I wasn't too convincing about the brain stuff because Alice started again, "He's going to be a vegetable, no better than a cucumber ... he's going to ..."

"SHUT UP, ALICE!" I finally screamed while my hands were shaking trying to find a vein that wasn't too scarred up. I put the syringe's dull point into the only clean vein I could find, pulled the plunger back, got blood, and then pushed the salt solution into it slowly.

"Is there any possibility he'll be a vegetable?" Tom asked.

"Look, I don't know! But can you imagine Sam a vegetable? Even if he had half a brain left he'd be smarter than most of the idiots at this party." This vegetable thing was nagging at all of us.

"WE'RE PISSING IN OUR DRAWERS OUT HERE!" the line screamed.

With my thumb on where his pulse should be, I started getting a little scared about the time it was taking for him to come around. It seemed too long, an eternity. I broke out in beads of sweat. Where was his pulse? He didn't even have a faint one.

"Didn't you know how many bags he did?" Alice turned on Tom. "You should have stopped him!"

BANG, BANG, BANG. The people were pounding at the door. "YOU ASSHOLES'VE BEEN IN THERE FOR AN HOUR!"

"I didn't know how many he did. How was I supposed to know?" Tom threw the towel on the tiles.

"You jerk! You could have stopped him!" Alice was hysterical.

"How could anybody stop Sam from doing dope?" he screamed.

"At least he was with him, Alice. What if Sam was in here shooting up all by himself and this happened!" When I said this I felt Sam's pulse returning slightly, then strong, then some pink was coming to his face, edging out the blue, and then there was a sudden movement under his eyelids like his eyeballs were watching some dream go by. In a second his long eyelashes fluttered. He blinked a few times, then opened them.

"Here he comes," I said, relieved. I sank to the toilet seat because my knees were buckling, they'd no longer hold me. Tom and Alice stopped glaring at each other to look at him.

Sam looked around. His eyes focused and he smiled. He became aware of who was in the room with him.

"Oh Sam, honey, baby," Alice was kissing him and crying with joy. She was hugging him, leaning way into the cold water so the bustline of her tight satin dress got all wet.

"WOW! That was pretty good stuff! Can we get some more?"

"YOU HAVE TO BE KIDDING!" Tom wiped the sweat away from his face again with the sleeve of his black sixties silk shirt. He sat down on the floor because his knees had given out too. "You're kidding, right?"

"He's not kidding!" Alice was angry again. "You just ODed, you asshole!" she screamed at Sam.

"You were almost fucking dead, man!" Tom said, laughing nervously.

"I just shot you up with some salt,"' I said. "Remember it. May come in handy someday."

"How do you feel, Sam? You asshole," Tom smiled at him. "What an asshole," he said to me happily.

"You had us going there for awhile, you jerk," Alice kissed him on his icy lips. "How do you feel?"

"I don't think I'm high anymore, dammit." Sam looked mad. Then he looked down at himself while he sat there in the tub. "Hey! You idiots put me in here with my best sharkskin suit on. You could at least have taken it off me!" He stood up in the tub, dripping and wobbling. "I'm freezing. Could you get me some dry clothes, babe?" he asked Alice.

"Of course, sweetheart," she said, and squeezed out the door.

"The two-tone purple one!!" Sam yelled after her. Someone tried to push in the door when Alice pushed out, but Tom jumped up and stood against it.

"I'M GOING TO PISS RIGHT HERE!" the person said. "I CAN'T HOLD IT ANY LONGER!"

"Go ahead!" Sam shouted back to the guy out there, "make yourself at home."

Obviously he wasn't a vegetable. Sam was Sam again, for better or worse. He took off his suit and wrapped himself in the IT'S THE REAL THING towel. Yeah ... it sure is, I thought.

His teeth were chattering while he took off the suit and

threw it in the corner. He looked kind of pitiful and still wobbly. It seemed like he had shrunk a little. His fingertips were all wrinkled from the water.

"I feel like shit. I'm not even high anymore!" he grumbled.

I left the bathroom. Some people are never happy.

Outside in the living room, the party was still jumping. No one had even suspected that the host had practically died a few minutes ago.

In less than five minutes, I saw Sam with a Nebuchadnezzar of champagne, walking around the dancers filling people's empty glasses. Someone gave him another birthday present, the book by Celine, *Death on the Installment Plan*. Another person handed him a familiar little package, probably more heroin. I shook my head and fought my way to the kitchen. A filmmaker handed me a glass of champagne. I drained it. I remembered that I hated champagne.

"So what have you been doing lately?" this filmmaker asked me.

"Not much," I shrugged. "You know … same old shit …"

Dogs I Have Known

I know that dogs dream: I've seen their feet running while they're asleep. They have horrible nightmares sometimes, and they whimper and jump up on the bed with me and quiver in the middle of the night.

"It's only a dream," I tell them. "Just a nightmare. Go back to sleep."

I had a dog named Frank once. I had him for eleven years. He was from a litter of only two pups: he came out first, and the little white dog with no neck and no tail came out last.

Frank was a black-and-white Border collie, but he had a weird exaggerated nose. He was an instinctual herder. Without sheep to herd, he would wait until low tide in the Provincetown Harbor to herd schools of little fish every day.

He was a smart dog. Too smart. He spoke a few words, it's a fact. He used to say waaater when he wanted water, and he used to say ooout when he wanted to go out. If I ever neglected him for too long, and he had to do his duty, he'd go into the bathroom and politely try to reach the toilet bowl, but he wasn't quite tall enough.

He liked to steal and eat people's hashish, and he loved to sit around and smoke marijuana with the humans. If someone didn't blow the smoke into his nostrils, he would lick the smoke from the air.

He was loved in Provincetown. Once he disappeared for two days and came back with red, blue, and yellow designs painted on his white face fur. Another time he disappeared for three days, and I was really worried, but he made it back, panting and dog-tired. That time, attached to his collar was a clothesline, complete with towels, bathing suits, and clothespins. Obviously someone had wanted to adopt him and tied him in their back-yard on the clothesline extension.

It's been years since Frank died, but Provincetown is loaded with his descendants. Every other dog around is a black-and-white son or granddaughter. He spread the seed. He was the duke of dogdom. Frank's in canine nirvana now, herding goldfish in hound dog heaven.

Dogs are the best friends; they assure you every day of your existence. They never grow weary of you. They love you no matter what. If you never had a dog, you don't understand this at all.

Two days after Frank died I was sitting at Chinese Chance, One University Place, the restaurant-bar owned by Micky Ruskin, who used to own Max's Kansas City. It was the hangout for all the established and rising downtown artists, writers, and filmmakers. It was a great place, very homey, everyone knew everyone else, and Mickey used to trade artist's work for food and liquor tabs. The walls were full of the best art in the city.

I was at the bar, crying in my vodka soda, when Jackie Curtis sat next to me and asked what was wrong. I told him about Frank and he said, "My grandmother just died."

I bought him a drink.

"Get yourself another dog," he said. "It's the cure for that one."

"Yeah, compared to you I have it easy. You can't get another grandmother," I said, feeling sort of silly comparing the losses.

"Hey, I know what it's like to lose a dog you love. It's really horrible, I know. You can't really replace your dog, but you can get a different one." He was very sympathetic.

"I know exactly what kind of dog I want," I said. "I want a little female Benji type, fluffy, all black, because I wear mostly black, so the dog hair on my clothes won't show."

"Don't say another word. Let's go now and don't ask any questions."

We left the bar and hopped into a cab. We went to Second Avenue and Eleventh Street where Jackie's grandmother's bar Slugger Ann's was. It was closed and locked up since her death. Jackie pulled out his keys and opened the door. In the darkness a bunch of dogs ran up to us, but I couldn't see any of them.

"There's five dogs here," he said, and turned on the light. Most of them were Chihuahuas, but there was one little black furry Benji type wagging her tail and dancing around on her hind legs. It was the dog I had described. It was love at first sight.

"Beauty! Come 'ere, honey!" The little black dog jumped into Jackie's arms. "Here's your new dog, Cookie," Jackie said. "Isn't she a beauty?"

"Really! I can have Beauty? But …" I said.

"You can't have her if you're not serious," Jackie said. "Beauty belonged to my grandmother and …"

"Jackie, this isn't some light thing to me. Once I take on a responsibility for an animal, it's for the rest of their life," I said, and it was the truth.

I took her home that night and she slept in bed with me. For five days I tried to get her to eat, but she wouldn't. I tried everything—Alpo, Mighty Dog, everything—but she turned up her nose. She would hardly even drink any water. I was really worried. I called Jackie.

"I think she's in mourning for your grandmother, Jackie. She won't eat anything."

"What are you trying to feed her?"

"I've tried every imaginable dog food but …"

"Dog food? She doesn't eat dog food! She eats beer nuts, potato chips, Slim Jims, pizza, and Chinese food," Jackie said.

"Oh, that's what was wrong. Okay, as long as I know."

"Oh, and Cookie," Jackie added, "She doesn't drink water either. She drinks beer. Sometimes she likes rum and Coke, too. In the mornings she has coffee."

I went right out to Smilers and bought some Slim Jims, potato chips, and a six-pack of Beck's. Beauty gobbled up the Slim Jims and the potato chips. I opened a beer and put a little of it in a bowl and put the bowl on the floor. She drank it right down and started barking for more. She was really thirsty. I opened a beer for myself and another one for her.

Beauty and I are drinking buddies now. We have lived happily ever after.

The Berlin Film Festival—1981

The whole time we were flying across the Atlantic I hadn't been nervous at all about my personal stash of drugs that I was carrying inside my overly padded bra.

I got nervous when we walked into the airport in West Germany and I saw all those security men in uniforms with their machine guns.

I had decided to go to the Berlin Film Festival with Beth Channing, the artist, and Amos Poe, the filmmaker, who had been invited to show his film *Subway Riders* there.

I had a part in this film. It wasn't a bad part, and I wasn't too horrible in it; the film itself was okay too, although not by any American standards. American audiences always wanted fast tight plots and big budgets and this film didn't have either, but it was viable enough and young Europeans looking for new art would probably think it was inscrutably hip.

Most people in the film world will tell you that the Berlin Film Festival is really fun, more fun than the Cannes Festival, less snooty than the Deauville Festival and less businessy than the LA Festival.

That sounded pretty good to me. Besides, German films were probably better than any other in the world at the time. Fassbinder was tossing his genius around. Herzog was busy influencing all filmmakers in the rest of the world and Schroeter was doing both, but to a more select audience. I wanted to see the stuff hot off the Steenbeck editing machine, fresh in the can, the films that might never get to America and maybe I could get some film work. Maybe. If I hustled. But I wasn't counting too much on that possibility. I suspected that I wouldn't have a lot of time to think about work … too many festival parties … things like that.

Basically I just needed some live European exposure.

All I had to do was get through customs.

This turned out to be harder than anyone would have guessed.

Everything might have gone smoothly if Amos hadn't absent-mindedly left his leather quasi-Nazi motorcycle hat on the seat of the plane.

Beth and I waited while he ran back out on the airstrip to get it. Of course it wasn't his fault really, but that put us at quite a disadvantage, since the customs people had nothing to do by the time we reached them. They'd checked all the other passengers.

The beer-belly bunch at customs were eager for us. They thought they might have some fun because we didn't look like any of the other passengers.

We expected a little delay, nothing much else. Amos and I didn't know that Beth was carrying marijuana in one of those little gray Tri-X film cannisters.

Unfortunately for her, customs people have been hip to the Tri-X cannister scam since the great marijuana days of the late sixties. They went right for it, found it, and then the place was alive. Suddenly a flurry of dogs and cops were circling in. Dobermans in S&M gear and aging uniformed Hitler youth cracking their knuckles like butchers snapping baby chicken wings gathered around us while visions of gas chambers danced in our heads.

I proceeded to melt into the Formica flooring. A puddle of sweat formed around my feet; after all, I was carrying hashish, cocaine, MDA, and opium, of course in small amounts, just tads really, but the variety was sure to turn heads once seized.

I wanted to confess, throw in the towel, but the whimpers stuck in my throat. My vocal chords froze in terror and I could only smile like Louis XVI on the guillotine gangplank. With the marble grin of an idiot, I stood there, goose pimples of horror rising on my flesh as the buxom bulldyke cop in full torture drag appeared in white gloves to strip-search me.

In the private room, I began to disrobe. Employing cold weather habits of fashionable bag ladies, and to cut down on the bulk of my suitcase, I was wearing most of the clothes I brought: tights, leg warmers, over-the-knee boots, a dress, two sweaters, a vest, a leather jacket, various fur pieces and a long black coat. It was hell for her. She had to painstakingly inspect every item. She fingered every hemline, felt every bulge, probed the hairs on the endangered species fur. She even dismantled my spike heels.

One can imagine the state I was in. A more stressful situation was difficult to conjure. The sweat was ridiculous.

Remember now that the stash was in my bra. It was no sloppy job. Back in New York I had carefully sliced open one of the seams above the gargantuan tit pads. Between the boob-contoured double foams I had deftly placed in a plastic Ziploc bag— all the personal needs of an underground film star.

Right before I removed my bra I realized that this big woman was watching me very intently. I was but a slip of a thing at the time, certainly unwieldy and so top-heavy with those huge fake knockers.

I took off the bra and my pitiful boobs hopped out. They must have looked pretty sad compared to the bra and all its womanly glory.

She looked at my chest, and she looked at the bra, and I noticed a hint of female compassion there. She felt sorry for me, sorry that I should have exposed my secret to her. My secret of little tits.

In deference to me, in pure sympathy, and not to humiliate me any further, she didn't touch the bra. She didn't finger it and probe it the way she had with every other article of my clothing. In her eyes, I saw that she felt sorry for underdeveloped girls. It had not gone unnoticed all her life, probably, that she was too well endowed in that department. She wouldn't embarrass me further by flaunting her superior bustline at me unnecessarily. God's meager dole to me was embarrassing enough.

And I thanked God right there and then. All the padded bras in high school were but a testing ground.

She told me to get dressed and go. She was all through with me.

I stopped sweating then.

Outside the little room, back at customs central, Amos and Beth had both been strip-searched too and Beth was on her way to deportation.

Amos stayed with Beth, waiting until she was safely deported, while I bowed out and proceeded on to Berlin to the hotel to take a bath and wait for Amos there.

I found Johanna Heer, the feisty little Austrian, part businesswoman, part thin-lipped kewpie doll, who was also the camerawoman for Amos's film, at the hotel waiting for us.

"Where's Amos?" Naturally that would be her first question.

I filled her in on the details, and we went to eat, which isn't easy anywhere in Germany because the food is so horrifying. All there is to choose from is pork, pork, pork, prepared in myriad different ways.

Later on, during a shopping spree at their German equivalent to Bloomingdale's, the Ka Da We department store, I understood all about the German cuisine. There was a whole floor devoted to meat: *Knockwurst, Schinckenwurst, Knockensnicken, Brattens-chicken* … endless displays of sausages, pigs in links, hung there bombarding the consciousness, the throwbacks of the Nazi mentality exposed and garnished with green parsley.

Seeing this, I understood the phenomenon of Hitler, I knew why Germans HAD to march. Pork makes one want to march.

Anyway, Amos appeared the next day just in time for the opening night party at the huge Intercontinental Hotel, where copious amounts of beer gushed from spouts into endless mugs. What Germany lacks in cuisine is well made up for in the quality of beer. A glass of draft beer is a meal.

I met all the German film stars, people I'd always wanted to have beers with: Udo Kier, Bruno Ganz, Klaus Kinski, and the German filmmakers, the ones I'd mentioned before. I was in Aryan heaven.

I became fast friends with Udo Kier, star of Warhol/Morrissey's *Dracula* and *Frankenstein*, star of Fassbinder films, and I fell in love with Tabea Blumenschein, a woman who was Berlin's underground celebrity film queen. I spent a lot of time with Udo and Tabea at Tabea's home when we weren't at a screening of a film during the day or at a festival party at night.

I decided that someday I had to write and direct a film because there are film festivals all year round in all different parts of the world. I could just live from one festival to the next, jet-setting with my can of celluloid, screening the film, looking for distributors, drinking local beverages, partying, living off the fat of moviedom's lush dreamscape, buoyed up into the land of ever-shifting realities where time was measurable only by ninety-minute feature-length intervals and space was measurable only by movie houses, star-laden restaurants, and festival party halls.

Berlin, like New York, is open all night and the clubs all have that decadent feel of pre-rampage-of-Hitler nights, those kinds of wild nights recreated by Christopher Isherwood in his *Berlin Stories* and the movie *Cabaret*. I wondered if Americans would feel this way about Berlins if they hadn't seen *Cabaret*.

It's true that all the Festival people except the buyers and sellers were great looking. All native Berlin nightlifers were gorgeous. Even the bookish intelligentsia in this city didn't look boring the way they do in the States, in fact it seemed that everybody I met was the intelligentsia, even the people with the purple mohawks and brown pet rats crawling around in their shirts.

John Waters was at the festival, and we saw a lot of films together, and went to all the night spots doing socio-behavioral studies.

Three days before the end of the festival, I ran into Udo at the festival headquarters.

"You better get out of your hotel room and move the rest of your things into Tabea's, Amos has left the hotel room and gone on to Paris. There's some problem with your bill," Udo said.

"What do you mean … some problems with the bill? The festival pays the hotel bill," I said, but nevertheless I had visions of going to the gas chambers again.

"The festival pays the hotel bill but there's some other things on the bill ... I don't know. Go there and talk to the man at the desk," Udo said. "Better hurry. They might confiscate your monkey fur."

I hustled off to the hotel and when I got there the whole staff was in a huff. It turned out that Amos had the false impression that the festival was going to pay for everything, including long-distance phone calls and room service. I thought that was fairly reasonable; I would have probably assumed the same, but I hadn't been staying at the hotel at all, just keeping some clothes there and living at Tabea's, so none of the bills were mine.

"You must pay this bill before you leave or we're calling the police," the desk people said, slamming fists on Black Forest wood.

"It's not my bill. I haven't even been here. Talk to the people at the Festival headquarters. I'm not paying this goddamned bill." I ran upstairs to pack. They yelled after me.

"We're calling the police. We're calling the police."

The thoughts of encounters with the German police again made my adrenaline glands go into overdrive. There had to be a way out of this. If I had been wise, I wouldn't have returned to the hotel at all, but I wanted my favorite clothes, the monkey coat, the rest of my money, and of course I needed the return airplane ticket that was lying in the top drawer of the dresser.

I packed in lightning speed, jamming the clothes into the bag and piling on layers that would never fit in the bag. I heaved the whole heavy mass under my arm, the contents spilling out leaving a trail along the hallway to the lobby.

I peeked around the stairwell wall at the front door and the desk. There was absolutely no way of sneaking out the front. In the next second I saw through the big lobby windows two cop cars pulling up to the entrance, so I ran back upstairs, thinking that there must be a fire exit somewhere.

I found it. Small stairs that led to a basement led to a door that was well bolted. I threw the bolts back, and the door was so heavy, but I got it open finally, only to find a ten-foot-tall wire mesh fence, and after that a twelve-foot wall with ivy growing on it.

"There's no stopping now," I said to myself as the heavy door closed and locked behind me, so I threw my heavy bag over the wire mesh fence and scaled it, ripping my blue leather skirt up to the hip on the barbs at the top, while the fence wobbled with my weight. I jumped down and then looked at the wall. What the hell was I going to do? I could use the ivy plants to climb the wall only if they were older plants with thick vines.

I quickly did some horticultural investigations and figured the vines were just old enough, so I threw the bag over the side. That took a few tries, and when I finally got it over I didn't hear it hit the ground on the other side for a very long time. That wasn't great. Once I was on top of the wall, where would I be?

I started up the vines and halfway I had to take off my boots and throw them over. It was easier in stocking feet.

On the way up I couldn't help thinking how perfect the scenario was. There I was in Berlin scaling a wall in fear, skirt all ripped, stockings now in tatters. It was the famous nail-biter scene from some anti-Communist film: youngish East Berliner female climbs the Berlin Wall to get into West Berlin with the East Berlin police firing machine guns at her. We all know this.

I got to the top of the wall. Below me on the other side was a construction site, a deep, wide pit, the future basement of some housing development or something. Far below in the dirt was my bag and my boots. Now what?

If I walked along the edge of the wall far enough, there was a place to jump down on a pile of concrete blocks. From there I could climb down and get my stuff, but then how would I get out of the pit and onto the street? I'd figure that out then. If I had to, I'd sleep in the pit and the construction workers could let me out in the morning.

I forged ahead, got my stuff and found a way out of the pit, but then there was another wire fence to the street and a few people were walking by. How embarrassing, I thought, a chic underground film star climbing a fence out of a pit in Berlin. How could I live this one down?

When I got to the fence, all dirty and ripped up, I yelled to a passerby who was gawking at me anyway. He could help.

"*Sprechen Si Englisch?*" I yelled frantically, glancing around for patrolling cop cars.

"Yes, but only a little. I studied it when I was ..."

"Never mind," I cut him off. "Can you just help me? Take this bag and then catch me when I jump down into the street." I started climbing the fence, skirt flapping in the breeze. Did I have underwear on? I wondered.

He helped me, he wasn't fazed a bit, just curious. Germans are always trying to understand the intellectual significance of every action.

"Now can you hail a taxi for me?" I asked him and looked down at myself in way of explanation. No cabbie would pick me up looking like this. There were no cabs. I expected the cops any second so I hid in the shadows waiting. Still, there were no cabs.

I saw a bus in the distance. I ran out into the street and flagged it down. Anything to get out of this neighborhood. When I crawled on board, the bus driver and the passengers were aghast. Nobody in Germany walked around half-naked from the waist down, barefoot, dirty, in the middle of February.

"Just get me to a taxi stand," I said as I hunted for some correct change.

Interminable minutes droned on. I stood there in the front of the bus, covered in dirt, humiliated, and the bus was alive with whispers. Everybody on the vehicle was talking about me.

Suddenly I saw a cab and I screamed for the bus driver to stop. He was very happy to let me out and I threw myself in front of the cab. The cabbie almost wouldn't let me in but I pleaded and showed him a handful of money.

While driving to Tabea's flat, I was thinking about how I was going to strangle Amos Poe when I got back to the States.

"Cookie, what happened to you?" Tabea asked, laughing, as she let me in the door. She was frying up some sausages while the music of Wagner was blaring on the radio.

"I just climbed the Berlin Wall."

Edgar Allan Poe on Ice—1982

It could have been a great play. We could have done aerial stunts in our hoop skirts, exposing our 19th century pantaloons to the audience. We could have wowed the theater goers with snappy thought provoking dialogue and witty dance numbers. We could have touched them with poignant song lyrics. We could have shaken Broadway.

As it was, this was difficult. Mired as we were, with our wind pipes yoked up in a tonnage of old lace and our tune belter's diaphragms strapped into whale bone corsets we hadn't a chance. Bound and gagged as we were, we sank in our hooks and eyes, our leaded hems, our layers of used method actor's petticoats.

Actually it wasn't so much the weight of the costumes, but the weight of the script. It tipped the scales.

Matt Beyer, a former Broadway Tony winner, and I got together one day over lunch and Matt started talking about Edgar Allan Poe. I told him about how I often took flowers to Poe's grave in Baltimore when I was a teenager. Somehow, we came up with the idea of writing a play about his life. We would co-write it and co-direct it. We were good friends. We wouldn't have problems. It sounded so perfect we started immediately. It took about four months to complete.

We were almost compatible co-writers except when we co-wrote.

At first we'd sit together and pound it out, laughing up a storm. We had a ball in the beginning. That wore off. After a while both of us would take the script home and work privately, sort of against each other. There was one major point we never really agreed upon. I thought the play should be shorter than it was and he thought it should be longer.

I thought we'd work out this detail in rehearsals.

With our script and innovative ideas plus Matt's laurels we found an off-Broadway producer. No off-off low budget stuff for us. We cast the play without too much deliberation and went right into rehearsals.

From the first day of line readings, I realized we were wallowing in too many words. I suggested minor edits immediately. Each day onward I trieed every tactic for script cuts but Matt was adamant about the importance of each word.

Okay, I thought, give it time. He'll see it weighs a ton in time. He didn't.

One night after four weeks of rehearsals and no edits, while we were deep into a snooze scene of far too many adjectives for the actor's tongue, I finally had had enough. It was right in the middle of a ponderously verbose monologue that I stopped the lead actor, mid sentence.

"I'm sorry," I said. "Can we break for a minute?" I turned to Matt, "I have to talk to you."

Everyone turned to me with their scripts poised. Matt glared at me.

"Yeah. You wanna talk? Come out here in the corridor with me for a second," he said to me.

When we got to the hall Matt's ears were red. His lips were up to his gums.

"What did you mean by destroying business he was building out there?" he asked. It was actor's vernacular.

His anger made me back down a bit.

"Look, Matt, we gotta cut some of that monologue. It's just too long and rambling ..." What I meant was the whole play was too long and rambling.

"The quality of the language in the 19th century was more florid," Matt said.

"Oh come on," I countered, "Poe was an alcoholic and a junkie. I'm sure he used some expeditious lingo occasionally."

"No," he said.

"Matt, let's face some real facts here. This play is too long. It's supposed to be a comedy. Comedies are better shorter. An hour needs to be cut off the whole thing. There's excess baggage here," I said but it was a weak argument. "Please. Let's just try it." I said it, but I was begging.

Matt just calmly put down his master script, let out a kamikaze whoop and pounced on my neck. I couldn't believe he was actually trying to strangle me.

Rose and John, two of the cast members, came running out of the rehearsal space. I was near a death rattle.

"He's trying to kill me," I screamed.

"We're too far into rehearsals," Matt yelled. "The actors love their lines." He looked at John and Rose, "Don't you love your lines?" He turned back to me, "Just try to take some lines away from them. I dare you."

"We don't love our lines enough for murder," Rose said.

"We're not cutting anything," said Matt andhe stalked back into the room where the rest of the actors were cringeing in their cups of coffee.

I looked at John and Rose. They were looking at the floor and puffing on harsh non filter cigarettes, the kind actors use when plays are only two weeks from opening and look like two months from opening.

"He's so obstinate," I told them. "Can't he see?"

They didn't answer.

"Oh he's a genius. Yes he is," I said. "But even geniuses need to be edited."

They didn't answer. Rose and John weren't interested in whatever Matt and I disagreed upon. Wisely, they just wanted to do their jobs without taking sides in internecine warfare.

In retrospect I realized the real problem with the play. Matt and I as the writers were trying to follow Poe's life too strictly. We got into hair splitting Poe's dead ends.

In reality Poe's life wasn't so theatrical. True, he did stand up to his romantic image. He used opiates and he drank himself to death, that part was dramatic enough. He married his 12 year old cousin who died singing. That part was kinky enough. But there are some very boring years in every immortal person's life.

All we had developed was authenticity. We should have pared away the mundane minutia, etched out a new dramatic life for him, and given the man a new history. We should have slashed the ho-hum, maybe with dancing life size feather pens or huge stage-engulfing ravens chanting "Nevermore." Poe might have liked that.

The night after the strangulation incident, the producer came into the theater to see a rehearsal. I watched him taking notes.

Afterward he took Matt and I aside. He was very diplomatic.

"Well … the direction is great. The characters seem strong, the actors are doing a superb job and some of it is really funny and it seems that it's also poignant when it has to be … but …" He paused here searching for words that wouldn't hurt us too much, "it's just too damn long! You've got to tighten it up. Sorry … sorry if I dampen the artistic sensibilities here."

Sorry?!? Don't be sorry, I wanted to say. He didn't dampen anything that wasn't already flooded. Finally someone else, the producer, was telling Matt what I'd been telling him for weeks. I felt relieved.

Matt didn't.

"I agree totally," I told the producer, "whole heartedly."

"You really believe it's too long?" Matt asked the producer. "I don't know what you mean."

"We could go over it scene by scene, if you want. I have my notes," he pulled out his copy of the script and leafed through it showing us the red pencil slashes.

"Ok. Let's go over this," Matt taunted.

We all sat down. It took a few hours, and it was a revelation. The producer knew exactly what had to be done, one, two, three. His objective eye was all we had needed. Matt would see it clearly, I thought.

The next day I called the producer to tell him that I agreed with all his edits. In fact, I thought there should be more.

"Great," he said, "but how does Matt feel?"

"I don't know. We'll see tonight at rehearsal," I said. "Can you be there again? I hope so."

"Not tonight," he said, "I'll come by on Monday and see the new cuts."

That night at rehearsal, before Matt came in, I got the actors together with red pencils to slash dialogue.

"OK, we have drastic cuts," I said, "starting on page four, cut line three to line eleven, page seven cut line six to fourteen …"

That's when Matt walked in.

"What's going on?" he asked.

"I'm cutting what's been suggested," I said.

"Oh, no. I never agreed to any cuts! The play stands as it is." He was all smiles. He looked really good that night, like a fox, I thought.

"Let's start rehearsals," he said ethusiastically, "Ok. John. Page twenty two scene five!"

"Hey, Matt … we can't do this …" I said but suddenly I realized something. Matt wasn't really trying to be difficult, he just hadn't heard a word the producer had said the other night. He had simply closed his ears. For Matt, the discussion with the producer had never happened. I guess he thought the producer didn't understand art.

I screamed but he was calm. He was looking good, I was looking bad. Only then did I realize for real that the actors weren't with me. They weren't really taking sides, but they just wanted as many lines as they could milk. It was a losing battle. I threw up my hands and decided against a huge confrontation in front of the cast.

I would have to talk to the producer again.

The rehearsal that night droned on, and things were tense. The next day, Bret as Poe called me and told me he was dropping out.

"I have another commitment," was all he said. This was devastating. The lead actress followed and begged out too.

"Did you tell Matt?" I asked her.

"Yeah, he wasn't happy. In fact, he yelled," she said.

I didn't ask why she chose to walk, I knew. This was a double whammy day. She'd been so good. It was going to be difficult to replace both of them.

Matt replaced both of them the next day.

Four days later two more actors with small parts dropped out. Matt and I took over these roles ourselves. At least I'd have complete freedom acting, I was being hobbled as a co-director.

I couldn't wait to get into that hoop skirt. I'd roll along in the hoop, I'd forget my anger, forget my astonishment at Matt's obstinance, try to not buck him unless I could do it tactfully. Maybe, just maybe, the producer and I were both wrong, maybe we were both looking at it without a postmodern conceptualist viewpoint. Maybe the play should be considered differently, as a deliberate attempt at a money losing profound art offering. Who could say? Matt wasn't talking anymore. He was a driven man, a man with a purpose, a man with a magnum opus.

I was confused. I weighed both sides. I believed in brevity, not redundancy, but maybe I was wrong.

I decided to concern myself with the cast's physical timing. If the pacing was brought up the play would be more cohesive. I gave the actors all kinds of new stage business, and it seemed to work better. Matt disagreed. He thought I was trying to challenge him.

So then I concerned myself with the visuals, the lights, the sets, the costumes. We had long since decided to spare no expense with the costumes, so we got them all from Brooks Van Horn, the theatrical costumers who supplied Broadway. We had a field day at the Brooks Van Horn warehouse looking for the right drag. That day we worked as a team, it was the best day of pre-production. With these costumes, at least the play would look great, even if it sounded bad.

Once we started rehearsing with the costumes, sets, music, and lights the play was really out of control. Fortyfive minutes hopped on to the running time. The pace slowed to a shuffle. Everybody was back-pedaling in heavy brocade. This was going to be a five hour play and even I didn't care anymore.

I called the producer to tell him that the play was looking retarded. The costumes might save it, but it was basically a snore-fest. I left this message with his answering service.

When he came at Monday's rehearsal and saw that the play was even longer than before, with none of the cuts he suggested, he blew his top.

Matt was contrite at first but then belligerent when the pro-ducer threatened to close the production. I thought it was all over. That was when I swear I saw the interior of Matt's cerebral cortex. Suddenly it seemed I had x-ray vision like Superman and I saw Matt's brain wheels whirring. He was thinking fast. He knew he ought to put on a new face and before our eyes he became the consumate actor, the Tony winner. He was charming. Superb. He made a deal. He said the play would tighten up in one week, no edits, just faster. He wanted the play to have an open dress rehearsal. We would treat it like a preview, sort of. Seats would be the regular price. If the producer still really hated it and the audience really hated it then he would cut the play to the bone if need be. He'd work around the clock on edits. He'd play the lead if need be.

He presented the scheme really well, so well in fact, it sounded very logical to me and the producer. He sure knew how to pitch it. He WAS a genius.

Thinking about it later that night I couldn't believe I had agreed to such a ludicrous idea. The producer was probably thinking the same.

The night of the open dress rehearsal, the house was standing room only. The lights went up and the play started rolling. Visually the play was incredible, a knockout. Into the first half hour the audience loved it. Into the first hour they still loved it, even though the plot hadn't even begun to unfold. Into the second hour the audience was restless, the laughter wasn't coming anymore. You could cut the droop with a knife.

We lost thirty percent of the audience at intermission, and a half hour into Act Two the seams just completely gave way. We were going downhill fast, very slowly. We lost the audience. They fell asleep. Somebody was snoring, even.

Finally, at the end of the play, I couldn't face any friends who'd come to see it. Some of them came backstage and lied. My more honest friends told me it was just too long. It was boring, but the beginning was incredible.

I couldn't even look at Matt, I was so mad.

The producer came backstage, shaking his head. "Too bad you had to waste valuable time. I hope you've learned a thing or two."

He pulled up a chair at the makeup mirror and sat down. "Now if word gets out it's a turkey we're lost. I didn't know so many people were going to show up tonight." He turned to face Matt. "OK Matt, you had your chance. Now the play is going my way."

"Sorry," Matt said, "can't do it."

The producer and I looked at Matt and then each other with our mouths open. We couldn't believe what we were hearing.

"Please, just wait and see," Matt said. "It's going to tighten up. The pace'll quicken on its own."

The producer was struck dumb, but I started yelling. I'd had enough.

"I want out," I yelled. "I'm not having my name on something I don't believe in. If you don't agree to cut this play now, the production stops. Legally I can stop it!" I wasn't sure about this legal stuff but it sounded good.

"Well you better sue then, because I'm not cutting this play. Never! NEVER!" Matt stomped his foot and the 19th century boot buckles burst.

"Is this your final word, Matt?" the producer asked him very carefully.

"YES IT IS!" Matt screamed.

"OK, then Matt, this play is officially closed." He stood up and didn't miss the trash can when he threw the script into it. "It's no skin off my teeth."

Matt's face registered disbelief. His resolve crumbled. The party was over. He had called the producer's bluff and lost. He forfeited the whole dream.

The producer put on his overcoat. "I have another play ready to open that'll fill your time spot in this theater perfectly. I suggest you clear outta here immediately. And get these costumes back to Brooks Van Horn by nine in the morning so I don't have a bigger bill on my hands. And get those props back too. Nine o'clock." He was all business now. He dismissed us as if we were lint on his lapel.

"How am I going to get all these things back by nine in the morning? I need a van ..." Matt looked confused.

"That's your problem," the producer said. He was curt. He looked at his watch, "I'm late for a dinner." He left.

A big silence filled the dressing room. The void settled in.

I didn't even look at Matt. There was nothing to look at. He was empty.

I went into the other dressing rooms to tell the actors to pack up. From Matt's dressing room came the sound of things being busted up. He must have been throwing his breakable props against the walls. He was probably biting some hoop skirts in half with his teeth and ripping out clumps of his hair.

As for me, I didn't feel bad. I didn't feel good. I didn't feel anything. I was going to miss that hoop skirt.

To this day, people ask me what happened to the Poe play and why didn't it officially open. They'd loved it. It was fabulous. A monument.

"Artistic differences," I answer. With fond memories clearer than the awful ones, I closed the book.

Another Boring Day

When she moved away, I began to approach the teller, but a man in the line next to mine grabbed my arm and pointed to the floor. There in front of me was a puddle of poo. Watery shit, right where the old lady had been standing.

Naturally I thought my dog had done it, but the man in the next line told me, "No, it wasn't your dog. That old lady did it. She must have forgotten to wear her diaper today." Someone else laughed and said, "She was making a deposit." Another said, "Yeah, doing her transaction." Everyone laughed nervously, trying not to think of the day when they might be incontinent.

I had an appointment uptown at three, so I went back to the apartment to drop off my dog. While I was opening the door to my apartment, I heard a sound in the back room. There was a man in a ski mask climbing in the fire escape window.

"Hey!" I screamed. He climbed back out the window and scrambled up the fire escape. I called the cops, thinking maybe they could catch him if they were fast. They weren't.

I went right out to the hardware store and spent the money I'd gotten at the bank for window gates. I put them on the window and put some garlic over the frames. That ought to keep out the VCR vampires.

Now I was really late. In the rain cabs aren't easy to find, but I got one finally.

"Don't I know you from somewhere?" the driver turned around and asked.

"Maybe." I said.

"You're a film actress or something. What'd I see you in?"

"Dunno," I said. I wasn't going to list the names of the eighteen films I'd done over the years.

"What'd I see you in? I know, it was *Female Trouble*, right? I know you. You were in *Pink Flamingos*, too! Yeah! You're Cookie, right? Those films changed my life. Could you gimme an autograph?"

He handed me his pen and a piece of paper, "Make it out to Lenny."

Luck, Laughs, Lust, Love, Cookie Mueller, I wrote on the paper and sealed it with a lipstick kiss. I handed it to him.

"Yeah, that's who you are, but I always thought you were a drag queen."

We hit midtown traffic. It was standing still and I was really anxious. I could walk faster than this.

"Hey, Lenny, I'm gonna get out here," I said. "I'm really late." I paid him, hopped out, and took a subway.

Everyone in the car looked so sad, the weight of all those subway years etched in their faces. I sat down next to a tired man who was reading a self-help book.

At the next stop a friend of mine got on the train. He sat down next to me.

"I haven't seen you in a while," he said. "How've ya been?"

"Ah well, okay I guess. Ya know New York. You?" I looked him over. I didn't feel like telling him the story of my day so far. He looked great. Spiffy. Prosperous, in fact. But there was something odd. He was carrying a brown paper bag, the kind with handles, just a regular grocery bag that was full to the brim with crumpled paper, orange peels, empty tin cans, and coffee grinds.

"What'd'ya got there, Bob?" I asked him and pointed to the bag. He looked down at his bag and blanched. Then he started laughing until he was crying.

"This is my garbage. I was taking it downstairs to dump it. I guess I forgot. I'm so embarrassed."

We laughed all the way to Times Square, where he got off and dumped his garbage.

I was going to the offices of a New York magazine to pick up a check and discuss a new article I was writing for them. I was very late, so the editor was going to make me wait.

I sat down and watched the receptionist who was crying on the phone. It sounded like she was talking to her boyfriend or her husband. Messengers came in and out, dropping things off, and she blindly signed their slips. A nervous man came into the room with a manila envelope and he asked to see the editor. The receptionist waved him away. He just stood there.

"You might as well sit down," I told him. He sat down beside me.

"I'm trying to get a writing job here," he said.

"You're a writer, huh?" I asked.

"Well I never had anything published, but I'm always trying," he said and smiled.

If he only knew, I thought. A journalist's job is second only to air-traffic control as far as stress is concerned. I read that in *Psychology Today*, I think.

"What the hell you want to be a journalist for?" I asked him. He looked me up and down, but said nothing.

Yeah, life is tough in the real world. Actors wait on tables, ballet dancers work as topless go-go girls, artists wash dishes, and that's not even the worst part. Someday you might bring your garbage on the subway, someday you might even shit in your own bank.

Later when I got back to my street downtown, I noticed my bike that had been chained to a pole was totally flattened and destroyed by a taxicab, which was now sitting in the Italian restaurant in my building. It had gone right through the big plate-glass window. No one had gotten hurt, even though it was a three-car collision.

Upstairs in my apartment, Max was home from school, and he was holding a party for what appeared to be the League of Nations' kids. The turbaned Indian kid from the newsstand, the cute Korean kid from the fruit store, the little Italian brothers from the pizza place across the Avenue, the black kid from the African restaurant down the street, the Colombian kid from the laundromat—they were all over the place, busting the house up, screaming, running the length of the apartment with the dog jumping and barking, chasing the ball they were throwing into lamps and vases. Half-eaten apples were rolling on the floor with smashed crumbs of potato chips. The refrigerator door was standing open and the Colombian kid was drinking from the gallon carton of milk, spilling it all over the floor.

"Hey, don't I hear your mothers calling you?" I lied. "Yeah, I hear them out there. You all better go and see what they want." After a while the kids left. The house was destroyed.

A friend of mine dropped by and needed the two hundred dollars he'd loaned me a week ago. I gave him the money from the check I'd just cashed from the magazine office. I'd had it in my pocket for exactly twenty minutes, not long enough to miss it.

Later that night I was going to a birthday party for a friend of mine. He was connected with the *Saturday Night Live* people, so some of them were there. It was in a Chinese restaurant.

After dessert, drinks, and the check, we noticed we were the last people there. The staff were standing around with their coats and hats on, waiting for us to leave. We got the hint, finished our drinks, stood up, put our coats on, and started filtering out the door. I ran into the bathroom quickly and while I was in a stall, the lights went out. It was pitch-dark. I couldn't see a thing. I got out of the stall, but I forgot exactly where the door was. I remembered it was a weird shaped bathroom, very large, with five or six stalls, and an adjoining powder room with a big mirror and chairs. But which side was the powder room on? I remembered it being on the right, but it had disappeared. I started laughing at the ridiculousness of the whole scenario, but it wasn't getting any funnier after ten more minutes of groping in the dark. I started screaming for lights, but no one heard me. I searched my pockets for matches but I didn't have any.

How did this happen? Where was the door? I bumbled around in the dark for a long time, feeling for the powder room, and then I finally found it and fell over a chair and hit my head on the counter and fell on the floor. I lay there for another few minutes, trying to remember where the door was, afraid to stand up again and run into another chair. So I started crawling around on my hands and knees searching for the door.

Finally I found the door, and I tumbled down the short flight of stairs into the restaurant. The place was dark, but there was light pouring in through the windows from the street outside.

The restaurant had closed, and I was locked in. The gates on the entrance door were down. Where were my friends? I looked outside. They were all there looking up and down the street, wondering where I was. I banged on the window, and they turned around to see me jumping around behind the glass. They started laughing.

I was locked in a Chinese restaurant.

They wrote a note and held it to the window. "We're going to call the police to get you out. Relax. Have a drink." I went behind the bar and helped myself to a vodka, then I found the phone and made a couple of long-distance calls while I was waiting for the cops. They laughed when they got there. They got me out through the back door that opened into a small cement courtyard and an office building.

I thought I was going to spend the night in there. After this day, I could have happily curled up on the Chinese carpet and slept.

"We have to go to that club opening," my friends told me when I was back out on the street. "Remember?" We got in a cab and headed there. We ended up at the Mudd Club afterward, where I knew that I'd see all my friends. It was jumping when we walked in.

The sun was breaking when we left Mudd, and after breakfast at Dave's Luncheonette, I said goodbye and caught a cab.

Inside the cab, there was something on the backseat. This was luck! It looked like a huge wallet bulging with thousands. That's what I wanted to see, anyway. I thought it best to sit smack down on it. I was afraid that maybe the cab driver had seen it in the eerie yellow light that all cabs have. I decided that I wasn't going to turn this wallet over to the driver. I was going to keep it. I'd had a long day.

I was hoping there was at least a thousand dollars in the wallet I was sitting on. It was uncomfortable and fat enough.

I planned what I was going to do with the money. The first thing would be to move into a better home. Then I'd buy an airplane ticket to some beach. I would rest. If a vacation didn't work to relax me, I'd use the credit cards to have a lobotomy. Then I would be stupid and blissful instead of stupid and stressed-out.

It was a long cab ride home, long enough to plan everything. Unfortunately I couldn't smoke in this cab. There was a sign on his sun-flap scrawled in child print that said, "Please don't smoke in this cab. I don't want my Granddad to die of lung cancer."

It was difficult to think without nicotine or some other kind of poison, but I had to think of a way to conceal the wallet. My pockets weren't big enough. I had to get the thing into my bra or down my pants. Cab drivers always want anything that's left on the seats, especially money, and he had been watching me closely in the rear-view mirror. For a minute I thought maybe he had intentionally planted the wallet there as a test, a game to pass the monotonous traffic time. But that was paranoia.

The red lights were interminable, the middle-aged woman that we almost hit was the slowest cow I'd ever seen, and gridlocks were suddenly appearing though it wasn't rush hour. Green lights weren't green enough.

I put the wallet into the top of my pants and hoped the safety pin wouldn't pop open and prick my belly button. I pulled down my pullover. I thought about all that money that pressed into my stomach painfully. I had never thought that money could be so uncomfortable.

It felt like so much money, I could even give some of it away. I'd finance low-budget films. I'd buy canvases for my painter friends. I had it all planned by the time we pulled up to my building.

In the cool safety of my bedroom, I found out that it wasn't a wallet at all, but an address and date book.

All my money plans dissolved.

There was absolutely nothing in it of value, not even an ID card in the zipper compartment. No cards, no money, nothing except a map of the NYC subway system. That was what had made it feel so fat all this time, not a wad of money.

It was with a sad heart that I looked into this person's life. A meager list of phone numbers and daily reminders was all that was there. It looked like the book of an organized person, an artifact from an uncluttered existence. This person obviously didn't ever have any bad days.

I put the address book in a Manila envelope and marked it C.O.D. with this person's address on the front. I took it out to the mailbox and dropped it in. Oh well.

The sun was shining and people were going to work. I had to get Max and the babysitter up for school and then go to sleep. It was bound to be another boring day.

Narcotics

I was at a sedate little cocktail party in SoHo. I can't really remember why I was there, or the purpose of the party, but I guess it was a post art opening party for the artist. It was one of those uneventful parties, the kind I wound up at once a week. It was a typical SoHo art shin-dig: there was a full bar, sliced raw veggies and clam dip, bread sticks, mini-wieners and pea-size meatballs floating around in red sauce in a hot stainless steel pan. The usual bunch of scrubbed, aspiring, New York art climbers were there mingling and tittering and chit-chatting discreetly, the women in sensible low heels and expensive stockings with no runs, and the men in silk ties, designer sports jackets, and clean jeans.

A few of the men, ones with goofy looking blood shot eyes were passing around marijuana, the ladies were giggling and tossing their sleek page boy hairdos around, acting like they'd never seen marijuana before. These women were young, fresh out of college, but they were always trying to make themselves look old for some reason. I never understood that. They wore gray baggy dresses and a few pieces of tiny, tasteful, conservative jewelry.

There was a man standing near me at the butlered bar, he was flirting with one of those bland-looking, milquetoast and corn-fed debs in gray. They were smoking a joint. The girl, this perky, peppy, preppie started to cough and he laughed and attempted to cuddle her for her cuteness. He turned to me only long enough to hand me the joint.

"Here," he said, "you look like the type that could handle this."

"No thanks," I said, "I don't use drugs … only narcotics."

That was the truth. I'd stopped using marijuana. It made me paranoid. I'd since moved on to the harder stuff.

The person I'd come with, Alvain Arles, the art critic and historian, came over to me.

"This is a real bore. A snore fest. Let's get out of here," he said. Alvain was many things, but never boring. He had a hard time tolerating people who were.

I hurled back my martini and we slipped out the door.

"Let's go cop some dope over on 4th Street. You think UFO or SHELL SHOCK will be out yet?" he asked.

"I don't think so. But ROADRUNNER, or SEVEN UP or NAUSEA ought to be out on 7th Street," I said as we tried to hail a cab.

"How about T.N.T. or DOLT BOLT?" he said in the cab, counting his money, "they're a little stronger."

"Let's just head straight for 10th Street for POISON or BLACK DEATH," I said, "they're always open. They have TOXIC and RADIOACTIVE there too."

"So where'll it be?" the cab driver asked.

"Just head for the east side," Alvain said, "How about IMPALE or PEG-LEG?"

"Is IMPALE any good?" I asked.

"I don't know, never had it. How about VIRGIN DEVIL or X-RATED? Or PARALYZE or WALLOP or LOT O'ROT?"

"Never had any of those except WALLOP. I don't even know if WALLOP still exists. You have to go for the newest stuff … after a week or two the quality always plummets. How about SWEET SIXTEEN or TRUE BLUE?"

"Hey, I know … what about STINKO?"

"Wait, wait! Why not TOILET?"

"Hey!! Okay!! Yeah!! TOILET's out now, so's TORTURE!" He got excited. "Driver, take us to East Third Street and Avenue B," he settled back, happy, "TOILET and TORTURE. Either one is great."

We were talking about heroin. These were the names that were rubber stamped on the little glassine packages of ten dollar amounts of the stuff sold on the lower east side streets. Junkies, weekend users, and other heroin aficionados memorized all the names by heart; they also knew where to get each one and exactly what time the "store" opened.

While we were talking I wondered what this cab driver thought when he heard all these names of different types of heroin. Maybe he thought we were going over the names of our favorite exploitation films, or talking about our favorite dirty book titles, or maybe he thought we were discussing S&M bars.

We got to the corner of Third and B, and Alvain hopped out of the cab. "You hold the cab," he said. "It'll take one second."

The cab driver waited for four seconds and then he turned to me, "Hey, I don't wanna sit here. I'm losing fares," he said.

"Don't worry. We'll make it worth your while," I said.

"No. Pay up, I gotta go."

I gave him the money and got out of the cab. That was a drag. Ordinarily, it wouldn't have been a drag, it was no calamity being without a cab, but I was looking a little too spiffy in my cocktail regalia for that neighborhood at that hour in that time of the decade. I was also holding the rest of Alvain's money, and junkies can smell money, especially if they're thieves or dope sick.

I looked around for Alvain and saw him down the block talking to a Puerto Rican in red and white running clothes. Alvain was probably flirting with the guy, because he was cute and he was Alvain's type. I walked up to them, and as I got there, I heard the Puerto Rican say to Alvain, "Yeah, TORTURE's smokin' righ now. I seen em carron out somebody who jes O.D.ed on it. Es some gooood sheeet righ now. You giv me ya money an I'll git it fa ya."

"And that'd be the last I'd see of you," Alvain Laughed. "No, I know where to go."

The Puerto Rican kept trying to think of some way to get some money from us, and he walked beside us talking non-stop. I could tell that Alvain was falling in love.

"Okay, I'm gonna give ya one of my bags," Alvain said and gently tweaked the Puerto Rican's beardless chin.

We walked over to the burned out building where people were lining up in the dark hallway, clutching their money, waiting to buy. Everyone was very quiet. Things were moving fast. The first guy in line put three ten dollar bills through a slot in a door in the back of the hall and out of the slot came three glassine bags of TORTURE heroin.

A big black guy standing at the hall entrance was keeping everything moving. He worked there. "Hurry up, move along, have your money ready, step up," he was saying.

A punk rocker in front of me was talking to a skinny oily looking Italian American guy, "Yeah, somebody jes O.D.ed on this shit minutes ago. Must be the best shit on the street right now."

"Told ya," the Puerto Rican reminded us.

"Great!" another person in line said, "I'm lucky I came out now."

"Yeah, my ol man was sa high on TORTURE yestada, dat he was throwin' up all ova da place," said a skinny birdy girl in a blue leather jacket, "Was goooood sheeet, man!"

"Shhh!" said the big black guy at the entrance.

Mixed in with the losers and hardcore users were a few prosperous types waiting in line: a Wall Street man, a blonde-haired model I'd seen in last month's *Vogue*, a famous post minimalist sculptor, a famous filmmaker, and a guy I'd seen once on some daytime soap opera, *Another World*, or *The Edge of Day*, or *City Hospital*. I can never remember the names of those shows.

When Alvain and I got to the dope door, Alvain slipped his money through the door slot and out came six little white rectangular packages, taped with clear tape and stamped with the word TORTURE. With the goods, we bustled out the building and walked fast off the block. Alvain gave one to the Puerto Rican, and the Puerto Rican disappeared. Alvain was temporarily heartbroken.

He got over it immediately when we saw a cop car cruising down the avenue. Instant paranoia. If they decided to stop us, we would go directly to jail for the night, even if we'd had just one measly bag between us.

I heard the lookouts, young kids, who worked for the dope houses from the roof tops, start yelling, "Bajando! Bajando!" That was the Spanish alert. It meant the cops were coming. We saw people walking very fast out of the building we'd just come from. Another watcher from the corner yelled "Don't run! Calm down! Don't run!" People on the street who were heading toward the building, looking to score, just turned in their tracks and walked fast the other way. In less than two minutes the street was empty. The whole thing was really organized. By the time the cop car appeared around the corner, and cruised slowly in front of the building, everything was peaceful.

I'd seen a funny scene one day at a dope spot on Rivington Street. People were lined up against a waist high wall, waiting to score. Suddenly the alert went out, a cop car was coming, so automatically the seller and all the people in line dropped on all fours and were then hidden by the wall. After the cop car went by, it was business as usual, everybody just stood up.

The sellers were always trying to be one step ahead of the cops. A few dope houses were doing the "lowering the basket from the window routine." The sellers would lower a basket on a rope, the buyer would put in his money and the basket would be raised. Down would come the packages of dope for the customer. When the cops came, the basket would be raised quickly and the crowd would disperse, walking quickly. The dope scene had no room for sloppy salesmanship. There were many workers.

Before the cop car got to us, we found a cab right on the next block. That was luck. We drove past 9th and B and there was a guy with a knife standing over a person who'd been in line at the building we'd just come from. The guy on the ground wasn't hurt, he was reaching into his pants pockets, and pulling out his heroin, and handing it over to the guy with the knife. As we whizzed past I heard the guy on the ground cursing, "Shit. Dammit, now I'm gonna be sick. Common, man, leave me jez one bag. Fuck!"

"Poor kid," Alvain looked back at the scene.

"He ain't gonna hurt im," the cab driver said. "He'll pralee leave him one bag too."

Anyone in that neighborhood at that hour knew what was happening on the streets there. Even the cab drivers.

"Good thing we found you when we did," Alvain told the cabbie.

"Yeah. I saw you two in line," he laughed. "Where to?"
Those streets could be pretty dangerous. It wasn't a good idea to carry much money when you went there to buy stuff and it wasn't a good idea to wear valuable jewelry or good clothes. Friends of mine who went there to buy dope were sometimes getting ripped off; they'd have their watches, earrings, rings, leather jackets, and all the drugs and money taken. An artist friend of mine had gone there right from an art opening and he'd been all dressed up in his leather jacket, his cowboy boots, his best wool tweed pants. The person who ripped him off at knife-point wasn't satisfied with just the dope and his money. The thief took that but also the jacket, boots, sweater, tweed pants and even my friend's boxer shorts. Stark naked, he started running home, freezing. On his way he searched the garbage cans for something to wear and finally found a dirty pink sweater so he put his legs in the sleeves and ran home, hoping he didn't see anyone he knew. At least his wang was covered.

I had laughed uproariously when he told me this story. In retrospect he too admitted it was very funny, but at the time he'd been more than mortified.

Things like this were always happening to people buying drugs there. Friends would occasionally get arrested and wind up in jail for the night, or they'd lose their rent money. I'd never known anyone to get stabbed, but I'd never known anyone stupid enough to refuse to give up their stuff to a thief with a knife. Some people, new to street copping would give their money to guys they thought were dope house runners. Of course these "runners" wouldn't ever return with the money. If you happened to find a real runner, he would come back with the dope, but he'd take one or two bags for the run. So it was expensive and sometimes dangerous over there. For that reason a couple of friends of mine started selling heroin from their homes.

Barbara did. She was a prose writer who'd written a mammoth novel, which weighed something like ten pounds. She lived with her paramour, named Jane, who was a rock and roll musician. They were good friends of mine before they started selling dope and while they were selling it I saw them everyday.

Way more pleasant than the street, there was always a fire burning in the fireplace, lots of books on the shelves and flowers in vases. The cats were curled up on the chairs, there was the smell of fresh coffee. It was a home.

A few close friends would visit her and buy some heroin. She made some money, everyone was happy. That was before a lot of her friends had daily habits, but they acquired them soon enough and then things got serious. A habit takes months, sometimes years of dabbling with the stuff before it creeps up on you. I think a lot of these people were shocked to find themselves dependent on heroin, even though they weren't shooting it, but snorting. Some people are dumb enough to believe you can't get a habit if you aren't using a syringe. That, of course, is ridiculous.

At a certain point, a lot of the people I knew were using heroin, and some of them had habits, but no one took it too seriously, everyone would always joke about it and everything was playful ... but ... being dope sick wasn't pleasant, or fun, or romantic. Baudelaire, Poe, Coleridge and all those writers who flirted with opiates didn't write much about the sick part. A heroin habit isn't a problem to the heroin user until there's no money.

I remember one New Year's Eve party, held at this chic French restaurant, where all the guests were high on heroin. Everyone's eye pupils were pin points; everyone was in a vegetable state, looking braindead, and acting cool like cucumbers. All eyes were dry at the stroke of midnight, and there wasn't a whole lot of laughter; there wasn't much outward display of emotion, like there was at drinker's New Year's Eve parties, but in their black little junky hearts, everyone was feeling warm and loving, they just couldn't show it, high as they were.

Everyone was standing up and mingling and talking, if they'd sat down they probably would have nodded out. They were all really good friends, people who'd gotten to know each other from the Mudd Club days before, and it was great to see everybody, even through the dopey haze of dope. These heroin users, like drinkers everywhere, had used the New Year's Eve excuse to get higher for this night, and everyone was as stoned as they could be. I remember at one point, after midnight, it finally dawned on me that we were all so stoned that we looked like zombies. I turned to a filmmaker friend of mine.

"Look around," I said, "Do you realize that every single person here is high on heroin? It looks like a Zombie Jamboree."

He scanned the group, "You're right," he said and laughed. I told everyone about this being a Zombie Jamboree and everyone laughed about it. We all had a good time that night, even though a lot of people were dozing off on their feet, buoyed up by the crush of people around them. Yeah, everyone had fun, even the people who missed most of it because they were in the bathroom throwing up, or snorting more heroin.

It wasn't like those typical SoHo art parties, like the one where they had passed marijuana around, where the guests had never known scary four a.m. walks in the heroin neighborhood, where none of them ever was dope sick, or ever ran home wearing a dirty sweater on their butt, or ever went without food for three days because there wasn't enough money for food and dope too. Those people, the dope innocent, the people who never found themselves suddenly in a lowdown compromising situation of heroin need, seemed like adolescents to a junky. They might have been smarter for never getting involved in dope, but somehow they looked less interesting through a junkie's eyes. The non-users were a whole different set of people than the users, and of course the users were actually the stupid ones, but it's a fact that when junkies become ex-junkies, they're somewhat the wiser, having seen hell.

The Stone of New Orleans—1983

I was so wildly miserable I was projectile vomiting at the very thought of facing another morning. I couldn't be at home for more than twenty minutes at a stretch; there were too many reminders. I couldn't eat; food tasted like rubber. I lost thirty pounds; I was skeletal. I couldn't sleep. My eyes, the proverbial mirror pools of the soul, were as mired as a peat bog. Beneath the mascaraed lashes were bags and dark circles. My crow's-feet looked like road maps. I was in pain. I was learning firsthand that one can actually die from a broken heart. What poets have always warned us about is true.

I wanted distraction every minute. I hung out at Danceteria and the Roxy every night till the wee hours. During the day I went anywhere I was led. One day I went to the blooming Japanese cherry orchard in the Brooklyn Botanical Gardens, but I found no solace in flowers. Another day I took a ride up the Hudson to FDR's house and the Vanderbilt mansion, but seeing those bedrooms where power couples used to copulate were reminders of someone else's past connubial bliss, which only made me feel more alone.

Jackie Curtis cheered me up a little on the phone every other day, with his rush of one-liners and his personal remedies for a broken heart. He was married eight times, he should know.

None of this helped. No nightclubs or day trips or phone calls could assuage the pain. What I needed was to leave town for a while.

I decided to hop a train to New Orleans. Nan Goldin suggested the Jazz Festival would brighten my spirits, so, with Nan and her cameras and Max with his bottle of calamine lotion for his Hyde Park poison ivy infestation, I got on the 2:30 P.M. Silver Crescent heading south to New Orleans. I had my little stash of white powders in pyramid papers. In times of past crises, powders had been the only recourse.

The train was packed with a contingent of Elsie Brown fans and family. Elsie Brown was a jazz singer, little known outside of Atlanta, who had died in New York City, probably before her time. Her body was in a coffin in the luggage car of the train. By accident or coincidence, we were on the funeral train, the only white people riding.

The funeral people were bound for Atlanta for the consecrated burial of Elsie. They were all partying, even Earl Brown, the beloved husband. The family and friends were clustered around Earl in the club car with bottles of California's Inglenook Navalle Vin Rosé supplied by Amtrak. Earl wasn't crying, in fact, he was jubilant in his strange clear plastic shower cap, playing poker and slapping his knee. I couldn't help but notice that most of them were wearing these odd shower caps at all times of the day and night, even though there weren't any shower accommodations on the train. (I noticed this more and more on every black person at every stop as we got deeper and deeper into the South.) This was a Southern fashion statement that I couldn't understand. I was befuddled, but too shy to ask questions. Did it have something to do with Southern processed hair jobs and beneficial head heat?

New York black people never wore these things. Was there some weird phenomenon going on, like when one wears a pyramid on the head for extra insight and pyramid power? I may never know.

It was an overnight haul to New Orleans. Sleep was difficult even in the cozy little sleeping compartment. But sleep wasn't something I cared too much about.

The minute the dining car reopened at six A.M., Nan and I were there. A couple of bizarre redneck guys bought us early morning Miller Lites, and one of these guys taught us how to shotgun a beer. He put a hole in the bottom side of an unopened can. Then he put his lips to the hole, flipped open the top, and all the beer gushed into his system at once.

"Ya git drunk ammeedlitly," he said wiping the beer off his neck and shirt. These Southerners sure know how to drink.

Early that evening the train arrived in New Orleans and I changed my outfit fifteen times before we detrained. I was unsure of the right look for New Orleans. I decided on black. I had little else anyway.

Our friend Sharon met us at the station and took us to the Olivia House in the French Quarter where she had booked us a huge suite with blue velveteen-flocked wallpaper and a wooden ceiling fan. There was a pool in a courtyard with ginkgoes and palms. There were big turquoise and red parrots sitting around talking and grooming their feathers in white filigree cages. But it wasn't quite a Tennessee Williams theater set; it was too modern.

"Don't worry about paying here," Sharon told us. "My best friend runs this place, so it's free."

That night we went to the Jazz Festival, held on a riverboat named *The President*. A lot of Cajun musicians played. The audience of Southerners cheered. They drank, they danced, they rocked the riverboat. The big black zydeco man, Clifton Chenier, ambled up onto the stage at the end. When the audience saw him, they went wild. He didn't move much because supposedly he had bad kidneys, but that didn't matter for the audience. He brought out an accordion that was almost as big as he was. It was silver, flashing with thousands of buttons and keys, and when he opened his mouth he had a front set of gold teeth that sparkled like the treasure of El Dorado. The whole effect was blinding, all that gold and silver. He brought the boat down.

When we got off the riverboat, we went to some party where the host was so drunk and obnoxious that Nan and I got into a fight with him. While we were leaving in a huff, Max said, "I wanted to punch that guy out so bad."

"I can't wait till you get a little bigger, Max," I said. He was only eleven years old.

Back at the hotel we took a swim while the sun was rising.

The next day we ran into a friend of Sharon's. His name was Mr. Gyros, the owner of a chain of fast-food Greek souvlaki joints, where Sharon had worked for a while. He wore a white polyester shirt, open almost to the waist, revealing a hairy chest and a bunch of gold chains with religious paraphernalia and gold cocaine razor blades. He invited us on his boat, a seventy-five-foot cabin cruiser. Never in my life have I seen a boat like this.

On the deck were plastic potted palms and plastic simulated bamboo chairs under an awning with ball fringe. Down below, there were synthetics everywhere. The wallpaper was that flocked velveteen stuff again, just like in our hotel suite, except this was beige. The polyester wall-to-wall carpeting was beige, too. There were marble statues of the Venus de Milo and Michelangelo's *David*, which turned out to be plastic. There were plastic flowers and fountains, and a low glass coffee table with a bottle of Retsina chilling in a plastic silver bucket.

I couldn't help but feel that this must have been a parody of a '70s suburban disco V.I.P. lounge, but no, this was no laughing matter. Mr. Gyros had a sign on a plastic silver plaque that said: "This is my ship and I'll do as I damn please." He meant every word, right down to the Naugahyde coasters.

On the boat was a crew of sleazy waiter types in white poly shirts and black poly pants. They were fluttering around Mr. Gyros's girlfriend, a Creole beauty who was the current Miss New Orleans. With her lacquered hair, turquoise eyeshadow, and her pink poly dress, she was in the perfect setting. She became one with the petroleum products.

Mr. Gyros went out of the room once and she turned to Nan and me and confided to us her big secret. "These aren't my real fingernails," she whispered, holding up her hands with the emerald rings and the two-inch pink pearl-luster nails. "These are attached with Krazy Glue." I guess she was trying to start a conversation, but with this topic she wasn't going to go far. My fingernails, and Nan's too, had been forgotten for at least fifteen years. Gossip about nail maintenance and grooming fell on deaf ears with us.

That night, after we listened to a bunch of gospel singers in a huge tent, we walked around the French Quarter and saw some black women dancing in the street with a bunch of tourists gawking at them. The dancing women were Haitians in purple and white eyelet crinolines. They worked the skirts. They were breaking bottles all over the place, and then they were putting the shattered glass pieces in their mouths, chewing and swallowing them.

This was impressive, even for such jaded New Yorkers as Nan, Max, and me. Of course we supposed that the bottles were those breakaway theatrical props, the kind made out of candy. We weren't convinced until they ate burning embers. They casually picked up torches that their children assistants had lit for them, and then they started eating the flames and the red embers. They swallowed everything that was hot, swallowed them like they were eating delicious French fries. That was proof.

I was so impressed I decided I had to talk to these women. If they could eat glass and fire, then they might know something about how I could stop eating my heart out.

After they danced, I approached them.

"Deez ez de tuffezt zing, ze brooken eart. We new ow to stomac de glass an de fire, but ze brooken eart? Deez we new no way to stomac, no," one of them said, while she was still breathing heavily from her dancing.

"You can't tell me anything? Not even some spell?" I asked.

"Some gris-gris stuff?" Nan asked.

"Something?" I asked, and I must have looked pretty desperate.

"Ahh … well … go zee me friend way et de end oof St. Anne Street. She meebee ken elp yoo," another one told me.

"Where on St. Anne?" Nan asked, and she took out her pad and pen.

"Jez look foor de bloo ouse, wee doon de end St. Anne. Aask do zee Yala, zee fatteest ladee zere. Yoo find er, yoo teell er wee zeend yoo. Ogaay?"

The next day I walked to the end of St. Anne street with Nan and we found the blue house. It was a two-story wooden house, the color of the sky at dusk. Once it must have been the color of the sky at midday, but now the paint was old. There was a banana tree growing from a little patch of dirt that was practically right at the front door. The windows on the second floor were open and the breeze was blowing the thin orange curtains. In front of the windows was a rusty black iron balcony that looked very feeble.

"What do we say when we knock on the door?" I asked Nan.

"We ask for that fat woman," Nan said. As usual Nan didn't seem one bit timid. She marched to the door. "Come on. You're the one that needs to see this woman."

"No, let's not. I don't really feel like it now. Let's go back to the hotel and swim and drink mint juleps or something."

Nan laughed, like always. One feels great when Nan laughs. "Come on," she said. "We'll give it a try." She knocked and after a while the door opened.

A man stood there. He was a thirtyish, light-skinned Creole wearing running clothes and sneakers. It was a Saturday businessman look. This wasn't what I had expected at all. Why wasn't he old and toothless with mojos hanging from his neck?

"Yeah?" he asked.

"We were looking for this woman, Yula," Nan said.

"Yala, yeah. I'll get er. Come on in. Those Haitian dancers sent ya?" he opened the door wide to let us enter.

"Yeah," I said and followed Nan into a room that looked totally ordinary. No candles or black drapes or incense. No St. John's Wort lying around. It was like anyone's living room, except there were Mardi Gras beads hanging at the doorways, and handwoven rugs on the walls and the floors that depicted the martyrdom of saints that might not have been saints—I didn't recognize any faces.

"Yala!" he yelled from the kitchen. We watched him between the plastic beads. He got a jar of orange juice from the refrigerator and came back out into the room where we stood.

"Yall sit down," he said. "She'll be down presently. Yall want any orange juice?"

"No thanks," we both shook our heads.

He took the juice back to the kitchen. "Yala, ya got some visitors down here."

We heard Yala coming down the stairs after a little while. Her footsteps shook the house. When I saw her, she wasn't what I'd expected either. She looked like a fat black woman in a green dress. She could have been a bank teller. There was nothing voodooish about her, except she had on her feet a pair of yellow scuffies with little mirrors on them.

We stood up when she came in the living room, and she looked us up and down. "Them dancers sent ya? They're good people. Ya like their dancin?"

"They were amazing," I said. "I've never seen anything like that, like eating the things they ate ..."

"We don't see things like that in New York," Nan laughed.

Yala laughed, too, deep from her diaphragm, "Ahh don no bout dat. Up there dey eat all kind of weird nonsense. How's New York these days? I used ta live there."

I couldn't quite look in her eyes for some reason; I kept looking at her feet in the yellow scuffies.

"Ya like my bedroom slippers? Dem mirrors on here ... Lordie, I don't know who's idee it was ta put mirras onna woman's shoe. Look in them mirras and you can see right up my dress," she laughed and the man with the orange juice and sneakers in the kitchen laughed. We all laughed and then there was music coming from somewhere upstairs. It was a scratchy record of a piano and a drum. Just that, real slow.

"Now yall sit down and tell me what sent ya to me," she said and settled herself into a big orange chair. She lit a Kool Mild and brought the hotel floor-model ashtray within arm's reach. "Wat's da praalam? Luv, money, or siknezz?"

"Love," Nan said.

"Hmm, yeeezz," Yala looked right over at me. "I ken see it all ova her."

"Yeah, I …" I started to tell her the whole story, but she'd heard it before.

"This ain't free," she said and heaved her weight to the ashtray where she flicked the Kool. "I hav a commodidee dat's valuable ta people like you. Part advice, part root remedy … works … it always works. Ya want peace or ya wantta git bak with da person?"

"I guess I want peace," I said after thinking about the getting back with the person part. "Yeah, I guess I want peace."

"Yeah, dat's better. Usually, it nevva works … gettin bak with da fella. I'm assumin it's a fella … you ain't a lesbian are ya?" she winked at me. "Lesbians don't have no praalams." She looked at both of us and laughed. Then she got up and went into the kitchen. I wondered if she was going to cook up some potion on the old Amana Radar range. Gris-gris gumbo? Eye of newt? Hair of toad?

She took the orange juice and poured herself a glass in an old Welch's jelly jar. She came back into the living room with the glass. It was the same glass I grew up with. Howdy Doody. This was a weird sign. It must have meant something. It was too weird. Yes, she was the right person for me, this must be the link between us.

She took a black stone out of a pocket in her dress and pulled two clinging bobby pins off of it, then she handed it to me. "This issa lodestone," she said. "The oldess magnet. Attracts everthan. Effyawrap this in white silk an douse it inna seawater an wear it on your person fa three days plus seben houws, den burry it in black cloth in dirt farway from where you live, then you'll have some peace. Guaranteed … nevva fails," she sat way back on her hips in the chair and raised her head to look at me like she was looking through bifocals. "Issa potent stone an hard to come by."

I took the stone in my hand. It felt right.

"Thatillbe fifteen dollers," she said and stood up. "Wadds your name? I godda write it down. I'm gonna repeat your name seven times aday for three weeks." I told her my name.

"Your real name, your baptismal name …" she said.

Then I gave her the fifteen dollars, and Nan and I left.

"Think that's going to work, Nan?" I asked when we were out on the street.

"Sure," Nan said.

Why not? I'd tried everything else. I'd been to a hypnotist twice and both times, straight from the trance, I ran smack into the person I'd been hypnotized to forget, so that didn't work. I tried what my psychiatrist suggested: "Make a list of all the things that disgusted you about this person. Dirty underwear. Farts. Obnoxious behavior. Stinky feet." That didn't work, the person in question had carried all those things off with such aplomb that none were disgusting.

Friends told me to write the loved one's name on many pieces of paper and flush them down the toilet, but the water pressure in my bathroom didn't sink them. The pieces of paper just floated around in the toilet water. No, nothing worked. This wasn't a minor heartache anyway; it demanded major steps. The lodestone thing would work. It had to.

On the train ride back to New York, Max jumped off somewhere in North Carolina and came back on with Mother's Day flowers. My son loves his mother on Mother's Day. My son loves his mother every day.

Ah, yes, my son loves me. I almost forgot! That's plenty. That's enough. What do I need with some dumb adult, some supposed lover? Some person whose angst rivaled my own? Some fully grown person who never grew up? Someone to share a cramped New York apartment and closet space with? Oh no. I will rid myself of excess baggage and sentimental flotsam! Who needs it?

I thought this way for a few days; the lodestone worked for that long, until a day after I buried it, then it didn't work at all. I fell right back into the pain pit.

Was there no way other than time to heal a broken heart? Time took too much time. By then I'd be dead.

I had to think of something other than hypnotists and mojos. I would have to think very hard, in a place very far away from all reminders. How does one forget? How do you empty yourself?

I was about to learn.

Out of the Bottle and into a Danish Remedy

It was spring in Manhattan, sidewalk café tables blossomed all over the place, and the homeless were sprouting up out of their winter blankets.

Spring lasted exactly two days, then it was summer, the city heat served as thick as lava gravy. Anyone with sense and a little money left town. Cool September was soon enough for most careers.

The gris-gris mojo I got in New Orleans wasn't working. I still had no appetite for life or food. The only thing in my stomach was vodka, rum, or beer, which sloshed around when I moved.

"I've had a full life," I told David, my photographer friend and drinking buddy. "I'm ready to die."

"Let's have some cocktails." He'd change the subject whenever I got maudlin. David liked to laugh, and he loved to drink. He'd buy a fifth of bourbon in the morning and polish off one or two more by the end of the night. His favorite bumper sticker read, "Don't drink and drive, you might hit a bump and spill some."

I never drank bourbon; one has to draw a line somewhere. I drank vodka or light rum with water.

David had just lost his apartment, and I needed company, so he moved in with Max and me. He slept on the lumpy mahogany and horsehair thrift-store sofa in the living room. It was one of those sofas you see in colonial museum homes, the kind that sit in austere parlors with velvet ropes keeping the viewers from jumping into the rooms and partying on the furniture. George Washington probably slept on my sofa before Martha Washington gave it to the Salvation Army, which was where I bought it for twelve dollars. It was in pretty bad shape, but David didn't seem to mind the lumps. I doubt if he felt them after three fifths of bourbon.

It wasn't easy to get Max up and off to school in the morning in those days, but somehow I did it, five days a week, at 7:30. Hung over, I'd lay out his clothes, then cook eggs and squeeze oranges.

When Max got out of school for the summer, David and I took him to Provincetown to stay with his dad for two months. David decided to visit his parents in Boston, and I went back to New York alone.

It only took four hours of being back in the city to make me wonder why I hadn't stayed in Provincetown. What would I do without Max and David? Then the phone rang.

"Hello?"

"Is this Cookie?" the voice said with an accent.

"This is me. Who's this?"

"Frieda. Remember me from Richard?" she said. I did remember her, although I didn't know her very well. I'd met her through Richard Hell. She was from Copenhagen. She said she needed to see me, and she sounded desperate so I said okay, come over.

Five minutes later she arrived at my door. She was close to tears.

Frieda was tall and thin, with very blond hair beyond unkempt, and pale blue eyes that she never used makeup on.

Lots of things about her face reminded me of women's faces in Van Dyck or Rembrandt paintings, mostly it was the attitude of the mouth, the white expanse of forehead, and the total lack of eyelashes. She wore dilapidated red cowboy boots with gaffer's tape around them to keep the soles on. On her narrow self she wore layers of tattered red and black clothes, and big sparkling mismatched fake jewel earrings. She had rags around her neck and her wrists, and on her upper arm she had a large black-and-yellow tiger tattoo that she'd gotten in Bangkok. In the hole in her pierced left nostril she wore a large emerald she got in India. One front tooth was solid gold from the Ivory Coast, and the other front tooth bore a diamond from the Cape of Good Hope. I remember the first time I ever saw her with Richard; I thought she was a lanky teenage boy, until she spoke.

"I know this is really presumptuous of me," she said, "but I need a place to stay for a while, until I get some money together. I had to leave where I was living, I feel really low-down ..."

"Yeah, sure Frieda, you can stay here. In fact you came at just the right time." She had.

She sat down in the broken-backed chair and brought one knee to her chin like a spider monkey.

"Where are your bags?" I asked her.

"This is all I have," she said, holding up a black leather sack that was a little smaller than a brown paper grocery bag. That was all she owned.

"Hey, know what?" she brightened. "I have half a bottle of Smirnoff in here. Wanna drink?"

"This is gonna work out fine," I said to her as I filled two glasses with ice and vodka. I didn't know anything about Frieda except that she was a world traveler. That day, with the afternoon heat closing in like the lid of a waffle iron, she told me about herself.

"Oh, I never did much, Cookie, I mean in the way of big success and things like that," she lit a cigarette and brought the other knee to her chin. She reminded me of a giraffe. This is what future women will look like, I thought. Ethereal, long, lean, able to see the scope of things from a higher altitude, ready to lope away when danger threatens.

She drained her glass. "Six years ago in Copenhagen I had a nightclub. I owned and ran it. It was a good place, good people. That sounds like I'm boasting, but it was the only place where anybody interesting hung out. It wasn't a huge space, it was sort of small.

"I had art exhibitions, new music, rock, punk, jazz, classical. It was like a home for friends. I lived upstairs with this guy—he was really famous—in Copenhagen anyway. A filmmaker. I was happy, the club was going fine, it was even making money, but then I left because … because the guy I was living with died."

"He died? How, Frieda?"

"He died on his motorcycle. A truck hit him." She paused, poured more vodka, drank half of it, then grimaced, "And then, of course, nothing made much sense to me, everything seemed hollow." She tossed back the rest of her vodka and looked at the grease-splattered wall over the stove. "Every time I tell this to anybody it sounds like a soap opera," she laughed.

A bunch of '50s B-movies came to mind. The cigarette smoke in layers, the half-full bottle, the low-down story, the exotic blond from northern Europe, the umbra in the windowless kitchen. It felt black and white, but Frieda didn't really belong in these movies, she didn't belong to anything, and besides she was in color.

"So anyway, I left Copenhagen. I left everything. I gave the club to a friend and bought a one-way airplane ticket to Calcutta."

"Why Calcutta?" I asked. "I've heard it's horrifying, the worst city in the world."

"Oh, I sat down with a globe, closed my eyes, spun it around and put my finger on a spot. It was Calcutta, so I went there; and you're right, Calcutta was horrible. But I met somebody there who told me I ought to be in Katmandu, so I went there and it was great. I made a lot of friends."

"I know a couple of people in Katmandu," I said and named these two women living there, one I met in Provincetown, who used to steal and import relics from Tibetan temples until she got her karmic kickback when she broke most of her bones falling off a Himalayan yak path; and the other, a vivacious ultra-modern girl, a major film star in the Philippines who appeared in one American film, Coppola's *Apocalypse Now*. I met her at the Berlin Film Festival.

"Yeah! I know them," she hooted, slapping her thigh. "They're fun." She told me about the rest of her travels, to Bangkok, Bali, the entire Orient, Asia, Africa, the Middle East, all of Europe, and the Americas. "I think I'll go back to Rio soon," she said, "except I don't have any Rio clothes. You know how they dress there ..."

"I've seen pictures." Her travels made mine seem paltry.

"I've got to get some money together. I don't have any money for Rio."

Frieda made money making jewelry, and she also worked in the flesh trade; she go-goed and stripped her way around the world.

"I need some new go-go costumes. Something flashy. I'd make more money," she said.

After the bottle was empty and we were walking to the liquor store for another, she asked me what I'd been doing.

"You don't look too happy; in fact, and I don't mean to offend you, but you look sort of sick."

"You're right," I said. "Heartsick." I told her my sad-sack story.

"You gotta get outta here," she said. "Why are you hanging out in New York, wallowing in your miserable soup? Traveling cures everything. I know."

When we got back home, she sat down at the table with both elbows on it.

"Bring me a globe or an atlas," she said.

I got the atlas off the shelf.

"Now, close your eyes and open the book anywhere. That'll be the country where you ought to go," she said.

"Sounds okay to me," I said, closed my eyes, and opened the atlas.

"Great! You picked Italy! That's perfect. You have to go right away. Now I'm gonna make you an omelette. You gotta eat. You're too skinny. Italian men like women fat," she pulled a six-pack of eggs from her black bag. "How do ya like 'em? With onions or garlic?"

The next day, I bought a ticket to Rome and started to get things arranged. A friend of mine would take my dog Beauty for the time I was away, and I found a permanent home for the rabbits. Frieda would live in the apartment and pay the rent until she left for Rio or somewhere. I'd still have my home when I returned, whenever that was. By the end of the week I was on an airplane.

The Italian Remedy—1983

It wasn't *La Dolce Vita* when I got off the plane at Leonardo da Vinci Airport in Rome.

Midday in July, Rome was an incinerator and I didn't have a plan. I was rudderless, lost, depleted, really hot and dry. Jet-lag wrinkles were growing on my face. I felt like a tiny, over-cooked, shriveled old meatball swimming alone in Italian sauce.

Sitting at outdoor café tables, squabbling American tourists with swollen ankles were clutching their bags to their breasts in fear of getting robbed. There weren't any Romans in sight. The stagnant air was heavy with turbo and diesel car exhaust. I decided I should head south for the beach.

Fortunately I was traveling light. I had one little bag with a bunch of black mini togs, a toothbrush, a bathing suit, my Italian phrase book, my crystals, and the monkey-paw talisman for luck.

I stayed in Rome only long enough to get on a train. It didn't matter where I went. I figured I might as well try Capri, so I headed for Naples, where I could get a boat.

Not too many tourists, especially Americans, ever set foot in Naples, because in every tour book for Americans, it says something like: "Avoid Naples at all costs. It's a human anthill. Take a tour bus from Rome to see Vesuvius and Pompeii, don't chance going on your own. At one time Naples was the beautiful summer playground of Louis XIV, but now it's laid to waste, crumbling, and in disrepair, a veritable shell of former glory. An undesirable ghetto. There's nothing to see. The Neapolitans are very dangerous."

With a buildup like this, it sounded like the perfect place for me. I didn't want to see American tourists, and anyway, after hanging out in the Lower East Side drug ghettos of alphabet land, there was nothing that could scare me about human anthills. Naples ought to be right up my alley.

There is an old saying in Italian: "See Naples and die." I didn't know exactly what it meant, but it sounded good.

Right off the train in Naples, I felt more at home. The station was full of life. All kinds of helpful men circled around me. I was probably the first solo female traveler they'd seen in a while. Certainly there wasn't another blond woman in sight. In fact, there weren't any women at all in the station, not even brunettes.

Having been without male attention for months in New York, I was loving it. Most of them were sweet-looking, fluttering their long Bambi eyelashes at me, talking to me a mile a minute.

I knew they were looking to me for something they thought I could give them, but I couldn't imagine what it was. They weren't cruising for money really, although they would have gladly taken it. Or sex, although that too they would have taken. It was entertainment they wanted. Something to change their lives for an afternoon, a way to get a few laughs.

I tried to converse with them in Italian. I asked them the best way to Capri, but none of them understood me. I then realized that they weren't speaking Italian; they were speaking the Neapolitan dialect, which is an entirely different language.

I went to the station's tourist information center. I figured somebody there has to speak Italian, maybe even English if I was lucky. They all followed me there like little ducklings. At the info center, this guy Angelo spoke English. We talked for about an hour, not about Capri. He was telling me jokes.

Angelo wasn't very young, or very old. He was around thirty, I guess, and he was handsome in that North African way.

"Naples is the northernmost tip of Africa," he said and laughed.

He didn't seem to be blatantly on the prowl for blond tourist girls like all the other guys there. But maybe he was. It didn't matter.

Angelo advised me that it was too late in the day to go to Capri, and that I ought to go out to dinner with him and spend the night in Naples.

"*Domani, domani*," he said. Tomorrow, tomorrow. "Plenty of time. My cousin who lives in Positano will take you there on his motorcycle tomorrow. Positano is a nice town. Nice beach. You'll be happier there. It's better than Capri."

Why not? What else did I have to do? I didn't exactly have a tight schedule. No itinerary. I was in no rush.

"Sounds good to me," I said.

"I have to finish work here. You can hang around or … hey, I have a good idea." He picked up the phone and had a conversation with somebody.

"This other cousin of mine lives right around the corner. You can go there and take a bath and rest. He'll be here in five minutes."

Naples is great, I thought. The tourist guidebook was totally wrong. What jerk wrote that book? Some bimbo afraid of getting his traveler's checks and money wad ripped off. I didn't have any wad.

I waited half an hour and Angelo kept telling me American jokes. He was hilarious.

"So where's this cousin?" I asked.

"Relax," he said. "Have an espresso." As I saw it, those two things were diametrically opposed. How can one relax with an espresso in their intestines?

"I've been traveling for twenty-four hours. I have to rest before dinner," I said. "I want to change and put on makeup and …"

"Okay, *cinque minuti*, " Angelo said. Later I found out that *cinque minuti*, five minutes, usually meant a half an hour, two hours, tomorrow, whenever.

Finally Angelo's cousin, Claudio, showed up. He was even better-looking than Angelo. He was my type. Obviously he'd just gotten out of the shower, his shoulder-length hair was still wet.

Angelo introduced us, but Claudio didn't speak English, and not much Italian, so there wasn't much we could say to each other.

"He'll take you to his place, and I'll see you just after dark," Angelo said. They started laughing and talking with one another and that took another half-hour.

Finally Claudio picked up my bag and I followed him silently. I was dying to talk to him. He was dying to talk to me, but it was ridiculous. I decided that minute that I had to learn Italian, maybe even Neapolitan.

Claudio took me to his place, which was actually his parents' home, not a grand villa, just a flat with four bedrooms, a big kitchen, a dining room, a living room, a terrace, and two bathrooms. It was dark and cool. I collapsed in a big overstuffed chair and surveyed this home. There were pictures of the pope around,

lots of red flocked wallpaper, tacky rococo china, ornate and useless knickknacks, gilt-framed photos of kids through the years. It
smelled like my grandmother's house.

Claudio showed me the bathtub and his bedroom, and
then explained in hand language that he had to leave. He gave
me his keys. He gave me his keys! He didn't even know me. I
could've ripped him off blind, stolen all the pope pictures and
tacky china and hawked them on the street. These Neapolitans
were something.

Before he left he pointed to the phone and motioned that I
should answer it in five minutes. Then he said *Ciao* and left.

When the phone rang half an hour later it was Angelo and
he explained to me that Claudio's family was away on vacation in
Sicily but his mother's cousin or aunt or somebody would be
coming in soon and that I should just say hi and ignore her
because she was a pain in the butt.

I took a bath, washed my hair, poured a glass of red wine,
and sat in the kitchen watching the courtyard below. A few kids
were tossing a soccer ball around. Then some old fat lady with
white hair and a navy blue polka-dot dress hobbled by with a
plastic bag. She yelled at the kids and pinched the ear of one of
them, patting another's behind.

Just as I was heading for the bedroom to take a nap, I heard
some keys turning in the lock of the door and in walked the old
woman in the navy blue polka-dot dress. She had a big hairy
mole on her chin and some bread and onions and plums in her
bag. She looked at me and started saying something, but whatever
it was I didn't understand. She got more and more animated.

I kept telling her in Italian that I didn't understand Italian,
but she didn't shut up. She kept ranting. When I finally went

into the bedroom and sat on the bed, she followed me, still talking a mile a minute. Finally she motioned for me to get up and she turned down the covers and fluffed the pillows and motioned for me to get in. Then she nodded and left the bedroom, closing the door behind her.

I love these Neapolitans.

I fell asleep.

After dark, around nine, Angelo and Claudio woke me up. We went to a restaurant where everyone knew everyone else and we ate some pasta and some fried calamari and drank lots of red wine. Everything was free.

"We don't have to pay?" I asked him.

"My uncle," Angelo said of the guy who owned the place.

After this we got into Angelo's car and went to some apartment house that sat right on the Bay of Naples. Two laughing girls dressed in yellow with fake flower hair clips in their uncontrollable dark hair got into the car and we went to a bar where everything was free again.

"My uncle," Angelo said.

The whole night I had no idea what was going on, because nobody stopped to explain things in English, and why should they? They were obviously having a ball.

After a few hours at the bar, we all went back to Claudio's house and the two laughing girls started drinking the red wine there. The same old lady who had tucked me in bed appeared and yelled for a half an hour and looked at the red wine bottle. She sounded mad but soon everyone was laughing, and she poured a little wine in a glass and disappeared with it.

All I wanted to do was sleep. My brain was reeling from trying to figure out what was going on.

While everyone was drinking and yakking I slipped off into the bedroom and got in bed. I closed the door. Angelo came in a little later and asked me if I wanted to "have love" with him.

"I'm really exhausted," I said. "I'll take a rain check."

"Okay," he said and left the room.

A few minutes later Claudio came in and asked me in gestures if I wanted to "have love" with him. I smiled and said "*Gracia*, no."

"No?" He asked like he couldn't believe it, but he left anyway.

The next morning when I woke up, I saw that he and Angelo were asleep under blankets on the rug in the living room between the two laughing girls.

The old lady was watching television right next to them.

"Café?" she asked me.

Later, when everyone woke up, Angelo told me that Arturo, his cousin, would come in about five minutes to take me to Positano. A few hours later Arturo arrived. He was even better-looking than Claudio, and he spoke English better than Angelo. He'd lived in Sarasota, Florida, for a year, he told me.

For an hour I waited while he and the rest of them talked and drank espressos in demitasse cups with six teaspoons of sugar.

Finally he told me he was ready, and we went out and got on his motorcycle. It was a big Moto Guzzi. Plenty of room on the seat. Plenty of power. Too much.

"We're going to make this a quick trip," he leaned back and said to me while we idled at a red light. "You ever traveled on a fast motorcycle before?"

"Don't worry about me." I said and tied a scarf over my ears, which were practically bleeding from the G force. This guy was a maniac biker.

"The first half of the trip isn't much fun," he said. "But just wait till we get to the Amalfi Coast."

We knocked off the first half in thirty minutes, then we reached the Amalfi coastline road and it was a sight that sent me reeling. I couldn't believe what I was seeing. The road was terrifying—narrow hairpin curves wound around three-thousand-foot mountains that plunged to the blue of the Mediterranean. But it wasn't the road that was so scary; it was the beauty of the place. I was afraid my eyeballs would explode. Could a human being hold this kind of beauty in their eyes without going blind?

Arturo was whipping around the curves so the bike was leaning almost parallel to the ground. I was really scared. I knew we were about to fly off a cliff and plummet into blue, but then I remembered that I didn't care if I died, so I took three deep breaths and let the fear go.

Around a curve, Positano in the distance opened up in front of us, and it looked like a town Walt Disney had built as a dreamscape. It was unbelievable.

When we arrived, Arturo got me a room in his uncle's pensione and told me he'd see me later for dinner.

Standing on the room's terrace, looking at the town and the sea, I had this strange feeling I'd been there before. I felt like I'd come home. That feeling never left me.

Two months later, still in Positano, I met a person I felt I had known. He lived there in the hills of olives with his strange noble family.

Five years after that we got married.

I knew I had known him before.

Edith Massey: A Star

On location for *Multiple Maniacs* in Baltimore's Fell's Point, after a long day of shooting, we'd all go over to Pete's Hotel Bar for a fifteen-cent draft beer, or a fifty-cent mixed drink. Pete's was a flophouse bar where Edith Massey was a barmaid. We'd all talk show biz there.

Pete's had fluorescent lights, peeling paint, and loose linoleum on the floor. It was a generic bar, just stools, a couple of tables, some mirrors, and a wooden bar that ran the length of the place.

The clientele of Pete's were old barflies, all of them down and out alcoholics, former stevedores, retired factory workers, ex-B-girls, and waitresses too tired and old to wait anymore. The years of booze had taken their toll on these people's looks, their faces were wrinkled and puffy, with bulbous rugged noses covered in gin blossoms (broken blood vessels) like pink golf balls with thin red spiders on them.

The liquor hadn't dampened their spirits though, they were always laughing in their beer. All of them lived in the neighborhood, Fell's Point. It was the low-rent district. The only other types aside from bums and boozers who lived around there were a smattering of poor visionary artists.

It was the oldest section of Baltimore, really just a bunch of little two-story houses built in the early 1800s. At the time, 1969, the streets were still cobblestoned, there were lots of quiet little bars, corner dime variety stores, family-run grocery stores. This part of town was not unlike the worst part of the Bowery, but unlike the Bowery it was pretty, it had lots of charm. It was the old harbor section, it sat right on the deserted, dilapidated docks with the expansive sky awash with light reflected off the water. This was the kind of place, this quaint enclave of the city, that would later be discovered by the developers and the yuppies who would buy the houses, renovate them into early Americana, sell them, or live in them.

But then there were lots of flophouses, soup kitchens, and bars, in fact, five bars to every block. My friends who lived there had houses for sixty dollars a month. Vince Peranio, the artist who created all John's film sets, had a huge three-storied former warehouse/bakery for a hundred a month.

Vince was the one who first started going to Pete's Bar, who met Edith, and like everyone else, loved his bartender. Vince introduced Edith to John there. He saw star quality in her; she was the real thing.

John cast her in *Multiple Maniacs* as Jesus's mother. She was thrilled, she had always wanted to be a star, in fact when she was sixteen, she ran away to Hollywood to become a star. She got as far in the film biz as working in a street booth selling pencils and combs and razor blades to aspiring actors and actresses. As she saw it, these were the implements of the trade: a pencil to write down the casting agent's address, a comb to fix your hair for the film audition, and a razor blade to cut your wrists when you didn't get the part.

Edith did get into show biz, on stage as a dancer in strip joints. She danced her way across the country, hitchhiking, hopping freight trains. She once owned her own bar in Calumet City, Illinois, and she was a madam in a place in Talihina, Oklahoma, that used a hotdog stand as a front.

She was one of the sweetest women, she fed the stray cats, she brought American cheese and Wonderbread sandwiches to the bums on the street. She could barely afford to do this. She wore her long dark hair in a forties' poof in the front, the back hung down almost to her waist; she wore the same dresses she'd worn in the forties. She had warts on her nose, there was a large space between her front teeth, she hardly ever drank, but when she did she was funny, she had a thick Baltimore accent, and she was everyone's mother confessor.

With her part in *Multiple Maniacs*, she was finally in films. She wasn't a quick study, though. When she memorized her part, she would memorize her screen directions too and say them right along with her lines during shooting. John had to do a million takes, but she was worth it; she was such a great terrible actress, the best.

When *Multiple Maniacs* opened she thought her life would change, she thought Hollywood agents would call her at Pete's Hotel Bar. They didn't.

In the years to come, she was the Egg Lady in *Pink Flamingos*, Aunt Ida in *Female Trouble*, the reigning queen in *Desperate Living*. In between films she opened a junk shop, Edith Shopping Bag in Fell's Point, where autograph hounds would come to be near her, and listen to her rambling chatter, while she sat at the cash register in her house dress and her skuffies. With her kitties and her fans all around her, she was happy.

I used to stop in there every day, since my thirty-dollar-a-month apartment was right around the corner. Sometimes in the junk shop I'd see something I liked.

One day I took off my jacket to try on a coat hanging on a rack and by the time I was finished, Edith had accidently sold my own jacket to a shopper.

"Aw, hon, I'm seow sarry. I'll geev ya the moneee, I gaot fave dallers foor it," she was very apologetic, "I dint neew what ta cheearg foor it, dere weernt neo teag oon it or nuthin. I'm sarry, hon. Yeoo woont aunther ceoat, yeoo teak it, hon. Leok reound, deres seom perrty ceoats heer."

It had been my favorite jacket, but one could never get mad at Edith.

"It's okay, hon," I said, "Maybe I can still catch the person who bought it." I looked up and down the street but the happy shopper was gone.

"Heer, yeoo teak the fave dallers," she handed me the bill.

"No, Edith," I said, "I'll just put on the coat I was tryin on. It's nice. I like it."

Years later Edith actually moved to Hollywood and opened a junk shop there. She was finally a star in Hollywood.

Once when she was visiting me in New York on business, singing in her nightclub review, we went out at seven A.M. to Washington Square Park to feed the pigeons. She bought nuts and popcorn especially for them.

"Ain't they cute?" she asked while the fat pigeons fluttered in around her. Sitting on the park bench, in the morning sun, amid the sanitation workers dumping the overflowing mesh garbage cans, and elderly people moving by with their aluminum walkers, she started her usual stream-of-consciousness chatter.

She talked about her new stray kitty that was once a street rat catcher, who was so mangy and hairless she put an infant's blue sweater on him until he could grow some more fur. They were all kitties to her.

She went silent after that. Then she said something I haven't forgotten. Perhaps she was suddenly taking stock of her life.

"John Werters is ah wunerfeol mean," she told me, "Heez been seo neez ta mee. Hee mead mee a stoar, Cookie. I'd prally stal bea barmead witheealt heam. Hee mead mee a stoar."

"You were always a star Edith. You would have been a star without John. He just made you a FAMOUS star," I told her.

She was a star indeed.

Fleeting Happiness

Many years and brain cells ago, I had this belief that everyone would be happy someday. I have since found that this isn't necessarily so.

Happiness is a fictitious feeling. It was created by imaginative storytellers for the purpose of plot building or story resolution. Fortunately most people don't know this. They think the lives they are living are actual screenplays or theater pieces. In earlier times people were convinced their lives were the fantastic tales told at the fireside. Because of this, I have seen people stop in their tracks for a moment and wonder where the plot is, but mostly they just forge on blindly.

Believing that life will someday be wonderful isn't a bad thing, in fact it is absolutely necessary. To know the truth—life is hard, and then you die—isn't a very comfortable thing to live with. If everyone knew the cold facts, the sky would be darkened with falling bodies in suicide leaps.

Most people have been led to believe that their lives would be better if they had money, and usually this isn't wrong. They know it's not impossible to come into money, in fact I've read that every thirty-nine minutes a new millionaire emerges in the world.

But what's the real reason people want lots of money? Food? Clothing? Shelter? Yes, these things are basic, even the poor often have these things in modest amounts. Usually, the more you have of each of these basics, the more complicated life gets. Having too much food makes you fat; you need to diet. Having too many clothes makes it hard to make a decision in the morning; you need to organize. Having too many homes must be really tough; you have to fill them. And why own all these things anyway, if there's no one else to share them with, or no one to hire to help you, or no one to be jealous of you?

I have pondered this and come up with the logical answer. People want money because they want to be loved. They believe that money will buy them love. Okay, we've all heard this.

Now, suppose you had lots of money, thus you had tons of lovers (perhaps it's superficial love but this blossoms), and you had lots of servants who loved you and hung around, and you had lots of friends who were envious. You would expect that everything would be great. Lots of love, lots of money. What else could one want?

Unfortunately, the pitiable human being will still want something else. It is human nature.

The next thing to want would be fame. So you need publicity. That's not difficult; you can buy a newspaper or magazine company and put your own name and picture in the headlines if you want; you can finance films and star yourself. Okay, now you have money, love, and fame. But still people laugh at you behind your back. Then what? The answer is power.

Let's suppose your magazine is successful and your film is a box-office smash. Then you have all four: money, love, fame, and power. Would you be happy? No. You would probably go mad.

Look at Howard Hughes. He had all four. In the end he went insane. He was so afraid of germs he was walking around with sanitary Kleenex boxes on his feet.

No one is ever satisfied.

Some people might remind you that the holy men of the East are satisfied, but I don't think so. Even those guys want something. They might want infinite wisdom or they might want to perform miracles to impress followers, or they might want to levitate. It's always something.

Being a human being isn't easy, what with all these insatiable physical, emotional, and intellectual desires.

If the ultimate goal in life is to be happy, then you have to admit that one-celled creatures have it all over us. Little germs are probably always happy. They are superior, they don't sing the blues. Think about that the next time you bring out the disinfectant bottle and start scrubbing them away.

Look at Howard Hughes again. He must have known that the happiness of germs was something terrifyingly enviable. He must have been jealous.

Manhattan: The First Nine Years, the Dog Years

I have lived in New York City for about nine years now. Since one year here is equivalent to seven anywhere else, that makes sixty three years for me.

With this kind of time passing, one begins to wax cool. It takes a lot to impress a New Yorker. The word cool was invented here, the etymological roots lie somewhere south of Fourteenth Street or north of One Hundred Sixteenth.

When I first moved here I used to bitch about everything.

"There are easier places to live," I used to tell myself in the mornings as I brought the toothbrush to my teeth and there was a cockroach hugging the brush, licking the toothpaste. Now I find myself admiring these roaches for their bold New York attitude.

They're so smart they've been around for three hundred million years, seven times that in New York of course. There's even a modern hybrid, a totally new breed, the albinos. Through evolution they've adapted themselves to white porcelain bathroom living. That's admirable.

"God love 'em," I say and smile. They seem like pets to me now, or like wild elk drinking at the edge of a watering hole.

I hated it when the pigeons used to wake me up, screaming and flapping on the window sills amid all their caked up guano droppings. Now I have discovered that eighty percent of all city pigeons are gay. Male pair bonding seems to make more sense for them here. I read it in some very reputable science journal. Now I respect them for this instinctive genius for population control.

I used to hate all the flies here, but I've learned that fat people benefit because they get exercise chasing them off their hamburgers. Because of flies too, illiterates find something to do with newspapers and magazines.

I used to hate the fact that there weren't any fish in the fountains and lakes in Central Park, but then I found that they've all been fried up and eaten by hungry people and that's good because it's really proletarian. I've been hungry and I have a fishing rod, so I get this.

Squirrels are good eating too, except they're so cute alive and look like rats when they're skinned.

I used to hate people with money here, but they're the ones who buy art from poor creative people and anyway on an average day there's always two or three people jumping out of Park Avenue windows or wielding the Wilkinson Sword blades on their blue blooded wrists. So I certainly can't dislike them now.

Toward the other extreme I used to look with impatience on the uneducated poor here. But then after I had to go on welfare and after waiting in lines for five days to get fifteen dollars' worth of food stamps that were supposed to last a week for a family of two, I decided that the welfare system was the thing to be impatient with.

I know now that ghettos are full of people with rich lives.

I know for a fact that the wild people on the street corners who are talking to themselves aren't crazy and lost, they just don't get enough carbohydrates to sustain the weight of profound ideas rushing into their cerebral cortices.

Even time is physically different here. It's faster. All clocks are aggressive and they warn you that every hour is zero hour.

I have found that all this is quaint and romantic, it is the stuff of which poignant movies about Manhattan are made.

"It's real life here in New York," the film directors visiting from L.A. say.

"Well … if you can live in New York you can live anywhere," I answer. There is no other response.

They wouldn't be so glib about New York City if they only knew that just getting out of bed here is like one of those hurdles on the way to wisdom that all the Buddhists talk about.

ESCAPE FROM NEW YORK

Lately, a couple of my girlfriends have committed suicide. One jumped off a building and the other one took pills.

As I remember, in conversations with them not long before they decided to do this, they told me they were depressed because:

(1) they were reaching forty

(2) their careers were at a standstill and

(3) they were lonely.

All valid reasons.

There have been times when I've been so depressed about these same things that I couldn't be emotionally positive enough to get up from bed at five in the afternoon to take a piss even when my bladder was bursting.

So I understood.

I have tried to commit suicide but the famous Dorothy Parker quatrain rattles in my head.

> Guns aren't lawful;
> Nooses give;
> Gas smells awful;
> You might as well live.

You might as well. You're going to die soon enough anyway and I guarantee when it happens you won't be ready.

In retrospect, I know what I should have said to them. I should have told them about my personal cure for deepest depression, which never fails.

"Girls," I would tell them, "Girls, don't be such pussies! Get the hell out of here! Take a break from the city! New York is only a small part of the world. Being forty ain't so bad in the rest of the world. Nobody on the Adriatic in Yugoslavia will see your hairline crows' feet wrinkles. In Lesbos, Greece or Fez, Morocco, nobody cares about careers and if heterosexual loneliness is the problem, get your butt on an airplane. There are millions of hetero men walking around in all parts of the world that would fall to their knees in front of you and lick your toe jam. And they're great looking, some of them have money, even. Not all men in the world are assholes or married or attached or anal or too career oriented or gay or balding like they are in New York."

It wasn't as if these girls couldn't get together the plane fare to somewhere.

And it wasn't as if these girls had inextinguishable burning desires for power and New York city fame that they would be throwing away if they left.

But it was true that each of them was sad because they didn't have a partner.

"Look," I should have told them, "if you're going to kill yourself anyway, why not go to some country where you can hook up with some fisherman on some coast in Turkey or Italy or Spain or Brazil and be anonymous? Why not start a new career as a fishwife? Fishermen always need wives. Or why not go into some European urban area and hook up with a restaurant owner? You could be the lover and bartender. Or go into the rural areas in southern hemispheres and meet a sandal maker. Think of the fine footwear you'd have."

I mean, hon, if you're going to kill yourself anyway what difference does it make if you don't get a mention in *New York* magazine and what difference does it make if a *Woman's Wear Daily* photographer finds you sheep herding in Sardinia wearing a peasant blouse?

The next time you find yourself climbing out on a ledge, give me a call. I can recommend a travel agent.

PART FOUR

FABLES

The Third Twin

In a suburban house with white shingles and black shutters, Ioona, a woman of forty, lived with her mother, a woman of sixty-four. The mother depended on her daughter now that she had emphysema and spent most of her time divided between lying in an oxygen tent surrounded by legions of waiting oxygen drums, and being propped on pillows in the front window, which over-looked the garden, on display to then neighbors.

That Ioona, back again with her mother after a fifteen-year sojourn in a lonely marriage to a man that was wealthy (money amassed though a patented adjustment to a ratchet wrench) was capable and independent enough to take on the responsibilities of the house and her mother's illness was questionable, but she had taken a mature stand to leave her husband and quit the ruse of love.

So now she was home again planting flowers for her mother with the seeds that her mother had given her. A profusion of color all over the lawn was what the older lady desired but Ioona threw away all the seeds but Impatiens, Bachelor's Buttons and Sweet William because these names were meaningful to Ioona who squeezed significance from everything.

She went to the shopping mall every day to escape the sound of breathing. In the mall the music was a cradle and all the mannikins in the windows wore clothes as bland as puree. She found herself, like the rest of the people there, speaking in hushed tones in reverence to the mall, intoxicated by the sheer size and force of the steel and stone and glass and endless displays of things to buy. But she wasn't very similar to these people at all. She was strong and fierce, despite the blue tablets of Librium she took four times a day. Unable to relax, always wanting new input or streamlined stimulus, she drove around at high speeds in her mother's beige Volare dreaming about transformation and destruction. Most often she dreamt of the Phoenix, living and burning, repeatedly rising from flames and the rubble of the shopping mall, wings spread, casting shadows on all of suburbia. When her dreams and driving went flaccid and weren't enough, she thought about meeting a man and how she would do it.

One day at the mall she went into the Bar, this place called Libby's Lounge. Her mother had warned her about this place, as if there was something horribly off-color about it, but Ioona knew that her mother simply had never been in any bar in her entire life. It was exactly like any other, dark and carpeted and quiet in the day.

Ioona expected to meet a man there and she did. His name was William Way. When they began to talk and drink together in the coolness of the lounge, she knew that finally she had met someone so much like herself that she felt almost as if miraculously her DNA double helix had uncoiled to make this man. Here was the man for her, someone who shared her every mood, someone who had been waiting just for her.

She brought him to her home and they fucked in her bedroom with the background noise of her mother's labored breathing and the oxygen whoozing from the tanks.

Whatever similarities that this new couple, Bill and Ioona shared, the fact that Bill had been a Franciscan Monk for the past fifteen years brought them the closest. In the fifteen years of abstinence and isolation, with only his pets as companions, he gathered a certain knowledge of the natural world.

He stirred her into the initial sexual response by telling her about male kangaroos and opossums which have forked cocks, the females forked vaginas and about Abyssinian bats which have cocks with bristles just like bottle brushes. He told her about the day he had taken a live cat and carefully cut it open to take a cellular tissue scraping from the heart to see the piece under the microscope pulsing all by itself. This fact now made her see the order of life that she only dreamt was true. This monk, he was perfect.

They didn't marry but he moved in and together they buried her mother (only grudgingly had she relinquished her tenacious grasp on life). They planted tomatoes, corn and sunflowers in the spring where all those flowers had been and in the summer they took his boat to the edge of the falls and in autumn they burned leaves on the front lawn and in the winter they went out on the frozen river to cut holes and when he finally bobbed up he was in a cube of ice and dead.

And now Ioona alone buried him and wanted to leave her own body but didn't have the courage to commit suicide nor the patience to coax astral travel by meditation. But when she found out that she was pregnant and there was someone else, a third twin perhaps, within her thinking all the wonderful uterine thoughts, she was consoled. This really was just the beginning and she was finally, after all these years, being included into life's mysterious order where tranquility's sweet bloodless arms would envelop her and rock her until the end.

Brenda Losing

She was five feet less than a year ago, but now she is four feet two because of a horrible, delicate operation where she had her thighs removed. Even though the operation had been absolutely unavoidable, she had not resolved it in her mind and she suffered terrible emotional anguish. She was always being overlooked.

The secret that she now had a vagina that began and ended at her knees was a source of much gossip but she held herself proudly and feared no one larger.

Luckily, she had a lover who she had lived with before the operation, this lover being a person who never let a minor physical aberration interfere with his feelings. Anyway their life together was enhanced by the operation, it had made each of them more independent yet closer. Their sex life was better too, because Brenda could easily bend at the vagina, giving her a remote feeling of distance from her mate.

Aside from her love, she began to socialize exclusively with midgets, and at first couldn't understand why they all looked older than their chronological age. But after considering for a while she realized that they aged more rapidly than normal size people because they're closer to the ground and as Einstein's theory proved, the closer you are to the earth and gravity the faster time goes. Because of this fact she knew she was going to die younger now than taller people but it didn't bother her in the slightest, because in her life she had already seen quite a bit, she had been around the block a few times, as they say, and Brenda, being the kind of person she was, would make it around the block a few more times, even without thighs.

Valerie Losing 2

Six months ago Valerie woke up and discovered that one of her toes was missing. True, it wasn't the really important first toe, the large one that keeps you from easily losing your balance. Nevertheless even though it was the next to the largest in size, it was tremendous to her in its importance. She had searched her bed painstakingly and had gone on methodically to dismantle her entire bedroom set in the search. She didn't have leprosy. Nothing like this had ever happened to her before so she made phone calls to various clinics, then decided to see a specialist, fuck the expense, but couldn't recall any category she might fit into or if in fact there was such a category.

"Doctor Rutin's office. May I help you?" the receptionist answered; Valerie wondered if she was an R.N. or a P.N. receptionist. All the better doctors had R.N.s as receptionists.

Valerie's voice didn't break; she didn't sob into the phone, "This is an emergency. I have to see the doctor."

"Are you a patient of Doctor Rutin's?"

"No, but a patient gave me this number. It's really an emergency. Can I see him today?"

"I'm sorry, but there aren't any cancellations today. I could put you in at 2:30 next Thursday. What seems to be your problem?"

Valerie made everything easier by hanging up. She got dressed, weeping. She struggled getting her shoes on, not because of pain, there was none, but because she was afraid that she might not be able to walk in many of her shoes. She went directly to the closest hospital's emergency room and waited with two other patients: one had been shot and was bleeding badly from the neck, the other looked physiologically sound but kept rolling newspapers into balls, trying to set them on fire in the corners below the plastic chairs.

When the doctor saw her, he registered little surprise. He took some blood, gave her another appointment, gave her some Valiums, and sent her home. When she got there she thought she should call her mother to tell her what had happened but her mother wouldn't be sympathetic either, probably blaming the loss on Valerie's alien lifestyle.

"You lost that toe because you stay up too late, you go to bars, you see too many movies, you don't write to me ..."

If only she could find the toe. There had to be an answer in the toe itself. She took the bed apart again and this time found a leaf. Unlike normal leaves it wasn't green or autumnal colored but grayish beige, a very unnatural color for anything once alive or living. She had seen the same color on walls of very unprosperous Chinese restaurants.

She thumbtacked the leaf to her desk and took two Valiums and laid down to sleep.

Many days passed. Everything remained the same. She went back to the hospital and the doctors told her happily that she didn't have leprosy, which she could have told *them*, also she wouldn't lose any more appendages. By now she was growing accustomed to the loss and she actually got a vague sort of sensual pleasure inside her shoes. She didn't give up hope of a regrowth: a friend of hers once told her that a friend of his had playfully bitten off one of his nipples one evening and in a few weeks he had grown another one. He had shown it to her and sure enough it was fresher and pinker-looking than the other one. But a few months went by and no newer, pinker toe grew. Even though she now felt the loss quite normal, she feared that someone might discover it. She kept the lights very dim at night and didn't swim at the pool anymore.

The leaf she had tacked to her desk was now one-sixth of the size it had once been. It was no larger than the thumbtack but was still as well formed with no visible signs of decay or disease. As before it was heavily veined, leaflike, and translucent.

After months of thinking the loss over very carefully she came to know why she had lost this part of her body. In the last fifteen years she had lost a lot, beginning with her virginity. She had lost two husbands, countless girlfriends, passports, bankbooks, wallets, one apartment, plants, a car, a dog, valuable jewelry; there were so many things. This was nothing new, only slightly different. She had lost so much it was just something else to mourn over for a bit. She took it in stride. There is a great art to handling losses with nonchalance.

The Mystery of Tap Water

Julie lost her mind one day, just like that. Well, really, it had taken two weeks to lose it completely. She had always been eccentric, but now she was past that. She believed very strongly in the principle, You are what you eat, so she experimented with water. She drank it—no food, no juice, just water—for two weeks. She was convinced that since she would be only water she could disappear at will.

I saw her the night before she disappeared and she was pretty lucid. She told me that she had lived forever, that she would never die, and since she was all water she must have been the iceberg that sank the *Titanic*, the heavy water used in making the hydrogen bomb, the basic element used with Kool-Aid in Jonestown, Guyana.

"I feel very guilty," she said.

Her last words before she left were: "When you see a gushing fountain, I'll be there. When you sip a glass of ice water, I'll be there. When there's a torrential downpour, a cloudburst, a flood, a blizzard, a lawn sprinkler, that's me."

"Okay," I smiled, "I'll look for you."

No one ever saw her again.

"Oh, she's so elusive," everyone said, "She'll turn up sooner or later in some mental hospital."

But she never did.

I know it's absurd and ridiculous, but now whenever I take a bath I see Julie pouring out of the faucet, and I begin to wonder just how many other odd people and complete strangers are in the bathtub floating around with me.

I Hear America Sinking or a Suburban Girl
Who Is Naive and Stupid Finds Her Reward

Gena grew up in the industrial Northeast of the United States. Like all the women for generations in her family she had hazel eyes, light brown hair and dish-water-colored skin. As a child she was very ordinary so whenever she walked out onto the little patch of land behind her parents' house, she would pretend she was Charlotte Brontë on the moors in the heather. In the distance as she stood there the flour and sugar refineries would belch out black smoke that damaged the sky so she would use this. She would lie down and pretend that she was Edgar Allan Poe in the gutters on his last day looking up at a sky that was in gray turmoil.

Until Gena was eighteen she lived with her parents but longed to leave the world of avocado formica kitchens and red Datsuns and get to New York where she was sure she would mingle with the arty types. She wanted to meet influential people, people who she believed were like herself … the sensitive types. She knew she was sensitive; she cried at all the animal shows about Africa on TV.

So she quit her job as an assistant credit manager … just dropped it as painlessly as a 5-year-old snubs a plate of liver. She forgot about her parents and their provincial souls and she merely put her thumb out on the highway that led to New York City. The first person she got into a car with looked seedy but she gave him the benefit of the doubt. He told her that he was a writer and naturally she was duped for a while until they got to the city in five hours and he pulled into a Ramada Inn and talked her into coming into the room.

He had angel dust and a gun and he asked her to remove her flesh-colored underwear.

"Never, never," she objected. "I thought you were different." Luckily she escaped.

Out on the street it was going to be a bad day. It was the middle of July and the heat had been so intense in the past days that cytoplasm in the cells of human beings had come near to solidifying like the whites of hard-boiled eggs. There had been no breeze for a week. Air conditioners weren't operating up to their normal windstorm standards; in fact many of these appliances had petered out from exhaustion like go-go dancers at the end of a three-day marathon. Normal people who ordinarily had wits were walking around with the effects of the sun on their brains. The vision was turning white. The insane homeless bag people walked around buck naked. In the winter these people wore plastic garbage bags as dress suit shelters.

On the street Gena saw a bum who was naked except he was covered from head to toe in yellow paint. She thought that he must have found a discarded can of yellow curb paint and doused himself with it. He was a human caution sign, a walking no-parking zone. This bag-man bum attempted to build a home in a garbage can that was laying on its belly, but he couldn't fit his big butt into it. She felt as homeless as he, but a wire mesh garbage can wasn't much of a hideaway as she saw it. She was lost in a city with bums four abreast on the sidewalks of every corner.

As she walked by, one of the bums screamed at her.

"Fashion mistake," he yelled.

She looked at him. He wasn't wearing anything at all. She looked down at her own clothes. Was he right? She thought she looked just fine for the city, in black spandex pants and a hot pink t-shirt. Was the look too out of date, she wondered.

As she kept walking nowhere she noticed a real true fashion victim overdressed for the weather.

This fashion victim was passing out in the middle of a street and the light was changing to green.

"Oh, heat prostration," Gena thought and she ran to lift the girl and drag her to the opposite corner.

Oh yes, it was heat prostration all right and the girl said, "Thank you."

Gena thought she had finally found a friend but as she tried to carry on a conversation while she walked beside this girl, the fashionette told her to get lost and the tone wasn't pleasant.

"Oh God," said Gena, "This city is merciless, beyond my ken."

Where were all the wise people? Where were the sensitive types?

The same day she came to Manhattan she thought she better leave.

She'd come back when it wasn't so hot. She found a rideboard at the New York University and went to upstate New York where she located an ashram.

She met a man in his forties who was intent on hammering a piece of bamboo into his forehead to open the third eye and she told him that she would help him do it because she knew that he probably wouldn't die because he was so wise. He was practically a yogi. He was almost to the point of levitation. He said he had always wanted to levitate because it was such a show piece, it would impress even his enemies.

On the night of the operation they ate millet with Tahini Taman dressing and goat yoghurt for dessert. A little later at the first sight of blood, Gena chickened out. In a state of nausea she left the ashram. She would never be a nurse.

So she gave up the search for wise men and settled down in a commune not far from the ashram on the edge of a little river. She would spend entire days in an inner tube floating, following the current. One day she saw the sky just as it had been when she used to pretend that she was Edgar Allan Poe but this time it wasn't darkened with chemical smoke but with the impending rage of a storm. The clouds looked like rats, all the birds were flying low, and the cows she saw weren't standing but lying on the grass. She knew that the animals were acting strangely because of the air pressure of a coming storm. Sure enough, it began to rain so hard that the water around her was singing with the whipping it was getting.

She knew she should get off the inner tube to make it to the safety of the shore but the river wouldn't stop … only meaner and rougher it got, until she could no longer see the line of the land.

When the river emptied out into a larger river she decided there wasn't much she could do, so she just relaxed. It rained for four days and four nights and she was sweeping past most of the Eastern United States so it occurred to her as she entered the ocean that she was lost. Big steamships passed her in the night … she got so close to them that she could see the bare light bulbs through the portholes of the engine rooms.

There had been no one to yell at for help in all this time and she thought perhaps that she no longer had a voice anyway. Her body was changing, pruning up, skin was looking different.

One day she was caught in a tuna net with tuna and porpoises. But when the fishermen took a good look at her they threw her back because by this time she had ingratiated herself so much with the sea that she didn't look too appetizing, as if she was some strange ineatable oceanlife from the Mesozoic epoch. Even the sharks shunned her.

In the distance were the shores of Key West, Florida. She had heard about all the gay men there so indeed there must be some wise men there dancing in the discos. But she began to realize that those fishermen that threw her back had been the wisest bunch of men she had ever met. They really knew a fish out of water when they saw one. Perhaps they knew that a whale's song was her lullabye.

The Truth about the End of the World

Late one night after Joanna put her two kids to bed, she sat down at the kitchen table with a bottle of Remy Martin, the Bible, an ephemeris, an atlas, a calculator and seven grams of cocaine. By eleven in the morning after endless exhaustive calculations, deciphering, deducing and reading she came to the conclusion that by the date Sept. 2nd of that year, only two days away, the world would come to an end. Very few people would survive. Civilization would be destroyed. Most of the planet would be under rubble or water. There were just a few places to go to escape the inevitable end.

It was all there in the ephemeris, the book of the chartings of the moon and planets. It was also there in the Bible in Revelations and then too, calculators don't lie. In her atlas she had circled points on the map of the earth where it would be safe to go when the cataclysm would begin. She had used the longitudinal and latitudinal numbers correctly, she knew. She then drew lines intersecting each point of safety on the map and these lines formed symbols and images that further proved that her discovery was correct.

It wasn't the occult. It was real, there it was in black and white. Scientists and physicists working on problems like these would have done no better, she prided herself.

There was no doubt at all. Truth was truth. There was no escaping it. She had overlooked nothing in her vast research.

She would have to act quickly, she hadn't much time. Her two roommates, who were just waking up, had to be warned and her children who were watching Saturday morning cartoons would have to go through a strict training period to steel themselves for the rigors ahead. She would call the news services, the papers and the radio stations and tv. She would naturally provide all the conclusive evidence.

She sensed that other people had been feeling it too. It was in the air, the feeling of impending doom. Everyone was sensing it, she had realized. Even her dog and cat, the psychic barometers, were experiencing uneasiness for the past week or so. Animals are more psychically aware, she had read many years ago. They always know about an impending disaster before it happens. Look at the way they act before a storm, when birds fly lower and cows in pastures lie down. She knew it had to do with the air pressure before a storm. It was denser. Well, the same type of vibration pressure had been weighing on her mind. She had had a picture in her mind every day for the past week. It came into her head every day until she couldn't stand it anymore and that was when she sat down at the kitchen table and figured it all out …

One of the roommates came into the kitchen.

"You look a little wiped out, Joanna."

"What do you mean, Alex?" she asked, rather on pins.

"Well … sort of wild eyed. Have you been up all night snorting that stuff again?" He pointed to the folded snow seal that now contained 5 1/2 grams of cocaine.

"I couldn't sleep … but it's not the cocaine. I'm in shock, Alex."

"What is it, Joanna?" Alex asked, concerned.

"I've just figured something out." Joanna's voice shook.

Alex felt the weight of the sentence, was floored by the intensity of her eyes, so he was speechless. Joanna stared at him, her eyes burning into his Foster Grant light sensitive glasses. When he regained his composure he said, "What is it? What's happened?"

"This is going to be a shock, Alex. You better prepare yourself. You better sit down and have a drink."

He poured himself a tall one. Actually, Alex never needed any encouragement when it came to drinking.

Joanna first wondered if Alex would believe her but she dismissed this thought as rapidly as it had fired across her brain pan. Of course he would believe.

She wondered if he would comprehend the complexities intellectually or would he be bowled over by the enormity of the crisis. He had always been a sensitive sort and very optimistic about humankind. But then she remembered that he was an astrology buff and she relaxed a bit. Yes, he would understand the ephemeris, at the very least.

So she told him slowly, evading the real point, setting up the figure first. Intermittently he swallowed his brandy and took snorts of cocaine. By the time she had gotten to the point, Alex had done a half gram. He picked up the ephemeris and pored over it. He inspected the map, checked the Bible and used the calculator. Then he sadly shook his head.

"Yes, Joanna. It's true. I can't believe it ... but it's true." He was pale and the pupils of his eyes were very large, the way pupils look when someone takes too much LSD.

They talked for another hour or two, did some more of the cocaine.

Calculations and facts kept falling into place, lining up perfectly, fitting like keys into specially made locks.

Joanna's kids came into the kitchen.

"Where's dinner, mom?" the fattest one asked.

"No dinner tonight. Peanut butter and jelly are in the fridge," she said, and thought, in a few days health wouldn't matter. We're all going to slide, slide, slide. At a time like this how could she make hamburgers and broccoli?

Alex and Joanna studied the world map, trying to choose a place where they should go to be safe. They looked at the places circled: Azores (where Atlantis must have been), the site of the great pyramid in Egypt, Stonehenge, Peru at the Nazar land scrawlings, the Tower of Babel site, St. Peter's Basilica in Rome, the Bermuda Triangle, Easter Island and Newark New Jersey.

"Why Newark New Jersey?" Alex asked.

"I don't really know, but I'm sure my calculator isn't wrong. Newark might have some kind of odd force we don't know about." Joanna was sure there must be some messiah growing up in Newark. There must be some explanation. Newark? Somehow it just wasn't anything like all those other places.

"Well then we have to go there, as soon as possible." Alex said with determination.

"Today." Joanna was relieved that it was only about an hour's drive away.

The other roommate came into the kitchen at this point and looked at both of them. Her name was Laura.

"What are you two guys doing in here for so long? Boy, you both look like you've seen a ghost or something." She poured herself a glass of orange juice. Joanna wondered how Laura could even think of drinking orange juice at a time like this.

"We're going to Newark New Jersey right this minute. We'll explain on the way. Get in the car, Laura and don't ask questions," Alex said and got up to get his car keys.

"Don't forget to bring the cocaine," he said to Joanna.

"What's all this about?" Laura asked.

"I'll get the kids ready," Joanna said and got up.

They all went to Newark and checked into a room at the Ramada Inn. There they waited it out. Laura left and went back to New York when she found out what was going on.

"You're both crazy. It's the cocaine. Don't you see that?" She laughed and told them she would see them back on the lower east side when the cocaine ran out.

A few minutes after midnight on Sept. 3rd, Alex, Joanna, the two kids, the dog and cats got back into the car and headed back for New York. All the cocaine had been gone for seven hours and the world looked to them like it was going to go on for another few million years. Looking at the lights of Newark New Jersey through world weary eyes, Alex and Joanna were incredibly depressed.

Which Came First

It was over breakfast at the Chuck Wagon Bistro that Sarah mentioned that she couldn't eat eggs in the morning in her own kitchen. It was something that had haunted her for many years, since she had left her parents' home, in fact.

"Even the idea makes me nauseous," she said.

"Even over-scrambled?" her friend Vera asked.

"Actually, I can eat hard-boiled eggs in the afternoon at home. Maybe it has something to do with my disgusting cookware. I need new cookware."

Sarah was not the sort of person who talked about home appliances. But Vera, a friend of more than seventeen years, was that sort of person. Sarah saw Vera rarely; she never knew quite what to talk about with her. She was always so concerned with the banality of kitchen minutiae.

Suddenly Vera said something that was so un Vera-like.

"I think I know why you can't eat eggs at home. It's because eggs are so congenitally girlie," Vera said, and Sarah knew she was right, but her choice of words was so uncharacteristic that Sarah laughed. Vera had never made Sarah laugh in all the years she'd known her.

"Also, I read that when you crack open an egg and drop it into the hot oil, it sends out agony vibrations and that traumatizes any house plants that are near. They go into some sort of vegetable shock," Vera added.

Now, coming from someone else, this would have been very matter-of-fact, but from Vera it was an eye-opener.

Sure, Sarah certainly knew all about the sensitivity of plants; she had read *The Private Lives of House Plants* and also the explosive piece on plants in the *Atlantis, Lemuria and Mount Shasta Journal*. It was about how scientists wired plants for their electro-psychic-vibration reaction to Beethoven, household violence, and slicing of vegetables. It was clearly proven that plants were highly sympathetic.

"Vera, I never thought you were interested in things like this."

"Well, I haven't seen you in a year, Sarah. I've changed. Six months ago I was living on Jane Sillman's ashram farm. I learned a lot there."

There was a grand silence, broken only by the slosh of a sunny-side's clear mucus, which accidently slithered off Sarah's suspended fork and back onto the plate.

"The famous Lesbian Occult Ranch?" Sarah asked. Was this really Vera?

"It's called the Feminist Life Force Farm," Vera corrected. "I'm experimenting with other meaningful relationships outside of heterosexual ones. You should know all this; your relationship with Janet is great, isn't it?"

A subway train went by under the restaurant. The table knocked the way it would at a seance.

"Well, yes, but ..." How could she tell Vera that having a

great relationship with a woman is the same as having a great relationship with a man?

At home Sarah thought about Vera. Miracles never cease. Perhaps Vera was experiencing the famous mid-life crisis. Maybe she was having a mind-expanding revelation. A spiritual rebirth? Maybe she even saw auras and talked about third eyes and Beings of Light with the ashram fems. Whatever the reason, Vera was happier.

But it was such a staggering turn. Vera had been a jaundiced homemaker—baloney sandwiches and iced tea at noon, the hum of her vacuum cleaner was music to her ears.

That night Sarah had a dream about the eggs in her refrigerator. Those eggs had been there for a long time. Obviously, she felt some deep-seated guilt about shunning them. In the dream she opened her refrigerator and each egg was shining with a blue light. The eggs then started to move, then hatch. The refrigerator somehow had incubated them.

Out of each egg came a full feathered sparrow. All twelve flew into the kitchen. The phone rang but she couldn't locate it amid all the fluttering birds.

Finally she found it and told the person on the phone that there were birds everywhere. But then she realized that there were no birds and the person on the phone was real and it had been a dream.

The person on the phone was Vera.

"I just called to tell you how much I enjoyed breakfast yesterday," Vera said, and she also told her that she was going away on an extended fishing trip with her girlfriend, a new lover.

"That's wonderful, Vera," Sarah said, and tried to imagine Vera baiting a hook.

Sarah was sure that this night she would dream about the frozen Mrs. Paul's fish sticks that had been in her freezer for three months.

For an old friend, would one dream any less?

The One Percent

Dodge Lee had a secret life. It was the kind of unimaginable, unacceptable, and grisly secret life that would horrify most friends and casual acquaintances. In fact this secret life was something that horrified ninety-nine percent of the population of the world.

For Dodge, who owned and lived the secret, it was something else. It wasn't so peculiar or terrible. He was comfortable with the secret and he knew that one percent understood.

Dodge's secret was his thirst. He was a golden showers guy, a man into water sports, a pee hag. During the day he was like everyone else, he ate eggs and toast and drank coffee for breakfast, and at dinnertime he drank mineral water or wine at the table, but late at night in damp pee bars he drank urine. On these nights his secret life came to full flower like a rare night-blooming jasmine under a swollen summer moon. It was wrong, he thought, to relish pee the way he did, but it was his secret which he proudly carried after midnight among the one percent who had seen a lot and hadn't blushed in fifteen years. There he was, sassy in the dark, the Dodger with a mug of gold.

Dodge truly loved urine, it wasn't just that it was fashionable in the bars he frequented, he really loved it. For him it was fluid of gods, a liquid elixir for bliss, and he couldn't get enough of it, couldn't get his fill, it was so dear. Sometimes he felt his heart would burst with love for pee.

This obsessional love he callously blamed on his mother, the battle-ax. She had messed him up. It was all her fault he turned out the way he did, he thought, even though most times he was not in the least unhappy with his little quirk.

His mother, Hilda Lee, had been a slob, a boozer. It was fortunate she was dead, otherwise Dodge would have had to kill her. He almost strangled her a couple of times out of sheer pissed-offedness. If she hadn't fallen drunk in an asphalt pit one night, after the bars closed, right on a busy city street, he would surely be on death row for her murder.

Dodge told the story of her death to fellow water sports people and his psychiatrist, Dr. Bernstein. He said she had probably moaned all night, and no one heard her. He said the next day when people were going to work they saw her down there covered in litter: empty beer bottles and Coke cans, potato chip bags, and candy wrappers. She was in the right place, he said, dead she was a shell, a wrapper, an empty bag, the contents were gone, the container to be discarded.

"Good thing she's gone." Dodge would shrug his shoulders. "Nasty broad was a witch. I'm this way because of her."

One has to wonder what a mother could have done to make a child so interested in urine. Does a mother wear a tasteful rubber dress and strap a toddler to a toilet seat in a bathroom that is warm and soothing and smells great? Or maybe the mother is just an innocent oddball, a weirdo, a knucklehead with a twisted take on reality that makes strange things seem perfectly normal. Certainly Hilda Lee was from white trash hillbilly stock, but so was half of the population of the United States. Being a hillbilly wasn't necessarily a factor that contributed to anyone's perversion.

"She never had an ounce of class," Dodge would tell his psychiatrist, "and if you didn't believe it all you had to do was look at her head. She always had her hair set in pink foam rollers and black crisscross bobby pins. I never saw what her hair looked like without these things in it. I used to wonder when was that big party she was getting her hair ready for."

True there was always something mysterious about Hilda, aside from the pink foam rollers that is, something to really blame her for. Once when Dodge was little he found in her possession a book of witchcraft with one cryptic passage underlined. It said something about witches stealing the penises of God-fearing men to collect them in boxes where they would writhe like worms. After reading this he immediately knew his mother had a ton of penises in her black pocketbook. There she kept all the family's dicks … his father's, brothers', the cousins'. Oddly enough he still had his own penis, thank God for that.

"So I looked in the pocketbook one night," Dodge explained to the quiet Dr. Bernstein, "but there were no penises there. Nothing except a wad of money, a hairbrush, lipstick, a pint of bourbon and a roll of toilet paper … toilet paper because she was too cheap and low-down to buy those mini-packages of Kleenex."

Dodge told the psychiatrist that he had to accept the fact that his mother hadn't really robbed anyone of his dick, not literally or physically anyway, but she had emasculated all of them just the same. She had robbed their power, and hid it from them.

"No wonder they all despised her," he added.

So Dodge blamed his mother for everything and that belief exonerated him. It wasn't him, it was her, he was a blameless victim of particulars. What he couldn't see was that she had been a victim too, just like him.

His psychiatrist listened silently for a number of long tearful years to Dodge's ranting about his poor mother and then one day, finally, after these years of being mute, years of literally not saying one thing, the doctor had something to say. Dr. Bernstein, the faithful, patient, rich psychiatrist, told it this way: "Dodge, look, here it is. You say when your mother was carrying you she drank a lot of beer. Beer is a diuretic and everyone knows how the baby in pregnancy presses on the bladder so that the mother has to urinate more frequently. Anyway you say when she started to go into labor she was sitting at a bar stool drinking beer. By the time she got to the hospital and you started to come down the birth canal her bladder was bursting. She must have urinated on your head the minute you were born."

Dodge's mouth fell open. This doctor could not possibly be serious, could he? Was this textbook psychiatry? Was there any validity to his wacky opinion? Probably not, this doctor was just an asshole, a moron grasping at gestalt straws. He almost lost his appetite for pee right there and then. He called Dr. Bernstein an idiot and stormed out. He never went back. Later, with a more benevolent insight, Dodge considered that maybe Bernstein intended him to lose his appetite for pee by telling him this. Well, it hadn't worked.

So Dodge decided to stop trying to analyze his obsession and just enjoy it. He let the past go, it was too dark, he gave up thinking about the future, it was too obscure. He concentrated only on the present, and this he found clear. He found bliss in this. Finally he decided to come out of the closet and openly admit to the world his love of pee. He shared his secret with everyone, thus he lost a lot of old friends, but made some new ones.

He found to his surprise that the majority of pee lovers weren't sleazy at all—in fact, they were much like him, they held down respectable jobs, had loving families, and were generally wholesome types. He had always had a prejudice against and felt superior to the people he used to call the "piss reptiles," the people who he believed were the worthless, soulless types, the kind that hung around in sex and pee bars waiting for urine to flow and not seeing the beauty of it. He also used to feel superior to the people he called the "wee-wee hobbyists," those people who were weekend urine enthusiasts. He wasn't at all those types, he wasn't a sleazo and he wasn't a mere weekender, he was a first-class guy and pee was his life.

After he eliminated his prejudicial judgments by opening his mind and the closet door, he became a happier person. New Year's Eve 1978 he even made a resolution to stop blaming his mother for everything.

So Dodge went along peacefully and normally enough, going to his job as a design consultant for a major international architectural firm and at night frequenting the bars. He was a polite man, and not too wild. He wasn't the type that would sit naked in the back-room piss tub accepting just anyone's fluids and he certainly had never waited in shadows at toilet bowls. He always went home at a reasonable hour, usually three A.M. He had a few long-term flings with leather men or guys that wore yellow hand-kerchiefs in the left-hand-side back pocket of their jeans. He had good and loyal friends, male and female. One winter he even attempted to settle down with a busty Irish fag hag who had admired his collection of blown-glass vases.

Everything was fine until one spring night when he heard about this disease called GRID and how it wafted through the air at gay discos. At first only handfuls of people were concerned about it, but after all kinds of people started coming down with it, and the name was changed from GRID to AIDS, and it was discovered that it was a virus contracted through body fluids, naturally Dodge got really scared. He worried constantly. It ate him up. Finally he got a test and unfortunately the results were positive for the virus. A few months later he got angry magenta-colored lesions on his thighs and went to the hospital to die. What else was there to do?

He was so confused. How could the beautiful golden fluid, the pure honest liquid, have been so bad, so evil, so unsafe? To him it had not only been an obsession but his sanity. Everything meant nothing now. Suddenly there were no footholds on reality for Dodge. He saw all the important things of his life become like the leaves on a tree after the summer. Those plump, green leaves turned brown, became shrunken and flimsy, and fell in October. By December the leaves were no longer existent, they had just disintegrated and totally disappeared.

He was ready to die as soon as possible. No one blamed him.

Feeble, despairing, and brokenhearted, he decided to get prepared so he could meet death with everything in order. Along with drawing up his will, planning a big furniture and clothes giveaway, and deciding on cremation, he also wanted to do some spiritual studying so he could greet God having done his homework.

As if the Bible, the Torah, the Koran, the Tibetan and Egyptian Books of the Dead were required reading to pass the grade, he pored over these pages of ancient texts and memorized the high points. The last book on his list was the Bhagavad Gita. He read it but didn't get it. Too many gods and goddesses.

He was told by someone that he ought to read the biography of Gandhi instead, because Gandhi was a Janist and pretty well embodied the spirit of the Hindu scriptures. It was while reading this biography that everything changed for Dodge. This book became his real salvation. Actually it wasn't the book itself but a fact about Gandhi that it revealed. If Dodge hadn't found out this fact, this secret, he would have died within the month. He had almost lost it all, his hope, his pride, his sense of humor, and his life, but he instead fell right into a pit of miracles.

To his wild delight, Dodge discovered that Gandhi, to maintain optimum health, drank his own urine every day. He discovered that many people, prime ministers and religious leaders in India, did likewise. Then he found out that lots of healthy people all over the world, including people in the United States, were drinking their own urine. It was a homeopathic remedy; it worked the same way vaccines work.

Well, Dodge couldn't believe it. It was a miracle! It was exciting! Mind-boggling! A new adventure! It made such perfect sense. He was a new man immediately. The minute he read the passage on Gandhi's urine-drinking he grabbed his urinal bottle and downed it with gusto. He was back on his feet in three days. As long as he drank his own urine he was going to be well.

He threw away his prescription pills. He ripped up doctors' phone numbers. He tossed away the aluminum walker.

He was happy with his own urine. It tasted really great. And what a cheap cure! Free in fact! And he'd certainly never misplace his medicine! It was all right there in his handy bladder!

Years later, after the discovery of Gandhi's secret, Dodge was healthy and happy. He even discovered a medical facility, an institute in New York City that was exclusively for "Life Fluids" drinkers. They held meetings and he decided to attend.

It took a lot of courage to walk into that meeting room the first time. He had been terrified until he finally lifted his downcast eyes and looked around. Lo and behold, all his old buddies from the pee bars were there, smiling at him, happy to see him, clapping for him. He felt like he had somehow, suddenly returned home. His joy cup ran over. He was once again where he belonged ... among the one percent.

The Simplest Thing

Floating on Confidence Lake, on a queen sized inflatable rubber pancake kind of thing, was Molly, the woman who lately had been thinking of herself as a joke. She almost was, but in this setting who was around to laugh?

This was a quiet hidden lake, way off the Cape Cod highway, accessible only by a narrow dirt road, where tiny cars could barely fit one at a time. The road and the lake were surrounded on all sides by a corpulent emerald green forest.

For Molly, this forest was very feminine, the trees that grew there were all like girls and old women. The haughty birch trees were tall and hip looking like runway models, the scrub pines were loud and bitchy when the wind blew through their needles, the oaks friendly like floozies, the Dutch elm trees were spinsters and half dead with that disease of theirs. Fat low bushes wore spreading green skirts.

The lake too was like a woman. All the lakes scattered around those parts. Confidence Lake, Patience Lake, and Sincerity Lake were old exotics, women of mystery, actual phenomenons formed in prehistory by glacier ice. Geologists had pondered these ponds since H. D. Thoreau, and said that they were glacier fed and deeper than anyone ever had the nerve to discover so maybe it was true, maybe there were underwater express tunnels direct from the North Pole. The water was cold enough and clear as clean windows to ten feet. Below that it was a mystery, murky and black.

"Just like women," Molly thought and smiled.

Someone would have to care a lot to go down there.

It hadn't escaped her thoughts also that aquatic dinosaurs could conceivably still be breeding around the bottom, wherever that was, maybe near to the earth's heart, the molten bull's eye core.

She had been getting paranoid while she was thinking about mammoth leafy women watching her from the shores, but she was more frightened thinking about huge things under her in the blackness, so she centered herself in the middle of the big floater so nothing dangled in the water. No toes or ankles to be bitten off by big snapper clamp jaws. A big mouth could eat the whole air mattress, she thought and laughed. It'd be just like eating a marshmallow.

Her imagination was always scaring her lately. It was bigger than she was, but at least she could laugh about it, the big joke.

On eddies she drifted to the middle of the huge lake and she drifted asleep. The sky around her was sapphire blue with a couple of back-woods beach birds in it. Molly would have seen them if she'd been awake. She was on her back.

She was there on that lake because of an invitation from two close friends. Barry and Emory, identical twins. Molly had been extremely overworked since December, seven months, and very hostile but fragile, much like a thin cracking china cup full of bitter hot tea. She deserved a rest more than anything, she was confused and frantic about the course of her life, she felt as if there was a secret about existence she was missing out on, so when the twins said, "Come stay with us for a while on the lake, you'll relax and learn a few things," she went. She hadn't been out of the city for five years straight.

The twins, born connected, had this lake cottage, an inherited grandparents' old summer home. After all the years and soil erosion this house was practically sitting squat in the lake, just a hop, skip, and jump out the door from the kitchen table to two feet of water where water plants, the kind in gold fish bowls, grew on the sandy bottom.

Barry was watching her from the kitchen window.

"Hey Molly," he yelled to her, "Let's eat."

She didn't hear him because she was so far away dreaming.

In the blue water, that was as placid as a plate. She reminded Barry of the Blue Plate Special served on Sundays at the EAT PAY AND GET OUT diner back home in Boston. She had been soaking the sun, and now she was as burnt as an over-cooked ham steak. Barry thought about how she'd probably be sitting in a bathtub of vinegar later that night, to ease the sunburn pain.

"What a dummy. She's getting crisp," Barry mused out loud and turned to his chicken salad. "Emory, you wanna eat?" Emory wasn't there.

Meanwhile Molly was dreaming that a giant woman was holding her in her palm and whispering about things under her, "All the living things down here, Molly, are much smaller than you." This was definitely a good dream because Molly never thought anything was smaller than herself. She was the smallest thing she could imagine.

"Hey wake up," Emory was hauling himself onto the mattress, panting. The cold water he splashed Molly with made

Molly really pissed off, but she didn't yell at Emory, after all it was Emory's lake, Emory's water.

"I almost died getting out here. I didn't think it was going to be so tough. It's really far. I almost drowned half way and then I couldn't turn back and I panicked. I yelled to you. I was yelling for help! You didn't hear me! God Molly! I could have died!" Emory whined like the runt he was. Wimpier than his twin Barry, like the negative of Barry's photograph, he was always less definable in the landscape, almost like his body outline was melting into what was behind him in life's picture. He looked just like Barry, except Emory's very being wasn't very substantial. If he had been a piece of fabric, he would be a chiffon veil, like the shadow material that came off of Peter Pan. Barry, as fabric, would be heavier woven stuff. Burlap twill maybe.

Molly liked both of them equally.

"I didn't hear you." Molly said, "I was dreaming, I think." Maybe it was something she remembered instead of a dream. Maybe she was experiencing a flashback to the time she was in a fetal state inside the big womb. It all made sense, the women all around, the whispers.

"God, you're really burnt. Better get out of the sun. Paddle us back, I'm too exhausted," Emory said and spread himself out.

"We can't drift back?" Molly asked.

"Drift back? No we're drifting over there." He pointed to the opposite shore. Molly looked there. That shore seemed a different zone. Foliage that bent reflections in that part of the lake seemed akin to Jurassic epoch flora. Over there it was like a slow stagnant swamp that hadn't kept in step. The water looked thick and slimy there.

"You have to kick or something. I can't do it all myself."

"Molly just paddle us back."

A half hour later they made it to the cottage and Molly's arms were very sore and trembling. She could hardly lift the bowl of chicken salad.

That night on the front porch after dinner, Molly got drunk with the twins. The mosquitos weren't biting, the mosquito authorities had just sprayed and there was a bug light and green mosquito coils burning.

"So this lake has no bottom? That's really frightening. I was scared thinking about it today."

Molly said. "There's a bottom somewhere. But it's so dark down there that you wouldn't see the bottom if you found it," Barry said.

"I got scared," Molly admitted, but she didn't want to mention the sweet water monsters or the lake trees that were just like women, unsavory women.

"You got scared of the bottomlessness? You think it goes all the way to China?" Barry laughed. "Molly, you have an active imagination."

"That's why we love Molly." Emory said. "She's always good for a laugh." "Shut up," Molly screamed because she was very sensitive about her joke quality.

The scream silenced the forest, as if it had been thunder. The chorus of bull frogs and nocturnal winged singers stopped for a full five seconds and every living thing there listened to nothing.

Emory was hurt because he had only intended affection.

When the frogs started again the conversation started again.

"Ever explore the other side of the lake? The side that looks swampy?" Molly asked them.

"Of course, we spent every summer on this lake," Barry said.

"That's the side that used to scare me when I was a kid. I used to pretend it was a primordial swamp with dinosaurs," Emory said.

Molly talked and talked. She ranted and demanded answers. She angrily threw her glass into the bushes at one point. The twins grew weary of her hysteria and when she finally wound down and fell asleep on the wicker porch sofa, the twins left her there. They felt that sleep for her was optimum. They figured she was headed for a nervous breakdown.

They left her there, Barry and Larry, to be surprised by morning flies, the kind that hover over dung. They had laid some measly thin shield of a blanket over her but when the first rays of 7 A.M. sun started cooking her she festered like something rotting and sat bolt upright on the porch next to the water.

Oh what had she told those twins last night? She had probably offered her soul and they had probably stolen it.

For a while she watched water bugs surf the ripples, then she decided to go across the lake to the shore she was so curious about.

On the mattress half way there, she started to get paranoid again about the trees and the darkness under her. In terror she paddled hard toward that shore. The water was laughing at her in splashes.

When she finally reached shallow water near the creepy shore, she discovered that the surface was covered with fine kelly green polka dots, little plants with no distending roots, just tiny life forms. It was like minestrone, a green magma. Iridescent hummingbirds and dragonflies drank from the lake like elk. The trees were already whispering and jeering, jealous, like most women, and she was exhausted, but all ears and on pins. She was vaguely aware that she might have been hallucinating.

The trees were leaning over her trying to put their shade on her, trying to snatch her from the strength she could soak from the sun. She didn't like these trees. In fact, she hated them. More than this, she hated everything. She felt superior, but cheated. Her life had never been easy, not as easy as the life of trees, or lakes. They had it good, she knew, so she hated them. Who did these trees think they were anyway?

"How dare you? Don't you know who I am?" she asked them.

And that was when she heard the loudest sound she'd ever heard in her life. A very tall dead Dutch elm tree began to scream. It tore itself in half and split from its branches down to its center. It chose to fall. The whole thing came falling toward her, but she didn't move. When it hit the sand and the water it missed her by a yard.

Why had this tree fallen right then? With her sitting right there? There wasn't any wind that pushed it. Apparently it had just given up the ghost. Something ran up her spine that made her shimmy, and in a flash, as if a light exploded in her, she remembered something she'd known a long time ago.

She looked at the sad dried up face of the tree, lying on its ravaged side, and she suddenly remembered that this tree *did* know who she was, knew her right down to her corpuscles. How could she hate that?

She looked at that tree and remembered that delineations didn't matter, didn't exist. Molly was right in there with the tree, she and the tree were just a bunch of swirling atoms, a jumbled chowder. Her skin appeared to bag her up, like all human skin appears to do, but that was just the way it looked. She suddenly remembered that she couldn't separate herself from everything around her.

"You're in the soup, Molly," she told herself.

Molly was indeed.

For the first time in months, she just sat there breathing.

In a split second she was flimsy Emory and tough Barry. She was pounding like a tall woman, stationary and grand as a girl tree, she was the whole of the lake, so so deep with miles of tunnels to the Arctic, cold, frigid and hot on the surface. She was the sun and the sky, the beach birds. She was the glacier ice, the earth's core, a fetus. She was the air she was breathing, the bathing suit she was wearing, the air mattress she was on, the tree beside her. She was all the work she'd done in the last eight months. She was in the soup, same as all the people, same as the frogs, same as the chicken salad in the refrigerator in the cottage across Confidence Lake.

Ahhh, no, she wasn't a nervous twit or a joke, or else she was both of those things magnified. She was a mass mess spaghetti jumble of nerves and the biggest joke in the world. Both. But neither. All. She was everything and everything made sense. She'd known all this simple stuff before, she'd just forgotten it.

A huge sense of calm settled over her like a fat mushy blanket.

She felt suddenly a fool. Everything was so simple it was hardly thinkable.

All at once now, she didn't hate anything because she didn't see any reason to take everything so seriously, things were okay after all. The sun would go up and down, she'd walk in it, days would go by, she'd eat and sleep in them. She was okay. Everything seemed a bit more friendly once she knew it was her everywhere she looked.

*A Letter from John Morton, Boston, Massachusetts, to Georgia Bank, Los Angeles, Californi*a

> *John Morton*
> 98 Newbury Street
> Boston, Mass.

Georgia Banks
1492 1/2 Mulholland Drive
Los Angeles, Calif.

Dear Georgia,

Maybe you don't remember me, you being such a big film star now, but we fucked about eight years ago. You were great. So was I, you should recall … gray eyes, brown hair, blue jeans, black shirt, big meat?

I love you. I will always remember your luscious lips, those fat full blooming labia. Blow job lips. Your flesh was so soft and tender, the kind of skin that feels like silk crepe de chine. I fell right down into your skin, like I was lying down in masticated steak tartare. Bunnies cuddle around flesh like yours.

You should remember me. I picked you up at the opening-night cast party of that tired Eugene O'Neill play you did in Provincetown, Cape Cod. We fucked out on that wharf in the fishnets. You got cod scales in your pudenda hair.

I love your career. I've been following it. I saw you in the first film you made, *Drums in Roanoke*. I remember your first line, "Indulge yourself, Harry, life's a short disease. Take your medicine like a big boy." And you threw him a bottle of gin. Then you started putting white shoe polish on your high school graduation shoes.

I know all the lines to all your films.

In *Swear Allegiance* in a hot pink dress and fluffy white hair you said, "I'm green with envy." In the same film you said, "Honey, I'm blue." Later you said, "According to your books, I'm in the red." You were wearing yellow. Did you realize what a colorful role that was?

I did.

You see, I know lots about you.

Save a place for me in your heart. I hope to be seeing you soon.

Love and Devotion,

John Morton

Write to me or better, call me anytime. 617–540–7849

Phone Call from John Morton in Boston, to Georgia Banks in Los Angeles

"Hello?"

"Yeah, hi Georgia! Did you get my letter?"

"This isn't Georgia. Who's calling please?"

"Tell her John Morton."

"She's not here. I'll leave the message.

Phone Call from John Morton in Boston, to Georgia Banks in Los Angeles

"Hello?"

"Yeah, hi Georgia!"

"This isn't Georgia. Who's calling please?"

"John Huston."

"From the grave?"

Phone Call from John Morton in Boston, to Georgia Banks in Los Angeles

"Hello?"

"Georgia Banks please. Steven Spielberg here."

Postcard to John Morton in Boston, from Fred Knowles in Jamaica, West Indies

John,

Weather's great. Wind's up. Snowing there? Not here. You oughtta be here! Georgia Banks is shooting a movie right down the beach. Eat your heart out sucker!

Fred

Phone Call to Fred Knowles in Jamaica, West Indies, from John Morton in Boston

"Hello?"

"Yeah, Fred! This John. I tracked you down through your girlfriend, Teresa. Georgia Banks still there?"

"Jesus, John, you're really sick. You still insane over her? Get a grip, man, she's out of your league."

"She still there?"

"Hey, John, you're nutty. You're thirty-five years old already, you're acting like a teenager."

"Fred, I've been calling her lately. I can't get through."

"John, you're obsessed."

"She was nominated for an Oscar."

"So what?!?"

"I had a thing with her … we were together and …"

"You had a one-night stand ten years ago!"

"Eight! Eight years ago. After I saw her two months ago in *Sidecar*, fucking some idiot in every scene … he didn't appreciate her …"

"Get real, John, they were acting. All film sex is simulated. "

"Yeah, I guess you're right. Actors probably don't really fuck …"

"How could they? They're employees!"

"Yeah, Fred, I guess you're right."

"Look, in a film sex scene there's fifty people standing around watching them in a fake bedroom, the director is yelling, there's light meters and boom mikes five inches from their faces."

"Yeah, I guess you're right."

"John, Georgia Banks has to be just a memory for you. She's a celluloid commodity now, competing for how much light she reflects …"

"And wow, her skin sure does reflect! Did I ever tell you about her skin? And the cod scales? And the way she …"

Postcard from Fred Knowles in Jamaica, to Teresa Minetti in Boston

Teresa,

I really miss you. My dad is better, so I'll be home soon.

Caught this big turtle, right when I was swimming. Huge guy, must have been a hundred years old, a survivor.—Could hardly pick him up. I think turtles have a different sense of time ... they're really in slow motion. Mom wanted to make soup, but I threw him back while her water was boiling.

By the way, you talked to John Morton? He called me. He's still nuts over Georgia Banks. How would she remember him? Hope he's normal by the time I get home.

How's your sister Mary? ... talking about nuts ... she still doing crack? She still hallucinating?

I'll be home before you get this card. Love you. Fred.

Phone Call to Teresa Minetti, Boston, from Mary Minetti, Boston

"Hello?"

"Hey, sis, Teresa, listen, you wanna buy a rug? You know that phony Persian one John Morton gave me last Christmas?"

"That's not a phony rug John gave you."

"Better, I'll get more for it."

"Mary it's ... what? ... fucking five o'clock in the morning! You wanna sell a rug at five in the morning? Whattaya selling that for, I thought it filled the floor perfect."

"I need rent money. You think your boyfriend Fred would buy it off me?"

"He's in Jamaica."

"You think John Morton would buy it back from me?"

"Why would he want to buy the same rug twice?"

"I need the rent money, Teresa!"

"Sure, Mary! You need crack money. You're an asshole!"

Phone call to Mary Minetti from total stranger (male), after she placed a For Sale ad in Boston Globe. *Ad reads:*

Persian Rug, Like New, 8ft. 4in × 12ft. 7in. 987–4357.

"Hello?"

"I'm calling about the ad in the *Globe*?"

"Okay. It's Persian, it's great. Hundred bucks."

"How about 9 and a half inches?"

"What? No ... it's 8 feet 4 inches by ..."

"I asked you. What about 9 and a half inches. You interested? I'll give you a hundred bucks."

Phone call to Mary Minetti from total stranger (male), after For Sale ad in Boston Globe *which reads:*

For Sale, Early American Four Poster Bed, Horse Hair Mattress Included, Best Offer 987–4357

"Hello."

"I'm calling about the ad in the paper. The *Globe*."

"Okay. It's a beautiful nineteenth-century mahogany museum piece. Three hundred dollars and you can take it away. Frame, mattress, and all."

"You sleep on it?"

"Every day. But it's really firm. Horsehair."

"All you do is sleep on it?"

"It's a bed ..."

"You don't suck and lick people on it?"

Letter from Teresa Minetti in Boston, to Fred Knowles in Jamaica

Dearest Fred,

You'll probably be back to Boston before this letter reaches you in Jamaica, but I have to tell you some news.

First of all I heard from John Morton again and he is still so crazy about Georgia Banks that he's planning to go to Naples where she's filming. Yes he's obsessed but I think it's better to be obsessed with a person than with drugs like my sister Mary. She's doing crack nonstop, so I've decided to call my Uncle Joe Minetti to ask if she can go live with him to clean out. You remember Uncle Joe? The one in the carbon paper business? He has a tiny row house in the hillbilly section of Baltimore … no cocaine there, so I thought it would be good.

True, Uncle Joe has a gambling problem. He plays the horses every day at the track, but maybe Mary could start out walking the race horses again like she did in high school. Or maybe she'd get off a drug addiction and into a gambling addiction. Either way, they could hang around the track together. It'd be a symbiotic relationship. Why not?

Call me, Fred darling and tell me what you think.

Love,

Teresa

Phone call from Teresa Minetti in Boston, to Uncle Joe Minetti in Baltimore, Maryland

"Hello?"

"Uncle Joe? This is your niece Teresa."

"Teresa, sugarlump, what's up? I know you're not calling to order carbon paper. How are things? How's your boyfriend Fred Knowles? And how's our little Mary?"

"Well, that's what I'm calling you about. Mary's bad off again."

"What?!? Cocaine again? That's a pesky drug."

"Now it's worse. It's crack. Maybe you've heard about crack on TV? It's like Dr. Jekyll Mr. Hyde stuff. She's hallucinating and she's selling everything she owns, even that Imperial Persian carpet that John Morton gave her last Christmas. The horsehair bed too."

"How can I help, Teresa?"

"Uncle Joe, could you put her up for a while? I don't want to put her back in a dry-out clinic again because all she did was perform fellatio on orderlies in exchange for coke connections."

"You know I adore that little Mary and I want to help, but I'm pooped right this second, I just walked in the door from a week-long business trip in Canton, Ohio, where a nice lady kept me up night and day. Give me a couple days to toss it around in the old brain pan. I'll call you in two days."

"Better be soon ... Mare's belly up."

Special Delivery Letter to Joe Minetti in Baltimore, Maryland, from Beth Edwards in Canton, Ohio

Dear Joe,

Hi Doll. Where did you come from? Are you Merlin or what? You sure put the hoo-doo on me. I can't shake you. My Ouija board spells your name all by itself.

The week we spent together was a dazzler, worth forty visits to the beauty parlor. I look gorgeous, like you ...

How about me and you? Let's cultivate this fling. I want to know you better. I want you to heat me up and melt my cellulite again.

How about me coming there? I'd live there. It's got to be better than here. I've heard the malls are better there than they are here. Climate controlled air, simulated light, Muzak, simple screwed to the floor plastic chairs formed to fit the size of my big butt. I can't wait.

Don't leave me fanning my feeler. We're at the crest of this thing.

I'm packing my mufti the minute you give me the sign. Please don't 86 me.

Luv Ya,
Beth

Special Delivery Letter to Beth Edwards in Canton, Ohio, from Joe Minetti in Baltimore

Dear Beth,

You're very special and I really like you a lot but your letter took me by surprise. Took the wind right outta my sails. What's this about you wanting to move here lock, stock, and barrel? With me? Sounds like your luggage is bulging already. I bet you even got your bus ticket.

Isn't this kinda sudden? You don't even know what religion I am.

You don't know anything at all and there's a couple of things I want to straighten out. I guess I misled you.

Member I told you I had a big mansion on the rolling hills here? Well it's not a mansion, it's a dinky row house … in fact it's not even my own row house … it's a sublet. It's not in the rolling hills either, it's in a part of Baltimore the urban renewers snubbed. The furniture isn't even mine. The Mercedes I told you about is really an old Plymouth Fury that belongs to my mother. All my clothes are my brother's hand-me-downs. To tell you the truth, I don't own a thing. Nothing. Not even my hair is my own! It's a hair weave.

It was the ponies cleaned me out. I'm at the track with the race form every day.

When I told you I was an antique dealer, I wasn't lying totally. I wholesale typewriter ribbons and carbon paper. Pretty funny, huh? My brother's twenty-year-old daughter Mary doesn't even know what those things are; this kid grew up with an Apple II and a personal mini Xerox copier.

So you see, the warranty ran out on my grubstake a long time ago, and all my ponies came in last. I'm not the person you thought you met. Sorry.

Even if you and I *WERE* serious about nesting down, it wouldn't work right now because my drug addict niece Mary Minetti is coming to live here for a while … I think …

Too bad huh? We did have a good time. Yes we did. Stay well.

Love,

Joe Minetti

Special Delivery Letter from Beth Edwards in Canton, Ohio, to Joe Minetti in Baltimore

Dear Joe,

That was pretty lowdown. When are guys like you gonna stop bamboozling fine women like yours truly?

Never mind, I didn't believe you anyway. I knew you were full of shit, goosing me up for the big tingle. Yeah, we had a good time.

Look, don't feel so apologetic, I still like you despite your sagging assets.

At least you have a hair weave and not an old wig. I didn't even know what a hair weave was till I asked my hairdresser. You're way ahead of me.

I have a couple of things to confess too. I'm not the person you thought I was either. I have green contact lenses, my eyes are really brown and I wear false eyelashes, my real lashes all fell out after my eyelift surgery. I'm not thirty-nine, I'm fifty-four. My fingernails are phony, like my hair color. The body's real.

You know what else? You know the dinner club and motel where we went every night? I wasn't the off-duty cocktail waitress there. I own those places. In fact, I own chains of them across America. No kidding. Unlike you, I'm loaded. I make it a policy to never let on how much money I have when I first meet a guy like you.

How about if I hop a plane and fly over and take you away from all that drug addict niece stuff?

Call collect. You have the number 216–719–6532

Yours Truly,

Beth Edwards

Phone Call from Joe Minetti in Baltimore, Maryland, to Beth Edwards in Canton, Ohio

"Hello?"

"Hi Beth, honeyduckling, this is Joe Minetti, your Merlin."

"JOE! HI! You called!"

"Beth, I think you have a good idea after all. I like this plane hopping stuff. I'm ready for a big entanglement. I can't live without you. Come get me. I'm yours!"

"WOW! What changed your mind? My money?"

"I'm no gigolo!"

"Never mind, I'll hop on the next plane … but what about your drug addict niece Mary? How about if I pay for her admittance into the Betty Ford clinic? Does that sound okay?"

"You don't even know Mary! You'd do that for somebody you don't even know?"

"Call me philanthropic. Remember Joe, I have a daughter too! And Joe … throw away that carbon paper. I'll buy you a port-a-pack mini Xerox machine. Okay?"

Phone Call from Uncle Joe Minetti in Baltimore, Maryland, to Teresa Minetti in Boston, Massachusetts

"Hello?"

"Teresa, this is Uncle Joe. I'm in love. I'm hopping a plane in an hour."

"What? Where ya going?"

"I'm being swept away by this Venus I met in Canton on that business trip I told ya about."

"But what about Mary?"

"All that's taken care of. She's booked in at the Betty Ford clinic. Can you manage to get her there by noon on Monday? I'll send you the travel tickets."

"Uncle Joe, you're a genius!"

Phone Call from Teresa Minetti in Boston, to Mary Minetti in Boston

"Hello?"

"Listen, Mary …"

"If you're calling about the rug, it's sold, the bed is sold, the dishwasher, seventy-five bucks or best offer …"

"Mary, it's your sister Teresa."

"HEY! Terr! How the fuck are ya? I've been sellin all this crap we inherited. You want some? What time is it? You got about sixty bucks I can borrow? Hey why don't you come over? Can you stop on the way and pick up two or three butane cannisters, I'll pay ya back when you get here, a box of baking soda … and some Winston Lights?"

"Mary, I'm coming over to pick you up in ten minutes. We're going on a vacation. Throw your frou-frous in a knapsack. Forget about the butane cannisters."

"Teresa? Ha! Where we going? Do I need my soul-healing crystal earrings?"

"Definitely."

"How about the pyramid power head gear? Hey, Teresa, are you taking me to a dry-out clinic?"

Letter from John Morton in Naples, Italy, to Fred Knowles and Teresa Minetti in Boston, Massachusetts

Dear Fred and Teresa,

You haven't heard from me in a while. I guess you wondered where I disappeared to. After I spoke to you, Fred, in Jamaica, I went to New York City and joined a Low Impact Obsessional Emotional Needs Therapy Group, LIOENT, and also FGA, Fans and Groupies Anonymous. I have come to terms with my sickness about Georgia Banks.

I decided to take a vacation in Italy. Get away from it all, you know? So here I am in Naples dipping into culture and tomatoes. It's great here. I'm living out my fantasy to visit Pompeii and Herculaneum, Paestum, etc. The digs are pretty impressive. A little antiquity goes a long way. I hired a guide who became my girlfriend. Yes, a new inamorata. She's so in tune with the past she puts human warmth into everything archaic. Her name is Allegra Pazienza. It means up-tempo patience. Isn't that great? She works in the Museum of Naples. I don't know exactly what she does there, something really important. I'm sure. She has shown me the real guts of Southern Italy.

How are you guys? How is Mary? I heard that Uncle Joe Minetti put her into the Betty Ford clinic. What a guy! I hope Mary's okay. I always think of her doing her ballet exercises on the Persian rug I gave her. Send her my regards.

Sta bene (Stay well in English),

John

Please write. My address is: Hotel Vesuvio, Via Caracciolo, Naples, Italy.

Letter from Fred Knowles and Teresa Minetti, Boston, Massachusetts, to John Morton on Art Hiatus in Naples, Italy

Dear John,

So glad to hear all's well.

WOW! We envy you … Naples … the seat of culture!

You must be letting the cinch belt go a couple of notches with all that pasta! Sounds like you're steeped in art culture too, especially with this Allegra woman! Glad to hear you forgot about that tart Georgia Banks. We heard you were going there just because she was filming there. Yes, she got the Oscar but so what!

We're fine. I bought a Volvo last week. Forest green. Teresa is flat out, recovering from a pinched nerve in her lumbar region. Last week she was moving her uneven parallel bars and her trampoline into the loft in her leotards all sweaty without a sweatshirt. She should have known better.

You asked about Mary. She cleaned up in the Betty Ford clinic, no more paranoid hallucinations. The latest is that she met this orderly there, an ex-junkie musician from Harlem. They ran off together to New York. Teresa talks to Mary and tells me Mary is happy in Harlem, getting ready to marry and have kids.

Can you see Mary the housewife? Unbelievable! I'm glad for her but I don't understand Mary's new African craze. She told me on the phone yesterday that the drums of Zimbabwe are beating in her loins. Sounds good to me.

As for Uncle Joe Minetti … he lives in Canton, Ohio, and is planning to marry that rich woman Beth Edwards. Isn't that great? We'll finally have rich relatives!

Call us when you get back to the States. Sop up that ancient culture! Be the art sponge you always were!

Sincerely,
Fred and Teresa

P.S. If you want to write to Mary, her address is: c/o Figuero Jeffers, 149 Malcom X Ave. Harlem, N.Y.C. 212–843–6990.

Postcard from Mary Minetti in Harlem, to Teresa Minetti and Fred Knowles in Boston

Dear Sister Teresa
       and Bro-in-Law Fred,
    I'm happy, finally. I found a person in the male form who is my peer. Don't worry about me in Harlem, it's just upper Manhattan.
    I'm having so much joy in life now that I'm beginning to believe that black people have more fun than white people.
    I heard that John Morton isn't on the Georgia Banks kick and is booked up with some Neapolitan Museum piece. Good for him!
    And isn't it great that Uncle Joe Minetti is going to marry that rich woman Beth Edwards in Canton, Ohio?!?
    Love to You and to Fred, Let's Do Christmas … all of us, O.K.,
       Mary and Fig

Letter from Allegra Pazienza in Naples, Italy, to Teresa Minetti and Fred Knowles in Boston, Mass.

Dear Teresa and Fred,
    You don't know me, but I feel like I know you because John Morton always talks about you two so much.
    I'm in love with John Morton, and I'm going to pour out my heart to you because I don't have anyone else here in Naples who knows him and can direct me about my love for him. I'm in love with him but I don't think he loves me. He keeps talking about some woman named Georgia Banks. Who is this woman? Was he

married to her? It's his big secret. He talks about her, but won't tell me what they meant to each other. He keeps telling me that if I tell him what I do in the National Museum of Naples, he will tell me the truth about Georgia Banks.

What I do in the Museum is MY big secret. But I'll tell you and maybe you can tell me if I can tell John. O.K.?

My big secret is this: I work with dicks. Yes dicks! HOLD ON! It's not what you think.

At this job, I'm confronted with penises everyday but it's not the oldest profession, it's the newest! To my knowledge I'm the only person in the whole world, perhaps the entire universe, who does what I do. Imagine the responsibility. Ponder for a moment my cool loneliness.

Penises are my business, yes, but in my job these aren't human penises, these are old impotent penises, castrated marble shafts whose northsides get very cold in winter weather.

Every day I'm in the basement, technically the underground catacombs, of the National Museum, where in front of me are hundreds of dicks laying on long banquet-type tables, a vast musty jumble waiting to be numbered, organized in categories, electrocarbon dated, matched aesthetically, and re-attached to the statues they were removed from in the 14th century by Pope Leo the 13th. This Pope de-dicked everything.

Fortunately for me, somebody, perhaps a secret art lover among the 14th-century papal dick disposal crew, had the foresight to collect the marble appendages from the castration garbage cans.

I'm terrified to tell John that I work with dicks. I can't even tell my family. This secret is a job related drawback, like the kidney pain I feel from the ancient moisture and mildew that chills me to the marrow. Job conditions are wet. Being in this basement frizzes my pageboy cut into a late-seventies sort of helmet hairdo, a work-connected fashion risk. I can't wear *au courant* spike heels either, because the spikes get stuck between the cobblestones, and all mucked up from the semi-petrified cement made from ground-up Christians' spinal column bones, marble dust, and horse manure.

Actually I love my work. Reattaching penises gives me a lot of pleasure. I like to restore these statues to their former glory. Without their penis they're like embarrassed eunuchs, defiled and rudderless, cast into a sea of sexlessness.

I match marble to marble, age to age, ancient crack line to ancient crack line. It's a painstaking procedure. It's not easy and the accuracy of my decisions is often questioned. That's the worst part of this job. My colleagues, other art historians and restorers, are always skeptical. They tell me that it's pornography when I attach a large dick to a little statue.

I can't work with the big dicks now. No one seems to believe that these big things fit on small statues. I just concern myself with the little dicks because after I replace little ones everyone is happy. Actually it's easier for me anyway, I don't have to use so much glue to hold the little ones in place.

Do you think I can tell John what I do here? Do you think I'll lose him when he finds out I work with dicks? I love him so much.

I have to close now.

Please find some time to write and answer my questions. I'm sleepless over this problem. I need some guidance.

Thank you.

> Sincerely,
> Allegra Pazienza,
> 316 Via A. Manzoni,
> Naples, Italy

Letter from Teresa Minetti and Fred Knowles in Boston, Mass., to John Morton in Naples, Italy

Dear John,

We just got a letter from your girlfriend, Allegra, in Naples. She sounds lovely, sort of verbose, but I know that Italians are that way with words.

We don't mean to reprimand you, John, but she tells us that you're still talking about Georgia Banks and this is a crime, because this Allegra says she loves you very much.

She told us about what she does in the Museum of Naples. It's an interesting and spooky but kooky kind of job and when she tells you, I'm sure you'll love her more.

Please forget about Georgia Banks and start thinking about Allegra Pazienza, Good luck!

Love,
Teresa Minetti and
Fred Knowles

Letter from Teresa Minetti and Fred Knowles in Boston, to Allegra Pazienza, Naples, Italy

Dear Allegra,

What an interesting letter! We felt like we were right down there in that job pit with you!

Don't worry about John Morton. I'm sure he loves you very much. Just stick something in his mouth every time he starts to yammer about Georgia Banks.

I suggest that you tell John about what you do in the museum basement. He understands the difference between a marble dick and a flesh dick, I hope! He's very modern!

Good Luck,
Teresa Minetti and
Fred Knowles

Engraved Invitation from Uncle Joe Minetti and Beth Edwards in Canton, Ohio, to Teresa Minetti and Fred Knowles in Boston

We joyfully announce the nuptials of Joseph P. Minetti and Beth Q. Edwards. Your presence is humbly requested for this blessed event. Reception immediately following ceremony. Kindly R.S.V.P.

Phone Call from Mary Minetti in Harlem, to Teresa Minetti in Boston

"Hello?"

"Tere, this is Mare. Did you get Uncle Joe's wedding invitation? Did they send you two airplane tickets too?"

"Yeah, how about that? I couldn't believe it. Beth Edwards must be really rich."

"Beth Edwards is really rich and you know what else? This is really wild. Guess who she's the mother of? You're going to die!"

"I can't guess. Who?"

"Guess! It's unbelievable! You're gonna kneel over! I'll give you some hints: Movie star. John Morton. Guess!"

"NO!!! STOP! NOT GEORGIA BANKS!!! Beth Edwards is the mother of Georgia Banks?!? Our Uncle Joe is going to marry the mother of Georgia Banks! I suppose Georgia Banks will be at her own mother's wedding."

"Yeah, Uncle Joe told me Georgia Banks was definitely going to be there."

"Oh my God, I hope they didn't invite John Morton! Can you imagine!"

Phone Call from John Morton in Naples, Italy, to Fred Knowles in Boston, Mass.

"Hello?"

"Fred, this is John Morton. Hi, buddy?"

"Where are you, John?"

"I'm calling long-distance from Italy. Listen, I can't hang on long, but I got the wedding invitation from Uncle Joe Minetti and Beth Edwards and they sent me an airplane ticket, so I'm going to go."

"Wait! No ... why leave Naples, John?"

"I want to go, anyway it's all expenses paid. This Beth Edwards must be loaded. I'll see ya then. Can't wait. Bye!"

Phone Call from John Morton in Naples Italy, to Mary Minetti in Harlem

"Hello?"

"Mary, this is John Morton calling from Naples, Italy."

"It's good to hear you, John!"

"Are you going to Uncle Joe's wedding too?"

"Of course, John. And I bet you're dying to go!"

"Yeah. A big reunion."

"More than that for you, John. Your old flame Georgia Banks is gonna be there. She's Beth Edwards's daughter."

"........."

"John? ... John? ... You still there? ... Hello? John? ..."

Phone Call from John Morton in Naples, Italy, to Fred Knowles in Boston

"Hello?"

"It's me again, Fred. John in Italy. You didn't tell me."

"Tell you what?"

"About Georgia Banks at the wedding."

"Yeah, she's gonna be there, but so what?"

"Fred, how can you be so blasé?"

"Jesus, John, you're really sick. You still insane over her? Get a grip, man."

"Fred, I think I'm having a heart attack."

"Maybe you'd better not go to the wedding, John."

"NOT GO??? ARE YOU CRAZY? I HAVE TO GO!"

"Take it easy, John. You sound like you're hyperventilating in the receiver."

"MY GOD, FRED!! IT'S GEORGIA BANKS WE'RE TALKING ABOUT HERE! THIS IS UNBELIEVABLE ... WHAT AM I GOING TO WEAR?"

"Hey, John, you're nutty. You're thirty-five years old already, you're acting like a teenager."

"SHOULD I WEAR WHAT I WORE WHEN I FIRST MET HER EIGHT YEARS AGO? YOU THINK SHE'LL REMEMBER ME IF I WEAR THE SAME STUFF?"

"John. You have to forget Georgia Banks. Are you listening to me? You're obsessed. It isn't healthy. Think about your days in Fans and Groupies Anonymous! Can you find some solace in that? Try John!!"

"YOU DON'T UNDERSTAND, FRED! THIS IS MY LIFE! GOD HELP ME!!! WHAT AM I GOING TO WEAR?"

PART FIVE

COLUMNS

Cookie Mueller,

Born 1949 Baltimore, Maryland

Biography and Education: I received most of my education traveling and working various inane jobs such as: clothing designer, racehorse hot walker, drug dealer, go-go dancer, underground film actress (otherwise known as independent feature actress), theater actress, playwright, theater director, performance artist, house cleaner, fish packer, credit clerk, barmaid, sailor, high seas cook, film script doctor, herbal therapist, unwed welfare mother, film extra, leg model, watercolorist, and briefly as a bar mitzvah entertainer, although I'm not even Jewish.

I started writing when I was six and have never stopped completely. I wrote a novel when I was twelve and put it in cardboard and Saran Wrap, took it to the library and put it on the shelves in the correct alphabetical order. When I was eighteen I left college for Haight-Ashbury and wound up a drug casualty, not unlike a bag lady. I learned a lot in the mental hospital, where I had shock therapy that didn't work except for eradicating from my memory all the contents from novels I had read in the past twelve years.

A few of the films I appeared in have attained a cult status and I am told that I have a fan club in Los Angeles.

I have a twelve-year-old son, who I believe has taught me the most.

I used to write poetry, but now I feel that poetry is archaic unless written specifically as song lyrics. I believe that my short stories are novels for people with short attention spans.

I live with my son in Manhattan and pay the rent as a journalist.

Ask Dr. Mueller (*East Village Eye*)

Dear Doctor,

I have very dry skin but I've found that so-called moisturizers don't really do what they're supposed to. A friend told me to use regular oil on my face. But which should I use?

Anne Marie Figette

Dear Anne,

Don't use Crisco or Wesson. I'm serious. They're made out of semi-drying oils; either corn, cottonseed, poppyseed, safflower, sesame, or sunflower. Use the heavy non-drying oils: almond, coconut, olive, or peanut. Also eat a tablespoon or two daily. Try a facial sauna to cleanse the pores while you're at it. Do this by boiling these nondrying herbs: licorice root, anise, peppermint, fennel, peach leaves, clover, and acacia flowers. Remove the pot from the heat and put your head over the pot, with a towel over your head and the pot. Stay this way for ten or twenty minutes. You'll feel great.

Love,
Dr. M.

Dearest Dr.,

I'm wondering about your true identity. Are you as beautiful as the little drawing makes you out to be?

Ronald Firbank

P.S.: I have a raging case of the clap. What should I do?

Dearest Ron,

Not only as beautiful but much more. No, truthfully, a

very dear friend and gifted artist drew this picture of me and he likes to think that every woman should look like this. What is my true identity. This is my true identity.

Now about the clap. Get some penicillin, but don't forget to get your intestinal floors back in line with acidophilus while the penicillin is destroying it. And don't think about beautiful women.

Love,
Dr. Mueller

O.K. Ms. Mueller,

Since you seem to know so much about herbs and things, can you suggest some real aphrodisiacs? My man has lost interest.

Signed,
Rosemary Leonica

Rose,

Look, there's lots of controversy about aphrodisiacs. Some say they exist, some say they don't. As I mentioned in one of the former columns, about male impotence, zinc and zinc-rich foods are vital for virility. Maybe he's too cerebral. Empty his brain a bit.

Anyway, here's a list of aphrodisiacal herbs that most herbalists agree on: saw palmetto berries, damiana leaves, muira puama root, southernwood, mugwort and myrtle teas. Other things are: marijuana, celery, kola nuts, honey, cocaine, ginger, oysters, cucumbers, avocados, artichokes, ambergris. If these things don't work, forget about him and go to the Roxy on Friday nights and pick up somebody else.

Dr. Mueller

Dr. Mueller,

I'm pregnant and I experience leg cramps every night when I go to bed. They're so overpowering I practically go into convulsions. This wakes my husband up and he gets really angry. Is there anything I can do?

Mildred Faun

Oh Millie,

Is the question "What can I do about leg cramps" or "What can I do about the husband"? The leg cramp problem is easy. Leg cramps are associated with pregnancy. They're very common at this time. I had them also. They're muscle spasms and can be due to sex hormone influence on calcium metabolism. They can be relieved by stepping up the calcium and calcium-rich foods such as yogurt, kefir, most vegetables, millet, oats, rice, sesame seeds, beans, and cottage cheese. Now for the other dilemma. Your husband should be more understanding at this time. Did you tell him that it's very common in pregnancy? If he still gets pissed off at night, tell him to sleep on the floor.

Love,

D.M.

Doctor Mueller,

How can I stop smoking? I've tried everything except something related to nutrition. Is there a way?

Beverley Talmadge

Bev,

The only way of breaking the habit is doing a juice fast. Nicotine is poison. We smokers have developed a physiological body dependence on this poison. During a juice fast, all the poisons will be eliminated as well as the desire. Women who smoke age twice as fast as those who don't. And I mean wrinkles. Buy a good book on juice fasting from the health food store. It's really too lengthy to go into here. By the way, juice fasting can cure any addiction.

Love,

Doctor Mueller

P.S.: I've tried the juice fast and it does work for smoking. I quit but started again because a friend forced me. He gave me a free carton. You know the old adage—the first one is free. It was a lonely smoker who gave me the carton; he had no one to smoke with.

Dear Doctor Mueller,

Can cocaine kill? How does this happen?

Sincerely,

Curious

Dear Curious,

You bet your boots it can. Unknown to many, there are more cocaine ODs in the United States than commonly thought. Cocaine devotees think it's harmless and many deaths attributed to heroin are really cocaine overdoses. In autopsies when both are found in the bloodstream it is usually blamed on heroin.

In an overdose, the diaphragm, the internal muscular partition that separates the chest from the abdomen and is used in breathing, "freezes" and the person can't breathe and suffocates. This also happens in extreme anxiety. Because cocaine increases the blood pressure and the heart rate, anyone with heart problems of any kind should *never* use the substance.

Love,
Doctor Mueller

Dear Doctor Mueller,

Lately I haven't been doing any drugs at all, but I must say, life sure is boring without them. What can I do for the boredom? There has to be something.

Signed,
Bored and Clean

Dear Band C,

Well, if it's any consolation, I know exactly what you mean. What I do is this: I make sure I'm never lonely. Plan your day with lots of activities. Start going to the movies often. Get a hobby.

I have an idea! Start painting and see if you can become a millionaire, one never knows. The money you would be spending on drugs you can spend on canvases and paints.

Love,
Doctor Mueller

Dear Doc,

I'm a writer and I must confess that I sometimes sniff whiteout. It has the same thing in it that glue sniffers loved. Now I'm told that the company has to change this because people are abusing their whiteout. Are they going to use another substance? What will happen?

Love,
A Secret Sniffer

Dear S.S.,

Well, it turns out the main integral ingredient in the whiteout is this stuff that makes you high, so they can't change it, so what they're going to do is make the whiteout stink. Gee, I guess us writers better stock up on the old stuff if we don't want our papers to smell too bad. Can you imagine the smell in the editors' room? I don't envy them.

Love,
Doctor Mueller

Dear Doc,

Please tell me something about psychic surgeons. There was a show on Channel 13 a year ago about this and I saw actual footage of some of these doctors at work. Do you know anything about this?

Henry Tormont

Henry,

I know a little. One of these surgeons is named Arigo (Jose de Freitas) who worked in the little town of Congonhas do Campo, Brazil. Arigo would perform surgery with rusty table knives and scissors. The method was simple … he would slash into people while they stood there unanaes-thetized, and in one case pull out the colon, chop off a piece, shove everything back inside and then close the wound by waving his hand over it. This I believe is the film you saw.

There are other psychic surgeons who don't bother with the knives, they just push their fingers into the skin and pull open the body. Then they remove various items, rusty nails, plastic bags, cans of film, plastic wrap. Don't scoff, there have been no cases of infection or postoperative shock. It's all in what you believe.

Now a precautionary note, don't try this on yourself at home.

Aside from these psychic surgeons, I once had a doctor in Provincetown named Doctor Herbert. He went down in the annals of medical history as being the only doctor who performed an appendecto-my on himself with the use of mirrors. His threshold of pain was so high that I think he probably even performed this operation without anesthesia, or just a mild local anyway. He was really pretty cool. You could ask him for anything and he would give it to you. Once I went in with a spider bite and told him that it was making me sleep too much thus I couldn't work … what I really wanted was speed. He gave me black beauties. Oh those were the days. This was about twelve years ago and I would never try such sleazy tactics in this age. Oh this guy had a great sense of humor also. In the waiting room of his office there was a framed-behind-glass picture of Marcus Welby, M.D.

Love,
Doctor Mueller

Brief Tips from Italy

One night in Capri (30 minutes by hydrofoil from where I live) on the dance floor of Numero Due, my identity as the questionable doctor was discovered. Immediately I was asked, "What is this herpes we've heard so much about?"

It dawned on me then that these people were really healthy, I answered. "In America, herpes is passé." Then I told him that he should relax but get

himself some brewer's yeast just for preventive measures because one never knows when it could hit Capri.

So the real cure for whatever ails you is a long stay in Italy, perhaps right here in Positano where it's shockingly beautiful and the food is straight from the vine and the Tyrrhenian Sea is so mineral-rich that breathing deeply puts ore into the blood. Also, one doesn't have to force oneself to do the daily exercise routine, because to get anywhere, for instance to the beach or to the bars, there are these labyrinths of steps up and down the cliffs so calf, thigh, and bun development is unavoidable. No wonder there are no cellulite problems here.

Another thing I couldn't help noticing is that everyone around seems to be downright euphoric and they do it all without drugs. In the States, to get this high one would have to snort something. Here I believe it's the tomatoes.

Obviously, any letters I write here would be fakes, so instead I've committed to memory some conversations about health that I've had at the table over *Costata alla Fiorentina* or *Scaloppine alla Marsala* or *Fritto Misto* or some other dish.

Someone asked me why Americans always eat the salad before the main course. I really don't know how this bad habit started but I think perhaps it had something to do with American impatience. There's this bizarre need to do something with the mouth and hands. It's totally incorrect to eat the salad first—I mean for health reasons—this has nothing to do with manners. The hydrochloric acids start to work on the first thing you put into your stomach and raw salads are difficult to digest so the acids start on this item and then when the main course comes down the chute it can putrefy, thus making gas. The same thing happens when you chew gum. The hydrochloric acids are triggered by the act of chewing, but then there's nothing to digest, thus making stomach acid. So chew gum only after a meal. Peppermint, by the way, is a great aid to digestion.

I noticed that people here don't generally overindulge in alcohol but they do drink wine all day. Only a few of these people have moved into stronger stuff and one of them asked me a very strange question about something he heard somewhere about alcohol being a desexer. He meant it literally. Well, it's true that alcohol weakens the adrenal and thyroid glands and also the liver. When the liver becomes exhausted it may not be able to fully inactivate hormones of the opposite sex. So, for instance, when a woman drinks a lot (now rest assured that I'm merely relaying information. I really don't believe this particular theory) the liver isn't able to detoxify the male hormones in her body and a new sex begins to emerge: a neuter sex. It sounds a bit far-flung to me but even if it is true, what's wrong with a little androgyny?

Stay well, don't worry about being sick. Eat some tomatoes.

Love,

Doctor Mueller

Dear Doctor Mueller,

I've got spider bites, mosquito welts, peeling sunburned skin, saltwater in my ears, sand in my crotch, burned feet bottoms, and sun-stripped, snapping hair. What is the general cure for these beach problems?

Frank

Dear Frank,

This is really an easy one. Stay indoors and watch soap operas. Douse yourself from head to toe with watered-down apple cider vinegar. It'll speed up the healing process to all these injured areas. Do this while watching *All My Children.*

Love,

Doctor Mueller

Dear Dr. Mueller,

I know you've gotten many letters about small penises, and about what could be done physically and emotionally. I have the opposite problem. I have a penis that's too big. It's really a problem because I'm a straight guy (not homosexual, I mean) and many girls are at first shocked and then unable to accommodate me. Can I have some removed? Do you think this would be a good idea?

Daniel Massini

Dear Daniel,

You might be better off as a homosexual. Nothing is too big for an experienced fun-loving gay man. It seems to me that the girls you're hanging out with don't know how to have a good time. Please don't have anything removed; you'll be sorry because they may just cut off too much and won't you be mad??? You have to look around more for a woman who fits. In most ancient philosophies there is a belief that there is always someone (if not many) that you will finally meet that will fit you. Take heart; you're definitely blessed and well-equipped for life.

I'm not going to talk about AIDS. It would be unwise and presumptuous for me to try to shed some light on a subject as serious as this epidemic. But there is one thing I have a burning desire to say and then I won't ever mention it again. If you have AIDS seek help from doctors other than ones connected with the A.M.A. Like some bizarre sci-fi C.I.A. plot the A.M.A. seems to be trying, albeit unwittingly, to obliterate the following groups: queers, voodooers, drug fiends, hemophiliacs who need transfusions often, and straights who share Sabrett hotdogs with gays. (But really, not only has William Burroughs thought that the C.I.A. and the AM.A. are creating strange diseases to eliminate certain segments of society, but just about everybody I talk to.)

I've had too many beloved friends die lately from diseases contracted when the immune system breaks down. I'm tired of going to wakes. I miss these people. So after you have an accurate diagnosis and before you take any medication or therapy, try a nutritionist, a homeopath, a kinesiologist, and a chiropractor/nutritionist. Go to them all. The first thing a really good chiropractor/ nutritionist will do is take hair, urine, blood, and nail paring samples to determine what your individual deficiencies and needs are. It's a very personal treatment. They put you on a diet that's correct for you alone. Three of my friends who had AIDS and didn't start any A.M.A. treatments but went instead to chiropractor/nutritionists now have white and red blood cell counts back to normal. They are virtually cured. So there is some hope.

If you have AIDS write to me and I'll give you a list of some of the people who may perhaps cure you.

Dear Doctor Cookie,
What is the difference between in-going and outgoing veins? Is there a dangerous vein? I'm talking I.V.'s.
Curious George

Dear Curious G.,
With all this AIDS that's floating around in the bloodstreams I'm surprised at this question. You're still using needles? It's time to stop. When you speak of ingoing and outgoing veins, I start to think of the highway into JFK airport. With veins and airport traffic,

it's difficult to tell what's moving where and who's exiting and who's entering. I suppose you're asking about the difference between the arterial blood flow and the venous blood flow. Arterial blood is distinguished from venous by its darker color and presence of carbon dioxide. The arteries carry the blood to head, arms, liver, and spleen, etc., and the venous supply moves *from* all of the above. I don't know which ones are which when I look at them, but I do know what to get to JFK. The train to the plane.

Have a nice holiday,
Doctor Cookie

Dr. Mueller,

You mentioned impotence in your last column. What can I do?

Robert Benchley

Dearest Robert,

I make house calls for this one. This is becoming epidemic in the United States. Hey, forget about the psychological causes, fear of failure, liberated women, etc., it's becoming evident that the cause is more dietary than psychic. Here's a list: Drink alcohol, it relaxes. Of course don't drink too much. Avoid lead (hard to do, it's smog), eat lots of raw seeds and nuts, especially sesame, pumpkin, sunflower, almonds. Halva is a famed virility food in the Orient. Avocados work. Take zinc, it's vital for virility: Studies show that a deficiency of zinc is associated not only with diminished potency but also with dwindling fertility. The seeds and nuts mentioned above are high in zinc. So is brewer's yeast, oysters, eggs, and onions. A lot of meat and poultry today contain the growth hormone diethylstilbestrol which destroys virility. East fish, I guess.

In Europe KH-3 (Gerovital) is widely acclaimed as a sexual rejuvenator, but, alas, it's not sold in the United States. Maybe you could get somebody to run it across the border from Mexico.

Take vitamin E, wheat germ oil, PABA (para-amino-benzoic-acid) lecithin, kelp, cod liver oil. Drink raw milk, ginseng, gotu kola, and sarsaparilla teas (no kidding). Eat some fertile eggs.

If after all this you're still having this problem, give me a call and together we'll work it out.

Love,

Dr. Mueller

Dr. Mueller,

One of my best friends just ODed on heroin. He wasn't a junky, he was an adult professional at the top of his field. It's terrible this drug has become so socially acceptable among people that have no real knowledge of it. A friend was with him when he died and this friend didn't know what to do to save his life. What can be done when someone ODs in your presence?

Phillip Tambur

Phill,

My sympathies. I too have lost a few friends this way. First of all, try to get the person up and walking. If this is impossible, put them in a cold water tub. Put ice cubes under the arms, on the chest, and up the ass (graphic but necessary here). If these things don't work, inject the person with a saline solution: 1 part salt to 4 parts water, intravenously. This works in seconds. A sure thing.

Dr. Mueller,

Just lately I've noticed that the A.M.A. is getting more tolerant. In an article in *Newsweek* a few weeks ago it was noted that the government has finally okayed the now-famous papaya enzyme treatment for slipped discs. Also in *Newsweek* I read that doctors are looking at fevers differently. They're just figuring out that when the body temperature goes over 98.6, the blood's T-cells are in mass production. The higher the percentage of T-cells, the better the immune system works. They're now saying that the overuse of aspirin should be avoided except in extreme fevers. So obviously it makes sense, as I've mentioned before, to raise your temperature about once a week. Go to the sauna. Or use the do-it-yourself method. Take a hot bath. Then get into bed with a towel under you and lots of blankets over you, including your head. The sweat will pour off. When you lift the covers and jump out you'll feel like a new person; and besides, all the blackheads will be gone.

Dear Doc,

Is it true that you can have syphilis for years and not ever know it? I'm just so worried about everything as far as health care goes these days, what with everything that's going around.

Jonas Corona

Jonas,

Well, how did you contract this French disease? I didn't think anyone was still having sex. Okay, this is just something I heard, but yes, apparently you can have it for years and not ever know it. Usually a blood test is pretty conclusive, though. But don't worry, there's plenty of penicillin around and the doctors are more than willing to give it out.

Take it easy. Relax. Try to think of what Christopher Isherwood said about venereal disease. "If you don't have it, you aren't trying hard enough."

Love,

Doctor Mueller

Where do epidemics come from? There is one theory that all the viruses and bacteria responsible for infectious diseases came to Earth from outer space. These people also believe that all aspects of life's basic biochemistry come from outside Earth's atmosphere. As a doctor I reserve my opinions. I'm skeptical of everything, until it's medically proven.

Things are getting serious in NYC. Everyone is scared and for good reason. No one's exempt from getting the new epidemic: AIDS. All the doctors I've talked to have thrown up their hands. Could it be that it came from outer space or the State Department? What a great sci-fi novel it would make—if there are any interesting authors left to write the book. That's the thing that's most disturbing and hardest to accept ... it threatens to wipe out a good deal of our creative minds.

Eat your acidophilus!

Dear Doctor Mueller,

I have a cellulite problem. You probably know all about it.

Please help. Nothing I've read has been beneficial.
Sincerely,
Ripped Flesh

Dear Rippled,

I beg your pardon. I know little about cellulite because I don't happen to be a sufferer. But I do have some second-hand knowledge. Here's what you can do:

First of all, stop eating the combination of salt with sugar and butterfat. This combination, as nutritionists say, is the main cause of cellulite. So basically you have to avoid cheeses and ice cream. Try warm water and lemon juice (real squeezed lemons) or carrot juice. These two juices help to break down fatty acids and also work as a liver cleanser.

Love,
Doctor Mueller

Dear Doc,

I have begun to notice something that I always feared was true. I think I may be allergic to milk. I tried staying away from it for three days and the insomnia, depression, diarrhea, and slight itchy skin disappeared. What do you think? What am I allergic to milk? I've been drinking it all my life. Is it possible that I've been this way for a long time?

Susan Chen

Dear Susan,

You certainly can be allergic to milk, and probably have been all your life. Descendants of people from countries who herded dairy animals and lived on a dairy diet are usually tolerant to milk. Their intestines contain the enzyme lactase that breaks down milk sugar or lactose. Now those whose ancestors never used milk are usually intolerant. So if your people are from Europe or the Middle East you probably can use dairy products. But if your ancestors are African, Chinese, Filipino, American Indian, Aboriginal, or Eskimo, forget it.

This doctor happens also to be allergic to milk and I guess it has to do with my Indian great-grandmother.

Don't get too upset. You'll miss the ice cream but there's

always tofu. (What a consolation.)

Love,

Dr. Mueller

Dear Doctor Mueller,

This may seem awfully strange to you but I had a thought about a month ago when what's-his-name was executed in the electric chair. Through the news coverage of this media event I learned that at the moment of death there was this puff of gray smoke emitted from the head. This happens whenever someone dies in this manner.

Now we all know that the soul (I know this anyway because I've done some astral traveling) leaves the body through the top of the head, around the forehead area. Could it be that when a person dies from electricity the soul dies too? Is this gray puff actually spirit smoke? Is it all that's left of the soul? I think that the soul is something like electricity anyway, so maybe I've hit upon a miraculous truth.

I'm trying to substantiate my theory. I didn't know any-one else to ask who wouldn't scoff. What do you, as an open-minded doctor, think of this?

Mr. S. Muldoon

Dear S. Muldoon,

Firstly you're right about my mind being open, in fact it's so open that at times I hear the wind whistling through it. No, but seriously, this is quite an interesting question. I guess I have to put on the occultist hat to answer this one.

Who knows, you may be right. Did you know that there are a few people who believe that the soul dies along with the body in a nuclear blast? The idea here is that the soul has energy and talk about the rearrangement of energy that goes on in an atomic blast … well you can only imagine from what you saw on *The Day After*. But these are the people who are *so* adamant about nuclear disarmament.

Let's just look at this for a moment. The space between the eyebrows is the location of the pineal gland which evolved from a light-sensitive spot that's still visible in some reptiles. In

1959 it was discovered that the pineal gland secretes a hormone called melatonin. The function of the stuff isn't clear, but it's derived from serotonin, a chemical similar in molecular structure to LSD. Serotonin is naturally present in the brain. So ... what's the catch? What has this got to do with anything? Supposedly people who have out-of-body experiences feel their spirit leave through this pineal gland. It would be interesting to know exactly where the smoke is emitted when these people die in the electric chair. Only the executioners know for sure and they're not talking. If I remember correctly from reading of this I think it comes out of the ears, but I'm not sure. This may mean that it's merely the brain frying. I'm sure real live prison physicians could tell you, or maybe you should pose this question to the parapsychological center here in New York. It's an interesting theory but can you package it?

Love,

Dr. Mueller

P.S. This serotonin is also present in dates, plums, figs, and bananas. Remember when people used to tell you that smoking bananas would get you high? Maybe it has some validity after all.

Dear Doctor Mueller,

There's got to be something other than barbiturates I can use for insomnia. I've tried hot milk before retiring. I've tried most of the well-known remedies but I just can't sleep easily. So is there anything besides the obvious drastic therapies?

Signed,
Myron

Myron,

I've answered this question once before but now I have something to add. First of all try magnesium chloride, calcium, B6, and pantothenic acid. Before going to bed have a cup of chaparral, licorice root, peppermint, valerian, lady's slipper, or hops tea. Or forget the tea part for the hops thing and go right to the other hops cure ... beer.

Love,
Dr. Mueller

Dear Doc,

I want to know, do people really die of a broken heart? Do they just stop eating and starve—or does love kill?

Celeste

Celeste,

It happens all the time. Look at Buckminster Fuller and his wife. The greatest cause of disease is stress and the most stressful situation is mourning. It's been proven. The loss of a loved one, and not necessarily death, creates the state of despondency, loss of appetite … you know the scenario. Any person can cause their own demise and most often illness follows the loss of a desired person, object, etc.

The second question, does love kill? The human body is at its maximum energy and optimum health peak when the soul is in love. There is no other time when one feels better, physically. Unrequited love can throw the body into a sort of shock but love that has been found and lost is by far the most disastrous situation. People can genuinely make up their minds to be sick or healthy but most people just aren't aware of this … there are so many other influences that can be sublimated. If you can't seem to eat anything at all … and I've said this before … take some brewer's yeast … at least it's food that is easily digestible and it contains all the B vitamins and essential amino acids that are so depleted during a stressful situation.

Love,
The Doc

Dear Dr. Mueller,

I've just returned from Berlin where my fingernails grew the longest that they've ever grown. Now I don't chew my nails or pick them but they never grow as rapidly in New York City. The climate was the same, I did change my diet. I ate meat because I just couldn't find too many vegetarian restaurants. I do eat lots of chicken in New York and beans and rice. I drank lots of beer there, and you know about the beer in Germany. Should I give my secret to the people that run the Revlon Nail Bank?

Love,
John Heyes

Dear John,

The answer is obvious. All the food you consumed there is richer in B vitamins and protein, even the beer. Also, it's a well-known fact that the food is less full of toxins, as the grass and fodder the meat-bearing animals eat is not saturated with poisons from the air. Talking about air ... the quality of the air you breathe anywhere outside of NYC has got to be better. I noticed that my nails and hair grow better whenever I leave New York for extended periods. Remember too that it's a total holistic thing. You were probably more relaxed there, free from career pressures and able to breathe deeply (literally). I believe that one of the most important things for a person who lives and works in New York is to get away from it for at least two months a year. There is just such a bombardment to the senses here that it gets taxing. Even walking out on the street for a leisurely stroll can be hair-raising. Car horns blare, people scream at you, you walk in dogshit, your feet get tangled in garbage, people bump right into you and don't even say excuse me, buses will mow you down, bicyclists will play chicken with you, taxi cab doors open in your path and some people will even laugh at your shoes.

Love,
Dr. Mueller

Dear Doc,

Last month I sent you a letter about a very famous person who had his asshole removed. I read it in the *Post* or somewhere. I wondered where the asshole was taken and what was left in the spot. I was serious and I wanted an answer. Also what happened to your old logo? It was great.

Signed,
A Person Who Wants an Answer

Dearest Person,

I answered your letter but my editor didn't print it. He always vetoes letters about assholes.

I think that this famous person's asshole was claimed by adoring fans. As to what is now in the spot ... the person must look something like a Barbie doll.

Here's my letter:

Dear Mr. Editor,
Why do you always exclude these kinds of letters? Also, I want my old logo back.
Love,
Doctor Mueller

Dear Doctor Mueller,
In Libya there is the Pesta Bubonica (Bubonic Plague) right now. (This disease hasn't been around since the Middle Ages.) What's going on? I live in Naples on the Mediterranean and Libya isn't far from Naples at all. Should I worry about swimming here? Should I worry about drinking the water? I ask this question because one morning on the beach I found a dead pig washed up in the tide. It looked pretty bad, like it had carbuncles or things on it. What is the deal here?
Signed,
Ciro Ianelli

Ciro:
Don't talk about this too much, the tourism in Italy, Greece, Morocco, and Tunisia will be ruined. Wait a minute, isn't there a cure for this? I haven't heard about this? Where did you read it? But then of course how would I hear about it? A lot of medical news is suppressed in the States. Look, I wouldn't worry about the plague here in Italy, not until people start dropping around you. Then it's time to evacuate the town.
Love,
Doctor Mueller

Dear Doctor Mueller,
Last year here in Positano there was this guy who fucked around pretty much. He fucked with girls and boys, but mostly boys. I won't mention his name but his initials are F.V. Anyway it turns out that he has second-stage syphilis and he didn't know it last year, of course. Now I slept with a guy who slept with him but the guy I slept with had a test and he doesn't have it. My question is: can I

get it even though my mate didn't get it?

Love,

. L.D.

Dear L.D.,

I know this person and there is cause for concern here not just for you. That person got around. Now it has happened many times that people with syphilis don't always spread it—sometimes it just doesn't carry, I don't know why really. I suppose some people are more disposed to it. There have been rumors that people can be carriers; some people never get it but they can give it to other people. The best thing to do is to go immediately to the doctor and have a Wasserman. I don't know what they call the test here in Italy. Go today. Now. This isn't the Middle Ages. There's lots of heavy-duty penicillin around and in Italy I'm sure it works like a charm. Thanks for this information. I know someone in the States who was here last summer that ought to be told about this.

Love,

Doctor Mueller

Dear Doctor Mueller,

I just broke up with my boyfriend after five years of living together. I'm thirty-three. Now I'm back out there cruising in the queer bars, but I feel like a dinosaur with all those young fags around. All the older homos wear leather, but I don't really like that, so I'm sort of displaced and lost. What do I do now? I am lonely. Is there a cure?

Signed,

Shadow & Myself

Dear S&M,

Ooops, Dear Shadow and Yourself, I'm not really authorized to handle these kinds of things but in this case, since I sympathize, I'll give you some answers ... although there aren't many. I hate to say this because it's such a standard retort and it's so (seemingly) insensitive and insufficient ... but you have to dive into your work really deeply. I like to believe things like this happen for a reason. Long-term relationships make one focus solely on the partner and forget about the importance of careers and things like that. You will get used to being alone in time ... at first it's really hard ... I know, I broke up with someone who I lived with for eight years and it took a while to realize that pillows were sometimes the only other forms in the bed with you.

But really, now's the time to make lots of money. Concentrate on this for the duration, don't even think about finding someone else so fast, give yourself a break ... it just happened ... no? As you grow older you become more selective and desirous of lasting relationships instead of one-night stands. But, for a while, I think this is going to be the shape of things. It's actually not so bad, it's great. And don't worry about AIDS, for God's sake ... if you don't have it now, you won't get it. By now we've all been in some form of contact with it ... not everybody gets it, only those predisposed to it. If everyone got it that was introduced to it, half the population of New York would be on death's door by now.

This is a stressful period for you right now, it's like mourning, which is the most stressful condition the human body can undergo. I read this in some medical journal while sitting in the doctor's office. People often die from the stresses caused by mourning. So take those B vitamins by the handfuls.

Love,
Doctor Mueller
P.S. If you concentrate on making lots of money, you'll have all those beauties banging on your door just to be in your rich presence.

Dear Doctor Mueller,

I've heard so much about collagen treatments for wrinkled and aging skin. I don't mean the application of collagen moisturizers, I mean the implanting of collagen. What is it? How does it work? I am seriously thinking about doing this because I am forty years old and I look much older and it isn't fair, dammit!
Collagen Curious

Dear C.C.,

You're right, dammit. Life isn't fair. I know this from experience. But there are ways to

cheat your way to fairness; one is collagen. The skin has two layers, the epidermis and the dermis. The major component of the dermis is the protein called collagen. It is like a nylon stocking. Over time the network of woven fibers weakens and there goes the water and the elastin gets slack like an old rubber band. Every time you frown or squint you put a strain on the collagen. In time you get wrinkles. Sunlight also damages collagen. Now physicians can inject collagen into the skin to supplement the skin's own. It's usually used for the worry lines between the eyebrows, the smile lines from your nose to your lips, and acne scars. So if you have the money, and you probably do since you're thinking about it, then go do it … why look like an old bag if you don't need to?
Love,
Doctor Mueller

Dear Doctor Mueller,
I don't tan very well. People tell me it's because I don't have enough PABA in me. What is PABA? Should I use the tanning creams that include PABA in their makeup?
A White Person

Dear White Person,
PABA is para-aminobenzoic acid. It's an integral part of the vitamin B complex. It is found in liver, yeast, wheat germ, and molasses. The truth about PABA as far as tanning is concerned is that it's a sunscreen. It prevents burning. Persons normally susceptible to sunburn have been able to remain in the sun for hours after applying PABA ointment. Adelle Davis suggests that the ointment delays old-age skin changes such as wrinkles, dry skin, and dark spots. She also says that PABA and folic acid can restore graying or whitening hair to its natural color. Throw away your Grecian Formula!
Love,
Doctor Mueller

Dear Doctor Mueller,
I have some coke-dealing friends who cut their product with all different kinds of things. They use lactose, inositol,

mannite, procaine. What are these things I'm ingesting? Will they hurt me?

A Substance Abuser

Dear Substance Abuser,

Lactose is the sugar present in milk. It's less sweet than sucrose. Inositol is part of the B complex. It has been found to be helpful in brain cell nutrition. It is vital for hair growth and can prevent thinning and balding. In combination with choline, it prevents the fatty hardening of arteries and protects the liver, kidneys, and heart. Caffeine and cocaine can create an inositol shortage in the body, so it's great that cocaine should be cut with this product. Inositol also is beneficial in the treatment of constipation but, then, whoever heard of a constipated cocaine user? Cocaine itself speeds up the metabolism and gives that immediate reaction of having to run to the toilet. This is not always because the cocaine is cut with mannite which is a gentle baby laxative. Procaine is altogether a different story. It is a chemical compound used in place of cocaine as a local anesthetic. Look out for the stuff cut with this. A lot of people have allergic reactions to it. Does this answer your questions? I'd try to find some pure stuff if I were you, but then we don't live in South America, do we? Inositol is the one to go with.

Love,
Doctor Mueller

Dear Doctor,

How can I regulate my periods? I've never had normal cycles. What's wrong with me? I've tried a few nutritional cures.

Sincerely,
Regina P.

Dear Regina,

Well these things are the secret of the sages. In the beginning, men revered women: the mystery of childbirth and menstrual cycles were akin to religious phenomena. Because the cycles were geared to the moon's cycles, the women had the say-so. This was before it was discovered that these female cycles weren't an act of the gods but biological forces necessary for procreation.

Now, you should try licorice root—to a powder in pill form. You can get these in any health food store. Licorice influences the estrogen levels in a woman's body (it doesn't work at all on men) and it also tends to keep women younger. It's a proven fact, in European countries, that women who take these licorice pills maintain fertility into their later years. Menopause and early menopause can be warded off until late in life.

One person asked me, no told me really, "Isn't this column too glib and facile? Sickness is too serious a thing to be joking about."

I believe that sick people can still perceive things that may be funny to them, even if it hurts to laugh. Of course some days may be less funny than others. To take for instance Richard ("And-I-don't-like-the-panties-on-the-curtain-rod") Dreyfus in *Whose Life Is It Anyway?*

But seriously folks, a patient needs to be free from emotional stress, worry, and fear. It has to be a total holistic approach to curing the disease. If the patient is so sick that he lost all his amusing friends that kept him laughing, then he has to stock up on a lot of funny books. TV isn't always hilarious.

Now to mention a little about the subject that is terrifying everyone, AIDS. I keep saying that I won't talk about it, but everyone approaches me with information and questions.

Here's a question, but I'm not sure who first asked it. Do mosquitoes carry AIDS? The anopheles mosquitoes carry malaria, isn't there a type of mosquito that could carry AIDS? To answer this I have to say that there's been no conclusive evidence, although you still wouldn't want to get bitten by a mosquito that had just sucked the blood of an AIDS victim. Now even if the little vampires can carry it, one has to eat lots of raw garlic to prevent them from biting. Really they just don't like the way the blood tastes when a person eats garlic.

Next year I predict a change in what is considered fashionable as far as body size goes. No longer will people want to be svelte and lean. Fat will be in because where there is fat you can be sure there is no AIDS. People by then will be terrified to align themselves with skinny people. Fashion, as we all know, is based on sexual attractions.

This brings up another topic. We all have noticed the way people are avoiding AIDS victims. Of course these are the people who aren't too bright or sensible and have little or no compassion. The victims are having a difficult time. Do not abandon them. *You don't get AIDS through the air, or from looking into the eyes of a victim or even from shaking their hand.* You don't have to put yourself in a plastic bag. You could just as easily be hit by a car and die while you're not looking where you're going when fleeing a very skinny person you think has it. Everybody now living in this city takes their chances every day. This is not the Salem witch hunt. Use some common sense. Relax. If you're not in the high-risk group you're really being ridiculous, and even if you are, there's no point in wasting time worrying. Take some precautions though. Keep your body very strong and don't forget your sense of humor.

Doc,

How come you don't see Siamese twins anymore? Aren't they being born these days?

Joseph Thomas Jacob

Dear JTJ,

Of course they're still being born. But they're being divided. Some are joined at the top of the head, or the abdomen, the chest, and they often share organs or limbs. Most of them are born dead or they die shortly afterward. These days, the doctors always opt for trying to save one of them. You might want to check your pals for telltale scars. At one time there may have been two.

Love,

Doctor Mueller

Dear Doc,

So glad that you're back from Italy. I'm pregnant and I go to a good gyn-ob, but I'm thinking that you might contribute some nutritional insights to the plan. Tell me some good things to remember to make me feel less exhausted and nauseous.

With Child in the Family Way

Dear With,

Pregnancy is a stressful condition and all nutritional needs of the mother increase. Protein, calcium, and iron are especially important to the development of the bones, soft tissue, and blood of the growing child.

Nausea and morning sickness will probably go away if you step up the intake of B vitamins, C, and K. You should always stay away from baking soda and common antacids because they increase fluid retention which can cause lethargy and a feeling of nausea and fullness. Please stay away from drugs, even aspirin. Believe it or not I did it for nine months and didn't have anything except for red wine. Take it easy, the hard part isn't the pregnancy, as you might think, but the hard part comes after the baby is born.

Rest often, read, eat lots but try to not gain any more than twenty-five pounds. Pamper yourself all the time. Cut out that emotional stress.

Read mindless stuff like 1950s comic books.

Good luck, Be Healthy,
The Doc

Art and About (*Details Magazine*)

October 1982

All summer in the city one was accosted by street art outcroppings as thick as a jungle of kudzu plants. Shapely foot-long girls in circles next to telephone receivers on wavy wires hooked to old-fashioned telephones; all this stenciled in black on steps, streets, walls. Out of the subway grilles a plethora of snakes filled the sidewalks, walls bore multicolored teaser paintings enclosed by invisible frames, marked by the code word AVANT. Men's faces with pipes floated in front of one's eyes and the shadow men still lurked around every corner. Trees cast shadows even when there was no sun or light and streets were divided by wide purple lines that zigzagged from curb to curb with the words: 17 Aug 82 Time Line 12:15 pm. The homes of the new International Dateline? Boundaries of the '80s twilight zones? The graffiti is still being waded through.

Here on the streets, aesthetic education is force-fed to New Yorkers whether they like it or not. It's making people feel something. "They need some culture, or maybe a panacea," one graffiti artist told me.

It turns out that all this street art is getting very valuable. New York is becoming the New El Dorado, but instead of streets paved in gold, the streets are paved in art. On black paper on subway platforms people look for new Keith Harings to tear off and take home.

But artists … this fall when you can't help but paint, when you get your high command, it will probably force your hands into the world of 3D. Sculpture. Or at least *trompe l'oeil*. Figures will rise from their canvas restraints.

One very hot Saturday not so long ago I escaped from the shoulder-to-shoulder cluster of torsos, arms, legs, and heads on the "dancing part" of the Coney Island boardwalk. In my blind retreat from this second throbbing mob I found myself in front of the "Hell Hole," the walk-in Fun House, although, judging from the exterior of this hole, the word "fun" was optional. The entire eighty-by-sixty-foot facade of the "Hell Hole" is a huge painting by Fabio (whoever he is … someone on the carny art circuit, no doubt). "Adante Shake Hammer and Blow Struck" is probably the title of this mural; anyway, that's what's written on a devil's book of music which is propped up on an organ. The devil faces the keys and when he hits a key, a hand from the top of the organ pounds a mallet on the toes of unfortunate people chained and hanging above the organ, thus the music of screams. Another devil in this mural is pouring Epsom salt solutions into the mouths of people strapped to toilets whose funnels empty into a river where about sixteen people in obvious agony are trying to stay afloat in this river of shit. What a commission that Fabio undertook! The mind reels when one thinks of the thousands of innocent children passing this hole each season who are subjected to scatological aesthetic education.

Farther along and down from the boardwalk on Surf Avenue is the Wax Museum, owned and managed by eighty-one-year-old Lilly. She sits in a bandbox out front with a microphone and barks about what's inside. Hardly anyone goes in despite the cheap ($1.00) entrance fee. They don't realize that they're missing art, and aside from the culture, the Wax Museum is the only place that offers a respite from squealing sticky children, dancers, screaming roller-coaster riders, drunks, the Polar Bear Club, disco dodgem cars, and slippery hotdogs desperately squeezing themselves between boardwalk planks. (Less agile, older folks fall on these slippery dogs, making a big mess!) What's inside is pure Americana, a jumble of wax folk art, effigies of well-known politicians, musicians, murderers, human oddities. There's Lina Medina lying in her hospital bed, staring coolly at the ceiling, not caring a damn that she just gave birth to a six-pound baby that a nurse is proudly displaying. Of course the fact that the little mother is just five years old and, as the news clipping says, "Lina Medina still had her baby teeth when she bore this infant," makes her rate a wax image. Nat King Cole and Muhammad Ali share a cubicle, although I doubt they recognize one another because the likenesses leave something to be desired. There's Elvis in full white-denim-stretch-plastic-gem-studded regalia. Lilly told me that this outfit was terribly expensive; in fact she mentioned the cost of Elvis's outfit so many times, I got the feeling that she begrudges him that outfit. Madame Chiang Kai-shek, Governor Dewey, and General MacArthur stare into space from behind their chicken wire, but their faces are still youthful and waxy, unlike the Duke and Duchess of Windsor, whose peeling and flaking faces make them look like mummies. Their box is too small for them—you can't see their heads unless you stand very close. Mayor LaGuardia, looking exactly like Lou Costello, is also having trouble with his face—it looks like thick crushed velvet. Lilly confessed that once, long ago while she was away, the temporary manager stupidly slipped sixty-watt bulbs into the dummies' pens to brighten the place up a bit. Sixty watts was just too much and the wax began to melt, thus the peeling faces. Now all the wax men and women live in murky dimness, a bit morbid under the bare low-wattage bulbs that hang near their skulls. Lilly has never entrusted "her people" to anyone else since.

Arms that had fallen off have been lovingly but unimaginatively reattached with scotch tape, clothes are safety-pinned. Bits of furniture have been used before by real people. John and Robert Kennedy and Martin Luther King sit numbly together at a table dressed in stained suits from local Salvation Army thrift stores. Across from them is Richard Speck murdering a nurse on a cot. John Lennon with the sign above him "ALWAYS SOMETHING NEW" stands in a dirty white linen suit dotted with peace buttons. The record album *Revolver* floats around his body. Hickman "The Fox," leaning over a bathtub cutting up little Marion Parker, is literally losing his head at the neck.

At a Halloween party at the museum last year, I happened to meet the wax artist who made all the newer dummies. I don't remember his name and Lilly couldn't remember it either, but he looked exactly like Lee J. Cobb with glasses. Lilly is thinking of selling the museum when she's ninety. That's a pity because, surely, without her it will lose all its charm. Lilly said that even though she is old she has never given up her enthusiasm for the beautiful things in life: trees, grass, clouds, birds, and Chanel No. 5. She won't give up the place until she has a Marilyn Monroe, because, as she says, "People feel close to Marilyn." A wax artist once tried to make her a Marilyn but the wax formula wasn't right and she came out too soft. "But then Jack Kennedy is too hard," Lilly smiled.

October 1983

In Bucks County, Pennsylvania, where in days past Arlene Francis put on her heart necklace in preparedness for *What's My Line* and Dorothy Parker puttered in gardens with rubber gloves while Lillian Hellman knitted, I lounged by the pool in the not-so-distant past on the horse farm where a few years ago Brooke Shields kept her dappled gray horse. Here I made up my mind that I should spend the summer in Italy. Behind me and the poolside blue spruces was an incredible landscape, like a painting by Eakins, with a huge modern barn where the horses, famous horses, the kind that jump eight-foot obstacles at Madison Square Garden, flicked their tails at occasional flies in better accommodations than my apartment back in Greenwich Village.

Later on, I sat in the Jacuzzi getting drunk on champagne while Jared and John, the people who lived there, splashed around and put in so much bubble bath that the Jacuzzi over-flowed and its contents seeped through the ceiling to the floor below, short-circuiting the chandelier and ruining the dining room table and the oriental rug. It was a disaster. After the Jacuzzi incident, we went straight to a drag show where an eighty-year-old show-person named Danny Windsor did cart-wheels in her floor-length sequined gown and high heels. Having experienced the Jacuzzi and Danny Windsor I thought I should indeed go to Italy for a little Old World influence.

Before I jumped on the plane to Rome I went to visit the Tibetan Museum. What a find. On October 16 it will have the Tibetan Harvest Festival, and on November 13 director Rod Preiss takes the visitors on a trek to the home of the Abominable Snowman and Shangri-la. This should be amusing. The museum is high in the hills of Staten Island at 338 Lighthouse Avenue, near the Frank Lloyd Wright home.

A few days later I jumped on the plane to Rome, sleeping the entire eleven hours, and when I got there I wondered very seriously why I was there. It was just as hot as in New York City and everyone I called to say Hi to wasn't there. I thought of the Amalfi Coast and Positano, where I know this rare person named Vali, so I headed south for Naples. There weren't any interesting people on the train except for very young American tourists from Connecticut wearing dirty backpacks. One of them asked me what Naples was really like, was it actually really scary, and did she have to keep her money belt close to her heart and weren't there an awful lot of horribly sleazy people there? I answered yes but they have the best sense of humor while they're cutting your purse strings. I also warned her that the Neapolitan dialect has nothing to do with Italian, so even if she thought she could speak Italian she wouldn't be able to understand anybody and the devilish plans they were cooking up. That shut her up for a bit.

I got off the train and there was Naples, the city and its people poor, like alphabet town here. I called an old friend, Enzo, and found him as he had been years ago doing his summer job as gigolo of the train station. With him and his two young Swedish conquests, I rode around the city and looked at the Bay of Naples by night; then we stopped at a strip bar and watched some incredible women remove their clothes ...

The next day Sergio came by on his 1200 Moto Guzzi, and he and I went off in a cloud of dust, headed for the Amalfi Coast. He warned me that no one ever rode with him because he drove too fast; he was right about that. The wind hurt my ears so much that I thought for sure the drums were punctured. In that forty-five-minute drive, moving along at 120 miles an hour without helmets, along curves thousands of feet above the rocks and the sea, I learned how to *give up*. If this was going to be the end, I would go without a whimper, like a yogi. Later at his sister's house in Positano, we had squid, mussels, octopus, shrimp, pasta Bolognese, pasta pesto, soup, rice, salad, cheese, arugula, asparagus, spinach, tomatoes, peppers, fruit, coffee, cakes, wine, and liquor with his cousins, aunts, uncles, brothers, sisters, mother, father, grandparents, sons, and daughters. The wife had disappeared a few years ago. After this I was exhausted.

The next day I woke up in Positano, threw open the ancient turn-of-the-fifteenth-century doors, and walked out on the terrace. Above me was the pre–Dark Ages, pre-Renaissance town, clinging to the rocks of the three-peaked Monte Sant'Angelo rising to five thousand feet, and below me was the turquoise water of the Mediterranean and the Church of the Holy Virgin with its gold dome. In the distance rose Capri, such a playland, and the Galli Islands, which are none other than the Odyssean siren islands. Could anything ever be better?

I met a girl from Berlin named Iris on the beach that day and I moved in with her. This began my weeks of villa-hopping. I had planned to do a lot of writing and serious things like that but after a few more days I realized that I'd have to shelve this idea because there was the water and the sun and all this wine to consume and food to get fat on and nightclubs to dance in. The sea there is so salty that I fell asleep floating on the surface. At night the music in the clubs is basically New York music except for an occasional Neapolitan hit such as "I'm Walking into La Dolce Vita."

One morning at seven, I was returning home from the Privilege, one of the clubs, with Antonio, who was extremely handsome and odd, and the DJ Marco, when a fattish, older man in a Maserati stopped us. He invited us to come to his villa for cocaine, which I didn't care much about, but I decided to go to do some comparative shopping as far as villas were concerned. When we walked in, we were greeted by awful art and a half-grown female lion. So while the men amused themselves I put on the padded gloves and played with the lion who, although she wasn't declawed and had sizable incisors, was surprisingly tender-mouthed and polite.

Later that week I met a urologist from Bologna who had his private four-seater airplane tucked away at the Naples airport. We flew for a day trip to Yugoslavia, across the Adriatic over the Hvar, Korcula, Mljet, and Vis Islands. I really did want to see the Borgo Pass and the Carpathian Mountains as described in Bram Stoker's *Dracula*, but as the urologist said, "Yugoslav petrol is far different than Italian," so we didn't land. The whole time he talked about his work … penile implants, various inventions for impotent men, his own personal ideas on the subject. I knew a little about the subject myself so we discussed the wire insert and the water-pump innovation.

I went to Capri a lot, since it was only thirty minutes by hydrofoil from Positano. It seemed like a good idea to go the first time on the six o'clock boat, since I had heard so much about the nightclub Numero Due. With a young plastic surgeon, who by the way assured me that my tattoos could be easily removed, we left, had dinner there, and stayed all night at the club. The place was packed with that special breed of playboys—I call them pappagallos (parrots)—the gold chain, tricolored Gucci shoes, and matching tricolored silk shirt types who, if you ask them what they do, will answer, "Import-export." We left Capri that morning at nine but I returned many times to see the rest of the island, which has been extolled for hundreds of years for good reason. But summer is not the best time to go there. It's too crowded.

On August 15, Positano, as well as the rest of Italy, closes up for the Feast of the Assumption (commemorating the day that Mary the Virgin bodily ascended into heaven). Of course there were fireworks. Practically every Sunday there were fireworks for some patron saint of the coastal towns, but the fireworks for Ferragosto, as they call this holiday, rival the Brooklyn Bridge centennial celebrations as far as ingenuity goes. The show didn't start until one in the morning, the appropriate time as far as I was concerned.

A few days later I met a couple from Naples with a sixty-foot sailboat with schooner rigging, and since I knew something about sailing I crewed with them for the day. We sailed to Galli Island, presently owned by Tania Massine, wife of the Russian dancer. We anchored and swam for a bit, and I really did hear the sirens wailing but then I had been drinking the local red wine with the strange sludge at the bottom. I watched the sun sink over the island, which is just sheer rocks rising from the sea with a bizarre castle perched on the top. In the distance there was Positano and to the north Capri, all in semi-twilight. I decided that I would learn how to read Italian so that I could understand Dante in the original language. I wanted to know in his own words what he had to say about Paradise.

December 1984

These days, if you aren't certain about the difference between a classically beautiful, enduring, engaging, expressive piece of art and a piece of froth, you are not alone. Lately, many people have told me that they aren't even sure of what they like anymore. But there is a way to spot the good stuff even if you don't know the first thing about line, color, minor shadows, rhythm, and the third dimension. It's easy. All you have to do is imagine the painting in question under a fluorescent light in a dingy little room, against a really ugly wall—one with cracking, yellow-stained, and finger-smudged wallpaper. If the painting looks good in this setting, you've found the masterpiece for you.

This is a glib and facile joke, but it makes the point.

Sometimes, walking into a gallery can be scary—not because the art is shocking or because the art-hopping hobnobbers are dressed in a frightening manner, but because you can never be sure that what you are seeing is the truth. The walls are white, so there is no color competition. The lighting is perfect. It is a whole package. This is the marketplace, the store. Its existence is determined by sales.

When I went to a gallery as a kid, my mother made me be very quiet, as if I was in a shrine or a museum. I could never understand this. She said we had to shut up because people were trying to make up their minds about how the artwork personally affected them. My father told me what the real story was. We had to be quiet because buyers were trying to figure out if the prices matched their budget. At a tender age I found that it was the hype that was important, that people could be coerced by good advertising. A gift looks better if it comes in a special box.

What a flimsy way to look at art. But lately, the owners, dealers, investors, patrons, and, of course, the artists themselves are looking at it this way. In this strange atmosphere, where businessmen are trying to have the eyes of artists and artists are trying to act like businessmen, nobody remains the same. The artist begins to lose his art and the businessman becomes temperamental. What used to be called the victory of art over tyranny doesn't exist anymore. There is no such thing. Everybody is working together in one big happy art pie.

May 1985

Suppose, just for a moment, that everything physical and tangible was an *art trend*. Everything: food, clothing, shelter, water, trees, animals, sex. This is a wild thing to imagine. But if it were so, the sun, which normally hatches hot from the East River and falls at dusk into the Hudson, would come to an abrupt stop right above Tompkins Square Park. Geographically, this is the dead center of the little hamlet known as the East Village.

Now, suppose instead that everything was art. Naturally, the word "art" is different for everyone. But we can all agree that art is spirit in matter, that it is the noblest of all noble things, that it is beauty, however we perceive that word. Now, if everything was art, then the sun would not stop above the East Village. It would travel normally. If everything was art, then the sun would still work the way it always does. It wouldn't halt or linger.

But limelight, that garish bright blaster, would. Unlike sunlight, limelight has, more or less, the qualities of neon. Sunlight has been around for at least a few billion years, while a neon light lasts a few months or, used sparingly, a few years.

So why is the limelight shining so bright on the East Village right now? How did this all happen? Simple. A few years ago, people who write about art in lower Manhattan publications started drawing attention to a bunch of less-than-rich-but-very-stylish creators who happened to live and work in the East Village. A trend never begins without journalists; given some space in a newspaper or magazine they will write about anything. And because of the dearth of other definable art trends, small waves, and then a little rumble started downtown. Then the uptown culture-seekers became hungry for news about the scene. Then the rest of the USA wanted to know. Now the world ... BAM! HISTORY!

Maybe in art schools in 2058 (if they exist), the textbooks for American art history courses will have chapters on East Villagism or the East Villagistic Period. Midterm exams will feature questions like: What was the East Village? When did it happen? Who were the forerunners? Students will memorize painters' names and even the names of some of their paintings (in light of this, you less literate artists should simplify things and use film and book titles for your work).

Environmentalism of art trends is nothing new. All over the world, in every city and burg, there have always been enclaves where creative souls hung out and did their creating. People, like rodents, tend to gather in groups seeking their own peers. And like rodents, human beings are always excited by group movements. By nature we are easily led to believe that groups are stronger, happier, and more solvent than lone individuals. If a group happens to band together because of art (the one word in history that has never had bad press except in fascist times), then that group must be okay, or at the very least interesting and romantic.

Now, in the history books on the East Villagistic Period there will also be facts, hard and cold, to swallow: that 80 percent of all East Village art looked the same; that 70 percent of it was inspired by money; that 60 percent of it was rendered by impostors; and 50 percent of it was expendable. But wait. This is not so horrible. Remember, every era has its style. Money is not necessarily evil. People who make art don't always have to be the aesthetic, sensitive types. And yes indeed, 50 percent of most creativity is expendable. One has to eliminate things that are less than sublime.

For those of you gentle readers who have just discovered that the big boom in the East Village was initially brought about by art, remember that East Village art is nothing new. Back in 1965, when at fifteen years of age I was visiting the East Village from my hometown of Baltimore on a mission as a bathtub LSD tester, there was plenty of art and creators and artists hanging around. In fact, the East Village then was in its glory. Now the hype is coming around for a second time. Only this time there is so much money pouring into the area that its face and spirit are not the same.

Still, nothing remains the same—not in New York City, anyway. The only constant we have here is change. Change is seen as something evil only by those who have lost their youth or sense of humor. Remember, with change comes hope—this is another constant. But I can't help but wonder if all those designer food emporiums will accept food stamps from the elderly Polish and Puerto Rican residents. And where in the neighborhood will poor people go when they want to eat out for an evening and don't want sushi? And what about the East Village artists who haven't quite made it yet? How in the world are they going to be able to afford the rent on their studios? What are they going to eat?

Oh, forget about food. Who needs to eat when you can feast your eyes on all this art. There sure is enough to see in the hamlet now. One can get fat—at the very least one's eyes will grow, the same way pupils dilate when you take a mind-expanding drug. Get ready for fat eyes.

June 1986

I am here this month to distract you. In this column, you are about to read—or skip over—some useless but interesting trivia, some topics for conversation, some well-guarded but cheap baubles, some dime-store details and some insignificant information about art. All of it is worthless but all of it is true, and that is something.

You see, there is little consolation to be found these days and we haven't too much unexpended ammunition left from the few weapons in our peculiar arsenal. One of our very finest weapons is art and it is being badly mistreated. It could be used strategically to influence events.

While mad dogs involve an innocent populace in their personal thoughts, while nuclear meltdowns are scaring everybody, while catastrophes and plagues are reducing us to base humans, and while our art is being bandied about in dumb commercials, stupid movies, mindless paintings, goofy theater pieces about insipid extramarital affairs, and dance works about flower blossoms in spring, we have to relax and hang onto a sense of humor … I guess.

Yes, we have to either relax or do the opposite. Perhaps we artists should plan a dramatic artful evangelical showstopper, some kind of world-newsworthy plea for peace. (Of course, we have to do some religious research first. We can't make complete fools of ourselves the way Warren Austin, the U.S. ambassador to the United Nations, did during the 1948 war in the Middle East. He went on record urging the Arabs and the Jews to resolve their disagreements "like good Christians.")

For now, take a respite. Worry about international traumas and personal politics later. Let me entertain you.

I was reading about how the restoration work on the Sistine Chapel is coming along. You may remember that I told you months ago about this task, which is being undertaken mostly by the Japanese, as the Italians don't seem to care much about all that old stuff. While I was reading, I pictured the painting and then remembered that great theological debate about Adam's and Eve's belly buttons. You may think this is really too insignificant to concern yourself with these days, but just stop and think about it for a moment.

Because Adam and Eve were created, not born, they should be depicted without navels. Some of the paintings from the Middle Ages and Renaissance show Adam and Eve with navels, some don't. You can imagine the personal anguish each artist went through deciding what to do about this. You can imagine the heated arguments. Michelangelo opted for a navel on Adam, and I'm sure the fundamentalists will never forgive him. Don't tell Jerry Falwell; maybe he hasn't noticed.

I began thinking about other restoration jobs and the restorers themselves. They are a patient lot. The woman working on Leonardo's *Last Supper* will probably be there for another fifty years at the rate she's going, inch by painful inch. I wonder if restorers have a social life? All those I know are obsessive about their work. They don't go out much unless it has to do with art. They are so well informed about art history that they really ought to be critics as well.

I have a friend who is a restorer. She is extremely beautiful, visually and otherwise, and works on mummies—a touchy, crumbly job. Those tired moldy old kings are lucky to be in her hands. She told me an interesting fact little known in the art world today. In ancient Egypt the royal embalmers used an ingredient called asphaltum on their dead. Asphaltum is a preservative and a great base for paint that gets even better—in fact is unsurpassed in quality—when it's aged. Four thousand years is quite a time to mellow. So lately, in recent centuries that is, some enterprising art suppliers and artists exhumed the mummies and ground them into powder to make paint. Think of the joy of owning a painting that holds on its canvas the body of some charismatic pharaoh. All the time-honored legends and archaeological greatness, the ancient strength, is right there. Hopefully the subject matter of these paintings isn't tacky. It would be a shame if one of those pharaoh's bodies wound up as a bad still life. Or just imagine King Mentuhotep of the Eleventh Dynasty, unsold and forgotten in some second-hand shop in a back street in Cairo, moldering as the medium for a chintzy fifties-style painting of the Great Pyramids at sunset.

Talking about human-being art, I am reminded of Chris Burden, the California artist who, with real nails hammered into his palms, was crucified on top of a Volkswagen. He also had himself shot with a .22 for another human-being piece of art. This is a painful way to make art, and without the sales of the photos of these pieces it isn't the most lucrative "body" of work.

Then of course there was that Milanese artist, Piero Manzoni, who gave part of his human self as art and about art. His piece was called *Mierda d'Artista* and it was just that—a few cans of the artist's fecal matter. I'm sure collectors weren't beating the door down for that sculpture. Was he trying to tell us something or was it just a simple relic?

Oh, just relax. I didn't want to get you started thinking about politics. Not with all this inspired work floating around. I could cite some more examples of other good art, but I'll wait until there's some other world catastrophe.

October 1986

ITALY—The only Americans who arrived in Italy this summer were the chutzpahniks, harum-scarums, born travelers, and of course the artists. The polyester-clad, camera-wielding, shopping-mall hags were too wary of having a Klinghoffer vacation. Their blood curdled at the mere thought of getting on an airplane headed due east across the Atlantic. In truth I don't blame them. The thought crossed my mind as well when I got on the Pan Am flight for Rome. But I left my mind open so the thought would whistle right through like the wind.

Nary an American could be seen posing for Polaroids at the fountains in Rome or digging around the digs of Pompeii. No American slang echoed in the marble halls of Florentine museums.

The banks of Milan exchanged few American dollars for lire. And Naples ... well, Naples never was popular with the Americans in the Italian tour package.

This year the Americans were happy to stay on home turf. We threw ourselves like lemmings into the comfortable abyss of patriotism—I say we, but I wasn't there. Still, as I watched the July 4th hoopla via satellite in Italy I felt a strange warmth, like patriotism swelling in my heart—but perhaps it was merely pasta pesto indigestion.

Actually, the reason Americans didn't leave home this year was directly attributable to journalists. American journalists are a fine breed. Don't you love American news ... the drama, the wild human interest sagas, the yellowness, the theatrics? It's show biz in its most accessible form. Being somewhat of a media hound, I read most newspapers, including the *New York Post* and the *National Enquirer*, and watch documentaries, docudramas, and television news. I know the reason why my fellow Americans were afraid to come to Europe this summer. Do you remember what the Post said about Khadafy back in June? He was running around in dresses, the journalists told us. This is the picture most Americans had in their minds:

Khadafy is patrolling Europe in a helicopter or some other surveillance vehicle. He is dressed as a mad dog drag queen and looks below at the cowering Europeans scattering in his wake. On the ground, armed with machine guns and primitive bombs, are legions of transvestite disciples ready to kidnap any person who is wearing polyester Bermuda shorts and has a Budweiser beer belly. In Paris, American tourists are roped to the top of the Eiffel Tower, cameras still swinging around their necks. In Venice, the gondolas on the Grand Canal are riding low in the water, full of Americans pleading for their lives with a sadistic Libyan macho man in lipstick, mascara, and pink Spandex. Scenes like this are happening in every tourist city in Europe.

Yes, American news is show biz. What is actually happening in Europe is a bit less dramatic. In fact, it's peaceful.

But let's change the subject to art.

Many years ago, sometime after the great Renaissance in Italy, a pope (the name of the exact one escapes me) woke up one morning and decided that most of the statues around him were indecent. What bothered him most were those male appendages—those vulgar things—so he decreed that these statues should be cleaned up a bit. He had most of the offending marble organs lopped off and replaced with fig leaves. He was proud. The statues now had pristine Ken Doll crotches.

But what happened to all those severed phalluses? Did some quirky rebel stash them? Apparently so, because in the National Museum of Naples (one of the best museums of its kind in the world) there is a room of hundreds of them, rows and rows of them. In this room, day after day, a woman bends over these marble pieces. It is her life's work to decipher which thing belongs to which statue. It is a mammoth job requiring superhuman dedication. When acquaintances ask her what she does, what can she answer? Is there some official title for the job she does? There must be a word for it in Italian.

On the isle of Capri this summer a New York contingent of the updated international artists gathered to savor a bit of *la dolce vita*. In Capri there is more than enough of that to go around. There were Paola Igliori Chia, David McDermott, Peter McGough, Philip Taaffe, and Diego Cortez, among others.

Diego was on the phone. "Okay, so sell the pink one. Okay? Yes, then ciao." He hangs up and the phone starts ringing again. He picks it up but it crackles and dies so he hangs up. "It's difficult to do work by phone here," he sighed.

"It's difficult to work at all here," I commiserated, "… too many divine distractions." But between diversions, McDermott and McGough are painting away and David Bowes, who is just a hydrofoil hop across the Tyrrhenian Sea in Naples, is painting while recovering from a broken leg suffered in a motorcycle accident. Accidents aren't rare in Naples, considering that if you stop your car at a red light, the drivers behind you start blowing their horns. "Why the hell are you stopping at a red light?" they ask incredulously. Drivers plow right through red lights here, sometimes for green lights they slow down a bit. Motorcyclists have an even tougher time.

Anyway, we were all sitting at a table having dinner and there next to us was Achille Lauro, the son of the Achille Lauro of recent Abul Abbas/Klinghoffer fame. (Achille Lauro is the name of the man who owns the boat which bears his name.) After he left we thought of the perfect way to make headlines here in Italy—and America too. Picture this as a headline: MADCAP VANGUARD NEW YORK ARTISTS KIDNAP ACHILLE LAURO and the first sentence of the story reads: "An international group who call themselves The Artists today turned the tables on Achille Lauro at a Mediterranean eatery." The real story might have been that we simply invited Achille Lauro to our table for drinks. But if in the vicinity there had been a wild-eyed journalist, desperate for a good story … well, you can see how these things snowball. That, dear readers, is journalism.

November 1986

NAPLES—Gravity is a burden. Human beings are overweight, a hefty bunch. Without anti-G suits we are a cumbersome lot; all these two hundred (and some) bones, water, amino acids, organs, and muscle pulp are nothing to scoff at. And then there are all those embarrassing bodily functions to make matters seem heavier: eating, moving about, eliminating. The act of being alive certainly is an oppressive job. We haul the mass with each step. Going up stairs is good for the buns but it's a mammoth chore. Getting out of bed in the morning is a Promethean task.

Is there any way to lessen the anguish of gravity? All we want to do is rise above the weight. How? Here are a few possibilities:

1) Love. You've heard the expression "walking on air."

2) Philosophy. Well-known as a medium for transcendentalism.

3) Religion. The highway for the freedom-bound.

4) Creativity. One seems to float when the piece is finished.

5) Culture. Remember when your second-grade teacher told you that books will open a new world for you? Art falls into this category, but not all art can ease the pain of gravity. Some art makes it worse. Last there is:

6) Humor. This is the more logical path toward levity. It is famous for lightening the load. It's no mistake that the word gravity can be used in two ways; somber seriousness and the earth's magnetic pull are quite alike. So humor is all the anti-gravity gear we need. It's the best aircraft.

A person who doesn't have a sense of humor sees every minute bringing a new insurmountable disaster. Hara-kiri often seems a pleasant, viable solution.

It has been proven that people are born with a sense of humor. Obviously some people are more well-endowed than others, but it is bizarre to think that we were automatically gifted with an eye for irony. And apparently we could lose our innate sense of humor somewhere along the line as we grow.

I saw a documentary not long ago that supported the biological humor angle. It was about two brothers, identical twins who were put up for adoption at birth. One (call him Bob) was adopted into a cheerful home of Italian-Americans. It was a fun bunch, so they claimed. He was happy, he got bicycles for Christmas and stuff like that. The other (call him Ed), on the other hand, wasn't ever really adopted by anybody. He stayed in the orphanage for many years and then went from foster home to foster home. It was grim.

When Bob was thirty-five he went on vacation to Rio. One night at a restaurant, the waiter asked him why he was eating there on his one night off. Since he was the chef there six days a week, didn't he want a break from the place? Bob didn't know what the waiter was talking about, but soon it became clear that someone named Ed who looked exactly like him worked there. The next night Ed and Bob met for the first time. They discovered that they were twins, but more importantly they discovered that they both had Austrian third-grade schoolteachers for wives, both used this obscure toothpaste called Vademecum, both drove the same model car, wore the same designer clothes … even had the same hairdos.

All this was so weird that scientists and doctors took an interest. They tested them for any peculiarity. One test involved putting them in separate soundproof rooms and playing a comedy tape to both simultaneously. The twins were wired for their heart rates and emotional responses (i.e., laughter). They responded exactly the same to every joke—the brain wave graphs were identical. A sense of humor is apparently not something you learn.

If you are afraid that you might not possess a sense of humor, there are a few things you can do to fake one. Faking something most often brings on the real thing sooner or later. If you are the kind of person who is usually deadpan, lumpish, and grave, and you're having an especially depressing day on top of that, stop for a minute and consider a few step-by-step rules toward achieving a sense of humor. Dissect your day in your mind. Rehash all the episodes. The one that is most hideously low-down will be better remembered. Okay. Look at the scene in your mind's eye. Let us imagine that you met your landlady in the hallway when you were off to look for work because you just got fired. The conversation with her starts off pleasantly enough, but she reminds you that you are two months late with the rent and she's also nosy enough to know that you're supposed to be at work Wednesday morning at 11:30. She mentions this. You get angry and you have a fight. It becomes violent. She has just returned from grocery shopping and she throws a head of romaine lettuce at you. Then tomatoes. You throw your job-hunter's newspaper on the wall-to-wall carpeting and storm out of the building as she yells at you about beginning eviction procedures. This would be considered depressing to even the best of black comedy aficionados.

Now, believe it or not, this incident can be funny. Worrying about it isn't going to change it anyway, so you might as well relax and turn it into farce. But how does one do this? Okay. Look at the whole picture. Imagine it's a movie you're watching in a theater or on TV. How do you see this episode? Is it in black and white? How big is your landlady in your mind's eye? Are you in the scene, or are you like the objective watcher?

Okay. You visualize the whole episode in color, the landlady is three inches tall and you are the observer. What you must do is to change the perspective on the scene. The scene isn't in color, it's in black and white. Your landlady isn't three inches tall, she's a giant, nine inches tall. You aren't the observer, you're in the picture too, but slightly bigger than she is. The scene you remembered had the landlady in a regular frontal shot. Change that, too. Look at the scene from overhead. The whole picture is suddenly much different. You can see the dark roots of the landlady's bleached hair. You can see the funny white antique bra she's wearing. You can even see exactly what she has in the grocery bag, stuff like imitation margarine and Charmin toilet paper. Already that makes you crack a smile.

With this changed perspective you see yourself not as the victim, but a little superior—you remember you're taller now. You see yourself a head taller than she, you have no dark roots, no fake hair, no dirty white bra. You look rather chic, taking care of biz with the newspaper, looking natty. She looks tired. You don't. While she looks wrinkled and haggard from shopping, you look fresh and well-combed, straight from the bubble bath.

Now we get to the verbal argument. You remember the words practically verbatim. But with the changed perspective, there is no dialogue, just music like that accompanying a silent film. Better yet, you could put a laugh track in there, canned laughter like on the sitcoms. This is getting good. Now she's yelling but you don't hear the words, you just see the mouth moving. Exaggerate it. Her mouth becomes as big as a watermelon.

That's pretty funny and you actually chuckle. Next you see the lettuce and tomatoes being flung at you. They bounce off you and land on the floor, but not in messy smashed disarray—suddenly they're a tempting salad and you strut out along a beautiful green and red path, out the door. Now you burst into uproarious laughter. You have definitely changed the perspective. You have done the sublime. You have taken a disturbing situation and caught the paradoxical comedy that lies there. Hidden and waiting in just about every ordinary event is potential humor. Now you know. All you need to do is to work on applying it.

There are other ways to attain a sense of humor, but I have given you the best shot first. Here is another but less effective way: Listen to jokes and make yourself laugh at them. Remember them as well as you can and recite them to the mirror until you have them down perfectly. Then try them on your friends. If you really are a person who doesn't have a sense of humor perhaps you have no friends, so you'll have to go to a bar, have a few drinks, and make friends with the bartender. He will always listen to your jokes. Bartenders not only listen to jokes but they are also great psychiatrists … providing it's a slow night. Once the bartender hears the great jokes he will get other people to listen to them and you will have an audience. There is nothing better than to have people laughing at your material. This will give you a well-hewn sense of humor.

There is only one problem with this tactic. If you admittedly have no friends then you probably haven't heard any good jokes lately. You could get them from a late-night TV talk show, but usually those are not very relevant. I will now tell you a few passable jokes that you have my permission to pass on.

The first one is about the very subject of having a sense of humor and not worrying about grave issues. A man goes to a doctor because his finger looks really bad. The doctor tells him that he has to cut the finger off because it's gangrenous. He goes to another doctor who looks at the finger, and this one says it is totally cancerous and fungus-ridden. It must be amputated, he says. The man decides to go to a third doctor for a third opinion. The doctor, who happens to have a sense of humor, looks at the finger for a few moments. The man tells him that he was told by two other doctors that he has to have the finger cut off. The doctor looks at the finger again and says, "Don't worry. You don't have to have it cut off. It'll fall off by itself."

That wasn't great, but here's another, quite an appropriate one too, considering we're discussing gravity. This one was Albert Einstein's favorite.

One day a man was speaking with God, asking him a few questions, seeking advice and help. The man asked, "God, what is a million years to you?"

"My son," God answered, "a million years to me is exactly a minute, a little minute."

Then the man asked, "Well then, God, what is a million dollars to you?"

God answered, "A million dollars to me is but a mere penny."

"Well God," the man said, "if this is so, I want to ask a small favor. Could I have one of those pennies?"

Then God said, "Oh surely. Just wait a minute."

This is supposedly an art column, so here is another joke, about art, which I made up just yesterday: How many artists does it take to screw in a lightbulb? Answer: None. Their assistants do it.

December/January 1987

This is a rare period in human history. Never have so many with so little become so big for a duration of time so short. Never before has such a shiftless bunch of life's lightweights hewn such formidable nests for themselves in so many people's minds. Never before have the woody, meandering paths of directionless plodders led to the blazing floodlit clearing in the forest, the center ring for the mini–history makers.

This is the age of the fleeting media stars. Watch the news. Read the papers. These stars are easy to forget.

If you're the kind of person who fiercely wants to be hot news but doesn't have patience and doesn't like to work hard, you're in luck these days. In fact, here in the late 1980s hard work is sort of detrimental if you really want to get famous fast. You don't have to do much—witness the people in comas who became media celebs for just lying there. Look at the jobless media hounds who air famous people's dirty laundry, or bring skeletons out of famous people's closets and then wind up as big names themselves on talk shows or in front-and-center magazine spreads.

Good for them; they're enterprising Americans. They've become celebrities for little or no reason, and while they were at it they created jobs for other people. They've put the journalists, newscasters, PR people, all the media movers to hard work. One hand washes the other.

Ratings-conscious TV news producers are here to help these meteoric stars, by pushing their newscaster journalists to find newsworthy stories. The journalists have to deliver, so they seek out the bright, brief rocketeers. There is no reason for anyone to be reticent about being a news item. If you care to be the newest fireball in the media, just give one of those journalists a call. They'd love to hear from you. Jump into the spotlight and dance. If your story is tawdry and sensational, human interest stuff, you're sure to be exploitable. If you're gaudy but simple enough, the world will understand you. Modern rapid-communications systems will have no problem with you. It is the age of the TV tabloid, the *National Enquirer* gone video.

When I speak of these fleeting media celebs, I'm not speaking of artists. They are another breed, untouchables, sacred. They find it difficult to make the pages of the supermarket mags and TV news tabloids. Woe to the poor artist who is still painting on canvas; he may well get rich, but such an archaic medium will never rate overnight success, and certainly not immediate superstardom. Real art will never make anyone famous really fast: there's too much hard work involved.

Besides, art sits on a throne. It is sought as an answer to intellectual problems. The highest expression of art isn't understood by most people.

Art, the old-fashioned kind, doesn't reach very many people. How can a bunch of paintings in a bunch of galleries reach as many people as a bunch of TVs in a bunch of living rooms? Obviously painting has to go beyond the galleries to accomplish this, like subway graffiti did. Keith Haring is one modern artist who has straddled popular culture and the elite intellectualism of the hallowed galleries, transfusing his vision into both. He brought art out on public walls. Andy Warhol crossed these barriers too. He mass-produced art, like Ford did Model Ts, but other than these two artists, who is there, and what other artist would dare the criticism now?

Everyone is patiently waiting for a new expression in art, but art is busy supporting itself as a religion. It doesn't have time to support an evolution, so it becomes mired in redundancy. Could it ever bounce around as mass media? If people understood it, it could, but it needs a public translation. Modern art should come with instructions for use.

Why is art in the position of a top-drawer fossil, an elite loner, a pedantic cultural dinosaur? Shouldn't art try to act as judge and jury to make public opinion change? Is the general public too retarded?

Perhaps this is the only way art can be, elitist and completely unproletarian. Who wants the huddled masses setting up shanties in the galleries anyway?

It can go on this way forever … all the artists will be wearing tuxedos in glittering ballrooms, greeting each other under crystal chandeliers, thanking each other for all the expressions of genius, praising the critics for understanding them. The congratulations will fix up eternity, but no one outside the art circle will ever comprehend. Shouldn't the circle be enlarged so that the rest of the population gets a chance at a larger IQ? Perhaps this is ridiculously optimistic.

How did this happen? How come the average citizen is art-ignorant?

In the past, during the Renaissance in Italy for example, when the church commissioned artists, the general populace was comfortable with art because they were comfortable with religion. Artists were commissioned by God, so art was backed up by a divine and formulated spirituality. At the time, God was the highest-paying sponsor. Now that God has been supplanted by things like Coca-Cola and pantyhose, art has found new sponsors with no ideology except sales. Commercial art usually expresses nothing more divine than the product it's advertising. Only gallery art has remained pure; it flowers as its own religion and exists on its own. No wonder it must have its own clique. No wonder it's misunderstood. No wonder the average citizen could care less.

Aside from this, the camera had a lot to do with mass social unfamiliarity with art. The advent of the camera ushered the arrival of surrealistic, pointillistic, expressionistic, cubistic painting—less strictly representational styles that provide both an aesthetic and intellectual experience. Art viewers began to feel that they weren't seeing the same things artists were seeing. They got shy. Or they felt excluded. Or they became critics.

With the development of cinema, painting became even more ignored. The static limitations of the canvas were over-whelmed by the possibilities of the giant silver screen. Only the lonely romantics remained faithful to the oil and brush. No hoopla, no stars. No wonder painters don't make the six o'clock news.

Doesn't matter, though. They don't care.

Nowadays the only thing a painter fears is being discovered too soon. Callow artists are seldom experienced enough to deviate from well-trodden paths, and mediocrity never changed the world for the better.

Now here's some art news:

Rolph Medgessy, a Canadian art historian and Goya authority, has come up with some earth-shattering news for the art world. According to Medgessy, Goya, while living in Rome around 1770, falsified about thirty paintings of Rembrandt, Raphael, Velasquez, Leonardo da Vinci, Michelangelo, Reubens, and Andrea del Sarto. This is quite an accusation, and he's not the only one who thinks this. It's also the learned opinion of the major French Goya expert, Didier Pouch.

According to the French daily newspaper *Libération*, these guys have seen very small Goya signatures hiding on a painting attributed to Rembrandt that hangs in a Berlin museum. The same signature has been found on many other important paintings, like the *Virgin of the Rock* by Leonardo da Vinci, which hangs in the Louvre, and a painting by Michelangelo in the Uffizi in Florence. A Velazquez in the National Gallery in London bears a Goya signature too.

Goya must have been very busy.

Renowned art historians, appraisers, and especially Goya experts are bringing out their magnifying glasses these days, bending over a cluster of very famous paintings, speculating about their authenticity. I can see them all now, going myopic from minutiae.

This is thunderous news in the art world, but as far as I see it, what would it really matter if these are fakes by Goya? Chopped liver Goya ain't. Besides, the controversy could make these paintings even more valuable than they are already. I'd rather own a Leonardo da Vinci that was maybe painted by the fun-loving practical jokester Goya, wouldn't you? It's a double whammy, and what a conversation piece it'd be over the sofa.

February 1987

It was a perfect day. The sky was cloudless and intensely blue. It was even bluer than the big sapphire my Aunt Nell used to wear on her pinky when she was in her cocktail drag. The trees weren't winter skeletons yet, they were fat with red, orange, and gold. The leaves looked even more livid through my rose-tinted sunglasses.

We were on an art excursion into the wilds of the Poconos, to a little town called Pen Argyl. In two hours, we found the two-horse town and the art site … a tiny graveyard where a heart-shaped headstone of pink Carrara marble marked the grave of Jayne Mansfield.

Under the dates on her stone was inscribed, "WE LIVE TO LOVE YOU MORE EACH DAY." So true. We were there to do a grave-stone rubbing at the shrine of big bold Jayne.

Looking at this town, it was hard to imagine Jayne Mansfield growing up there, right on Schank Avenue, Nowheresville, USA. She had been a brazen broad, becoming a legend because of her tactics, nothing else. The very act of making herself remembered was the reason she was remembered at all.

It's all different now, 1988. It's difficult to be remembered. You don't want to tread the earth with too much gusto, especially if you're an artist. It might be misconstrued as fanaticism, and we all know this just isn't *fashionable* anymore. It's not a marketable commodity; no one wants to invest in *that*. It's not stable.

"Things change. Life goes on," Robert Crumb once succinctly said in a Zap comic book. "Learn to adapt," I would add. That sums it up. You have to be very sober now. You are allowed only to hint, to glance the edge of your manifesto, if you want an audience of fans. The only way you can sneak in your soapbox platform is if you do it with classical decorum. Be calm. Tongue in cheek you must slither. The wild crazy days are over. Most of the great creative fanatics are dead, many are forgotten.

One genius fanatic who isn't forgotten is Vincent van Gogh. His *Irises* are worth $53 million. Irises are perennials. The very same irises he painted are conceivably still growing in that St. Rémy garden.

Van Gogh was a fanatic, but he tempered it by painting pictures of flowers. His earlier painting *The Potato Eaters* was bolder, more intense. This subject matter wasn't immediately understood or acceptable like flowers. Fortunately his personal fanaticism has weathered the time. His talent was big.

The great talented creative geniuses were impossible to be around. "Get lost," the fashionable Parisians would say to van Gogh, "Don't cut off your ear in *my* living room. All that blood on the carpet. Get hold of yourself. Clean up your act. Paint something we'll buy or go commit yourself to an insane asylum." If he came back now, from his grave, they wouldn't say that to him. As long as he left a painting, they'd let him cut off his ear anywhere in the house.

There isn't one living artist who wouldn't want to be immortal like van Gogh.

Forget about it. The water in the wishing well looks rather polluted now. Unrewarded genius is becoming a proverb and geniuses are getting even harder to discern because there's five billion people on the earth and there's a baby boom. Geniuses are a dime a dozen. Forget about genius. Invest in beauty. It's a perennial. If you invest in beauty, the chances are you'll get the slice of genius anyway, because it comes in the beauty package.

Forget about being immortal. Unless you have talent, like van Gogh, plus media-blitz ability like Jayne Mansfield—and unless you aren't afraid of sometimes being considered a bold, fanatical asshole in the eyes of your more serious friends—then forget about your name in the art or film history books. Human beings will be fighting for space on the globe, and the space in history books won't get any bigger because of waning paper pulp because all the trees have been leveled. Accounts of great talented artists will flutter like dried brown leaves. Stories of water and oxygen shortages will be more important.

May 1987

Revelations about oneself usually take the wind out of one's sails. Sometimes it has the opposite effect.

The other day, with back issues of *Details* piled in front of me, I started reading my most recent column and I was elated to realize that I am truly an unsparing critic of certain visual and intellectual atrocities. All I do is bitch, bitch, bitch.

One can hardly hold the tongue all the time. Glance around. Don't you see lots of spiritual vexations trying to drag you down?

One must stand up and be a grouch.

Grouchhood is great. Being a malcontent, lodging complaints right and left can make you a better person. You have to have opinions while looking for art or searching out the other forms of divinity in daily life.

Doing it in print is exhilarating.

In my last column I lambasted computers. Prior to that, I berated malls and suburban banality. Before that I attacked insensitive morons, then I discounted unromantic types, then I chided art buyers who bought work that didn't fit their personalities. There was more.

All this vituperative slamming was for the purpose of edification. High duty was calling.

"Elevate art understanding," the voice told me, so I studied the very foundations from which art flows and found that, of course, all one has to do is look at social science and basic human behavior.

This column might even be used as a map for treasure hunts, with all the indications of the dangerous everyday pitfalls, all the benevolent guideposts to lead you to art nirvana.

You don't want to make any mistakes. You could wind up like the house painters at the Venice Biennale. You read the recent story. Those guys were hired to paint all the doors white in the exhibition building, so they went around with their rollers and paint cans and painted all the doors white, just like they were told. It turned out that they also painted white a piece of sculpture—a door by Marcel Duchamp. Oops!

How could they know? They were doors, weren't they? If the Three Stooges had done it, the act itself would have become art. It's a fine line between what's art and what isn't.

Some people buy art and then ask the painter if they can hang it upside down on their wall because it goes better with the lamps and the symmetry of the room that way. Most artists would naturally say no or get offended and of course think the buyer had no taste. The only redemption would be the act of hanging every other painting in the house upside down. Now that would be class. The act and the result would be art.

So you see, it's difficult to tell. One needs experience in all the subtleties.

Since it's spring, there's gotten to be a whole kettle of new hazardous eyesores that make it difficult to tell the art and beauty from the graceless and base.

I could complain about a lot of things this time of year but one major pitfall is most outstanding.

I have discovered a whole mass of the base and I just can't keep from bitching. As I walk down the street and see it I grumble to myself the way Popeye does.

Anyone would complain.

One might think there's no reason to make disparaging remarks about this, but I think it's a major distraction to finding art.

What we're confronted with now are mobs, human units of flesh. Touring cows searching, waddling down the blocks looking for knickknacks or food.

Tumbling out of those new squat, ugly, expensive cars, they've come from all the neighboring boroughs and environing states. Their hairdos are moussed into place and they're wearing all the stuff they gathered the last weekend when they were here marauding.

These are the locusts, the packs of confused touring alien shoppers who wake up the natives with their blaring car-theft sirens, the rustle of their new leather outfits, the clicking of Gold Cards and margarita tumblers at outdoor restaurants.

Once awake, we natives slither out of bed and hit the streets to walk our dogs or take the sun and there they are, obstructing the paths, hogging the sidewalk.

Two by two, bonded in insular pairs, they wander, usually clustering in areas where money can be spent blindly.

It's difficult to find untrampled beauty after the ravaging effects of plunder. If you decide to visit a gallery where you think you'll find solace, you find none. They're in there too, shoulder to shoulder, veritable sardines making comments like, "Holy cow! You call that art?!"

Looking into the eyes of one of these people can make your art IQ drop. Finding yourself walking in the herd with these types can destroy your sense of sanctity.

Don't bother trying to visit a gallery on a sunny weekend. Go on a rainy weekday.

You might think that the wee hours of spring weekend nights would be a respite from these people, but no, they still haven't returned to their homes.

Probably because they are woefully inexperienced as hard-core drinkers, they become, with only one or two meager beers filling their bladders, not unlike banshees. These types, so tame and apparently civilized in the daylight hours are now outside the bars on the street at 4 A.M. breaking beer bottles over each other's heads, yelling, "Fug you, fugger. You fugging trying to fugging tell me I was fugging around with your ugly fugging wife/husband?"

What could be a less aesthetic experience than listening to them from your windows overlooking this bar? While trying to paint or write the great American masterpiece, or trying to have a nice peaceful late-night conversation with brilliant cultured types sipping fine wine out of imported crystal stemware, your senses will reel.

The history of culture is suddenly thrown into the dark ages. What can you do? You might throw a fat hardcover copy of *Roget's Thesaurus* at them. Perhaps this could improve their word power. Perhaps it would put an end to the redundant overuse of that one tired adjective they love to use.

Now that I've castigated the philistines, let me praise the nobility.

"I wondered what it was that had made all those people scream. I'd seen kids scream over Elvis and the Beatles and the Stones—rock idols and movie stars—but it was incredible to think of it happening at an art opening. Even at a Pop Art opening. But then, we weren't just *at* the art exhibit, we *were* the art exhibit …"

> —from *POPism: The Warhol Sixties*, by Andy Warhol & Pat Hackett

The "we" was Edie Sedgwick and himself, Andy Warhol, the human art icon incarnate. New York City has changed because of his death. Not just the art scene, every scene, including his last, the memorial, where he was very much alive in spirit. It seemed just like the old days. Now it's a new New York. There will be no human replacement ever in our history.

March 1988

In the stinky backwater swamps that stagnate on acres where looming power plants assault the senses and churn out the energy needs of cities like New York and Newark, there has just been an amazing discovery. In that foul water, mucked up by the scary vomit of belching, smoking monoliths of energy, scientists have just found a new breed of being … a new fish, ultramodern. Never seen or categorized before, this weird fish has knocked the socks off biologists. It has lungs and glows in the dark.

Somehow this creature has evolved and adapted itself to the toxins and pollutants that it had to flounder in for years. So now we have a lovable mutant, a living ray of hope, a viable silver lining for human beings, a reason to light votive candles for the future. Worried scientists and biologists who chart humankind's destiny have just heaved brief sighs of guarded relief. The discovery sheds a very small glimmer of optimism for the nail-biters.

Taking a cue from these fish, human beings will have to follow suit or become extinct like dinosaurs. Just look around. Things look grim for people. Look at the gray sky, the dying oceans, the disappearing wildlife. View the mess. Turn on PBS and hear the bleak story.

Fifty years ago people weren't starving in Africa. Now they are. Deforestation has destroyed the deep roots that hold rich soil to grow food. Years ago, too, the ozone was a seamless enveloping layer, but now it's become much the same as your great-grandmother's dry, rotted lace doilies. How were we to know that Freon wrecked ozone? We needed that Freon for frozen orange juice, deep-freeze meat lockers, and ice cubes for the world's Coca-Cola. Many years ago, people who lived in sweet air didn't have cancer or AIDS, but these new environmental diseases are a byproduct of toxic water, poisoned air, and nuclear fallout. Mutated viruses, weird pollution, and cell degeneration have finally weakened the race.

There are only two options for humankind. Number one: Shut down all power plants that produce all this lethal stuff. Shut them all down immediately all over the world. Turn off the switches and we'll start all over again. No cars, no lights, no ice cubes, no polyester clothes, no computer cash registers, no TVs or airplanes. No business. Or, choice number two: adapt.

Since we could never get everyone in the whole world to turn off the power switches (there would always be some cheaters in the world who would want to wear poly, hop on airplanes, watch *General Hospital,* have ice cubes for their Diet Pepsi, and keep their grandmothers on respirators), option 2 is our only obvious recourse. Who really wants to go back to churning butter and making candles?

Like the mutant fish, we just have to learn to adapt. We have to evolve to meet the modern toxic demands that tax our internal organs. Unlike the dinosaurs who stubbornly refused to get modern, we'll have to change. Most species learn. Recently scads of mutant mice were found after years in a frozen-food vault, living it up in sub-zero temperatures, eating frozen meat. They had long, lush fluffy fur, and looked like teeny cuddly fur puffs. They adapted.

With this in mind, I have been pondering what we'll look like in the future.

First of all, we'll have to get smaller to fit on the world because of population overcrowding. We'll be about three and a half feet tall at the most. Secondly, we'll have thick skin, no pores, because we can't have any skin assimilation of toxins. We'll also all have the same skin color, sort of ecru, from interbreeding of white, black, yellow, brown, and red humans. We'll have no body hair because soon the greenhouse effect on earth will warm everything up, so who'll need a head of hair to keep body heat in? We'll have bigger eyes with thick corneas in order to see through smog and be impervious to it. We'll have smaller ears, because who'll want to hear all the billions of voices, footsteps, and whirring of vehicles and power plants night and day? Our hands will be really agile and sensitive for adept button-pressing. We'll have no mouths, because kissing spreads germs and we'll be able to communicate telepathically anyway.

Our brains will be huge for obvious reasons (how does one deal with modern life without intelligence, smarts, savvy, and common sense? In the future we'll need more of each). We probably won't have a digestive tract because there won't be anything to eat. We'll live on food for thought. Very few of us will have sex organs, only those people who'll act as queen bees and drones, because it just makes evolutionary sense for population control. People won't get old and die, they'll just pass into another one of the countless dimensions we'll have discovered by then.

I'm sure science could back me up on this description of our future appearance. Remember the aliens in *Close Encounters of the Third Kind*?

As far as personality, character, and soul are concerned, we'll all be sensitive, creative, and funny. There'll be plenty of jobs in the architectural design field, what with all the interiors of homes and airships we'll use to escape the harsh environment. Planes of reality, too, will have to be considered in design. Clothing designers will have to come to terms with clothes that can pass easily through dimensions and time warps without wear and tear. Artists will have myriad mediums and art will be like a cross between mind-bending science projects and soothing cocoons to wrap up in. Comedians and entertainers will be treated like royalty because the heavy intellectual atmosphere will need some leavening. The concept of God won't be just a concept.

Seen optimistically, the future looks pretty good.

But doubtlessly in the future there'll be those old codger types that will say, "What is this world corning to? It's a mess." Just like they say today. And just like the ancient clay tablet excavated in Pompeii read: "What is this world corning to? It's a mess."

August 1988

For a few years now, we've noticed that most of our friends still standing have adopted the 99.44 percent pure way of life. They can almost walk on water. Of course there are paltry few means of recourse other than this way. … We humans are in danger of wiping each other out if we don't start cleaning up our acts.

While reminiscing and wincing over embarrassing past pie-eyed and blackout states, you might take heart and ease your guilt with the information I'm about to enlighten you with. Allow me a few paragraphs to set up the scenario before I get into the juicy stuff.

Archaeologists in Central America who concern themselves with Mayan culture just discovered an old floor. It's a big deal because this floor is the oldest handiwork of man ever found in the Americas. Once the floor of a community center or "party temple," it dates back to the time prior to the great Pyramid of Cheops, even prior to Stonehenge, and that means more than 4,000 years, give or take a few thousand. So this makes the "new country" seem even older than the "old country."

Anyway, near the floor they found a wall with ancient graffiti art and they also found pieces of some sort of bowl with paintings on it. On the wall was the image of a bound and restrained man whose intestines were falling out all over the place and his face distorted in pain. … No wonder. The archaeologists didn't know what to make of this except to suppose that this image represented an unlucky sacrificial victim, and they chalked it up to the cruelty of the times.

But when they pieced together the bowl and saw what was painted on it, they had to rethink their theories. On one side of the bowl was the image of a guy disemboweling himself, and he was smiling. Then on the other side of the bowl was the image of a guy who was about to cut off his own head with a sword. Sure, those times must have been tough and weird, but come on, there must have been a better reason to go *this* far.

After careful analysis, further study, and the help of some anthropologists, the archaeologists found out that these ancient Mayans weren't just some high livers or lowlifes committing suicide because of personal problems—*no*. Those Mayans pictured were: (1) completely plastered (2) grand priests and rulers (3) trying to see their gods.

Through the use of intoxicating substances they hoped to see, feel, hear their deities, so they took every drug and liquor known to man for the purpose of seeing those gods and maybe communing with them. This, most likely, wasn't antisocial behavior. ... Any man with enough chutzpah to kill himself could join the fun. It was probably the center of their belief system, their salvation, the quick road to their muses. And what a road! It was probably also good entertainment for the wise womenfolk. A couple of chuckles, anyway.

Okay. After all these drugs, if they still didn't see their gods, they figured they'd better kill themselves, because then for sure they'd see something. And besides, how would they ever live that night down? So take heart, all you ex-druggers and ex-boozers out there. Don't let your tiny transgressions of the past smudge your memories. At least you didn't stagger away from the bar and decapitate yourselves, not literally anyway.

Yes, take heart, but don't allow yourselves an imperious attitude when it comes to judging old Mayans. Sure, those times must have been really dark, sinister, and creepy, with restless spirits everywhere. But look around. Take a gander at the Middle East and give those guys a piece of your mind. Tell them something like this: "Hey, you crazed bloodthirsty maniacs over there … You better clean up your acts. Your enemy isn't who you think it is."

November 1988

The host of the party looked sad. He was sitting in the corner on the gray wall-to-wall industrial carpeting watching his shimmering, gilded, celebrated guests with his sloe eyes full of apathy and his oft-kissed lips frozen into a disingenuous smile. He was ignoring his famous guests, ignoring the sambas and tangos from the twelve-member marimba band, ignoring *La Dolce Vita* humming on the mammoth Advent video screen, ignoring peals of laughter from the group frolicking in his Jacuzzi, ignoring the Nebuchadnezzars of champagne, the Mr. Chow–catered food, even ignoring the bad manners of the two French poseurs, dressed in fashion-casualty drag of black-and-red plaid shirts and leopard-skin trousers, who were on top of a table crouching over the kilo of beluga caviar that Alba Clemente had presented the host as a party gift. These awful frogs were right on the table, right in the lettuce leaves, eating caviar by the tablespoonful, as if it were cheap livestock oatmeal.

The host was unruffled. He batted not one Bambilike lash.

It was a good party, you could tell by the party barometer man, Andy Warhol. All the stars were crushing in, bubbly, perfumed, crackling with sparks, but the host was just looking melancholy. And when he wasn't looking wistful, he was looking bored and sullen. He even yawned a few times.

I thought he might perk up when I saw the gaggle of gorgeous girls and the bevy of blond bombshell beauties cluster around him, attempting to titillate him, but this did nothing to arouse him. He was monosyllabic in his answers to their giggly questions.

Yes, our host, Jean-Michel Basquiat, the bright graffiti artist turned suddenly wildly successful genius painter, was in a ho-hum kinda mood.

Watching him, I filled in the blanks myself. Maybe he was, for the first time, thinking what a sham this success nonsense was. Maybe he was asking himself if this was all there was. Where was the joy that's supposed to come with fame and money? Wasn't life supposed to be fun and glamorous and fulfilling after one was successful and rich and had a beautiful home, famous friends, lovers, esteem, respect? When was the real deal going to start? When came the Fun at the Top stuff? When was the panorama up there going to look better than any other vista? When was it going to mean something?

Maybe Jean-Michel had found that packing for the trip was better than getting there, the climb more rewarding than the summit. True, Basquiat had always seemed more vital and happier, more involved, bright-eyed, and bushy-tailed when he was just a poor graffiti artist crashing on friends' floors. He used to laugh a lot.

Looking at him now, I wanted to shake him and say, "Don't you appreciate all this, Jean? Don't take this success jive so seriously. It's just a ball, it's all a party, enjoy it. It's all a façade.... *You're* the one that has to give it depth."

But maybe that's exactly what he was discovering while watching his party drama unfold around him, while he was just sitting on the floor in the Party Pooper Corner. But whatever was on his mind, he was lightyears away from where his body was, he was just a Jean-Michel Basquiat shell sitting there. His genius, which he so deftly displayed on canvas, was somewhere else.

Looking at him, I began to feel somehow protective, but kind of angry and sort of sorry for him too.

It was later in the evening, around 3 A.M., after people had eaten and drunk and were whipped up and sweating in samba frenzies, when I looked up from my dancing partner's face and saw Jean quietly slipping out the door. No one noticed that the host himself was leaving. No one noticed because the party was that good, it was ripping, one of the year's best. No one noticed and half the crowd, the hollow party people, the ones that appear uninvited at every party not even knowing who the host might be, didn't care an iota.

The host had had enough of his own party. Let them eat cake, the guests, let them laugh and dance and slop drinks all over the floor, whatever. The host was going out into the night. A gust of wind bearing a few gold and red leaves and a stray piece of newspaper blew in after him and that was all. The door closed behind him and as Chuck Berry had said in one of his songs, the host was gone … "gone like a coooool breeeeeeeze."

In my very first *Details* column (Summer 1982), I featured Jean-Michel Basquiat, who I believed was one of New York's, in fact America's and maybe someday the world's most talented artists. Young, gifted, and black, "that's where it's at." Basquiat was clearly destined for the art history books. Already his paintings were selling furiously, even still wet and oily. Fresh from his studio, he was making hotcakes. His name was on all the buyers', gallerists', and art students' lips. Already he was considered an old master, soaring to the ranks of the studyable and copiable. He was dancing in the dizzying heights of fast becoming a *great* twentieth-century artist. There was a school of Basquiat imitators, but no one could top the master, no one could paint as prolifically or brilliantly with such incredibly shocking ease. He even outdistanced himself by being so prolific. He turned out a few canvases a day sometimes.

He was becoming internationally famous, he was having shows all over the world. A photograph of him sitting in a chair with his sweet eyes and his luscious café au lait coloring graced the cover of the *New York Times Magazine*, and he was doing collaborative work, sharing canvases, with Andy Warhol. Warhol had become a close friend. They phoned each other every day.

Beside all the superficial stuff, Jean-Michel was really talented, and no one questioned it, not the critics, not the poo-pooers, not the public. We all knew he was doing some kind of shaman work, some voodoo hoodoo, like automatic writing, he was like a copper wire for art electricity, a conductor telling visual tales that were ancient profound history. There was a strange force that was moving his hand, forcing him to commit to canvas something that was at once much larger than he was. After all, he was but only human, a fragile, vulnerable being, a tiny speck on the globe, one of the world's citizens who was translating the universe on a canvas. He was making transmissions, unrestricted manifestations were appearing in front of him.

Labeled first as a graffiti artist with his famous SAMO tag on all the New York subway cars, he soon transcended this moniker and went right for haute art's fine swanlike throat. He was rising like a meteor, like a lot of artists before him, but he was slightly different than most. He truly had a piece of the old romantic self-destruction stuff inside him, lurking there, ready to spring, given just a glimmer of a chance.

He was not destined for old age; he flashed on our aesthetic retinas and took flight at age twenty-seven. It's almost 1989 and Jean-Michel Basquiat flew right past us in the eighth month of 1988.

Writers who want to eulogize might take a few steps back in Basquiat's case: he sort of defied pigeonholing. Sure, he used drugs, there is meaty gossip here and ripe tales to tell. Yes, his star had been slipping of late because he was making a mess of himself, it was rumored. He was having a fallow period, and after Warhol died he looked as though he was going to flounder as an artist, as if he might sink altogether. … But then he made a brilliant comeback at Vrej Baghoomian, Inc. at 611 Broadway this past spring, he was starting his second climb.

But the strains of the song of the "rapture of the deep" were calling to him and he succumbed but not in pain. Like the greatest of all the purest and most tortured of the sensitive artists, he died during his own party blaze. Once again he left, gone like a coooool breeeeeeze. "It's my party and I'll *die* if I want to," was the song they played that night.

Jean-Michel Basquiat had a full life. He did everything he could and did all of it well. Don't feel sorry for him. It's the rest of us, left behind, we should feel sorry for.

August 1989

I'm a fan of Vittorio Scarpati. I'm also his wife, so I guess you might say I'm his biggest fan, aside from his mother. I know his art well, so I have some insight into it. I know what it looks like even before it's a gleam in his eye.

Despite this, I have found writing about his work to be the most difficult task I've ever had. In April I wrote text and captions for a book of his art (to be published this fall by Kyoto Shoin International as part of their Art Random series) and I was in agony over this job. It's not because I try to be diplomatic and kind about mediocre work but because I have to restrain myself from gushing. Obviously this simplistic explanation only scratches the surface of my dilemma. I've discovered that in bold black-and-white print it's hard to express one's love, a love that has always been silently understood. There are things that are too profound to commit to words on paper. In this situation the critic/commentator, so closely related to the particular artist, has to become a complete stranger. Emotionally it's the only recourse. So I shall reintroduce myself to a stranger.

I met Vittorio Scarpati seven years ago in Positano, Italy, a town that defies description. It's so beautiful it takes the breath away. It looks like it can't be real; it's too incredible, perhaps Walt Disney made it. In this paradisal setting I got to know Vittorio. I discovered he was an artist, at that time a cartoonist, and I was amazed at his ease with pen and ink, brush and color ... the images he drew just flowed out of him effortlessly. While many artists struggle with their work, Vittorio didn't. It was as if he had already planned every stroke, every detail long before it was committed to paper. He was so fast. Also, his "cartoons" weren't empty; they always delivered subtle messages or wisdom.

In the seven years since then I have seen him work in all kinds of art modes, in architectural design and commercial animation, and I've seen what he's done refurbishing large marble statues, carving and replacing lost hands, noses, and arms on these cool, austere stone people. But this was work for other people; he wasn't working for himself in complete creative freedom. For some reason he just couldn't bring himself to sit down and do his own work.

That all changed when Vittorio's lungs collapsed. Maybe it was his breathing the marble dust–laden air, maybe it was years of smoking everything he could get his hands on, but one day his lungs just literally ripped and he was taken to the hospital and confined to a bed. He stayed there for five months (at this writing he's still there). He was immobile, attached to two lung machines, and there was nothing to keep his mind active or spirits high. But a friend saved him, brought him some ink pens and drawing pads. Vittorio picked up those pens and didn't put them down. Did he need to be physically tied down to finally do his important work?

From these restrictions and limitations came his brilliant emancipation, a luminous disengagement from his restraining bounds. In the depths of his plight came a grasp toward the pinnacle of inspiration. Now suddenly he was gripped by a frenzy of pent-up art communication that exploded out of him. The man was being touched and guided by something invisible, as if this were automatic writing, like speaking in tongues in pictures. It was obvious that he had tapped into something mysterious, unearthly even. He seemed to be a channeler of recognizable truth. The work transcended small concerns and became grand, beautiful, honest, and somehow ancient. The most incredible work poured out of him at an amazing rate, as if his gods were working him overtime. So prolific was he during this period that no one who saw this work could believe their eyes. Miracles were pouring out of a mortal.

He finished about three hundred pen-and-ink drawings in three months, and each little drawing held an astute and wily message. Each was drenched with wisdom, humor, and poignancy. The drawings impressed two of Vittorio's hospital visitors, Bill Stelling and Dean Ralston, the men who run 56 Bleecker Gallery. They agreed that Vittorio should have an exhibition there.

In this show were included one hundred thirty-two small eight- by eleven-inch pen-and-ink drawings, some with color, some without. This exhibition was really a visual narrative that told of deep despair, sadness, and pain, but also hope, happiness, and joy. It was actually a pictorial diary, literally leaves of paper from the drawing pad; it was a tale of hospital horror, a black comedy, a singular experience of institutionalism, and what it does to the soul. Somehow Vittorio, with his spiritual stamina, rises above all the woe.

The subject matter of this work is diverse. Some concerns itself with otherworldliness and personal fantasy, and some of it is earthly, stark, and real as can be. There are "piles of angels," or as Vittorio calls them, "puti puddings" flying en masse above the Italian Mediterranean coastline. There are dolphins leaping from the sea wearing their rightful halos, pictures of Socrates, Alaskan oil spills, trees full of colorful birds, monks, chained life warriors, strange animals, a sumo wrestler, tigers in pitch-dark, broken bleeding hearts, St. Sebastian tied and pierced with hypodermic syringes, a self-portrait of Vittorio with an elephant sitting on his chest … there is so much more, as if this show comprised a whole lifetime of captured images and memories. This work speaks eloquently and sensitively about the deity that lives within, the inner nature, the life force, zeal, and human courage. Everyone who saw the show was genuinely touched and certainly moved. It was like a course in theosophy. Laughter wasn't forgotten either; Vittorio's sense of humor and wry wisdom read loud and clear. He instilled his spirit into his work and strongly communicated it to his viewers. The artist, Vittorio, came off like a sagacious, ageless, comedian teacher/angel with wings.

Vittorio's work (new work—a lot of this exhibition was sold) will travel this winter to San Francisco to be exhibited at the gallery/museum Artspace. Fans will spring up across the country. One can't help but be mesmerized by this work; art that so coherently expresses the artist's generous compassion for life and its forms (humans, animals, and nature) can't be ignored.

Vittorio continues to draw in his hospital room, to compile his illuminated visions, spreading some light around. There is a communiqué here for all of us that tells of strength of character, bravery, and courage in the midst of adversity and intense physical pain. Vittorio has learned that like a flood of sunlight, hope can vanquish gloom. Things are never so bleak and threatening as we believe. Vittorio is fortunate he has his incandescent wit and his work to keep him out of darkness.

I hope he comes home soon.

Ronnie Roach (*High Times*)

I would bet that Ron Reagan's favorite maxim is "only the strong survive." Well, if you look at animals, you see this is pretty true. The less spunky ones are winnowed out, and the ones with stamina and blind determination are getting bigger everyday. Take a look at an average cockroach.

Three hundred million years ago, during the Carboniferous Age, cockroaches were walking around amid the ferns and amphibians. That 300 million year-old roach looked just the same as the one that lives in the cabinet under your kitchen sink. Same cute little hard-shelled body, same shapely legs, same eager antenae, same bouncy stride. The only difference that I can imagine is that now they have modernized their perceptions to fit the atomic age and civilization.

The cockroach should have been Ron's campaign mascot. A picture of the roach should be the symbol of his term in office.

The tenacity of the roach is what Ron admires most in human beings. I wonder if, when he steps on a roach, he realizes that he is actually destroying a higher, more evolved life form? I wonder if he knows he is squashing the creature, whose spirit epitomizes the spirit of his presidency?

There are a few other animals who would fit into this category too, like sharks, scorpions, clams. Despite what they look like, clams are not lazy; they're all muscle and we all know that they're the happiest of animals. I'm sure, since Ron's language is all idioms, sayings and maxims, he often uses the phrase, "happy as a clam," when asked how he feels about some issue.

This is Ron's religion, his house of worship … not the tangible physical structure, but a bunch of maxims strung together. His religion is based on the strength of the human being to pull himself up by the proverbial bootstraps. Strong to him means hardshelled, food-fierce, and work-oriented. Work, work, work "and you'll win, win, win. It's true, but who wants to work that hard just for a dumb bank account?

Talking about Ron's religion, have you ever seen him going to church? At least he's not a born again Christian or a fake Presbyterian. Unfortunately, he isn't a thoughtful, intelligent pagan either. That would be an ideal president, a pagan, because there would be a certain amount of open mindedness and lack of prejudice. Well, at least he doesn't ask us to pray with him.

Evidence of Ron's beliefs about the human work spirit are everywhere these days. Tum on the TV and flip the channels starting at 11 p.m. There're all these programs about millionaire makers, people like Ed Begley who, with no money down and no credit, became a millionaire in real estate. Ed Begley goes into it, telling us step by step how we all can do it. Propaganda, kids. Ok, but what if a person isn't bright enough to work with all those pesky figures? What if some people don't seem to have that business savvy?

Ron has a plan for the people he thinks are the quasi-retarded of America and it all starts with the new planned budget cuts.

You know about the cuts he recently proposed? He wants to cut education, housing, medicaid, welfare and government aid—in fact, everything, except defense of course.

Okay, suppose these cuts go into effect. Obviously the poor would be even poorer. In fact, they would be starving, a lot more than they are already. There would be no way for them to find a place to live, no way to find food or work. And where would young people who really wanted an education possibly find one they could afford with no government help? The answer is obvious. They'd have no choice but to enter the army. There they have a roof, meals, education. There is no other option for them. So tricky Ron, by making these budget cuts is really strengthening the militia. There'll be lots more people in the army, which is exactly what he wants. I don't know why he is so paranoid.

Okay, now for the other kinds of people who wouldn't dream of joining the army no matter how hungry they are, there is only one other viable alternative to make enough money to live: they have to turn to crime like robbing and stealing, or more peaceful means like drug trafficking.

Now when the upper middle class bunch is being ripped off of the dumb things they bought and worked so hard for they're going to be awful mad. There's going to be a call for more police protection, and the poor people who didn't join the army will join the police force, another guaranteed job which puts food on the table.

So in the end, we have a total military and police government, all because of these budget cuts, I warned you.

Really, Ron has gone off the deep end this time with these budget cuts. It's all about the spirit of the cockroach: the great work ethic smashing ideas, creativity and intellectualism.

The core of the problem here, as I see it, is Ron's imagined superiority. He truly believes he is the smartest man in the world and everybody else is dumb—your basic uncultured, hillbilly attitude. Also, probably the attitude of working insects: ants, bees, flies and roaches.

But I have to stop now, I get too mad when I think about Ron. He is one human being that really bugs me.

PART SIX

CODA

My Bio—Notes on an American Childhood

The year I was born, 1949, the North Atlantic Treaty was signed, the Dutch were ousted from Indonesia, and the first Russian nuclear bomb was exploded. So what. It didn't happen in America so who cared? Not me. I was too small.

I cared about the flannel blanket which I sat on naked under a Norway maple tree in my Baltimore backyard. I cared about the kitchen sink that I was small enough to take a bath in, and I cared about my right thumb, which I sucked.

Somehow I got the name Cookie before I could walk. It didn't matter to me, they could call me whatever they wanted.

In 1949 my eyes were the same size as they are now, because human eyes do not grow with the body; they're the same size at birth as they will always be.

That was 1949.

In 1959, with eyes the same size, I got to see some of America traveling in the old green Plymouth with my parents who couldn't stand each other, and my brother and sister who loved everyone. I remember the Erie Canal on a dismal day, the Maine coastline in a storm, Georgia willow trees in the rain, and the Luray Caverns in the Blue Ridge Mountains of Virginia where the stalagmites and -tites were poorly lit.

Unfortunately I remember all too well Colonial Williamsburg, where the authentic costumes were made out of Dacron and poly and the shoes were Naugahyde. I remember exactly how much I detested seeing these fakers in those clothes, as I was very concerned with detail. Even more than the outer garments, I imagined that, of course, they weren't wearing the historically correct undergarments. I knew in my heart that, for instance, the person who was dressed up to look like the 1790s blacksmith was wearing Fruit of the Loom underpants. Hiding under colonial skirts that the women wore were cheap 79-cent nylon pantyhose from Woolworth's. This bothered me very much.

My father's travel itinerary was mighty strange. We visited a saltpeter mine somewhere in the woods of someone's rundown farm. It was listed in some defunct tour guide manual, but it wasn't much of a tourist attraction, maybe because saltpeter has such a bad name. Still does. It's the stuff used in American cigarettes to make them burn up faster.

Actually the saltpeter cave was really quite beautiful because it was all white salt crystals that would have sparkled if it had been a sunny day. The farmer who showed us the little cave had to keep a dirty red-checkered oilcloth over the entrance so the crystals wouldn't dissolve in the rain.

At home in the quasi-country lands of Baltimore County I would spend idle summer months in the woods behind my parents' house. In these woods was a strange railroad track, where a mystery train passed through a tunnel of trees and vines twice a day, once at 1 P.M. and then again in the opposite direction at 3 P.M. I would climb a steep hill which sat right on the tracks and I would look down into the smokestack and always the black smoke would settle on my white clamdiggers.

For miles and miles in the direction the train was heading there was nothing except a seminary and an insane asylum, so naturally my assumption was that one of the boxcars was full of loons anxious to be committed. The other car was, of course, full of future priests, students of theology, who, as everyone knows, have to use public transportation because they're far too religious to drive their own cars. The 3 P.M. train would return the other way carrying the dirty laundry: I guessed both boxcars were full of stained straitjackets and sweaty clerical collars. There was always a caboose full of shirtless men with fistfuls of cards, probably playing strip poker. They would always wave as they went chugging by.

In these woods I found lots of pets. I brought home box turtles; one I named Fidel, because I had a crush on Castro at the time. My sister named another one Liberace, because she had a crush on him.

Fidel, the turtle, was great in captivity. He used to crawl up into Jip's dog food bowl and chow down. Jip would get angry and run over to the bowl and growl at the turtle who was eating all his food, but Fidel ignored Jip. He kept eating. Turtles are the plodders in nature's scheme. They're the ones that know the term "easy does it," the ones that don't let minor setbacks and petty jealousies bother them much. It's obvious when you study a turtle. Their skin is as thick as linoleum and their shells are as hard as the undergirdings of a concrete overpass. My parents hated Fidel, only because of his name; they named one of the turtles Joe McCarthy, to keep a political balance.

There were eleven box turtles roaming around in the house one summer.

I would also bring home black snakes and tadpoles that turned into frogs all over the house. Once I brought home a nest of baby opossums that turned out to be rats. My mother was not amused by this.

One day, along the tracks, I unearthed a yellow jacket hive while I was rearranging boulders. Stung seventeen times, the doctors didn't see much hope for me, but I recovered.

After facing death, I became a young novelist and wrote a book about the Jonestown Pennsylvania flood in 1830-something, where Clara Barton threw her weight around. I did research. Clara Barton was the American version of Florence Nightingale. She was a nurse in Gettysburg during the Civil War, just like Ms. Nightingale in the Crimean War … or some old war over there.

On Barton's hemlines there were always bloodstains and she carried morphine in her pockets. She wasn't as much of a tramp as Florence Nightingale, though, Nightingale spread syphilis to all the European soldiers, but Barton was probably an American pioneer celibate.

The book was 321 pages long, and I finished it the day before my eleventh birthday. I'd heard somewhere that the girl who wrote *Black Beauty* was eleven, so I wanted to be the youngest novelist in the world.

I didn't have any idea how to get the book published, so I typed it all up, stapled it together, cut up some beer-case cardboard, covered this with white butcher paper and Saran wrap. Fashioned after any legitimate library book, I smuggled it into the library and put it on the shelves in the correct alphabetical order. I never saw the book again.

I learned early that writing was hard on the body. Blood turns cold and circulation stops at the typewriter; the knee joints solidify into cement, the ass becomes one with the chair, but I kept writing.

One Sunday, around this time, my brother died. It happened at the railroad tracks. He was climbing a dead tree and it fell on him. It was quick. He was fourteen. He hadn't seen a whole lot and he saved himself a myriad of future problems. He was one of those kind of people who was too sensitive to hang around for long.

My mother's hair went gray practically overnight, but she dyed it black again after a while.

"Whenever you're depressed, just change your hair color," she always told me, years later, when I was a teenager: I was never denied a bottle of hair bleach or dye. In my closet there weren't many clothes, but there were tons of bottles.

Ten years later, at the beginning of 1969, I was in a mental hospital in San Francisco, having been committed by my roommates. They did it out of desperation; they'd tried everything including potatoes, nature's tranquilizers: au gratin, mashed, boiled, baked, and fried.

All that you've heard about mental hospitals is true. Patients cut paper dolls, and they weave baskets, and they have a lot of wild fun late at night when there aren't any doctors around. Crazy people have a hard time sleeping at night.

In the wee hours there were only nurse's aides and bouncers. The bouncers were huge, just like bouncers at sleazy bars. When a late-night gathering would get too out of control, the bouncers would bodily pick up the loudest of the lot and throw them into solitary confinement. I found out that solitary confinement isn't as romantic as it sounds.

One day I accidentally had shock therapy, when I got in the wrong line. I thought I was waiting for drugs. It's the truth.

You have heard a lot of bad things about shock therapy, perhaps from reading too many renditions of the Frances Farmer story, and you may have an opinion about it. But it really isn't as bad as you may think. It really isn't so horrible, as a matter of fact, it's rather pleasant, because it eradicated from my memory all the contents of stupid literature, the required reading forced on me by liberal English Lit. teachers in school. It all came back in a few months.

In this hospital everyone got lots of Thorazine, Stelazine, and hot chocolate. The hot chocolate was doled out constantly after the sun went down for the patients who couldn't sleep, and that was everyone. Even after megadoses of tranquilizers, the brain pans were still overflowing; the cogs of wild imaginations were still whirling, so there were lots of loons walking around like the people from the film *The Night of the Living Dead*. Everyone clutched their Styrofoam cups of hot chocolate. The floors were sloshed up from the spills; after all those tranquilizers, people got pretty sloppy.

I met some very entertaining people there.

After two months in the California hospital, I was sent to a Maryland hospital. The staff of doctors wanted me to be near the place I was born and raised.

And wouldn't you know it, ironically, they sent me to the very hospital that was in the woods behind my parents' house. I found out that the mystery train, the one whose smokestack used to sooty up my clamdiggers, didn't stop at the mental hospital at all, but I could see it from my barred windows as it passed at 1 P.M. and then again at 3 P.M. Somehow, seeing this train did bring me down to earth again. I got better.

In the caboose of the train, the same shirtless men were playing the same games, just as they had ten years before.

Ten years later, after moving around in the world and then to New York, I got a phone call from my mother on a rainy Sunday. She told me that my father had just died when the Plymouth ran over him in the driveway. My mother got out the hair dye bottle again.

No, some things never change.

Even if they do, it doesn't matter; you can cover all of it with black hair dye.

A Last Letter

"It's like wartime now," my aunt told me a few weeks ago. She lived in France during World War II. "You young people are losing friends and relatives just as if it were bullets taking them away."

She's right, it's a war zone, but it's a different battlefield. It's not bullets that catch these soldiers, and there's no bombs and no gunfire. These people are dying in a whisper.

In 1982 my best friend died of AIDS. Since then there have been so many more friends I've lost. We all have. Through all of this I have come to realize that the most painful tragedy concerning AIDS death has to do with something much larger than the loss of human life itself. There is a deepening horror more grand than the world is yet aware. To see it we have to watch closely who is being stolen from us. Perhaps there is no hope left for the whole of humankind, not because of the nature of the epidemic, but the nature of those it strikes.

Each friend I've lost was an extraordinary person, not just to me, but to hundreds of people who knew their work and their fight. These were the kind of people who lifted the quality of all our lives, their war was against ignorance, the bankruptcy of beauty, and the truancy of culture. They were people who hated and scorned pettiness, intolerance, bigotry, mediocrity, ugliness, and spiritual myopia; the blindness that makes life hollow and insipid was unacceptable. They tried to make us see.

All of these friends were connected to the arts. Time and history have proven that the sensitive souls among us have always been more vulnerable.

My friend Gordon Stevenson, who died in 1982, was a filmmaker. His insights turned heads. With his wife, Muriel, who starred in his low-budget films, he was on the road to a grand film future, one that would serve to inspire and influence a lot of people. When Muriel died in a car accident in Los Angeles, it wasn't long after that that Gordon started getting sick.

We thought it was mourning that was wasting him, until he was eventually diagnosed and admitted to the hospital with AIDS. He demanded that I didn't visit him there, and I honored his wish, so we talked on the phone every day and he wrote me one letter.

It was written on his own paper, with his designed letterhead: a big black heart, inscribed with the words Faith, Hope, and Charity on a background of orange. It was the last letter I received from him. He died the day I got it. I still have it, it's all frayed but the message is crisp.

Dear Cookie,
    Yesterday when I talked to you on the phone, I didn't know what to say.... Yes, you're right, all of us "high riskers" have been put through an incredible ordeal—this is McCarthyism, a witch hunt, a "punishment" for being free thinkers, freedom fighters, for being "different."

I think if you told kids that measles was caused by excessive masturbation, and were made to wear T-shirts to school that said "contaminated" so that no one would sit near them or play with them, and then put in a hospital ward with other measles patients to have swollen glands ripped out, spots cut off, radiation bombardment, and tons of poison to kill the measles, all the while their parents telling them that it serves them right, masturbation is a sin, they're gonna burn in hell, no allowance, no supper for a week, and the doctors telling them that it's the most fatal disease of the century ... I think you could produce a large number of measles deaths.

Instead the child is kept at home, given ginger ale, Jell-0, and chicken soup, and reassured by a loving mother, whom they trust absolutely, that it's nothing serious and will go away in a few days—and it does.

Our problem is that we are all alone in the cruelest of cruel societies with no one we love and trust absolutely.

All we really need is bread, water, love, and work that we enjoy and are good at, and an undying faith in and love of ourselves, our freedom, and our dignity. All that stuff is practically free, so how come it's so hard to get—and how come all these assholes and "professionals," friends and foes, family and complete strangers are always trying to convince us to follow their dumb rules, give up work in order to be a client of theirs, give up our freedom and dignity to increase their power and control?

I still don't want you to visit me here. I'm much worse, visually, than when you saw me last, so until I'm feeling stronger and looking better, let's leave it this way.

I hope this letter finds you in good spirits. I hope you're not upset that I don't want you to visit me. I wish you happiness, love, prosperity, and a limitless future.

I KNOW, I KNOW, I KNOW that somewhere there is paradise and although I think it's really far away, I KNOW, I KNOW, I KNOW I'm gonna get there, and when I do, you're gonna be one of the first people I'll send a postcard to with complete description of, and map for locating ...

Courage, bread, and roses,
Gordon

Sources

Many of these texts were collected previously in *Ask Dr. Mueller: The Writings of Cookie Mueller*, edited by Amy Scholder (New York: High Risk Books, 1997). *Ask Dr. Mueller* included the original versions of two texts which appeared in different forms in *How to Get Rid of Pimples* (New York: Top Stories, 1984), the entirety of *Fan Mail, Frank Letters, and Crank Calls* (New York: Hanuman, 1988) and *Garden of Ashes* (New York: Hanuman, 1988), much of *Walking through Clear Water in a Pool Painted Black* (New York: Semiotext(e), 1990), and the selections from Mueller's columns in the *East Village Eye* (Ask Dr. Mueller) and *Details* magazine (Art and About) which reappear here. *Ask Dr. Mueller* also included two previously uncollected texts: "The One Percent," first published in *High Risk: An Anthology of Forbidden Writings*, edited by Amy Scholder and Ira Silverberg (New York: Plume, 1991); and "Provincetown—1970," first published in *Ferro-Botanica*, no. 3 (1982). Additionally, eight texts were published for the first time in Ask Dr. Mueller: "Another Boring Day," "Dogs I Have Known," "The Italian Remedy—1983," "Jamaica—1975," "John Waters and the Blessed Profession—1969," "No Credit, Cash Only—Baltimore,

1967, "Out of the Bottle and into a Danish Remedy," and "The Stone of New Orleans—1983."

How to Ged Rid of Pimples included twelve stories (or "cases"), some of them developed from previously published works and four of which are collected here: "Brenda Losing," first published in *Bomb* 1, no. 2 (1982); "I Hear America Sinking or a Suburban Girl Who Is Naïve and Stupid Finds Her Reward," first published in *Lo Spazio Umano: Rivista Internationale di Scienze Umane, Arte e Letteratura*, no. 11 (April–June 1984); "The Mystery of Tap Water," first published in *Bomb*, no. 6 (1983); and "The Third Twin," first published in *The World*, no. 34 (1981). In all four cases, presented here are the original versions of these stories, rather than the versions from *Pimples*. (*Ask Dr. Mueller* previously collected these same versions of "Brenda Losing" and "The Mystery of Tap Water," while the original versions of "The Third Twin" and "I Hear America Sinking" are collected for the first time here.)

Fan Mail, Frank Letters, and Crank Calls published for the first time Mueller's piece of the same name. Likewise, nine texts here were published for the first time in *Garden of Ashes*: "Alien—1965," "Breaking into Show Biz," "Cookie Mueller," "Divine," "Edith Massey: A Star," "Female Trouble," "Fleeting Happiness," "Tattooed Friends," and "Waiting for the New Age."

Mueller's *Walking through Clear Water* included fifteen texts, nine of them previously uncollected: "A Last Letter," first published in *City Lights Review*, no. 2 (1988); "British Columbia—1972," first published in Wild History, edited by Richard Prince (New York: Tanam, 1985); "Go-Going—New York & New Jersey, 1978–79," first published in *Cuz*, no. 1 (1988); "Haight-Ashbury—San Francisco, 1967," first published in *The World*, no. 34 (1981); "My Bio—Notes on an American Childhood," first published in *Bomb*, no. 11 (Winter 1985); "The Pig Farm—Baltimore & York, PA, 1969," first published in *Bomb*, no. 4 (1982); "*Pink Flamingos*," first published in the artist's book *Spunky International: Translux*, edited by Billy Miller (Paris: Billy Miller, 1988); "Route 95 South—Baltimore to Orlando," first published in *Just Another Asshole*, no. 6 (1983); "Sam's Party—Lower East Side, NYC, 1979," first published in *Long Shot* 5 (1987); and "Two People—Baltimore, 1964," first published in *Bomb* 1, no. 1 (Spring 1981). Another five texts were published for the first time in *Walking through Clear Water*: "Abduction and Rape—Highway 31, Elkton, Maryland, 1969," "The Berlin Film Festival—1981," "The Birth of Max Mueller—September 25, 1971," "Sailing," and "The Stone Age—Sicily, 1976."

Finally, a considerable amount of material is original to this volume. Four texts are collected for the first time here: "Ronnie Roach," first published in *High Times* magazine, June 1986; "The Simplest Thing," first published in *Bomb*, no. 24 (Summer 1988); "The Truth about the End of the World," first published in *Angel of Repose*, edited by Nancy Peskin (Buffalo: Hallwalls, 1986); and "Which Came First," first published in *Out of This World: An Anthology of the St. Mark's Poetry Project, 1966–1991*, edited by Anne Waldman (New York: Three Rivers, 1991). Another four texts were discovered by Max Mueller among documents recovered from Cookie Mueller's floppy discs, and are published for the first time here: "Careening around in Career Vehicles," "Edgar Allan Poe on Ice—1982," "Narcotics," and "Manhattan: The First Nine Years, the Dog Years." We thank Raymond Foye for bringing this material to light. A cover letter to an agent found with these stories indicates that Mueller intended to include them in a collection of autobiographical writings that was never realized, and suggested the order in which they have been sequenced here. At least two working titles for this manuscript seem to have been *A Life of Many Faces: True Stories* and *An Acutely Present Past: True Stories Remembered.* "As for the title of this book, I'm still not sure," Mueller's cover letter ended. "Here's some more to mull over: NO CLOTHES, MOTION STUDY, MAKING TRACKS. FULL TILT is good too. The title is the hardest. Let me know what happens. I'm hoping for the best."

ABOUT THE AUTHOR

Cookie Mueller (1949–1989), nee Dorothy Karen Mueller, played leading roles in John Waters's *Pink Flamingos, Female Trouble, Desperate Living*, and *Multiple Maniacs*. She wrote for the *East Village Eye* and *Details Magazine*, performed in a series of plays by Gary Indiana, and wrote numerous stories that would only be published posthumously. She died in New York City of AIDS-related complications at age 40.